I0818260

Bunny

Bunny

a romance

D. K. Smith

KANSAS CITY RIDEAU LAKES

Published in the United States by Cedar Point Press
www.cedarpointpress.com

Library of Congress Control Number: 2016920761
p. cm.
1. Unrequited love—Fiction. 2. Fathers and daughters—Fiction.
3. Separation (psychology)—Fiction. 4. Revenge—Fiction.
5. Fairy tales—Fiction. 6. Romance—Fiction.

Smith, Donald Kimball
Bunny: a romance / D. K. Smith. –1st ed.

ISBN 978-0-9914737-2-4

for Annie

Part One

Bunny

Everything that happens is real.
That's the first thing you need to understand.

BUNNY

1.

She is sitting on a large pink suitcase in the middle of Willow Rock Park dressed in pearls and a pale grey suit. The shining silver hair is not her own, though the color is true. She'd gone pewter grey by senior year in college—that was the joke between them: a life of privilege had aged her prematurely—and the next eighteen years have brightened it to a fine, metallic sheen. Though the chemo has doubtless dulled it again. She's been traveling all night, Chicago to Connecticut, home to here. A bus and then a cab and then walking for what seemed like forever. She has barely slept. Now, peering around, she wishes it all looked more familiar—the shape of the trees, the slope of the grass. This scene has stood out for so long in her memory it is a shock to realize how wide the gap has grown between what she remembers and what is true.

Partly it's fatigue; she knows that. But mostly it's the medications playing with her mind. Poisons fighting poisons fighting poisons: how can that end well?

She rises carefully, trying for another perspective, and in turning notices the pink suitcase. It isn't that she's forgotten. She looks down and, of course, there it is. But lately she has room in each moment's thought for only a single thing, as if her mind is constantly remaking itself.

Now she tugs the suitcase on its little wheels over the grass, and as she does she feels the quick, sharp pain of the skin graft drawing tight, a new seam threatening to open between her shoulder blade and the base of her neck. It's been two months, but still she thinks of it as an intruder who has hitched a ride and now can't be shaken off.

Dappled light, the feel of grass, the scent of the breeze. She tries to concentrate on each. It is only gradually that she notices the man. He is sitting on a bench beneath a tree: a slender figure in dark hat, suit, and sunglasses with a book open just beneath his eyes as if not wanting to miss a word.

Two months ago she would not have spoken: strange man sitting in a park. But there is something about bad luck that makes you think. If enough of it accrues you begin to wonder if maybe it doesn't mean something, so that every event becomes weighted with doubt. Besides. There's something about a reader.

"I hope you won't take this the wrong way," says Bunny, pitching her voice against the silence, "but I thought you might be a figment of my imagination."

The man glances up, considering the idea. "What makes you think I'm not?"

She steps into the shade; her eyes adjust. The suit, she sees, is thick with dust. Jacket, vest, and pants all different colors, though blended under the dirt. He isn't wearing a hat; dark hair hangs to his shoulders in a series of tight braids framing a pale face, and his beard seems to echo the effect: a double handful of patchy whiskers gathered into five tight strands. They vibrate like little antennae when he moves.

She understands this is not a good a idea. She should just keep walking. But it's a beautiful day. The air is rich with the scent of spring. And she is too tired to walk away. Instead she sinks onto her suitcase, like a woman waiting for a taxi in the middle of a field.

His voice is low and pleasant. He is squinting at her, though the light through the branches overhead isn't bright. "Are those pearls real?"

She hesitates, touches them. "I've always assumed so. But they were a gift from my husband, so I suppose there's no knowing."

"I bet you could have them tested."

"Sometimes I think it's nicer not to know. You're not planning to rob me, are you?"

"No."

"Are you sure?"

"I don't think so."

"You don't think you're sure?"

"I don't think I'm going to rob you."

"That's good."

She raises her face to the morning air. "They say the sense of smell is the most evocative. It brings back memories out of nowhere."

Companionably he tilts his nose. "What are you smelling now?"

"A picnic. Long ago. My friend and I, under a tree. That tree." Though even as she says it she hears the doubt creeping into her voice. "Or maybe that one over there. My memory is not what it was."

"Was it an elm or a maple? That should narrow it down."

"I don't remember. I'm not one for trees as a rule, but this stayed with me."

"Actually," his voice is gentle, "it doesn't sound like it did." He folds down the corner of the page and closes his book.

"You shouldn't do that. It's bad for the pages."

"That's okay," he says. "It was a gift."

And because, in the proper frame of mind, everything is reminiscent she says, "My friend would have hated that."

"The one from the picnic?"

"He was very particular about his books."

"So was mine. That's part of why I do it."

She's not sure why that makes her smile. "My name is Bunny."

"Surely not."

"Well. Barbara Jean. Barbara Jean Bingham."

"That must be fun to say."

"Not as much as you'd think. As a girl I always imagined I should be wearing a pinafore."

He shakes his head. "I don't know what that means." A grimy hand smooths the cover of his book. "People call me Clean."

"Mr. Clean?"

"Just Clean."

"Is that your name?"

"It's one of them."

"Do they ever call you Bill?"

"They never do."

"You look like a Bill," she says.

She's balancing now on the suitcase, on the moment. She hugs the purse on her lap. There is a slick of moisture beneath the tight grip of the wig, but her lips are bone dry.

"Are you okay?" he asks.

They have planted a capsule under her skin, a slow timed-release of toxins. The pills she takes are not so much against the ravages of her body as the ravages of the cure. She imagines it as a war now, an ongoing contest requiring all her vigilance. "I think maybe I should eat something," she says.

Clean touches his pockets with the helpful air of one who already knows they are empty. "Skinned, I'm afraid."

"Oh, I brought a picnic. How could I not? Would you like to join me?"

He glances around at the obvious lack of food. It almost makes her laugh. "Don't worry," she says. "I'm sure there's plenty." She turns back toward the way she's come. "If you could just reach it for me. I'm between pills right now."

"What kind of pills?"

"All kinds. It's something new I'm trying."

"Maybe you should take one."

"They make me a little uncertain."

"Nobody here but us," he says.

She opens her purse. A careful search among amber bottles and she shakes a pink oval onto her palm. "Would you be a dear? There's a bottle of water."

He walks over and finds the grocery bag lying in the grass. He opens it with the air of someone willing to be pleased. "There's wine."

"Just the water for now." She accepts it gratefully. "There are pink pills for the aches but they make me queasy. Blue pills for the queasy but they make me dizzy. White pills for the dizzy, but I'm not always sure what they do." To the expression on his face she says, "Isn't it funny how the world works."

She swallows the pill and waits uncertainly. After a moment she reaches into her purse again. "Since we have the water." She shakes out two more: blue, and another one, bright, unexpectedly yellow.

"What does that do?"

"It holds me all together."

This time, after a moment, she begins to feel them work. "Oh my. They are a little dreamy." From the depths of her purse a timer goes off: a muffled beeping and then silence. "And there we are. Right on time." Wearily she smiles. "Life's an adventure, isn't it, Bill? Isn't that what you always said?"

"Is it?"

Another sip of water and she straightens herself primly. "So, what do we have for lunch?"

"You're the one who brought it."

"Surprise me. A girl likes to be surprised."

"Why don't you sit on something more stable. Just so you don't tip over."

Bunny rises from the suitcase. The ground's a little tricky: more uneven than she expects and softer in places. She settles onto the bench with a little sigh of relief. "Isn't this nice."

He arranges on the surface between them her various parcels. He is thinner up close, and as he opens them he touches the tip of his tongue to his lips as if reminding himself of all the possibilities of taste. Out comes the bottle of chardonnay. "A Jug of Wine," he says, "a Loaf of Bread, and thou."

"What luck," Bunny murmurs. "A reader."

She draws a corkscrew from her purse. "Would you mind?"

He handles it uncertainly, looking pleased when it eases the bottle open. "That's a neat trick." He pours the wine into a plastic cup and holds it out.

"You're not having any?" she says.

"Maybe later."

She sips. "Do you think it's true that you leave a little bit of yourself in every place you're happy?"

"I wouldn't know. It doesn't seem likely."

"But isn't it a lovely idea?" She considers the plastic cup. "He brought glasses the first time. Wasn't that sweet? Tall and delicate. I think they were the only two he had. He bought them just for us. And a tablecloth. A table and chairs. Plates. And all the stars and fireflies. It must have taken all afternoon to set it up." She looks around, not quite finding a place in the wide expanse of grass and trees for everything she recalls. "Do you remember that first picnic? Do you remember what we had?"

"I'm sorry. I don't think I do."

"Wine and bread and cheese. Olives and tiny tomatoes. Cold green beans and a single apple. Do you remember what he said when he unpacked it all?"

"Why don't you remind me."

"We can't have paradise without an apple. Isn't that sweet? It made me blush." The smile fades on her lips. "I used to think about it over the years. Much more than I should. I used to think about it all the time. But now, wouldn't you know? I can't quite remember."

She drinks the wine, feeling the drift and flow of the pills in her blood. When she holds out the empty cup he says, "Are you sure about that?"

"Bunny," she replies. "Are you sure about that, Bunny."

"Maybe you shouldn't be mixing."

Her smile is of the gravest sort. "My husband left me for a Pilates instructor. My daughter just got married without me. I have a hole in my shoulder the size of a teacup." She gazes at the dappled sunlight on the grass as she waits for all the far flung thoughts to settle. "Oh, Bill. It's a hell of a time for a gal when she loses her looks."

"That sounds like a line from a movie."

"It's the pills. They make everything seem like something else."

Reluctantly he refills her wine. "Say when." But she watches the mounting level without urgency until finally he is forced to stop. The cup is steady in her hand. "Here's to love," she says.

He looks uncertain.

"Got to have a toast, Bill. For luck." She takes a long sip. Then she runs her tongue over dry lips, measuring the effect of this, as well. "So what shall we talk about?"

He hesitates, casting about. "This picnic is nice."

"Oh, let's not talk about food."

"What, then?"

"Current events?" she says.

"I'm not really up to date."

"Sports?"

"Sorry."

"The weather?"

"It *is* a beautiful day," he concedes. His eyes drift over the abundance of food, the elegance of her clothes, the large, pink suitcase. "So, what did you do today, Bunny?"

She smiles. "A question. What a lovely way to begin."

"My daughter just got married. Did I say that already?"

"I think you did."

"I came out for that, I suppose. We'd been planning it for so long. And now here I am."

"And how did it go?"

"Did I tell you she eloped?"

"Maybe you should have called ahead."

"Oh, don't," she murmurs. "That's unworthy of you. It

sounds like something Roger would say." She fingers the clasp of her purse. "I wonder. What would you think? Maybe just a little pick-me-up? You wouldn't begrudge me that, would you, dear?"

"Certainly not."

She shakes a pill out onto her hand and sits there contemplating. "A girl is supposed to be married out of her mother's home. Isn't that a lovely way to put it? We always talked about it when she was little. How big a reception, what to serve. She always had her own ideas. And it's not that Patrick isn't a nice boy. But he's twenty-eight, and she's only seventeen. Isn't that too young to be married? Wouldn't you say so?"

"What did she say?"

But Ruth had said so many things. And Roger. It had never ceased to amaze Bunny, just how alike her daughter and husband were. So ready to argue. So determined to be right.

And so, as if January first were the starting gun, she lost her family by degrees. Roger first, just a trial separation; he thought it would do them some good. Then Ruth's engagement, young as she was. And then it was Bunny's turn to rebel, but her body did it for her.

And with that everything changed from *what was* to *what if*. She thought she had convinced them both a May wedding would be beautiful. She'd be on her feet by then. Roger was so reassuring. Ruth, back in prep school in Connecticut, let her make all the plans she liked.

And then, just before the second surgery, Bunny had stopped by Roger's apartment. She just wanted to talk. Nothing melodramatic. Just in case something happened under the anesthetic. But Roger wasn't home. The cleaning lady let her in. It was a beautiful apartment, looking out over the lake. They had never lived anywhere so nice when they were together. There were some things on his desk. Travel brochures. Caribbean resorts. Wedding menus. A small list of guests. A thick envelope of cash. She helped herself.

Usually only the daughter elopes, but for Bunny it was a family affair. Ruth and Patrick; Roger and all the pleasures of Pilates. Bunny had told the doctor just a short delay; plenty of time for the surgery after. She'd be there and back in no time. Though by then she could barely get out of bed. And when he had frowned at her, that was all it took. Better safe than sorry, he had said. Well. She was sorry, sure enough. For the rest, they'd have to see. Roger was all sympathy. It was just bad timing, he had said. And that was true, as well.

"I think, in the end, Ruth was just embarrassed. She didn't want to wait. All the arrangements, all the people. She didn't want to be a pregnant bride in a tight white dress. That was always a little joke in our family. And I guess, in the end, Roger agreed."

"So why did you come?" he asks.

"This is the date. The one we planned originally. This is when I said I could come. I guess I just wanted to prove that I could."

But she worries it's more than that. She worries that she has come uncoupled from her actual life, and is committing herself to all that might have been. "I imagined what it would be like: coming to see her, talking to her. The mother-daughter chat before the wedding. I wanted her to learn from my mistakes. I wanted her to know what I had done."

She still has the pill in her hand. She considers it for a moment, then takes it, chases it down. She sits for a moment. "She's so stubborn. She didn't get that from me. I've never been as stubborn as I should. She said she wanted to manage her own life. I think she felt we weren't doing such a good job. I don't suppose she's wrong." Her smile is wistful. "You're an awfully good listener, Bill. I've always thought so. You don't often meet a man who can listen. Are you sure you won't have some wine?"

"I'm not much of a drinker."

"Neither am I. That's what Roger always said. I was a cheap date. I'm not all that sure it was a compliment." She holds out her cup. "Would you mind?"

He hesitates.

"Don't be like that. What's another drink between friends?"

"Is that what we are?"

"A friend is someone you can talk to. Someone who knows you at your worst."

He glances around at the green grass, the leafy trees, the sunshine puddling on the lawn. "And this is the worst, do you think?"

"Oh, I hope so."

"Why don't you eat something? There's a lot of food here." She watches as he tears off a piece of bread and lays it on the bench where she can reach it. He adds a piece of cheese.

"It's such a comfort, to be attended to," she says and smiles. "You wouldn't think it, I know, but I had nice shoulders once. Once upon a time. The rest was a little meager, but a gal's got to be proud of something. And, of course, wouldn't you know it, that's the spot they chose. Do you ever wonder where all the happiness goes? I mean, it must go somewhere. It can't just disappear."

He shakes his head. "It's not something I know a lot about."

"But wouldn't it be nice? Little pockets of it here and there. Like buried treasure. But how do you find it again? That's the problem. How do you dig it up?" She is a little unsteady on the bench, as if parts of her body have become weightless without her realizing it. "He kissed me there. On my shoulder. Do you remember? In the moonlight. That very spot. And sometimes, late at night, when I've had a glass of wine or two, I can still feel it. Just the touch of it. As if nothing had changed." She feels her eyes close of their own accord.

"Bunny?"

"Hmm?"

"Are you okay?"

"Do you remember getting married? Wasn't that something? In the Chapel of the Forest on a Thursday evening in early May. But that's the thing. It was all early May. When you only have three weeks to remember, you can be sure about the month."

She opens her eyes again onto the bland and ordinary lawn. "I remember that first night. Do you? You haven't forgotten that, have you? You took a sip of wine. Then you leaned forward and kissed me. We hadn't kissed before; we were determined not to. Do you remember? It was all perfectly harmless, perfectly honorable. I think you even said that, how honorable we were being. Two friends enjoying a beautiful night. But then you leaned forward and we kissed—in the silence, with all those fireflies—and the wine spilling over my tongue."

"And his name was Bill?"

"Stop it," she says almost teasingly. "You know Bill. Good old Bill. Don't say you don't."

He hands her another piece of bread. She takes it gratefully but just holds it in her lap.

"Bunny?"

"And now she's married. Our little Ruth. *Where you go I will go, and where you stay I will stay. Your people will be my people and your God my God. Where you die I will die, and there will I be buried."* She looks up at him. "You always had such a memory for things. Do you remember where that's from?"

"I'm sorry, no."

"You never met her, did you? I'm sorry for that." She peers out onto the wide green sweep of the park, considering it all for a moment. "I'd like to have talked to her. I'd like to have told her some things. I'd like to have given her something. A ring. You remember that ring, don't you, dear? That first one? I was mad for rings in those days. One on every finger. But that was my first. It was my mother's ring. You know, she passed away years ago."

"I'm sorry. I didn't know," he says. And then, in the silence, "I never knew my mother. My father, yes. Though I'd probably have been better off the other way around."

"Is he still alive?"

"No. He died a long time ago."

"What was he like?"

"Big. Mean. But he was my father, and that's got to mean something, doesn't it?"

"It all has to mean something, dear."

"Tell me about the ring."

The wine is cool and sweet on her tongue. She sips as if the mere sensation could bring back almost anything. "She gave it to me when I was a girl. It was a simple thing. Just a gold band with a big square garnet. Something she'd bought for herself when she was a girl. She wore it until she got engaged. When she said she was giving me her ring I thought she meant the other one, a beautiful diamond my father had given her. I was so disappointed. I'm sure my mother could tell. It made me very sad when she died."

He is watching her. She is grateful for that, as if his attention, alone, can help prop her up. "At least you have her ring," he says.

"I wanted to give it to Ruth. I wanted to give her something of mine. Something of my mother's. She's got too much of Roger already."

"You'll see her again. You can give it to her later."

Bunny peers into his face. Despite the hair, despite the terrible beard he looks so understanding, so sympathetic. Though that could be the wine, the pills. She isn't foolish, however much she'd like to be. "But you see my problem now? You see what I've done? I've lost them both. I've lost them all. Everything. Everybody. Ruth, Bill. Even dull old Roger. And the ring. I've lost the ring."

"You'll find it."

"No. It's gone. Don't you remember? We buried it. Eighteen years ago. We dug a hole at the base of our tree, and planted our happiness there." She turns and stares at the long sloping hillside, at all the nameless trees. "Oh, Bill. Can you imagine being so young? To bury a ring? To think that nothing was more important than marking that time? Tell me you remember. We sat beneath the stars. We sat and drank our wine and kissed. And all the fireflies moved around us. And he read me a poem. And we buried it. The poem, the ring, his father's watch. Oh, my."

She is at a loss.

"Tell me," he says.

She offers up a wistful smile. "Can you imagine? Those moments of happiness. They're unlike anything else. And even then we must have known it. How easily the whole day would just disappear. So we wrapped our treasures in a handkerchief, the most precious things we had. And a year later we would come back together and dig them up. Isn't that a beautiful thought?"

She isn't crying. Her cheeks are dry. That's good, surely. Or have even her tears been taken away?

"But we never went back. How could we? Not after all that happened. And now."

She looks around at the trees, one after another after another. "Do you ever think about death?"

"I do," says Clean. "Every day. But never my own."

Hesitantly she smiles. "Tell me it's going to be all right."

"It's all right, Bunny. It's just the pills. It's just the wine."

"Oh, Bill. We weren't big drinkers, were we. Not really, I mean. I wasn't. How did you manage when I left? I worried about that. I was afraid about what you might do."

"No need to worry," he says gently. "Everything works out in the end."

"Does it? Does it really? We did have our moments, didn't we?"

"Of course," he says. "Who could forget?"

But she can hear her own voice changing. Between the pills and the wine, she can feel herself deflating. "Oh, Bill. I didn't think I'd ever see you again."

"It's okay, Bunny."

"At least we were happy. Weren't we? I think we were. I like to think we were. And there's Ruth. At least there's Ruth."

"Your daughter."

"Oh, don't be cruel. I should have told you. But that was such a hard letter to get. Even you must have thought so. It's what I deserved, I know. But it broke my heart a little. The part that wasn't broken already." Her eyes are filling now, her heart already full. "But you might have come for me. I thought you would. I thought you might." She is cradling the wine for comfort, but she can't bring herself to drink. Not with the memory so close at hand: sipping the wine from mouth to mouth, nothing but days and days ahead. "I don't know what you expected. After all that happened. What could I do? What else could I do? I mean, Roger was there. He'd come to take me home. I had a wedding to get to. My wedding, for heaven's sake. I put it off. I put it off as long as I could. I thought you'd come. But you didn't. Just the letter."

"It's okay," he says gently. "You should probably eat."

But she can only shake her head. "Now there's nothing. Not even this." She gazes around at the park. Impulsively she stands. "Come on, Bill. Let's find it. Come with me." She reaches for his hand, drawing him up from the bench.

But even as she turns there is no place to go. "Is this right? Is this the spot? We sat next to a hillside near an old stone bench. And you kissed me." But she is gazing bleakly now. Pearls, silk suit. She sinks to her knees as if she might dig with nothing but her fingers, but the grass is impenetrable. All her strength gone. She can feel his eyes on her. A crazy woman. That's what she's become. He settles down beside her, gathers up her hands.

"Don't," she says.

"There's no digging up happiness. It's not like that."

"But it should be, shouldn't it? It should be like that." And now she can weep, at least. At least there's that. "Tell me it's here. After all that's happened, just tell me that." But she's crying so hard now, tears adding themselves to the flow of all she can't hold onto. "Oh Bill," she sobs. "Oh Billy Bill. I miss you so. Oh, please don't be dead. Oh, please."

BUNNY

2.

She wakes slowly into the new day, with so little memory of what's come before that all she can do is lie there, unfinished and strange. For a moment she allows herself to wonder if this is simply another dream. If she closes her eyes again, will she wake up as herself? But then the ache in her shoulder returns, roused and ready for the day, and like a thread running back through the long maze of her dreams, it leads her to herself.

She gets up, washes, dresses. The hotel suite is comfortable. It was reserved for Ruth and Patrick, the bridal suite, and no one thought to cancel it when all the plans had changed. Finding it empty on her arrival, the only vacancy in the hotel, she thought it was a sign. Though now it only makes her sad, as if she's always a step behind the rest of her life.

Automatically she checks her purse. The thick envelope catches her eye, though she doesn't remember opening it; beside it the glossy brochure of white beaches and a peaceful world. *Come to the Caymans to Play.* She wonders why she took it. Why she hadn't just left it on his desk. At the time it seemed like a point she was making, but now. Now she wonders if this is just what she's become? A magpie, drawn to the glint of other people's lives?

In the last few months the line between *is* and *absolutely not* has grown blurrier every day. It's something she has noticed, along with all the rest of her symptoms. In the course of a day she will catch, out of the corner of her eye, one impossibility or another. A penguin, say, amid the Spring display at Saks, or a resting dromedary among the bushes on the Kellermans' lawn. Just for an instant. A second only. When she looks again, of course, it's gone, resolved into something more ordinary: a pile of branches, a bicycle.

But still.

It troubled her at first, the unreliability of it all. Though now she has begun to wonder, begun to resist that second glance. She has tried to embrace the possibilities, to see them not as a series of small mental breakdowns, but as something new, an addition to her life.

And the fact is, she has begun to wonder if it might mean something.

She half-imagines—with what she hopes is sufficient irony—that the universe is somehow talking to her, laying out its possibilities to her senses, now made more delicate and perceptive, more open, to the shifting state of things.

And though it worries her, a little, that she would think this, it is only when she emerges into the hotel lobby and sees, through the wide glass doors, the figure sitting at the bus stop—wild beard and hair like a Norse god in a dusty suit—that Bunny wonders if she has slipped too far. There is nothing about him that could be real.

She waits for him to shift or vanish, but he doesn't, of course. (There is a part of Bunny proud of that *of course*.) So she pushes out through the heavy glass doors. The sun is bright. She thinks at once of his sunglasses, of his squinting discomfort, and hurriedly reaches for her own. When she looks up again he has closed his book and is waiting.

"Good morning," she says.

"I'm not Bill."

"I know."

Her eye falls on the grocery bag from the day before, slumped on the bench beside him. "I didn't think you'd mind," he says. "I didn't want it to go to waste." There is a little cardboard Starbuck's tray with three large cups of black coffee, two of them empty.

"Is one of those mine?" she asks.

"It can be."

"How many sugars?"

"I didn't really count. They just have them there on the counter."

She sits down beside him and takes a grateful sip. "Here's a funny thing," she says. "How did I get back?"

"We took a cab. I've never been in one before. It had a particular smell. I collect them. It wasn't one I'd noticed before. You fell asleep. I found the room key in your purse. And money. The driver said I was supposed to tip him, but that didn't seem right. I have change from a twenty." He glances at the tray of cardboard cups. "Two twenties. I bought extra."

"Change is good," she says.

He is eyeing her with what can only be concern. Bunny savors it like the coffee. "How are you feeling?" he asks.

The truth surprises. "Not awful. This coffee is nice."

"Have you eaten?"

"I'm not hungry."

"Maybe a pill."

"I don't think so." She hesitates. "I wasn't really myself yesterday."

The news doesn't seem to disturb him. "What about today?"

"It's probably too early to tell."

"You have an appointment at ten," he says.

She glances over. "And you know that how?"

"You asked me to come with you. You said I was your guardian angel."

The shape of the words is familiar. A fragment from the day before along with the slow ebbing of her sobs, the unexpected comfort of his arms. He'd smelled of earth and old wool. Wordlessly now she sips her coffee. He reaches into the grocery bag and nibbles on a piece of bread.

They take another cab. Clean wears a thoughtful expression, stroking the upholstery with his fingertips, though Bunny doesn't smell anything strange. They emerge before an elegant brick townhouse in the middle of a leafy street. She climbs the steps with his hand at her elbow, an elderly woman of thirty-nine. Every movement rings from her body a little chime of pain. There is a small brass plaque: Philip Hilliard, attorney.

"Is it time for a pill, yet?"

"Not yet."

"Do you want me to wait outside?"

"Don't be silly. Nothing frightens a lawyer."

She tugs on the heavy door, trying not to use her left arm at all. A receptionist's desk sits empty at the base of a curving flight of stairs. There is a deserted air to the place. The man who steps out from the back office is dressed for the weekend in a t-shirt and jeans—a thin white mouse rousted from its hole, all pointy face and irritation. He hesitates at the sight of Clean. "When I heard you'd fallen on hard times, this isn't what I pictured."

"Hello, Phil. It's nice of you to see me. I wasn't sure you would."

"Old time's sake. Curiosity, I guess." He takes in the sight of her, but she can no longer imagine what he sees. "You're looking a little peaked there, Bunny. Happy days?"

"I've had my ups and downs."

"You're not going to be sick on my carpet, are you?"

"I'll try not to."

"She needs to sit down," Clean snaps. He is already guiding her into the office toward a deep leather chesterfield.

"A little more upright," she murmurs, and he brushes a folded blazer off a chair and settles her like a dove on its perch.

Phil regards the fallen jacket for a moment, then stoops and picks it up. "I heard you'd been living on your own. I didn't realize you had a valet."

"Are you still in touch with Roger?"

"Not much. Alumni stuff. Odds and ends."

"Anything recent?"

He considers his answer. "I'm sorry you're sick, Bunny."

"You don't sound sorry."

"No one deserves to get sick."

"But you think maybe I do?"

Her phone beeps three times. Clean is rummaging through her purse. He shakes out a blue pill, and then a yellow one just to be sure. "Blue is aches and pains, right?"

"Is he your nurse?"

"Pink for the aches. And that lovely yellow one." She slips them into her mouth and closes her eyes to swallow.

"Give us some water," says Clean.

Bunny sips gratefully, listening for a moment as if the pills are singing in her blood. Her voice, even to herself, is a kind of afterthought. "Do you remember senior year?"

Phil looks impatient. "Not a bit of it."

"Just at the beginning of May? You were headed off to Amsterdam. Remember? To paint. To find yourself. You were so excited. We were sitting in the living room, just the three of us. Who was your girlfriend? Nancy?"

"Nancy," he admits.

"She knocked on the door. You said goodbye for the last time. Out in the hall, because we were there. She was crying, I remember. You kissed and whispered. I thought that was so sweet. She left, weeping. We could hear her through the open window. But you just looked relieved."

"Did I? That doesn't sound very considerate. It was a long time ago."

"Roger said you married her."

"I did. It didn't last."

"He said you married again. A nice young man."

"We'll have to have you over sometime," he says drily. "We'd all have so little to talk about."

"But do you remember?" Bunny says "That afternoon? We spent the whole time waiting for the limo to come and take you to the airport."

"I was waiting for the limo. You two were just waiting to be alone. Where was Roger, by the way? Do you remember?"

"D.C. Just a few more weeks. The end of his clerkship. You talked about painting. About starting over. About going to a country where no one knew anything about you. You could not stop talking about that."

"Really?" He looks a little daunted. "That didn't last, either."

"But you remember it? That moment? When everything was possible?"

He is regarding her more gently now. "What do you want, Bunny? You call me out of the blue. For what? Talk about old times?"

"Tell me."

"Why come to me?"

"Who else can I ask?"

"It's been a long time. It's not as if you kept in touch."

"Oh, come on, Phil. You're his friend."

"I'm his lawyer."

"And his friend." She regards him steadily. "Isn't it funny? I haven't seen you for eighteen years, and you look exactly the same. I can barely remember what Bill looked like."

He almost smiles at this. "You were the only one who called him that."

"Good," she says. "Now tell me how he is."

"I don't know how he is."

"Just tell me, Phil."

"He's gone, all right? Is that what you want to know? He heard you were coming and he left."

She is silent at that, catching at some last, receding echo. "You always were a little cruel."

"Not cruel." He hesitates, smoothing the drape of the blazer over his arm, then he sinks down onto the arm of the sofa. "People have their ups and downs. It's just what happens. He was okay for a while. Early on, when you left. He drank a bit, but then he stopped. He bought a house. But that didn't last. Sold it, oh, a long time ago. That wasn't so great."

"You were supposed to look out for him."

"I did. I tried. I took care of him where I could. A few different jobs. Some he kept, some he didn't. He got to looking pretty threadbare. But he was okay. He was sleeping in my garage for a while." He offers up a wan smile. "How about that for a friend?"

"You let him sleep in a garage?"

"I told him he could stay with me. As you might imagine, he declined. He said he was doing fine. Then out of the blue, he stops by. Couple of months ago. He looked bad. I think he'd started drinking again. I tried to give him something to eat. We shot the breeze. He left."

"Just like that?"

He reaches into the blazer pocket. The newspaper clipping is thin and rumpled. He smooths it on his lap and hands it over. Bunny's heart tightens, but it's nothing. An announcement. A wedding announcement. *Ruth Marie Bingham to wed Patrick Buxton Falls in Cheshire, Connecticut.* A photo of the happy couple. There is a bright determination behind the girl's smile that makes her seem older, all finished and grown up, as if Bunny is looking into the future or as if, like Rip Van Winkle, she has slept through long portions of her life.

"I must have missed this."

"He didn't."

"Doesn't she look beautiful?"

Phil is frowning slightly, as if he's looking for just the right place to begin. "He didn't want to be around for it. All the festivities. Happy families being happy together. He didn't want to see you."

She takes a sip of water, feels the cold trickle down her throat.

"He's disappeared before," says Phil. "Just up and gone.

But never like this. Sometimes I'd find him at the homeless shelter. Sometimes in the park."

Bunny tries to imagine it, but all she can picture are the table and chairs, the fireflies and the glasses of wine. "That's awful."

"That's not awful. I'll tell you what's awful." A moment's hesitation and he steps to his desk. There is a short stack of files. "I started looking around. Anything the police might have. Anybody down on his luck."

"Still chasing after him?"

"Just trying to give him a hand. That's all he's ever let me do. Too little and too late. This is nothing," he says. "Probably nothing." But he hesitates now, as if, having picked up the files, he can't quite bring himself to show her. He hands them instead to Clean, who opens the first. A typed report. A photograph. A man lying, ragged and pinched, beside a dumpster. His face is hollow-cheeked and grey. It's clear that he is dead.

Bunny forces herself to look. "That's not him."

"No," says Phil.

Clean leafs through the next file and the next. "That's not him, either," she says. "That's not him."

But the first relief vanishes with the unrelenting photos. The men are beaten, starved, stabbed. The last one is terrible. Railroad tracks. Blood. A sprawled figure, horribly damaged. But not him. None of them him. Each one clearly no one she has ever seen. It is just the bleakness of it all, the shabby depths of such unhappiness. What are her memories compared to that?

She says, "You don't know he's dead."

"I don't know anything."

"Then why are you showing me these?"

"Because you asked," he says. "Because I'm tired of being the only one who's afraid. Because I don't know where he is, but where he's been is bad. And you weren't the one who got him back on his feet. You weren't the one who found him a place to stay. That wasn't you, was it? All these years. You don't know whether he's alive or dead. He could have been hit by a train for all you know. And now you show up out of the blue. Remind me, Bunny. Tell me again about the power of love."

She swallows. She is grateful for the pills, the watery numbness. "You were supposed to look out for him." It is all she can say.

"You broke his heart, Bunny. What was I supposed to do about that?"

Clean is hovering, leaning close. "Do you want some more water? Do you want another pill?" He is in her purse. "Here. Here's another yellow one." But she just holds it in her hand. It feels as if all the weight of all the dread of all her life is finally here.

Phil watches her. Even his sympathy is hard to bear. "What will you do?" he asks finally.

"I don't know. What happened to the house?"

"What do you mean?"

"Bill's house?"

"He sold it. I told you. Fifteen years ago."

She sits there quietly, waiting him out.

"I suppose it's still there," he says reluctantly. "That's the thing about houses. They tend not to move. Is this a pilgrimage, Bunny? Do you really think this is such a good idea?"

"And where, exactly?"

When they leave they take a cab—the third and final cab of Clean's life—and climb out in front of the house. Bunny stares at it without expression.

"Are you all right?"

"Let's walk around the block," she says.

Halfway along they find the entrance to the alley. She hesitates, then leads the way. Tall lilac bushes, broken asphalt. A faint, misplaced chime of familiarity hovers on the air. They stop before a picket fence and a narrow, unremarkable yard. A sturdy young man is sitting at a table. No, a woman. About twenty. Her hair is very short, a soft chestnut inch or so, furring the curve of her head. She wears a pair of heavy earphones and holds a dish antenna in her hands. She is frowning in concentration.

"Miss?" calls Bunny. She raises her hand and waves. "Excuse me? Miss?"

The girl sees them and her frown deepens. "I'm working here!" She points the antenna away in annoyance, and even Clean flinches in the face of such obvious antipathy. But Bunny is not to be undone. How do you know if the universe is talking to you? What would it look like? How would it feel? Not a misfire of the brain but a sudden possibility? Not a breakdown but a gift?

Part Two

Delilah

DELILAH

3.

Serenity has always been tricky for Del. She recognizes happiness and gloom and the low, ruffling sounds of approaching danger. She can do terror and excitement and boredom, which is really just the same as hope if you modulate the sharper notes and mellow out the middle range. But serenity is key. That's the one you need. That moment toward the end of every adventure, when you know it's going to be fine. When everything is looking rosy and bright, and all the worst has happened.

But it's a hard sound to capture, and it's nothing you can fake. You can't just find an insincere version and brighten it up. No shifting the phase or punching up the high end. You have to catch it fresh on the wing, fully formed and flying. So here she is, sitting with her eyes closed, earphones on her head, shifting the parabolic dish in its slow, prospecting arc, getting more and more irritated and impatient and outraged. Serenity. It's nothing to live by, but she knows it when she hears it.

She is dressed in baggy jeans and a grey sweatshirt, but she's thinking about changing. It's only three p.m. and she knows she should wait—in fact she's made it a rule, has actually written it on the list: no St. Regis Café until five. But Del has always hated weekends. They go on forever; they sap your will to live. During the week she keeps busy. Café Ion divides her time into manageable bites, revving her up on espresso and an air of faux-European impatience. And there is always work to be done on the website; each week she tries to record at least one Voyage. And occasionally there's Russell. If he feels like it. And she can be bothered. And he can make the time. But the long stretch of a Saturday afternoon is bleak as mid-winter, and today she's not sure if even her mother's clothes will be enough.

It used to be she'd look forward to the weekend, back when her father was still stopping by. He had mounted a mailbox for her on the white picket fence on the alley, and he would leave her notes, letters, little objects he might find on his travels, and she would write back with questions about the house or school. And sometimes if she needed to see him she would raise the little metal flag on the side of the box, and the next morning he'd come strolling along. She'd make coffee, she'd bake something, and they'd spend hours side by side reading in silence, sometimes looking around. Passing an occasional comment back and forth. He didn't come very often, but he was always happy to see her.

Wait.

One hand on the earphones, she reaches after the sound. The sighing breeze like a silk curtain drawing back. No voices. That was key. Luanne had taught her that. People were a disaster, and not just for serenity. What was needed, she used to say, was a setting both empty and welcoming. An imaginary world that could lend itself to romance and peace. A landscape each and every listener could slip into like a favorite sweater.

And there, right there, as if on cue, dropping into the center of it all, five silver notes of birdsong up and down, clear as a teardrop. She tilts the microphone just a smidge, coaxing the dip and sparkle of it. Just the right balance of loneliness and peace. Just that little bit of longing before—.

"Miss? Excuse me, Miss?" The sudden voice scours her earphones.

Del shifts away, trying to stay focused on the songbird, closing her eyes against the noise.

"I'm working here!"

"I'm sorry to interrup...."

"Can you be quiet please? I'm looking for serenity!"

The slender woman gazes at her in mild-eyed surprise. She has stepped half into the garden and now stands uncertainly by the low picket fence. "And how is that going for you?" she says at last.

Delilah dislikes her at once. She knows the kind of woman: thin and elegant. Effortlessly pretty. She wears a grey silk dress that hangs so smoothly there seems no room for a body underneath. Her hair is perfect, and she stands with such inconspicuous grace that Del finds herself hunching in response. "It's going fine," she says. "At least it was."

"Serenity?"

"And other things. Last week I trapped some excitement, a little trill of danger, and a whole unbroken minute of hope."

"Is that a lot?"

"I've never heard so much before."

The woman considers that for a moment, the tip of her tongue hesitating over dry lips. "I'd be interested to hear it sometime."

Beyond her shoulder a slender wolf of a man hovers in a dusty coat. The tangle of hair and beard makes him something out of a storybook. But then he turns and hurries away. The woman calls after him. "Clean? Oh, dear. He's a little shy."

"He's with you?"

"He is."

"He doesn't look a little scary?"

"A little," she concedes. "But angels are never what you expect."

She rests her hand now on the open gate, seeming suddenly less arrogant, more unsteady. Del lowers the microphone. "Nothing's ready yet. Not from today. It needs some work. But I have older episodes. On the website. You can listen to those, if you want."

"You have a website?"

"It's more like half a website. I share it with my mother. It's called The Voyage of Del. I'm an artist. An adventure artist."

"That sounds interesting."

Her voice without the microphone is delicate and thin. She looks increasingly fragile now beneath the flawless hair. "Do you want to sit down?" says Del.

The woman manages to close the gate courteously behind her, but then she stops to peer up at the gnarled old horror that fills the corner of the yard. "That's a beautiful tree."

"It is?"

"Would you mind terribly?" And without another word she lowers herself onto the grass and lies like a toppled mannequin gazing up into the flowering branches. The breeze sends them into a motion of pink and cream, and she lies so stiffly attentive she might be waiting for some message to be delivered through the heavy, delicate blossoms.

"Are you okay?" says Del. "Ma'am? Are you--?"

"Please don't call me ma'am. I'm lying here under your tree. I think you should call me Bunny."

"It's nice to meet you, Bunny. I'm Delilah." And because its sometimes better to get the worst of it over with right away, "Delilah Belle."

"Isn't that beautiful?" The woman smiles up into the branches, as if perhaps she has confused the names; as if it is she and the tree who have just been introduced.

"Do you think you're supposed to be doing that?" says Del.

"I think so. Yes. Would you like to join me?"

"I'm good, thanks."

"Do you believe in accidents, Delilah Belle?"

And her mind is suddenly filled with possibilities: a mugging, a car crash, a ringing blow to the head that leaves the victim wandering and disturbed. "You mean like a traffic accident?"

"Not so much. Well. I suppose so. Yes. But more generally. Do you ever think about the way things happen?"

"You mean like fate?"

The woman seems to consider that. "I don't think I believe in fate. Do you?"

"Sometimes I'd like to."

The sudden smile is wistful. "Well, that's another matter, isn't it? There was a time—a moment, actually—I thought things happened for a reason. One moment would lead to another, taking you where you needed to go. I believed in that. I thought it would lead me home."

"And it didn't?"

"In the end, no. It all just petered away. That's when I decided to believe in accidents."

The perfect smoothness of the silver hair keeps catching Del's eye, the elegance of the clothes, even lying on the grass. "I'm not sure I understand."

"Accidents. They happen, that's all. They just do. But here's the thing. Every accident is an opportunity. Like coming to this house. Meeting you." She glances over, turning her head on the grass. "Or do you think that was fate?"

"No. I guess I wouldn't say that."

"Exactly. But still. Every so often you can't help wondering. Take this tree, for example. I've seen it before."

"This one?"

"I think so. But I can't be sure. I've had an issue with trees lately. Are they familiar because you're staring at them now or because you saw them once, eighteen years ago, and you'd almost forgotten all about it?" There is a note of concern creeping into her voice. "Do you ever feel time isn't working the way it should? That things don't seem to be following the way you'd expect?"

"I'm sorry," says Del. "I'm afraid I don't."

"Is this 1816 Romany Avenue?"

"That's right."

"I used to know someone who lived here. A long time ago. Or rather, I knew him and then, after I moved away, he lived here. Just for a little while. But here's the strange part. Before I moved away, before he bought this house—years before—we came here together. I swear we did. Right to this spot. And now he's disappeared and I'm afraid he might be dead."

"I'm sorry," says Del. She tries to make her voice gentle. "I have no idea what you're talking about."

The woman sighs. "I'm not at my best. I think it's this tree. I think that's what's doing it."

Delilah doesn't reply, but there is something familiar in the moment. Something comforting that comes back to her. If this were her mother she would know what to do. She would make her a cup of tea and try to coax her up off the ground. Try to let her know that everything, as bleak as it may seem, is going to be all right. She would hug her and brush her off and try to make her comfortable.

"Can I get you anything?" says Del. "Would you like a cup of tea? Why don't you come and sit down."

"That does sound nice. This isn't as comfortable as I remember. I wonder if you could help me up?"

She is much frailer that Del expects, much thinner beneath the perfect dress. It's a tricky moment: a sharp wince, a gasp, and then she's on her feet, straightening up, catching her breath, and Del notices the perfect silver hair has shifted. It's a little bit askew.

The tea seems to help. There is half a pound cake, a slice of banana bread, half a dozen chocolate chip cookies, and most of a pan of brownies. Bunny sips the tea and nibbles, but with a dutiful air as if her mind remains on something else. Up close her face is more youthful than Del expects: a young girl made of parchment.

"Oh, dear," says Bunny. "Do I look a wreck?"

"No. Not at all. Just a little...." Del touches her own hair by way of explanation, though there is very little there. It is short and soft, an unremarkable brown, though Russell has said he likes it—Russell, who, she has begun to suspect, will say anything. As a girl she'd worn it long. But then, at fifteen when everything happened—her mother gone, her father just barely there, her life feeling like the merest figment of her imagination—she'd cut it off. Mostly she'd been angry. But gradually, over time, she has settled on the decision, first as a reminder of all that went on, and then as a kind of protection against anything worse. It makes her look strong, she thinks. And by now, of course, it's one of her rules.

Bunny reaches up to the wig. "I try to think how convenient it is, but I'm still not entirely used to it." A tiny adjustment and it's perfect again.

"I'm all about wigs," Del confides. "I have a collection."

"Well, I hope you'll show it to me sometime."

They settle into the patio chairs. Bunny turns to regard the house. It's a bright and cheerful yellow in the sunlight. "Was it ever white?" she asks.

"Not that I know. Part of that wall was lavender once. My mother thought it would be more serene. But it didn't last, and my dad painted it over."

"Didn't care for lavender?"

"I think he would have been all right if she'd finished the job. He pretty much let her do whatever she wanted. But it stayed like that for most of the summer, and finally he painted it yellow. He said a yellow house is easier to find."

Bunny smiles. "Well, we certainly found it easily enough, my friend and I. All those years ago, yellow or not. I remember walking down that alley in the twilight. The most perfect evening. We came to this spot. Not a soul around; the whole world was asleep. And we let ourselves in. We lay down under that tree."

"That tree?"

"Just the two of us. We whispered and kissed, but not for long. We made love. Under the moonlight and all those blossoms. Isn't that something?"

Delilah sits very still. She can feel her face growing warm.

"I know," says Bunny. "It sounds so unlikely. Sometimes I think…Oh, so many things. That I'm making it up. I imagined it all. Or that I was simply a different person back then, and now I can't remember who. Isn't that a terrible thought? As if you'd kidnapped your real self and you've been holding her hostage for so many years you've forgotten where you put her."

Her lips are dry, but there is a line of moisture at the edge of her perfect hair. Del lightly touches her hand. "Maybe you should eat something."

"I was worried at first. That color isn't familiar. But the fence is right. I'd swear to that. And the cherry tree is exactly the same."

Del hesitates. "It's a crabapple."

"Are you sure?"

"I'm afraid so."

Bunny can only peer at the arching branches, heavy with blossoms.

"Don't worry," says Del. "I'm sure it doesn't mean anything."

"But don't you see? That's exactly what I'm afraid of."

Del's mother had started her website, *Self-Healing Woman*, in a fit of exasperation, and against all likelihood made a business out of it. She founded the company just after she married, when Delilah turned seven. It came to be something they could do together. Del provided the computer skills and her mother the inspiration.

It was in many ways an odd career choice. Even as a girl Del used to marvel that a woman who was so upset, so much of the time, would think to found her fortunes on serenity. Or that anyone so constantly and convulsively driven between resolution and despair could launch a line of self-empowerment meditations.

But it turned out Luanne had a feel for such things. The microphone gave her a soothing voice, and she knew how comfort sounded, even if she didn't always know how it felt. Her last work was a series of four guided visualizations, each one building on a different element—earth, air, fire, and water—and each one affirming a different aspect of inner strength: awareness, breathing, passion, contentment. She had gotten the idea of organizing them as a ring, so that the final image: a spring rain nourishing the dry winter soil—a great loop of sound Del picked up in the park among the reeds by the pond—carried the listener directly back to the beginning and launched the sequence again. Her mother had gotten some good comments online. Fifteen thousand four hundred and fifty-two people downloaded her file in the first six months. She had more than twenty-two thousand likes. Though in the end even that wasn't enough.

Her mother died in the week after Del's fifteenth birthday, and even at the time she had tried to see it as a relief. A coronary, her father had said. Surely a life of such unhappiness must put a strain on the heart. And wasn't it better that it catch you without pain or dread in the comfort of a familiar place? She'd been grateful her mother hadn't fallen, that she wasn't bruised or hurt or embarrassed in public. Instead she collapsed in the garage, in the front seat of her own car, before she even had a moment to turn the engine off.

In the months that followed Del worked hard to remember it just right: a sudden painless attack that carried her off too quickly for fear, that left her, perhaps, with a brief, puzzled feeling before sweeping her away into peace. Though later, of course, as she got older, she couldn't help but know.

She tried to take over the website. But if Del had an imagination for disaster that more than matched her mother's, she had nothing of the comfort and reassurance that made Self-Healing Woman what it was. It began to weigh on her, affect her dreams, fill her muscles with fatigue. She needed something else. And what she found one afternoon was a single audio file from months past—from the week before her birthday. It lay lost among so many, but when she clicked it into life, the bright song of an evening-bird rose clearly on the air and a boy's low voice said, "Wow. Isn't that something."

It was at that point she made a decision to move beyond disaster. She actually wrote it down, the first of her rules. *Move beyond disaster.* And she began with the sudden, unspoken belief that, with a little care, in the narrow confines of a thirty-minute audio episode, things could be exactly as you wanted. She began to think of them as voyages. The Voyage of Del. And she began constructing them, drawing on the meager adventures of her own daily life, but reimagined, invested with all the wonder and satisfaction they lacked.

She kept her mother's site online, and in the early years after she was gone Del liked to listen to her recordings. With the earphones tight on her head she could sink into the messages of comfort and resolve. And if she recognized that a message of such soothing reassurance had little relation to how her mother had actually been, the voice remained perfect and preserved for when her daughter needed it most.

Though, for her mother at her very best, Delilah has always turned elsewhere.

Now she leads Bunny into the house and up to the second bedroom. She pulls from the bedside table a heavy leather volume of *The Anatomy of Melancholy*—her father's in a previous life—and draws from the hollowed out compartment a rolled baggy of pot and a pad of papers. Bunny eyes it mildly. "I think I'd better not, dear."

"Have you ever tried?"

"I think Roger objected on general principles."

"Roger sounds like a pill."

She rolls a joint, holds it out with her lighter ready. Hesitantly Bunny accepts, purses her lips. She draws in a delicate sip of smoke, then seems to brace herself for the effect. When nothing happens she takes another and another, finally breathing out with a testing, thoughtful expression. "I'm sorry, dear."

"Just give it a minute."

Del helps herself, then passes it back. This time when Bunny exhales she pauses, as if a message is gradually appearing in the faint grey haze. "Oh."

"And there's something else," says Del confidingly. "But you have to promise not to laugh."

"Not for all the world."

As a girl Del hated shopping. Nothing fit the way it should, and it always embarrassed her to try things on. But her mother loved it above all else, and when they finally bought whatever it was that Delilah could not avoid, they would turn their joint attention to Luanne. I suppose, she would say, I might look at one or two things.

They were wonderful clothes, lively and bright, stylish and extreme, and almost uniformly inappropriate for any but the most extraordinary occasions. There would never be a time to wear them all. In fact, whole weeks went by when her mother never changed out of her robe. But even so, it never struck Del as foolish. It was an expression of something fine and untrammeled in her mother's daunted life, the bright, brief embodiment of unbridled optimism.

So it was that, after her mother's death, when her father had all but left and Delilah was first living alone in the house, she had stood before the open closet, taking in the vast and parti-colored array, and from her first wildest hopes she assembled an outfit. She spent a long time thinking, making lists, composing the story of who she might be. And then she began.

It took some getting used to. At first she was overcautious, stymied by any dress that was too bright, too demanding, or just too snug. So Delilah had to concentrate. It required some nerve. But the first time she stepped before the mirror in a bright magenta party dress with an orange scarf and yellow velvet gloves, she knew she was onto something.

Now they are standing before a bank of white louvered doors. "We have to figure out who we're going to be," she explains. "That's the trick. You have to decide before you look at the clothes. You have to know who you are."

"Maybe I'll be Martha Stewart."

"No," says Del patiently. "You can't be a real person. Here. Have some more of this."

Bunny pauses delicately to refuel. "Maybe I'll be Bunny Bingham," she says through the smoke. "Sometimes I think she's not a real person."

"This is serious. You can't joke around. You have to choose. That's how it works."

"Okay," she says. "You can call me Colette."

"Colette was a real person."

"Not that Colette. Just a Colette. A different Colette."

"All right," Del says. "So what's Colette's favorite color?"

"Don't talk about me as if I'm not here."

Bunny draws on the now-dead joint and exhales, gazing meditatively at where the smoke should be. Shyly Del smiles. "I like you, Bunny. I like your hair."

"Bunny who?"

"It's perfect."

"It's a wig."

"I know."

"It keeps me company."

"I'll keep you company."

A moment's hesitation, a moment's thought. Then Bunny reaches up and removes the silver bob. Beneath it her ivory scalp is just beginning to blur with a growth of fine grey hair like the down of a chick. It startles Del—a pale and delicate version of her own sheared brown. Luanne's hair had been blonde and straight; nothing Del could have done would have made them the same.

But this. Del's heart catches at the sight. The unprotected face looks thinner, the nose sharper, the eyes dark and doubt-filled. "You look beautiful," she says.

"Old. Old and used-up."

"Don't say that. Look. Look at this." Del steps to the closet and draws back the doors, releasing into the plain white room a rainbow of color.

It takes a moment for Bunny to speak, hesitant in the face of such extremity. "Those were all your mother's?"

"You think it's creepy?"

"Oh, no. They're beautiful."

"There's more." She steps to the second closet and then to the last.

Bunny's hands settle lightly on the placket of her dove grey dress. She is sagging a little before the bright good cheer. "I haven't played dress-up since I was a girl."

"It's not dress-up," Del says earnestly. "It's adventure."

"Yes. I see."

"Don't worry. We just have to think this through."

She steps to the first closet and opens a cupboard within. Four wigs sit on their own little stands, pensive and full of purpose. They are Del's own addition to her mother's trove. She bought them when, in spite of every dress and accessory, she could still recognize herself in the mirror.

"How about this?" She lifts the black pageboy from its stand and hands it to Bunny, who slips it on with practiced ease. The transformation is abrupt. In the mirror her pinched and peaky look is gone. The dark wig frames a dramatic paleness, and when Delilah hands her the rekindled joint she stands for a moment, letting the smoke drift out of her mouth like a silent film star.

"Goodness."

Del chooses a short bob of rust-red hair, but she is suddenly shy, unnerved by the company. The red wig looks different this time. Dowdy. In the sweatshirt and jeans she resembles no one so much as her fifth-grade gym teacher. Ms. Klonsky. She feels clumsy and big beside the transformed slimness of Colette, who now becomes more and more of a stranger as she begins to remove the staid grey dress.

"Wait."

The thought of taking off her clothes makes Del anxious.

Even with Russell she is always dressed. Disarranged, perhaps—clothes tugged roughly out of the way—but still the pale embarrassment of her body remains behind the scenes. "Maybe I'll change in the next room," she says.

"Don't worry, dear. It's just a little awful at first. Don't look. We'll find something to cover it."

"No. It's not that."

"There's no running away, I'm afraid."

Unbuttoning the dress she steps out of it gracefully and lays it on the bed. She turns and regards her shoulder in the mirror: a movie starlet's pose.

Her body is slim and pale, bones a little prominent now, the flesh gone slack as if stunned by all it's endured. The wound is shocking. As big as a fist, it nestles into the curve of her shoulder up against the neck, a crater of raw artificial skin, joined at the rim by a fiery seam. The silk strap of her bra looks out of place beside it, from another life altogether.

"Does it hurt?"

"It does, actually. Along with everything else. I try to look a little longer each day."

There is something in the way she turns with a faint, birdlike hope, as if the proper angle might make it vanish or fade. It's too late now to leave the room. Hesitantly Del can only peel off her sweatshirt and drop it on the floor. She unbuckles her jeans, pries off her sneakers. The widening expanse of her own pale skin emerges into view.

They are a study in opposites. In her grey dress Bunny looked undersized and thin, reduced against her will to something less than she had been. But now, in the pale simplicity of white satin, with that striking cap of coal-black hair, she is sleek, freed from the baggy remnants of her previous self. Beside her Del feels bulky and large in white socks and plain grey underwear, another order of creature altogether.

"You look so smooth, dear. You have beautiful skin."

Del feels her face go hot.

In the end, her mother's clothes preserve her. As they always do.

The two women work their way through the Pucci prints and jersey shirtwaists, the too-bright rayon. Bunny is delighted with each dress, the wilder the better; they outfit her like a Barbie doll. Though nothing seems quite right.

But they're in no hurry. Del rolls another joint and they move on to the acetate and lycra, the wilder boundaries of Luanne's imagination, ending, against all likelihood, in a snug, orange sheath with a high neck and a hemline stretched taut above the knee. There are raspberry gloves and earrings, a yellow scarf, and most surprisingly, a pair of Luanne's own shoes, wobbly and high, that slip onto Colette's feet without a murmur of effort.

Together they regard this stranger in the mirror. She should look clownish. In all her wildest flights Del is always half-embarrassed by herself, turning before the mirror in uneasy satisfaction. But Bunny has come alive beneath the layers of disguise. She lifts the joint to her lips and sparks the lighter; exhales thoughtfully. "She looks interesting, doesn't she?" Bunny says. "I wonder what she'd do if her husband ran away with a Pilates instructor?"

"You should ask her."

"Oh, no. It's impolite to pry." She shifts her gaze to Del, one of those cardboard cutouts in bra and panties just waiting for her clothes. "And what's your name, hot stuff?"

And though this is a game she has been playing for almost seven years now, a game whose rules are entirely her own invention, Delilah suddenly has no idea what to do. Confronted with Colette, so elegantly constructed out of all the parts that have been available to her for years, she feels oddly bereft.

"Wait," says Bunny. "Let me think." She is smiling into the mirror. "You look like a *Bertrande*." Her French accent is careless and superb. "Or *Dauphine*. That's a possibility."

Even the names are impossibly slim. "Do you think?"

"Definitely. Dauphine Inez."

"What does she wear?"

"You tell me."

But Del stands helpless before the cascade of bright dresses.

Colette raises a thoughtful hand to her lips. "Let me see."

In the end she wears a pale green sheath, simple and, much to her surprise, elegant. It is very tight, but somehow that only makes her feel sleek and tautly confined. It glows against her pale skin and the red of the wig. No gloves, no scarf. No clashing colors. Bunny lifts her own pearls from the bed and fastens them around Del's neck. "Dauphine always wears pearls."

They stand side by side in the mirror. Del has an odd fluttery feeling. She used to think that without bright colors she would disappear. But there she is, pale and unexpected.

"So what do we do now?" asks Bunny.

"Now we go and tease the men at the bar of the St. Regis Hotel."

Bunny allows herself to be led out to the garden and seated at the patio table. She is smiling expectantly. "Should we call a cab?"

But with her new friend's eyes upon her, Del feels suddenly foolish and ashamed. For this is as far as it goes. This has always been the nature of adventure. Delilah in her mother's clothes with all the imagined possibilities. An hour or more, lost in the smoke and the bright details. She shapes them, transforms them into their own perfect voyage. Then she captures it, enlivens it with sound and description, and releases it onto the net. It's not just pretending. People recognize that. Her followers, her fans. Fifteen hundred downloads a month. They like it. They Tweet it. They post their comments: we love you, Del.

"So this is it?" says Bunny gently.

"Welcome to the bar at the St. Regis Hotel."

Her mother had taken her once on Del's fourteenth birthday. The elegant old hotel had been going to seed for fifty years but it clung to its shadowy elegance. Together they had dressed up and eaten their meal in a fairy tale setting of ormolu and oak.

"Can I tell you about the room?" Del says shyly.

"I wish you would, dear."

It was large and wood-paneled and warmly lit, with the glow of years past and all the promises of candlelight. They had come in after shopping, slipping out of the bright sunlight and into a booth in the elegant gloom of late afternoon. They had eaten their lunch and watched all the handsome older men and beautiful young women smiling and talking. Occasionally leaving together. Del had marveled at how quickly strangers could meet, how she could watch them fall in love. Years later she had been amazed that her mother had thought to take her there, but perhaps even Luanne had only seen what she wanted to see. They had both of them been transfixed.

"It sounds lovely."

"So that's who we are," Del explains. "A pair of glamorous women who have just stopped in on an elegant afternoon to fall in love."

Bunny smiles. "And just how glamorous are we?"

"We're here at the end of our busy day and we're waiting for our boyfriends. They're already late, but we'll give them another hour, because we're so understanding. But since they're late, we can talk to other men. Just to teach our boyfriends a lesson."

"What if they want to buy us a drink, these other men?"

"If they offer, we can accept. But only one. Because we wouldn't want to take their drinks under false pretenses. And if they try to kiss us, that's okay. But only kissing. We're not that kind of girls."

"I can tell," says Bunny, but she is gazing around at the limited scope of the garden: the tool shed, the narrow lawn, the crabapple tree.

"You don't like it," says Del.

"I do."

"We could have another joint. I can get you some wine. I have some in the fridge."

"You know, dear. It's all very nice. But I think maybe we need a real adventure."

"This is real."

"I think maybe we should go out."

DELILAH

4.

They sit in the back of the cab like birds of paradise, the two brightest objects in the wide afternoon. Del is appalled. She cannot pull her hem down far enough. She is afraid of running into someone she knows, afraid of running into anyone at all, but when the taxi stops no one gives them a glance. Pedestrians hurry past. Before them the university art museum rises: a plain stone block of a building with a wide glass door and a banner: Sunday is Art Café!!

Small groups of women in brightly colored dresses are entering with such careless self-possession that Del is frozen to the seat. "I don't think I can," she whispers.

"But we look so nice."

"This dress is too tight."

"No one will think so. We owe it to Dauphine."

"I can't even pronounce it like that."

But Bunny is already climbing out. Del's palms are slick. It's like that nightmare of arriving without pants. Bunny turns and helps her out, and while there are glances of attention, no one laughs. The glass door opens; they step into a big white room made meaningless by a scattering of abstract canvases. Del is entering a foreign embassy with neither passport nor a word of the language to her name.

The men are dark-suited, the women bright with color. They move from painting to painting with an unsurprised air. Del can't raise her voice above a whisper. "We're the only ones without nametags."

"We know who we are," says Bunny. She is breathing in as if orienting herself to the faint smell of dust and floor polish. There is a low hush of air conditioning and, only slightly louder, the answering murmur of conversation. "It still smells the same."

"You've been here before?"

"Not dressed like this."

"What were you doing?"

"Just this. Strolling. There wasn't anything in particular we wanted to see. But it was raining, and we had no place else to go. As long as we stayed here, it was fine; we were just looking at art. We could run into anybody we knew." She smiles. "Though we didn't. We walked through every gallery, up and down the stairs. We looked at every picture." She breathes. "It smells like a Sunday afternoon, don't you think? Slow, and a little heart-breaking."

They walk. There is a smaller version of the outside banner on the wall above the stairs, and underneath a drawing of a wine glass: Drink in the Art.

"I can't help but think that might do us some good."

On the lower level a selection of works from the permanent collection are hung according to the whim of the curators, and the public can sip wine and stroll among the artwork or out into the sunken courtyard as dusk approaches and a pianist fills the silence. "I don't think we're supposed to be here," whispers Del.

"Of course we are. Can't you feel it?"

Against the wall a table, draped in linen, holds a scattering of nametags: a few remaining answers still awaiting their questions. A young women in waiter's white smiles dutifully as Bunny chooses two nametags and presses one firmly over Del's heart. "Welcome, Mrs. Wheeler."

"We are going to get into so much trouble."

"Honestly, Dauphine. I had no idea you were such a worrier."

There is a table of wine glasses. Bunny helps herself to two. "Drink this. It's the antidote."

"To what?"

She slips her hand through Del's arm. They are floating through the world. "There is something I want you to see. Ah, here we are."

They have stopped before a wild painting of reds and yellows, bright and thickly impastoed. "Did you come here a lot?" asks Del.

"Just that one time."

"With your boyfriend?"

"I was engaged."

"Your fiancé, then."

"No. Somebody else. Roger was out of town. He had a clerkship in Washington that year. He would fly back for visits, or I'd fly there. But this was a busy time for him, so he missed the end of the semester. A few months later I got married. Then I had Ruth. Things got going after that. I sometimes think this was the last time I really paid attention. I was so aware of everything. And right here he took my hand."

Del is conscious of the empty hand hanging between them. She takes it. And after a moment Bunny interlaces their fingers. "And then what happened?" says Del.

"We didn't say a word." She is gazing at the painting. *The Night Café.*

"It's not exactly pretty."

Their hands are warm together. Del sips the wine, though she has never liked the taste.

"I've often wondered what it meant that this was the painting we were looking at. It's so frantic, so full of... something… I don't know what… Trouble."

"What did you do then?" Del feels strangely breathless.

"He leaned over," says Bunny, "without a word. And he kissed me." Her voice is small, a whisper of reminiscence. "Would you kiss me, dear? Just for old time's sake?"

Del hesitates. Then she leans forward and presses a kiss gently onto the warm, dry lips. Bunny's eyes close; everything about her leans into the moment. When she opens her eyes her smile is wistful. "We walked around the museum, holding hands."

"And then?"

"Oh, then. Everything."

Del is out of her depth. Even Dauphine, snug beneath her perfect wig, can make no sense of it all. She is afraid to move; afraid to do something wrong. But now there comes a murmur of voices and a little flurry out of the corner of her eye, and a man is standing at their side. Slim and smiling. No one she has ever seen. A perfect grey suit and horn-rimmed glasses; the top of his head is not so much bald as shiny and clean; the dark fringe over his ears well-barbered and smooth. "Bunny?" he says. "Is it Bunny Bingham? Aren't you a sight for sore eyes."

Bunny turns with a smile, and Del can see the years of cocktail parties coming to her aid. She starts to release her hand, but Bunny's fingers tighten in hers. "Hello."

"It's Bertie," he says. "Bertie Clutter." Though clearly a little dashed, he is determined not to turn it into a question. "I work with Roger. We met... well, it's been a few times. Back in Chicago."

"Of course," says Bunny. "I'm sorry. You caught me by surprise."

"I almost didn't recognize you." He's confiding now, sheltering his wineglass in both hands as if to shield it from the news. "You've dyed your hair."

"It's just something I'm trying."

"Well, you look wonderful." He turns to Del. "You both do. You look like a pair of butterflies in a roomful of caterpillars."

Del is once again aware of how snug her dress is, how bright. And the image of the butterfly somehow pins her to the spot. But she manages a smile.

"This is my friend Dauphine," says Bunny.

Bertie reaches out his hand, but Bunny's grip remains firm in her left hand, and her right is taken by the wineglass. She offers what she hopes is a Gallic shrug.

Bertie hesitates, then offers a little bow. "*Enchanté. Je suis tres heureux á faire votre connaissance.*" And somehow, despite it all, he is less comic than she expects. She feels the warmth rising through the exposed skin of her throat. She recalls only a single word of high school French. "*Merci.*"

"Where are my manners?" he says. "Another glass of wine? *Un peu du vin, Mademoiselle?*"

Del can only murmur, "I'm not really French," but Bertie seems oblivious. His smile is for Bunny.

"Thank you, Bertie. That would be lovely."

Del's glass is three-quarters full. As the man turns away she drains it and offers it up, pink-cheeked and gasping, when he returns a moment later with a full one. He gives not the slightest suggestion that her dress is too small, or too bright, or too foolish. He continues to address her occasionally in French, though now it is with a friendly smile, and she cannot be sure if he is teasing or not. To be safe, she says not a word. Even her silence delights him. He nods and smiles as if everything she does is managed beautifully. And Bunny, too, is rising under his attention like a daffodil in fresh water.

He isn't handsome. But he guides them through the gallery, showing them this and that, pointing out what is already clear. Sometimes he makes them laugh. And through it all Bunny holds her hand so firmly that Del cannot tell if she is giving comfort or receiving it.

"Did you ever paint as a child, Dauphine?" he asks. They are standing before a canvas of vivid yellows and blues.

"No," she answers. "I nay-vair did." It is not exactly a French accent, but she is on her third glass of wine, and if Bertie finds it unconvincing, he doesn't seem to mind.

"I know it's wrong," he replies, "but I can't help wondering if, with a little help and a little more wine, I couldn't have done just as well."

In the end he has to run. "I would rather chew off my leg

than leave right now, but I'm afraid I have an appointment." He lifts Del's empty glass from her fingers and clasps her hand, gives his little half-bow—she thinks for a moment he's going to kiss her—and she fights the urge to curtsy. He turns to Bunny. "Are you in town for long? Maybe I can take you out for dinner. Both of you. A woman on each arm. That's not something I can look forward to every day."

When he strolls away Del is sorry to see him go. Even Bunny stands a little straighter, as if, unexpected as it's been, this, too, is part of what life can be.

DELILAH

5.

When she was first on her own Del cleaned the house whenever she liked, a little bit each day. Dusting and polishing, sweeping up after herself. She bought a new vacuum. Then she saw the Miracle Swiffer on late night TV and bought that, too. Nothing wrong with cleaning, she thought. Nothing wrong with cleanliness. Though after a while she began to grow self-conscious.

So now she schedules it. Once a week, Monday, top to bottom. Vacuum, dust, wash; drawers and cupboards; bathroom and kitchen. Starting at eight, finish by three. That's the rule: she has to stop by three. And if sometimes she goes over a little, fifteen minutes, say, or twenty, if there's just a bit left. Well, what's the harm?

As a girl she had picked up ferociously after her mother. The more Luanne's attention wandered, the more spotless their apartment became. When her mother married, part of the growing promise of their lives was that she now had a father to clean up after, as well. But then her mother was gone, and her father. And one morning Del realized there was no one else to care about dishes in the sink or laundry in the hamper or mud on the carpet. It was a moment she never forgot. Her list of rules started that day.

It's surprising what you get used to. Her father had always traveled. That defined him as much as the gentle voice and the ease he had brought to their lives. In the early years, when he'd go for only a day or two, he would leave behind him the lingering shape of a family life that hadn't existed before. Del and Luanne would open his closet door, just to be reassured by the rows of hanging shirts, by the shoes and socks. She could feel her mother drawing on the deep reserves of calm that drifted off the clothes.

But it didn't last. Her mother began to take his traveling personally. And often when he returned—and as the years passed and Luanne's responses grew more extreme, the trips became longer and more frequent—she would be cold and angry, resentful, as if he had taken something of hers when he left and forgotten to bring it back.

Her mother was unreasonable, Del had always known. Though it was only with her father's arrival that she recognized an alternative. She began to brace herself for the homecomings, comparing, even without meaning to, her father's calm with the ragged uncertainty of her mother's irritation. Del came to believe, in a way that went beyond the limits of science, that she had inherited all her better self from him. She explained it once, when Luanne had gone to lie down one Saturday afternoon. "I'd be happy to think that's true. Yes," he said. "Let's decide to believe it." And in that moment she actually thought—Del remembers this long after her mother has gone—how much smoother life might be if it was just the two of them.

There was a big argument on the night before she died. Del returned home to find her mother hysterical and her father almost stiff with impatience. Someone had broken in, she cried. Had tried to kill them both. He doesn't care! We could have been murdered in our beds!

But it was nothing like that, her father had said. It was just some homeless kid looking for food. Though his weary tone just inflamed her more.

If her mother had been afraid, Del would have comforted her. But Luanne was in a fury. And Del was in the grip of her own disaster. It was her birthday, after all. She had met a boy. Calvin. They had made plans. But by the time she returned home that evening, all her plans were in tatters, and her mother was incandescent. "You think I'm crazy and unreasonable. You think I don't see? Your stepfather would rather take the side of some homeless vagrant than his own wife."

And Del had lost her temper. She never lost her temper. "You are such a drama queen! You're not the only one in the world who's sad!"

And the next day she was dead.

There were times in later years when Del would wonder if she had made up any part of the story. It seemed impossible so much could happen on a single day. But when she thought back she saw it as the beginning of a whole new life: her mother dead, her father drifting away. And she never saw Calvin again. Everything from before became a kind of daunted opportunity, a moment of preparation for a life that would never occur.

She went about her days. She dissolved into sobs that left her face dripping and the breath thin in her lungs. She went to school. She cleaned.

She waited.

With her mother gone she began to wonder if all the anger and distraction, all the wild flights of fury, might simply fall away. They got along well, her stepfather and she. They were a comfort to each other. In those first months after her mother's departure—and for a long time Del could only think of it as a departure, as if Luanne had actually put the car into gear and driven out of their lives—he hovered beside her. He rose to fix her breakfast, came home early to be waiting when she got back from school. He tried to care for her.

And Del should have let him. But she couldn't quite stop herself: the cooking, the cleaning. She found herself taking over. Not just to keep busy but to keep her life in place, to keep it from collapsing like an empty tent. And as if that weren't enough, she found herself saying things: You're late for lunch. Dinner is cold. Can't you see I've already mopped the floor.

They appalled her, the things that leapt out of her mouth.

But he would nod and smile. He'd apologize. He took off his shoes at the door and sat down for dinner at an earlier and earlier hour as Del found herself with less and less to fill her afternoons. And then one morning late in the summer he said, "I'm going to be gone overnight. Just a short business trip. I'll be back by dinner tomorrow."

And she watched him go with a sinking heart. There was no way to avoid the realization. After all, there was no one else there. Now, when her father left, even for a day, he was leaving her. The thought came to Del that, having just turned fifteen, with the whole vast space of her life before her, she had somehow and against all effort turned into her mother.

She cooked him breakfast, packed him lunch, made him dinner. She washed his clothes, cleaned the house. It was a normal life. Then one day he came home from work, holding his right hand as if it were a small animal he wanted to protect. It was wrapped in gauze, stained with blood as if a red pen held between his last two fingers had leaked all over the bandage. "It's nothing," he said.

A lawnmower had kicked back. The motor had taken the tips of his last two fingers. She burst into tears when he first unwrapped it, but he smiled and patted her shoulder. "I'm okay," he said. "I'm okay."

"Is this because of mom?"

"It's just an accident. Just something that happened. It doesn't mean anything."

But, of course, it did. And it worried her that he couldn't see. Piece by piece, right before their eyes, their life was disappearing.

Then one morning he left his lunch behind, and she determined to take it to him. She looked up the company online. *Greenville Lawn and Garden*. She had seen the name for years on the pocket of his shirts, bright letters outlined in a green pick-up truck. Now she put the lunch bag and a cold can of coke in the basket of her bicycle and pedaled off.

The nursery was like a little village on a cul-de-sac in the hills to the west of the city. She pedaled up and around the base of Willow Rock to catch the tail end of the old Hartford Turnpike, then she followed it past houses and trees to a sign that said simply *Greenville*.

It pleased her, the sign, the curving gravel road, the great squares of trees looking so established and broad, so set in the earth. It was a village of plants, a suburb of roses, and then the rising peaks of greenhouses. She was smiling as she parked her bike. In the office she spoke to the pleasant-faced woman and then to the gruff and dusty foreman who sat at a desk before a map of the nursery and explained that her father hadn't worked there for a year-and-a-half.

When he arrived home that night his pants were caked with dirt, his hands glazed with a faint wash of mud. He sat down at the table and said, "Hey, tulip. How was your day?"

"I rode my bike all the way to Greenville Nursery."

"Pretty place, isn't it?"

"They hadn't even heard of you."

"Yes, they had."

"They thought you were dead."

"No, they didn't."

"They said you'd been carried off by pigeons six months ago."

"I thought they'd never heard of me."

"Or eaten by squirrels."

"If you can't trust a squirrel...."

She waited with a thunderous look on her face.

"I don't work there any more, sweet pea. I work somewhere else now."

"Why didn't you tell me?"

"I didn't think you'd care."

"I rode all the way out there."

"I'm sorry. It's a pretty ride, isn't it?"

"It's such a beautiful place." Her voice was wistful. "It's like a little town of flowers."

"It wasn't as nice as it looked. I work at a really beautiful place now."

"Really? Let me see your shirt."

The patch above his pocket was vacant now except for a broad smear of dirt, but he turned in his chair. Across his back was printed *Lawnkeepers Grass and Grounds*.

"It's not a very good name," she said.

He smiled.

And with that smile her father became unreliable.

She would show up at the greenhouse with an extra sandwich or a piece of fresh gingerbread. She sent him letters that he could only answer if he picked them up at work. She asked him at the end of every day what he had planted, what he'd done with his time. His answers were not reassuring. They had struck a water main and the whole yard had flooded. They had put the wrong mixture in a fertilizer gun and the grass had turned blue. A caterpillar had crawled up the foreman's leg and butterflies fluttered out of his sleeves. She caught at every answer, testing it for strength, but in the end she was unable to distinguish between what was true and what just made her laugh.

One afternoon when she was home from school, in that second year after her mother's death, she was baking banana bread in one of Luanne's parti-colored housecoats. She heard the truck pull up and saw the Lawnkeepers insignia on the side. She wished she'd started sooner so the whole house would smell of baking. But then she saw that, of the two men who stepped from the truck, neither was her father.

Hello, they said. They smiled at her housecoat. The boss asked them to stop by. It had been a couple of weeks. It wasn't that unusual with companies like theirs. People came and went all the time. But they liked her father. Did he want his last check?

Would he pick it up or should they mail it? Del told them he'd been sick in bed, but he was getting better. There was no need to worry. He'd be back at work. She waved goodbye and poured the batter down the sink. She washed the bowl and the mixer and dried everything and put it away.

He arrived home at five-thirty, smiling and relaxed. He wore his Lawnkeepers shirt, but he was covered with dust instead dirt. He settled into his chair with a sigh. "I've been on my feet all day."

"How was work?"

"Good."

"Do a lot of digging and planting?"

"Sweet Aunt Agnes, yes."

"Would you tell me if you were lying?"

He continued to smile, though she saw the smile had changed. His voice was gentle. "It's okay, sweet pea."

"Is it about mom? Are you sad about mom?"

"Don't worry," he said. "There's nothing wrong."

And then for a week in the late fall he never came home. He said he'd be gone overnight. A business trip. On the second night he called her. Said there had been a delay, but everything was fine. Another day, he said. Maybe two. But it wasn't until Saturday morning that she came down to find him fast asleep in his bed. He looked tanned and freshly scrubbed. Untroubled. Snoring lightly.

She checked the name on his shirt, then rode her bicycle to *Evergreen Landscaping* and stepped into the office. She had her pitch ready. It was a whole week, she knew, but she hoped it would be all right. He'd been too sick to call. He was better now, and he'd be coming back to work. She hoped it would be all right.

A round woman with bright blonde hair clucked sympathetically. She consulted the files, though when she turned back she was frowning. No. He'd been to work every day this week. But don't worry. Sometimes it's like that with these men. They're so tough, nothing gets in the way of their job.

When she got home he was cooking breakfast: pancakes, bacon, coffee. Her hands were shaking as she ate the food. She wasn't stupid. She had read about this sort of thing. Do you have another family? she asked. Do you have another wife? Do you have another little girl that you go and visit?

He smiled at her so gently that she was certain of the answer before he even spoke. But what he said was, "Of course not, sweet pea. Where would I find the time?"

Once, when she was young, during one of her mother's darkest rages, she had caught sight of her father out the bedroom window. It was late. She was ready for bed. But she saw him slipping through the falling darkness toward the low gate in the fence. She was out of bed instantly, her robe and slippers on, hurrying down the stairs, aware, even then, of the need for silence. She caught him at the gate. She was twelve. He seemed much too tall, a stranger in the darkness. And he turned on her a hesitant, pained expression she had never seen before.

"Where are you going?" she asked.

"Just out for a walk." He seemed to brace himself for whatever message Luanne might have sent.

"Can I come?"

"All the good girls are in bed right now."

She went back inside, peered out through the window. He stood for a long time as if letting the silence settle. Then he turned and started down the alley. She hurried out again.

Perhaps it was the slippers, the robe, the flannel pajamas that gave it a feeling of wonder. They carried her through a world larger and more empty than she had ever imagined. She was quiet and secret, peering through branches and around leafy corners. He slipped along the ordinary streets, a slender shadow sharpening under every streetlamp. He seemed to be moving at random, one street and then another, as if the formless path were drifting with his thoughts. He came at last to the park and sat down on a bench.

She waited for the longest time as he did nothing at all. Then he turned. She was at the edge of the grass, hidden in the shadows, but he looked directly at her. He didn't wave or gesture or shoo her away. But she could see, in that one moment, that she was ruining it for him, and when he finally stood up, Del turned and hurried home. She lay awake that night, waiting for the muffled click of the gate, and when it came she couldn't be sure if it was a sound she heard or just part of her dreams.

It was years before she went out at night again, and then it was with Calvin and it was completely different.

She found him one morning in the park, a week before her fifteenth birthday. He was sleeping like some forest creature. She'd been out collecting sounds for her mother, tracking the dimpled trickle of water beneath the whisper of cattails—Luanne had wanted just a few minutes of hope and promise to suggest the larger transformation to come. When she looked up she saw the boy, young and thin and smudged with earth, rising on his elbows, peering through the drooping branches of a willow tree with an expression of wonder.

If he had been older she would have run away. If he'd been angry or big or rough looking. But he was thin and young, just a year or two older than she, and tired and sore and hungry. And he was her very own adventure. She ran home and brought them each a peanut butter sandwich and bag of potatoes chips and a box of apple juice. Even then, from the beginning, it had been as much picnic as rescue. "Do you want to eat down by the pond?" she asked.

"It's a little bright out there."

So she had crawled in beside him and they sat together under the overhanging willow. She had never seen anyone eat so fast. The sandwich was gone in four bites, the potato chips in three. He drained the juice box and looked up, bright and eager. She gave him hers.

"Are you a fairy child?" she asked. He probably wasn't, she knew, but the question seemed an important part of how they were supposed to proceed.

"A fairy?"

"A valiant wood sprite. Condemned to a life of hardship and adventure until you recover your stolen treasure."

"Oh." He seemed to consider it. "I guess. I was chasing a guy. I almost had him, but he pushed me off a train and I had to walk back through the forest at night. I got to tell you. If I hadn't been so valiant I'd have been scared silly."

"Why were you chasing him?"

"I'm going to kill him."

"You are?"

"He killed my father, so that's what I have to do."

Del was almost whispering now. This was so much better than she'd any right to expect. "Who was your father?"

"Frank the Bear. He was king of the forest. Or anyway, king of the bridge. And that made him king of the forest. Least, that's what he said. But I think it was just something he was trying."

"Was he a troll? I think of trolls as guarding bridges."

"Might have been. People said so, but you can't believe everything." He looked shy under her questions.

"You must be a long way from home," she said. "I can bring you more food."

"You don't need to. That was good. Thanks." But his eyes grew quick at the thought.

"I've got to go," Del confided. "I have to help my mother. But I'll bring you something later."

"Maybe another sandwich? That bread is so soft. And those chips?"

"We'll meet back here. You better not wander too far. Wood sprites can be very delicate if they get too far from their tree." He seemed to accept that without argument. "I'm Del," she said.

"Sometimes, in magical situations, you need to know the person's secret name."

"Calvin," he said.

"Is that your secret name?"

"It's the one nobody uses."

"I'm pleased to meet you, Calvin. Don't leave the tree."

But when she returned late that afternoon he was sitting on a park bench up the hill from the pond, reading. He was holding the book just inches from his face, and when he looked up at her he squinted hard against the sunlight. They ate as they walked, and they walked well into the evening. But it was different than the walk with her father, and not just because she wasn't wearing pajamas.

There was one moment. She had been nervous about the darkness so she had brought along her parabolic microphone. They were each wearing a pair of headphones, listening to whatever they could find. He was aiming it, and at first it was all the rough fluttering sounds of the breeze across the dish and the grating noise of their footsteps, or the sudden rising bark of a dog. But once, as she reached up and steadied his hands, they heard a single tremor of birdsong, a tiny cascade of notes, bright as diamonds in the dark. And Calvin said, "Wow. Isn't that something." And his voice laid itself alongside those notes so that months afterwards, when she came upon it by accident, she would play that small seven-second loop over and over and over.

Even now she almost smiles. Vacuum in hand, dust mop at the ready, she lets the memory play. The memory of a memory. The soft wonder in his voice that transformed even that partial statement into the beginning of something mythic. Maybe that was his gift. Looking back on all that hadn't happened, she sees it was his imagination that sparked her own. He had only one story, and she was helping him tell it. Giving it its proper shape, making it more vivid with every retelling. They spun it out between them—that's what she remembers—weaving it on the air as they walked.

And by the end of a week, it was something. A piece of wonder. Frank the Bear, Troll King of the forest, master of the bridge. His rule cut short by guileful murder. The intruder, the sneak, the wanderer, who had come out of the night, a small and unimpressive man, fleeing some terrible crime. And the woman, a pale spirit of the forest, kidnapped against her will, dragged into the darkness by the hateful stranger. He needed to cross the bridge, to escape into the woods with his prey, but the Troll King said no. He would rescue the maiden if he could. There had to be a test: questions answered, a riddle proved. A trial of strength. But the intruder was sneaky and fierce. Evil is always more unexpected than good. And he surprised the Troll King. They struggled and fought. The young prince came to his aid, but the stranger was treacherous. He threw a potion in the young man's eyes, blinding him for just the moment he needed, and with a trick, a spell, before anything more could be done, he had thrown the king from his bridge to perish in the river below. And in a mist of pain the maiden vanished, and the evil stranger fled back across the bridge. And for all the years to come the young prince was fated to hunt him down, to find him and to kill him, and to set the fretful spirit of his father once again at peace.

Every morning of that week she brought him food. Every night she snuck out after twilight. They walked and whispered against the wide open silence of the night. It was her birthday coming up. That must mean something, mustn't it? That he had appeared like this, just in time? She talked about what it would be like to be fifteen. He talked about his father; he talked about growing up in foster care. And at some point in their walk Del glanced down shyly and saw that they were holding hands.

On the night of her birthday Del had crept out and made her way to Wyldwood. She waited under the moonlight, listening to the sound of the water and the breeze. But he never came.

Not the next night or the next.

It was a month before she stopped going there.

Afterwards it was hard to make it mean nothing. She never told her parents. She came home the night of her birthday and they were still in an uproar. Then her mother died, and any meaning the week might have had just drifted away in the general cloud of unhappiness.

But what emerged was The Voyage of Del. It arose from the realization that nothing so important, so satisfying and exciting, should ever be left to chance. And so it was, with her mother dead, her father drifting free like an errant balloon, that Del plucked up the remains of her life and began to re-weave them into a more pleasing shape. A story you could tell and retell.

She began to go out at night, alone on her bicycle. She would roll herself a joint, bundle up against the breeze, and ride her bicycle around the neighborhood, letting the air snatch the fumes from her lips. She looked around at the lighted windows, the dark lawns and trees. She told herself she wasn't looking for anybody, and after a while it became true. After a while she was just riding along streets whose meaning was like a low vibration of memory that could just be made out if she coasted quietly, the low ratcheting click of her wheels like a murmur of reassurance, riding the same routes over and over—all the paths they had walked, all the streets—until they became layered with meaning.

Looking back, those early years after her mother died were like a learner's permit for life. She was nervous, frightened, lonely. Her father came and went. He brought her presents, packed her lunch, helped her with her homework. He attended parent conferences. Talked her up and talked her down. And sometimes he'd be gone. There was no shouting, no arguing. There was none of the heavy, overhanging sadness that had so often formed the main current of her mother's life. Delilah learned to have the house to herself.

6.

The doorbell rings when she is upstairs cleaning the tub. She walks slowly down the stairs, giving whoever it is plenty of time to give up and leave, but the bell sounds again, and she opens the door to find Russell standing there with a slowly widening smile. "Is this a bad time?"

She has a moment to remember what she is wearing. She slips the bandana from her head but then is left holding it like a janitor doffing her cap.

"What are you doing here?"

"I just wanted to see you. Nothing wrong with that, I suppose."

He is cheerful, unembarrassed. There is something in the way he smiles that implies she has dressed in this particular costume just for him: stained and baggy t-shirt, ragged shorts, the smear of cleanser across her cheek. As if this is a new character she is doing just for him.

"It's Monday," she says. "I thought you said no Mondays."

"I changed my mind. Aren't you going to invite me in?" But he is already in.

He leans forward to kiss her.

"I've got Comet on me."

"I don't care." But of course he does. He kisses her lightly, careful of his clothes.

He isn't particularly tall but he holds himself as if height is just a matter of jumping higher than anyone else. He has thick, reddish hair and a square face, handsome if not exactly appealing. He is dressed this afternoon in his slumming clothes: jeans, pressed white shirt, soft leather jacket and loafers. He is a professor at the local community college—it's something he mentioned within five minutes of ordering coffee—and she has always thought of him as somehow collegiate ever since. Youthful but not young. Teasing but not quite playful. He moves around her house as if he has chosen it for her and is still amused by some of the details. He takes in the little forest of spray bottles and bleach in their basket on the counter. "So this is you cleaning."

Of all the things she has managed since her mother's death, boys have been the least successful. In much of life a certain measure of scornful bluster can carry you along; a certain feigned indifference. But things get away from you. Problems arise. In high school there was the principal's office—all but pulled from the arms of Jimmy Threewit or Clancy Drummond or Jeffrey Clive. In those days it didn't really matter which; they were pretty much interchangeable, smelling of cigarette smoke and too much cologne, with snarky, demanding mouths, and all the nerve she could ever hope to learn.

Mrs. Garvey was a diligent woman, and she had, she explained to Del, been keeping an eye on her. It was very dangerous what she was doing. It was leading her somewhere she wouldn't want to go. Life can present us with tragedy we must work to overcome, but we mustn't go out of our way to do things we'll regret. Mrs. Garvey called her father. They waited a long time.

"He works a lot," Del explained after a while.

The principal shuffled her papers. "He works at the Blueville Nursery?" She frowned at the clock.

"He's not very good with his phone."

"Go back to your classroom," she said in the end. "This behavior has got to stop. Do you understand, Delilah? This isn't who you are."

She got home to find her father at the kitchen table, having found the stack of letters that had accumulated. Mrs. Garvey had included a great many names. "What an unsavory group.

Timmy Klinger? Didn't his father rob a grocery store?"

"I don't really know him."

"Buster Crem, Ted Blinker? They set fire to the maintenance shed."

"It was an accident. And it's not like I hang out with them."

"Denise Roscoe?"

"She's okay."

"It says she shoplifts. What am I reading? The police blotter?"

"I don't shoplift."

"At least tell me you're not smoking," he said.

"It's okay. I don't inhale."

"You know smoking is stupid."

"Not if you don't inhale."

He peers at her, a little wide-eyed. "You don't inhale, you don't shoplift. So what do you do for fun?"

For a while the answer was Brian Ford, who was in the math club, and then Tommy Jenkins from her AP English class, and then Bruce Watkins, who was a tight end on the high school football team. Del thought about telling her father about him, it might have reassured him. But he clearly enjoyed his own secrets so much, she thought she should have some of her own.

Del had a lot of boyfriends, though only one at a time. She found they required all her attention—she could never be certain what they would want next. And they usually didn't last. A few weeks, a month. In this day and age even the Math Club president will lose patience if there was no prospect of getting his girlfriend into bed. And with Delilah, there wasn't. Her longest relationship was with Bruce Watkins, tall, handsome, nice, who in addition to being a football star was the school president of Teens for Jesus, and whose prickling combination of desire and guilt was an almost perfectly complement to Del's own needs. She broke it off after six months when Mr. Riley, the football coach, came to tell her she was ruining his life. In that first moment Del hadn't been sure whether it was Mr. Riley's life or Brian's, but it might well have been both.

She knew she was an unsettling element, and it was that as much as anything that drew her to boys. And it was always she who ended things, breaking up in a little flurry of scorn and impatience that left them wondering at all the ways they must have fallen short. And in a sense, they had. She liked the hot, imploring looks they gave her, the importuning kisses. She liked the hesitancy with which they first touched her breasts, and then the eagerness, slowly rising to a simmering desperation, with which they put their hands and lips, and, in the case of Brian, his tongue, on the narrow and electric portions of her skin that she allowed them to make available. But there was never any question of going further. It wasn't that she had no interest. It was that the sense of balance that came with hurtling forward and drawing back gave her such satisfaction, such a feeling of reassurance and control, that she couldn't imagine getting carried away.

And she didn't. Not exactly.

She had met Russell at the Café Ion. He had come in with a pile of student work, from what would turn out to be his Intro to Abnormal Psychology class, and he set up shop at one of the little steel tables. "Double espresso, and keep 'em coming even if I tell you to stop. I want all the caffeine you've got until I see the bottom of this pile."

"What do I do when your hands start shaking?"

"Just hold me down until it passes."

His eyes crinkled when he smiled in a way someone older might have recognized as less than accidental, and if his tone gave her a little tickle of something just behind the belly button, she told herself not to worry. She recognized flirting. It wasn't anything she couldn't handle.

But Russell had left high school far behind. He was married but separated. "My wife doesn't understand me," he said in a way that sounded both rueful and true. He was all grown up, and he treated her the same. It wasn't that he was impatient of delay; the prospect simply never occurred to him. His unthinking assumption of the straightforwardness of things brushed aside all her various resolutions without her quite understanding how. He assumed a level of experience Del was too proud to deny.

It wasn't so much that sex caught her by surprise—in fact it seemed to happen in slow-motion. But there was nothing she could think of to do or say that would hinder all that assurance. He kissed her. He smiled. He was very gentle. In the end she thought, for Pete's sake. If Denise Roscoe could do this.

There had been a little blood. Del explained that her period was occasionally irregular, to which Russell had replied, with equal parts rue and irritation, "Why the heck didn't you tell a guy?"

The business itself wasn't anything bad. After the first discomfort it felt all right. And in place of the reassurance of holding boys at arm's length, Del discovered the satisfaction of a man who had clearly been around, a man who found in her a grown-up whose performance seemed in every way satisfactory. And if he wanted to do things, well, that's what a woman did for her man. And even that added another little brick of reassurance to her growing foundation.

"Do you want a drink?" she asks.

"I'll just help myself."

Her first response, which she is careful to hide, is annoyance. That he would burst in on her routine, catch her off guard looking so drab and streaked with dirt. But gradually there is something else, a poised, proprietary air with which he keeps turning from the bright furniture and shining floors to look at her. He has come to see her, after all. And she imagines this is what desire feels like: that familiar tickle of anticipation tightening the muscles of her stomach.

He takes a beer from the fridge as if it were his own. Del

tries to see this as something intimate. She likes that he is older. He won't tell her his age, but she is aware of the crows feet at the corners of his eyes, a few faint creases on his face that never quite disappear after he smiles. She watches him. She is always watching him. Trying to collect all the information she can, trying to decide what he sees in her, what it is that he'd like her to do. Though that's rarely a mystery. He says she's the strongest woman he's met; the most independent. It's great to be in a relationship of equals, he says, and he has no difficulty asking her to do whatever it is he wants. This startles Del again and again, but she hides her uncertainty. It's like on-the-job training. Learn as you go.

"You don't seem very happy to see me," he says.

"I am."

With a beer in one hand he is poking through her cleaning basket, lifting rags and rubber gloves, but he glances up at this. "I could leave if you wanted to get back to work."

"Let me go change. I'll wash my face, put on something nice."

That isn't quite what he wants, she can tell. She watches as he comes around the kitchen counter, slips his hands around her waist. "You look good just the way you are."

"You'll get your clothes dirty."

"Aren't you glad I came?"

"Of course I am."

And certainly the touch of his hands always does something to her breathing. The sudden heat in his eyes. She suspects he can turn it on and off at will—but here it is now. And his fingers are already plucking at the hem of her shirt. He always does this. Once he learned she was so easily embarrassed it seems to be where all his interest lies. "Come on, Russell!"

"Just a peek." He is smiling now.

"Let me go put a dress on. It's the one I wore last night. You'll like it. I promise."

"I like this."

He has his hand under her shirt now, reaching up to frame her breast. No matter how peremptory his voice, his hands are always gentle, teasing, so obviously admiring. She draws the hem down firmly over his hand. It makes him laugh. The t-shirt is getting all stretched out. His lips are on her throat, her mouth. He tries to raise the hem. "Uh-uh."

Laughingly he concedes the hem, but abruptly reaches up and drags down the neckline, stretching it out, pulling it low until he can press his lips to the pale rosy smudge of her nipple. She shuts her eyes. His lips close on her. He wants to draw a moan from her, low and against her will, but she bites it back. "Upstairs," she murmurs. "Let's go upstairs. Please."

He likes the please, she can tell. He likes the quivering in her legs. He steps back. He is still holding the beer. He takes a sip, smiling, but his eyes are serious. "Where are you cleaning next?" His tone is light, as if he's only just stepped in through the door.

Del swallows, tries to slow her heart. Smile, she thinks. Laugh. It's a game. He likes that you play the game. But the memory of Bertie from the gallery arises, officious and silly, elegantly dressed, but thoughtfully handing her a wineglass, guiding her as if she were something fragile. "I was just doing the bathtub. Upstairs."

"Well, don't let me interrupt. Oh." He bends down and picks up the fallen bandana. "You don't want to forget this."

She's uncertain for a moment, but then she slips it back on her head, half-gypsy, half-cleaning woman. It's something new. He's never acted quite like this before, but she's aware of his eyes on her as she climbs ahead of him, and she thinks: what is he expecting? what would a normal girl do? Del tries to put a little sway in her hips as she climbs, but she can feel herself blush. She hopes it doesn't look foolish, and when he laughs she's still uncertain. But then he slaps her lightly on the bottom. "Oh, you chamber maids. You must have some stories to tell."

At the top of the stairs she is still uncertain. Are they heading toward the bedroom? Sometimes he doesn't like her to ask; let your imagination run wild, he says. But that never really helps. She has no idea what he imagines. He slides one hand up her leg, reaching beneath the fabric of the cut-offs. "How does that feel?"

"Let's go lie down," she whispers.

"Shame on you." He seems to have no trouble with his voice. His fingers stroke her skin. "You have work to do. That bathtub is not going to clean itself."

She hesitates at the door of the bathroom. The air smells of Pine-Sol. The scrub brush is lying by the edge of the tub, her rubber gloves overhang the rim.

"Don't forget the gloves."

Del tugs them on, making the mistake of glancing in the mirror: frumpy and heavy-hipped, soap-smeared cheek. She quickly looks away, standing uncertainly as Russell leans against the door looking easy and handsome, sipping his beer. He sets the bottle down. She steps toward him, forcing a smile, forcing a sway into her hips. "Is this what you want?"

He catches her gloved hands before they touch his shirt. Then he leans forward and kisses her. No trace of a laugh in the kiss. That's good, isn't it? She closes her eyes and presses against him, but he's fending her off. And she thinks, Is this about his clothes? "I could put on a dress," she whispers. But then she feels him tugging at her belt, unbuttoning the shorts. She feels the hand, softly smooth, slip beneath the fabric, molding itself against her. His mouth is back, hot and demanding. But her own hands, awkward in the gloves, hover in the air.

"How does that feel?" he whispers. She can only nod. "Does that feel good? Does it? You're so wet. You feel so wet. I've never fucked a maid before." Del cringes. Not just the language but the rough gracelessness of it all. Her eyes are still closed, concentrating on the feel of him. Telling herself to loosen up, not to be such a little girl. But just for an instant she remembers the evening before, the low sound of music, the comforting warmth of Bunny's hand. They had shared a cab to her hotel. Del offered to walk her up to her room, but she had declined. Even in the bright party clothes and black wig Bunny had been so certain, so smilingly confident as she walked away, as if all that good cheer was a cloak not quite big enough for both of them.

"That's right," whispers Russell. "Here I was, just minding my own business, and I wander in on you, bent over the tub, hard at work. What could I do?" he murmurs. "What choice did I have?"

He once told her he loved how tough she was, how she didn't care about anyone else's opinion. But when they make love he shapes her like a doll, this position and then that. The touch of a hand, a whispered instruction. And she tells herself it's exciting to be the sole focus of someone's attention, to know that, for these moments, at least, everything she does is what he wants.

The tile floor is hard under her knees; the edge of the bathtub bruises her hip bones. She hasn't had a chance to rinse the tub, and the smell of cleanser is sharp in her nose. She keeps a grip on the hem of her t-shirt to keep it snugly down, but the shorts are around her knees. She tries to concentrate on the feel of him. She hears the pleasure in his voice, the low building rush of his breathing.

Afterwards, clothing readjusted, face washed, she makes coffee, while Russell stands at the kitchen sink, irritably scrubbing at the sleeve of his shirt, where a smear of Comet has made a small mark and now refuses to come out.

DELILAH

7.

The Suds'n'Duds is not beautiful as laundromats go, nor particularly convenient, but there is something in the reliability of its warmth and hubbub that keeps Del coming back. She passed it once years ago on one of her evening rides, and with the twilight turning the streets gloomy all around her, the wide storefront window glowed like a beacon. She had stepped inside, empty-handed as she was, and settled in one of the comfortable plastic chairs while women washed and folded and chatted away in brisk, companionable Spanish, not a word of which Del could understand.

Now she steps in with two pillow cases of dirty laundry, her house-cleaning clothes chief among them. This is not her usual day. Bernicia glances up. She is a heavy and currently blonde young mother of three, who runs the place and will give you change if you ask politely. "Hey, Thursday. What the hell?"

"Just trying to keep ahead," says Del.

"Betsy Two's on the fritz again. She'll take your money and break your heart."

Two women are cursing genially in front of the vending machine, and at the long formica table a woman in a grey hoodie and bright green tights is reading an ancient copy of *Forbes*. In the corner, where she has set up her own ironing board, a woman whose name is Estrella fills, on any given day, a whole bank of double-washers with other people's sheets and towels and napkins, and then spends two hours on the folding alone.

Del has never told anyone how far away she lives, or about the washing machine in her basement. The first time she brought laundry—a garbage bag stuffed with her mother's dirty clothes—the women watched without comment, though when

Del began to cry, a thin, grim-faced woman pressed a flat, dry hand against the back of her neck.

It's a thin crowd today, with the usual homeless person or two, dozing in the warmth. Del loads her washers—separating lights, darks, and colors, though there are barely enough items for one machine—and sits down at the folding table beside the pile of magazines.

In the beginning the laundromat had played a major role in her adventures. The place was serially transformed into a dungeon, a doctor's waiting room, a holding cell, and a psychiatric ward where Del had been confined to keep her from telling anyone about her discovery of the great Rune of Power. (She'd been reading Tolkien then, and it took her a long time to get out from under him.) She had been starved, handcuffed, bundled into one of the evil wizard's special torture machines where she had tumbled around over and over in the heat and noise, until released—in that instance by a grim-faced woman, whose named turned out to be Elodia, and who had muttered at her in Spanish and then walked away shaking her head. That had been a hit. She'd gotten forty-five hundred 'likes' on that.

But over the years her voyages have changed, and Del worries they've turned into nothing but stories. Early on, every adventure had been like a continuation of that week with Calvin. A chance to hold onto it a little longer, to re-weave the memory of it over and over.

But in all these years alone, even as she has become more self-sufficient, she has grown uncomfortable in the darkness. Not afraid exactly. But she hasn't ridden out in the evening for years. And as her voyaging has migrated into the daylight hours, her adventures have grown ever more wildly improbable. Her fans like it. But she knows she has somehow mislaid the heart of things.

Another homeless man shuffles in. No laundry to do. Here for the chairs and the murmur of company. He stands before the bank of triple-loaders, squinting under the fluorescent lights. He is tall and thin, with something vaguely Lincolnesque about him, despite the dreadlocks and heavy, crooked glasses. He wears a long coat over a dusty suit, and he is shaking his head, as if, having mistaken the front-loader for a television screen, he is marveling at the truly terrible reception. It takes her a moment to recognize the wolfish man who'd arrived with Bunny.

"Three dollars a load," he murmurs. "Who can even count that high?"

But then his eye falls on Del and the smaller, top-loading washers, and he ambles over. "This is the stuff. This is what I'm talking about." He glances up to see if Del shares his leap of understanding, but she keeps her head down, poring over a *Reader's Digest*. "These babies are the answer," he explains. "A dollar. That's what I'm saying. Four little sweethearts, four friendly little quarters, and you're clean as the day is long."

She is unable to help herself. "Five," she says.

"Five quarters? What's that? That's not a dollar."

"Dollar and a quarter."

"That's got to be wrong. That doesn't make any sense." Now he's fiddling with the coin slide, its little slots lined up and waiting. "Who's ever heard of five quarters?"

Reluctantly Del admits, "I have an extra one if you need it."

He gives her a sideways glance. "So you say. I don't believe in extra quarters. What makes it extra, that's what I'd like to know."

She hunches a little behind the magazine.

"Oh. So now you're not talking." He is smiling now, as if each new discovery adds a little something to his day. "I'm hearing five quarters, but I'm not seeing 'em. I'm seeing zero quarters."

Del lowers the *Reader's Digest*, whose long exile in the laundromat has clearly stripped it of its powers. "How many do you have?"

He is less spooky when she looks at him directly. She braces herself, but he smells fine, a thin scent of sweat and fresh dirt that adds its own reminiscent note from her childhood. Up close the beard looks almost jaunty, its little braids quivering on the air. The squinting eyes behind thick lenses give him the puzzled look of a game show contestant who has practiced for years and can't quite believe he has ended up with this question. "Four," he says finally.

She reaches into her pocket and slides a quarter onto the top of the machine. He observes it for a moment. "Now isn't that a nice thing to do." He touches the quarter with one grimy fingertip. "And will you be missed? That's what I'm wondering. Do you think you can be spared?"

"I have plenty," says Del, then wonders if she should admit to such wealth. "Do you have detergent?"

He stands for a moment then gives the coin a decisive tap. "I do not."

She nods at her jug of *Arm and Hammer*. "It's concentrated. Don't use too much."

The man picks up the quarter and, after a moment's hesitation, the detergent. He marches away to the very end of the row, and then takes a moment to line up the five quarters in the coin slide. Squinting, he pours out a careful capful. Then he stoops down and begins unlacing his heavy boots, pulling them off, setting them aside. Straightening up he gazes down at the front of his overcoat and after a moment's consideration, fastens every single button. There is a brief, confined struggle as he draws his arms back out of the sleeves, and then he is standing like a narrow caterpillar wrapped in a wool cocoon.

He begins to move. The process isn't easy—he seems to be wrestling with himself beneath the shelter of his coat—but after a moment a suit jacket slips to the floor around his feet. He kicks it away. The shirt slides down, still within the loosening embrace of the vest. Then the pants topple into a little heap around his ankles. A last effort, like a stork in a straightjacket, one leg and then the next, and a startlingly cheerful pair of flowered boxer shorts settles like a leaf on the pile, followed by a plaid pair and then a blue. He reinserts his arms into the overcoat sleeves, and he is done. Everything goes into the machine. It buzzes into action. He returns the jug of detergent and sits, several chairs down, his eyes bright with interest.

"Is that coffee?"

His gaze has fastened onto her thermos. She'd made enough for Russell, but he left without drinking his. "Would you like some?"

"You know how they say, stop and smell the coffee? I get that now. I stopped. And now I smell it."

She wonders how to reply, but then sees he is smiling. "It's pretty strong" she warns.

"You can't frighten me."

"Do you have a cup?"

He draws from the pocket of his coat a folding camp mug and sets it down on a chair between them. "I've been having a dream about coffee," he says. "This is probably why." He watches her pour with great interest. When he drinks, it is all he does. "Oh, my. You could make this for a living."

"I do."

"I'm sure you're much beloved among your customers."

"I do all right."

She hesitates, then opens the Tupperware box. "I have brownies. Chocolate chip cookies. Two slices of coffeecake from the day before yesterday."

"Is that all for you?"

She frowns. "I'm offering, aren't I?"

"Is there something wrong with it?" But he's smiling again. He reaches out, helping himself to a brownie. One bite, and half the brownie is gone. He sits with a bemused expression as he chews and swallows. "That is maybe the most wonderful thing I have ever tasted."

"Okay then," she says.

Russell is always laughing at her baking. He says go ahead.

He says he likes his women well padded. That almost stopped her. She threw out everything and put her mixer away. But she missed the stirring, the measuring, the fragrant companionability of it all. So now she hides everything when he comes over, and doesn't eat in front of him.

Abraham Lincoln is watching the Tupperware box as if he's worried it might disappear. Del opens it again and holds it out.

"I don't mean to be greedy."

"There's plenty."

"Thank you."

The hand holding the brownie is grained with dirt, but his teeth, she notices, are strong and white. Even in this short time she's gotten used to the braids and beard. She keeps the *Reader's Digest* open protectively on her lap, but she watches him as he chews and nods. The brownie seems to have started its own tune in his head.

"There are usually more people here," says Del.

Her first machine gives a loud click, then slows to a stop. She makes a job of transferring her laundry to the drier. This would be the moment to gather up her things, shift her seat. A nod and smile, nice to meet you. But the two other machines stop, and when the clothes are loaded and the dryers launched, Del finds she has sat down again. The stranger sits with the empty cup in his lap.

"My name is Clean," he says.

"Del."

The second brownie is long gone, and when he glances down at the Tupperware she says, "Try the coffeecake." She refills his cup.

When his own machine shudders and clicks to a halt Clean rises and lifts the edge of the cover as if expecting it to weigh much more than it does. His arms are full of the sodden, felted bundle of his suit.

"Have you ever washed that before?"

His expression makes her wonder, just for a second, if she

has spoken gibberish: it displays such polite incomprehension.

"The suit," she says. "I'm not sure you're supposed to wash it."

"Wouldn't that be awful." He turns to the wall of dryers.

"You probably shouldn't dry it, either."

But he throws it in and starts it up. The suit bounces like a body in the drum. Del pretends to read. He looks gawky in the overcoat: delicate wrists, naked ankles. He helps himself to the coffee and to a chocolate chip cookie. "What's that funny taste?"

"It's mint."

"How about that."

"Have another," she says. "They kind of grow on you."

She watches the timer out of the corner of her eye so she is ready when his dryer stops, but it catches him by surprise. The clothes fall heavily to the bottom. He opens the door reluctantly, like a host who has twenty guests waiting and knows the turkey isn't done. His face turns thoughtful.

"It'll just take a few more quarters," she says.

"Might as well say another fifty dollars will make everything just perfect."

"I don't have fifty dollars," she says and holds up the last of her change.

She thinks he'll take it without hesitation, but he gazes at her for a moment. "Am I the lion or the bear?"

Del shakes her head blankly.

"The bear is walking along, steps into a trap. The hunter is coming. But a little rabbit comes along. She's frightened at first. But the bear says 'please, oh please,' and the bunny releases the trap."

"Well, that's lucky." Del hesitates. "What happens then?"

"Bear eats the bunny. Breaks the hunter's legs. Runs away."

She considers his smile. What is a smile, after all? But there's something in it, not sweetness exactly, but a kind of distant and considered sadness that holds out its tiny, delicate burden. "That's a terrible story," she says. "And the lion?"

"Same story, but there's a little girl. And a thorn in his paw."

"I thought he and the girl became friends for life?"

"Nope. He eats her and runs away."

"Are you saying you don't want the quarters?"

Reluctantly he picks them up and turns to the dryer.

Del's life has made her brave, that's what she likes to believe. It has prepared her for surprises, for sudden flaws and disasters. It has made her independent. But there are moments that come unexpectedly. They slip into that hollow place, the lonely part she tells herself she doesn't have anymore. She wonders how it is that even a homeless man is better company than her boyfriend.

Her clothes finish. She takes them out and folds them. Clean stands before his own dryer as if afraid it will stop if he looks away. There are a couple of cookies left. She wonders what she should say. When his dryer tumbles to a halt she waits. He opens the door. The suit looks less heavy now; fluffed and rumpled by the effort.

"Nothing like clean clothes," he says.

"They're going to be wrinkled."

"Have you ever been soaking wet? Down to the skin? And cold? You don't know how cold until you live wet for two weeks in November. You pool your quarters, and all your clothes go in. You dry them and dry them. Round and round. Standing there in your skivvies hoping the police don't come, getting colder and colder, as if your whole body is shrinking down. Then you lift them out, hot from the oven, and put them on. It's like baking yourself in a loaf of bread."

But still he doesn't move, as if the thought alone is enough for now. "I made bread yesterday," says Del. "Potato bread. I ate half the loaf right there on the spot, with butter and salt. Don't you think that's sad?"

"Real butter?"

"I made a whole chocolate cake last week. I ate three pieces and threw the rest away."

"I like cake," he concedes. "But I'm still thinking about that loaf of bread."

She draws a five dollar bill from her pocket and holds it up. "Can you use this?"

He peers mildly down at it. She has expected eagerness. Does he look disappointed? "Never say no," he says, but he makes no move to take it.

Reaching into the dryer he draws out the boxer shorts, three pairs, and turns modestly away to step into them, drawing them up under his coat. The wool pants look as if they've been stored inside a football for a year, but he shakes them out and pulls them on, hands fastening and tucking beneath the coat. Out comes the shirt, the vest, the jacket. Del sits with the stuffed pillow case on her lap like a young girl getting ready for a trip. Clean is squirming under the overcoat, but with a final twisting flourish his arms reappear in the sleeves. He opens the coat and gives it a little settling shake. "Thank you for the hospitality," he says.

"So when do you wash the coat?"

"Everything in its time."

"I come on Thursdays usually," says Del. "I could bring a loaf of potato bread. Or more brownies. Something to look forward to."

He smiles. "I will be thinking about that potato bread." And he turns with a little wave. "See you, sweet pea."

Her eyes follow him in surprise, but before she can speak he is gone.

Part Three

Clean

CLEAN

8.

He smells the savory smoke of a pot on the fire, and the ache of his hunger almost matches the pain in his eyes. He is seven years old. Every step catches him by surprise; he is shaking uncontrollably. But Peach hurries them along—now that he can smell the food, nothing will slow him down. He lets go of his grip, and the boy is floating, adrift in the darkness. But not alone. The terrible scream is still in his ears—the clamoring fight at the edge of the trestle, the shouting, the blinding pain in his eyes. And then the scream like something torn from the air. His father going over. Falling, falling, a shrill toppling cry that will be with him forever.

But now, as he steps into the clearing and feels the dusty softness of well-trodden dirt, a new sound rises through the low murmur of the flop. ...*widow she cried over me, and called me a poor lost lamb, and she called me a lot of other names, too, but she never meant no harm by it. She put me in them new clothes again, and I couldn't do nothing but sweat and sweat, and feel all cramped up.*

He has trouble locating the voice. The rough bandage Peach has tied around his eyes covers his ears, as well. But as the voice drifts to a halt he can tell, from the sudden space it leaves, that it was coming from off to his left, near the warmth of the fire. A prime spot. He tries to hold onto the sound of it, but now that he's come to a stop, his legs go wobbly, and it takes all his attention not to fall.

No one's in any rush to speak. The silence opens around them. Then a voice from the back, "Anybody know 'em? You got a name?"

Peach is overeager. His voice has that sugary note. "We're just here for the night." Maybe he's thinking, given all that's happened, this spot is too close for names.

"Got anything for the pot?"

He hears the unconvincing pat of hands against pockets. "We just need a spot by the fire."

Peach's tug on his sleeve guides him down onto a tilting concrete block. But once down, he can't keep still. His stomach is an empty ache. His eyes are on fire.

"What's with the kid?"

"Yeah. Can't he cut that out?"

Peach gives him a shake, and he realizes he's been moaning, little sounds escaping under his breath. He tries to lock them in his chest. "He's just hungry," Peach says. "If we had a piece of bread or something it might shut him up."

Sounds of rummaging. A moment later the soft pat of something landing at his feet. Gratefully he reaches, but Peach is there, gathering up the small offerings: rolls, slices of bread, a hard fragment of cheese left over from the shelter. "Much obliged," says Peach and presses a stale roll into his hands. Gratefully he gets to work.

"What's wrong with him?" someone asks.

"He's just tired."

"What happened to his eyes?"

"Accident. Just a piece of bad luck."

"Got no use for bad luck here," someone warns. "Don't want the chimps around."

Peach's voice is all honey. "Nothing like that. Just a little mishap. Long ago and far away."

But nobody is stupid here.

"You're planning on being gone in the morning."

It isn't a question. "Yeah," says Peach reluctantly. "Or next day."

"Make it tomorrow."

"Yeah. Sure. Got to get the kid off my hands. Got a grandmother in Cleveland. We're headed there."

"Tomorrow."

"I said tomorrow. Catching the freight."

"Just after sunrise, then," says the man.

"Okay, okay," says Peach. "Everything's cake." The words are all smiles but he can hear the anger like a bent hook behind them. "When we came in, thought I heard somebody talking. Is that a Story I heard?"

"No shit," says a man. "Not just a Story. We got ourselves a Book."

"Sounded nice. Might be a help to little Pisser, here."

"We're not runnin' a resort," someone mutters, but after a silence long enough to make the point there is a murmured consultation. The voice's slow comfort rises again.

He gnaws at the roll. The warmth of the fire is wonderful. It soaks into his clothing, seeps into his chest. He's surprised no one's slapped him away from such a choice spot. The reading goes on. It's not a story he recognizes, but he's caught by it anyway. Young boy, mean father, older friend on the run from the law. He can feel the different parts of it latching themselves to his mind even if the words, themselves, slip past. Somehow the voice smooths the edges, bends the old-fashioned strangeness of the words into their own perfect shape. The warmth, the voice, the hovering presence of the other men all hanging on the sound. He eases into sleep.

"Hey! Mustache!"

He jerks awake to the cold ground and a dead fire. In that instant he is terrified all over again. The blackness, the pain. He scrabbles in the dirt, jams his elbow against the concrete block. Then he feels for the long rag wrapped around his eyes, and if it isn't exactly a comfort, it helps calm his heart.

"Where the hell you think you're going!"

"Easy. Take it easy." Even from a distance, Peach sounds peevish. "You said to leave. I'm leaving. Don't need to stay where I'm not wanted. Catching the freight."

"Ain't you forgetting something?" He feels a new hand on

his arm, firm but not unkind. It helps him to his feet. "We ain't running an orphanage."

"I'm just scoutin'. Wasn't going to leave him."

"Good to know."

"God's sake," Peach mutters bitterly "How's a blind kid supposed to jump a freight? It's gonna snap him up. Gonna grind him under the wheels."

"Not my problem."

"Fuck's sake!"

But that's not an answer. And then the familiar grip is back on his sleeve and he's in motion, stumbling, working to stay upright. There are branches, weeds. It's like he's being slapped awake over and over and still can't open his eyes. His mind is racing. *Snap him up. Grind him under the wheels.*

Dirt gives way to gravel, then dirt again. His ears are reaching ahead for the sounds. And then Peach is easing them onto a bench, and he can smell the diesel on the air and hear the engine winding up. *Grind him grind him grind him.* He can't keep his thoughts in check.

Beside him the sound of breathing, the patter of nervous hands on knees. Peach shifts, turns. He starts up from the bench. *He's leaving!* No. He's dragging him up. *Here they go!* And his heart jolts in his chest. But they're just pacing now, back and forth. Just pacing. He can hear voices in the distance against the low-throated roar of the engine.

In the past it has seemed like nothing. Creeping along the length of a train, choosing your spot, choosing your grip. Scramble up and you're done; nothing but a game. But now his feet are blocks of stone. He catches every scuff and stumble. They're creeping toward the sound of the engine, zigzagging back and forth across the yard. But it's not cunning. No strategy: one eye on the railroad chimps and one eye on the train. It's just that Peach can't find his way to the end. Can't see that last leap. Not like this.

You got to see it, that's the thing. You got to see yourself landing clear. You got to hold it in your mind. Scrabbling for a handhold, pulling yourself high. The boy tries to imagine it. He tries to make it real. But all he can picture are the huge hungry wheels. Closer now. And he can hear the creak and grind of their edges against the track, the rolling bite of them. Fear clamps his stomach. His hands go numb. He imagines his legs dangling, kicking, sucked in by the wheels and pinched off, just like that.

"Jesus, Pisser! Your grip's slippery as shit. Get ready."

And he is rubbing both hands against his pants, but it makes no difference. And the engine's rising now. He can hear the bump and creak of the couplings. "Okay. That's the one. Right there."

"Where! Where is it?" He turns his head as if he can see, grabs at the rag, wrenching it aside. But his eyes are blurred beyond help. Peach is there, foggy and dark. Oh, please.

"It's no good, Pisser."

"I can do it!"

But he feels a sudden shove. His feet catch, he stumbles. His mind is screaming at the thought of the wheels, but it's gravel he hits, not track. Scrapes his hands, bruises his shoulder. He hears Peach calling back, "You're a kid. They'll go easy." And there comes a grunt, the scuff of a leap. The last words drifting back to him, carried on the rushing train. "Just go soft, Pisser. Don't tell 'em a thing."

So he lies there on the gravel, blind as a bug, as the train cranks away into the distance. He can hear the whistle fade, hear the angry voices rise as the railroad chimps catch sight of him. He struggles up, but he's all turned around. Without the noise of the train he's got nothing. He hears the shouting in the distance, the crackle of a radio. Hears them closing in. It's the deep dark for sure. Then a sudden grip on his arm, just like that. Jerking him up. How did they get so close? And a voice. "Can you run?"

He's only got a sob for an answer, but it doesn't matter. He's hauled into motion. Each step catches in the gravel, but the grip on his arm keeps him aloft. He might have been flying over the ground.

"Tracks," says the voice.

"What?" He tangles in the rails, but the man keeps him up. Next time he is ready.

"Branches. Down." They're in the woods. The man steers him this way and that, slowing down, trudging now, dirt under their feet.

Then they're squatting, panting, in among the sheltering branches. The man's voice comes out in little gasps. "I think... that I ... shall never see ... a poem as lovely ... as a tree."

Without his own blood pounding, he recognizes the voice. There is still something in it of the night before, the low tremor of a story only partly told. "You're the Book."

"I guess I am," he says—a low hiss of laughter and surprise that will grow into such a comfort in the years ahead.

It's a long trudge back to the flop, and Calvin is nervous about the reception; even blind it was clear how much they hated Peach. But settled in the warmth of the fire there's no grumbling. "Thought you'd left us."

"Change of plans," says the Book.

The pot's scraped dry but there's coffee and some ancient bread. Book hands him a piece of something. He thinks it's bark, then jerky, but when he starts to gnaw, it turns into cheese.

"Let me take a look." And then Calvin feels gentle fingers on the rag, tugging at the edge, peeling it back. There's a long, low breath. "I think maybe we need to take a walk."

Calvin has never been to an emergency room. They sit in uncomfortable chairs breathing in the antisceptic air. He cannot let go of Book's sleeve. The whole visit is a series of hands. Untying the rag, cleaning his face, rinsing his eyes again and again. The light is too bright. The nurse clucks as she pries the eyelids open, and he is embarrassed by the sounds he makes. There are drops for his eyes, ointment for his face. Then gauze patches and a long strip wrapping round and round. When they walk out, it is into the warmth of the afternoon

"That wasn't so bad," says Book. His voice is too cheerful.

"What did she say?"

"You'll be fine."

"Did she say that?"

"We change the ointment, change the bandage."

Calvin hesitates. In that moment it's hard to make his voice loud enough. "Then what?"

"Then we'll see."

"Will I?"

"She says yes."

"What else? What else does she say?"

"She doesn't know when. Or how well. She said it'll take some time."

They sit on a bench. The first of many in the years to come. "You hungry?" he asks.

Calvin shakes his head.

He feels the shift beside him, hears the rustle of a canvas bag. Then Book begins to read. He can't help it; he feels his eyes start to leak. He sags against him. He can't stop sobbing. It's only when he does that he realizes Book is still reading; there's an arm around his shoulder, and he's been reading steadily throughout. "Wait," he murmurs damply. "I missed that. Go back."

"How far?"

"All the way. Start over."

They return to the flop. Over the next few days it's like they're settling in. The weather is fine, the woods are quiet. In the daylight they move in a constant circuit around the streets, finding pockets of sunlight, hot air vents, wasteful restaurants with brimming dumpsters. This isn't a city he knows, but now he learns it the way a hand learns a pocket. He is less and less frightened by the constant darkness, and given the pain that comes with even the dimmest light, he is grateful for the bandage. He grows shyly confident of the arm that leads him, of the grip he keeps fastened on Book's jacket. The voice in his ear is low and conversational. "Sidewalk here. Low branch. Up now; here's the curb." He murmurs steadily as they walk, telling the story of each day as it unfolds. At night in the warmth of the fire he listens as Book reads, feeling like the hero of his own story, feeling like Huck, himself.

But on the third morning they wake to the crash of footsteps. It's like a crowd fighting its way through the woods, louder each moment. Shouted commands, the crackle of radios. Around him men are rousing, shoving each other, waking up the sodden. He feels the sudden blade of helplessness. Climbing to his feet, he stands in an instant of uncertainty, his reaching hands closing on nothing. And then Book takes his arm. "Where do we go?" But he's not talking to him.

"Stay clear of the tracks," comes a voice. "Out of the woods. Keep away from the shelter. When the chimps get a bee up their bottom like this, you just have to lay low."

And Book is leading them cautiously through the trees. Calvin is surprised by the man's uncertainty, his nervousness. It's only the chimps. All you can do is let 'em have their fun. But Book is unnerved. They're on a wandering route. And after a while he's startled by the softness of a lawn under his feet. "Where are we?"

"In the park."

"Not the park! What are you thinking? Chimps look in the park! That's the first place they look."

"Where then?" says Book. His voice is tight, rattled. "What do we do?"

"Where are we? Where in the park?" He is cursing the darkness, reaching up to tear off the bandage, but a hand settles over his.

"On the corner. Just up from the pond."

"No, no, no. Not here. We've got to go. Anyone around? Can anyone see us?"

There's a moment's pause. "There's a guy with a dog."

"Big dog?"

"Tiny."

"Anyone else?"

"No. All alone."

"Alley. That's what we need. Out of sight. Hurry. But don't rush. Don't draw attention."

Book's hand is back on his arm. His feet hit asphalt, and then gravel. He can tell by the muffled sound of traffic that they are in among houses and trees.

"Now where?" says Book.

"Downtown. But not the shelter. Chimps'll check the shelter. Just get out of sight. We should have stayed in the woods."

"Cops were in the woods."

"Just go," he says. "Slow and steady. Got absolutely nothing on our minds."

And they're walking. He tries to measure their progress but the panic has cost him all points of reference. There's concrete under his feet again. And people. The steady movement of people. Book just comes to a stop.

"What are you doing?"

"Just finding my bearings."

"Don't stand still. You never stand still. Don't you know anything?"

"Then where do we go?"

"When it gets late enough, back to the flop. Chimps won't spend the night there. Maybe check the dumpsters on the way. We can bring something for the pot."

Book's hand on his arm finally draws them into motion, but it's like he wouldn't have thought of it himself. Like his mind is on other things.

And so, as they make their way back through the cool of the evening, he worries about what the Book is thinking. He must be wondering about the chimps in the forest. How could he not? Chimps just happen to show up a couple of nights after Calvin?

You don't have to be a possum to figure out they're connected. They must have found The Bear's body. What else could it be?

So now with every step he waits for the Book to speak, to bring it up, to put two and two together. And to cut him loose. Leave him with nothing to do but wait for the chimps, the grip and grab, the long dark hole. Darker now, he thinks, than he's ever imagined. He can almost hear the man thinking; hear the circle of his thoughts, back and back, edging toward the truth. "Anything on your mind?" says Calvin.

"Nothing to worry about." Though he doesn't sound convinced.

Fewer people back at the flop. A low murmur of tension. Even the Book is suspicious. When he reads he gives it only half his attention, ears pricked for the sound of footsteps. Finally the boy can't stand it. When they settle down to sleep he leans in close, his voice a whisper. "It's me," he says. "I'm the one. The chimps. They're after me." And fool that he is, he waits in a little curl of hope through the whole long hesitation.

"You don't know that," says the Book.

"Don't leave me."

"It could be anyone."

"We've got to skip. We've got to brush before morning."

"But how?" says Book. "Where do we go?" Even now he sounds uncertain.

The boy finds himself talking faster, more urgently, trying to carry him along. As if it was just this bit that was hard and then everything else would be cake. "We've got to lift a freight. There's one before dawn. You've got to help me. Please. Don't leave me behind."

"A train?"

He can hear the doubt. And the pictures start up in his mind again. He tries to shut them down, but there they are. *Grind him under the wheels.* He grips the sleeve. "Don't worry. I can do my part. I won't hold you back. I just need a hand. A lift, that's all. Just a skip and a lift. I won't slow you down."

But he can tell in the way they approach the yard—the stopping and starting, the doubling back—that the man is unconvinced. The boy tenses himself, waiting for the shove, for the jerk and snatch that would leave him alone, grasping at nothing. "Is it there?" he whispers. But it's only for assurance; he can smell the diesel, hear the engine breathing. "Not too close. Why are we stopping? Keep walking. Stay dark. Are we dark?"

They draw back, and he can feel the weeds around his legs, hear the branches overhead. "Did you pick our point? You got it? You got our spot?"

"I don't know what that means. I don't know what to do!"

"Don't leave me," he whispers. "Please don't."

But the Book doesn't reply. Instead there is the breathing of the train, and it sounds like his own. *Don't leave me now. Don't leave me now.* And out of it rises a dry, murmuring voice somewhere off to their left. "A minute more. Just a minute more. Just a minute more. Just a minute."

An old man huddled maybe ten feet away, muttering to himself. The boy can hear the rocking in his voice. Some crazy old man. "No need to rush," he is saying. "No need to rush. Just another minute. Just another. Gotta loosen your arms. Gotta loosen 'em good."

Book's hand is on his shoulder, his breath warm in his ear. "Hear that?"

Calvin nods.

"It's a gift."

The old voice is droning on, the murmur like a catechism. "A running machine. That's what you are. You're a running, leaping, catching machine. Don't think about the wheels. Your legs are quicker than the wheels. That's what you are. Quick. Quick. Your hands are claws. You catch with your claws. You leap and catch and you don't let go. And don't forget your legs. They're your friends unless they dangle. You want to take 'em with you. That's the thing. They get you there, but then you have to take 'em along."

The boy feels his mouth go dry. The sigh of the brakes; the sharp creak of the wheels. The longer they wait, the more impossible it seems. He pictures the high walls of the freight cars, like trying to climb a barn.

Book leans down and whispers in his ear. "You're a running, leaping, catching machine."

His knees are shaking. His muscles are like bags of sand. His heart won't make it: it'll race ahead or stop. A rustle in the darkness, a shift beside them. "He's up," whispers Book. "Get ready." He can't feel his feet, but he can feel the grip on his shoulder. And then from the shadows beside them the scrape of a running start, the slap of footfalls.

"Can you run?"

His lungs aren't working; he can't make them work.

"It's slow; it's long. Cattle cars."

"I don't think I can."

But they're moving ahead. Not running, but hurrying now across the gravel. "Just a little faster. That's it." Book is pulling him along, bearing him up. "You're a running machine. You leap and you catch and you don't let go."

"Don't let go," he repeats, but it's a plea, not a promise. They're closer now, he can hear it. The hand slips from his shoulder. "Don't!"

"Stay here."

"Don't leave me!"

But the Book is gone.

It's like hovering over a well and being released. He is afraid of the fall, afraid of stopping, afraid of everything it will mean if he is left here all alone. "Book? Book!"

"Here." His breathing is rough and ragged, panting through every word. "There's one unlocked. Easy as pie."

Then the grip is back; they're moving. And he thinks of the wide, high cars, each one a building he cannot see. *A running, leaping, catching machine.* He hardens his fingers into claws, but there's nothing to grab.

He can hear it rushing past, wheels clanking now, the great springs lurching. His heart is catching in his chest. His legs are done. And he knows, with sudden clarity, that he'll never make the leap.

"There's an open gate," gasps Book. "Up onto the floor. I'll give you a boost. Three steps and jump."

"What about the wheels?"

"No wheels," he says. "It's just floating on air. Three steps and jump. Three steps and *jump*!"

He's not ready. He stumbles. One step. Two. His foot catches, dragging. He starts to sprawl. His legs! he thinks. Legs! The grind and thump of the wheels. Fear lights him up like a flame. And then a jerk on his belt, and he really is flying now, rising through the air. And there's time for half a breath before he thumps and scrapes and skids across a wooden floor scratchy with straw and sharp with the smell of cow shit.

And he lies there, gasping. He feels the rocking of the train, the motion translated from a distant threat to the steady, comforting movement underneath. And with a grunt and a scrape Book is there, as well. He hears the gate clang shut. He reaches up a hand to touch the smear of something muddy on his cheek. "It smells awful in here." And with a laugh Book sits down beside him and in his low and cheerful voice describes the lights drifting past, the buildings gone, the trees and the darkness of the night.

9.

Memory has its own colors. In all the years that follow he remembers the journey taking place in the honey-warm light of dawn, though he doesn't see a sunrise for months. He recalls being warm, though the open slats of the car must have let in their share of cold night air. And he remembers the sleepy, comforting murmur of cows, though what cows are doing on a train in Connecticut he has never figured out. Together it carries the wild implausibility of fate: pulling into the yard on that particular night, the only sort of freighter a blind kid and a newbie could ever possibly have snagged.

They ride it for fifty-seven hours. They will never ride one as long or as far. It sets the shape of things to come. Whatever else they do, wherever else they go, wherever they move or stop or live, it will remain at heart just a version of this. It's not simply that he remembers it until his dying day, but that somehow, inevitably, of all the things that happen, it is this one trip that turns into the rest of his life.

They find a place in the corner, cleaner than most, where the wind through the steel slats doesn't quite reach. They sit shoulder to shoulder inhaling the scent of straw and manure, savoring the unaccustomed warmth of so many animals gathered in one place. At some point it starts raining, but that is nothing to them now.

The train stops and starts, letting cows off and taking on, and the hours of sitting still are marked by occasional shouts of men and the lowing of cattle, as if behind the dark bandage they have drifted into some western dream. In the train yards they are wary. Men feed the animals or clean the cars. But they are overworked and underpaid; new to the country and uninterested in the strange ways of men who would stay in these filthy cars any longer than necessary. In their little corner they begin to feel protected, all but invisible.

And because it is the beginning, they are careful with one another. Everything is a question. You feel like getting out? Do your eyes hurt? Are you getting thirsty? No one has ever been careful with him before. Book stuffs a wad of crumpled paper into the latch of the gate, and now when the train stops they stretch their legs. They never wander far, but under cover of rain and darkness they gather supplies. There isn't time to panhandle so they steal what they can from convenience stores and commissaries and unattended lunchboxes. There is one Quik Stop where he distracts the manager for ten full minutes, asking for help with his bandage, feigning an injury to his fingers, as Book cleans out the snack aisle. They work together well.

They live on candy bars and coke, sandwiches, potato chips. The trip passes in a haze of sweets, the tight-wound spring of all that sugar stretching out the time, lacing it with a delicate and manic glee.

"Still hungry?"

He has the bag of food in his lap and is running his hand over the wealth of chocolate. "I just like to feel it."

"Have you ever had so much candy before?"

"I went trick-or-treating once."

"Did you have fun?"

"Not fun, exactly."

The Bear had said it was too good a chance to miss; he didn't even need a costume. Ring the doorbell, say the words, and they'd fill his bag with candy. He hadn't believed him at first, wary of all the kids in their shiny outfits. Then he mustered his nerve. How hard could it be?

Maybe it was the way he said it. Or how he stood. Or the look he gave the pink and startled freddies in their little doorways. They started telling him to go away. One old lady said she'd call the cops. The other kids decided he was bad news and even the older boys wouldn't go with him. He kept thinking about that old lady, and in the end he went back and cut her tires, tried to set her tree on fire. Trick or treat.

Now he feels his way through the bag—all crinkly paper and cellophane. He holds up a candy bar. "Three Musketeers?"

"Milky Way."

"Even better." He unwraps the chocolate bar, takes a bite.

"How old are you?" Book asks.

"Twenty-seven."

"I mean really."

"Hundred-and-five."

Silence.

He is given to moments of panic as he's waking up or falling asleep. Sometimes the constant darkness seems too wide and empty, and even holding out his hands he can't reach across. "You still there?"

"I'm here. Where else would I be?"

He takes another bite and chews but without much pleasure. The candy is cloying, though he'd never admit it. He eats it because he can. "My dad used to say we were gypsies. Before he died. Made it sound better than it was. Used to say we were tinkers, travellers. I think he saw a movie or something. Rovers, that was my favorite. I liked the sound of that. Once I told him we were just homeless, but he said, who needed a home? The whole world was our home. Anywhere we wanted; that was our home."

"What about your mother?"

"He didn't talk about her much. Said she ran off with the mailman, but that might have been a joke."

"And now?"

"Now nothing. Same as before."

"Don't you have any other family?"

"Does Peach count?"

"He mentioned a grandmother somewhere. Cleveland?"

"1016 Cuyahoga Boulevard. My dad showed me the house about a hundred years ago. Must have thought it would be a comfort." He plucks at the bandage. Sometimes it just doesn't sit right, bites into his eyes or slips too far down. "How about you?"

"Chicago."

"Is that where you're from?"

"It's where I'm going. Someone I know. I'm thinking about going to see her again. Maybe give her something."

He listens to the edge Book has given to the words. "Something nice?"

No response. Though after a moment there is a rustle beside him. Book shifts amid the straw, and then something is pressed into his open hand. It takes a moment to decipher the warm, hard shape. "Is it candy?"

"It's a ring."

And now that he knows, he can feel it. A delicate band. A stone in a tiny claw-like setting. He touches it with the tip of his tongue, tasting dirt and the fine, neutral tang of metal. "Is it gold?"

"It is."

"Feels nice. What does it look like?"

"It's a red stone. A garnet."

"I like red. You going to give it to someone?"

"I'm going to return it."

But something in the voice makes him think of the moment with the old lady's tires.

"We buried our treasure so we'd have something to come back to. But when she left I dug it up again. And all I found was some cold jewelry and an empty hole."

Calvin listens, holding the ring, reluctant to give it back. If he had seen it, it might have meant nothing at all. Something else stolen, something else to pawn. But this way, Book's voice in his ear, all the concentration in his finger tips, it takes on its own weight and importance.

Book will take out the ring many times as the hours pass, just to hold it, to consider. And the boy—who isn't Clean yet, not even Calvin, really; who is still Pisser or Bug or Spitwad—will recognize each moment by the quality of the silence. The way even the murmur of the cows seems to die down and all attention is drawn back to this alone. There will be stories of the woman, of their time together. Of how easily she was able to leave him in the end. Just walk away when he needed her most. And Calvin will listen, and he'll put out his hand to hold it for a moment, and in doing so he'll feel the silence like a continuation of Book's thoughts, as if he is sharing not just a moment but a small, hard piece of his heart, and he will grasp the ring as if trying to make it a part of his own. And when he finally takes it, months from now, picking it up from the ground where it has dropped, it won't feel so much like theft as like transferring all those memories to himself, as if they are already a part of him, as if he is reclaiming some lost portion of his own life. And even Book's obvious heartbreak, even the sight of him bereft and heavy-eyed at the prospect of it being lost forever, even that won't be enough to make Calvin give it back.

But now he does, he hands back the ring. And in the moment just after, when he feels the shadow of the pressure it made still marking his palm, he reaches into one of the deep pockets of his coat and brings out something of his own. He fumbles a little. Perhaps after the tiny weight of the ring it feels over-substantial. Perhaps he just hasn't grown accustomed to its cumbersome shape. He holds it like a rock cradled in his lap, measuring the answering silence with satisfaction.

"What are you doing with a gun?" asks Book.

"It was my dad's. He left it to me. Do you want to hold it?"

"No."

"He was shot by some stupid freddie. In his own woods. On his own bridge."

He is pleased with the silence. It seems to add to the weight of the already solid gun. Book, when he replies, says, "He had his own bridge?"

"That's right. He said it was his job. Had to pass it down father to son. He said, someday this bridge will be yours, and then you'll have to guard it."

"You're not guarding it now."

"No. I got another job now."

He feels his way around the gun, letting his fingers wrap the butt, one hand tracing the revolving chamber, the stubby barrel. Then he feels Book's light touch on his fingers, turning the gun, pointing it gently away from them both. "Just to be on the safe side."

"I'm not a chump."

"I know."

"I know what I'm doing."

"I can tell."

"I'm going to find that freddie. And I'm going to give him something nice."

Book seems to consider that, though he says nothing.

"I heard him fall. My dad. All the way down. I heard his voice. He was trying to protect me. And that freddie jumps him. This skinny little freddie. They're punching, they're tussling. And my dad just tosses him off like a skinny little piece of garbage. But the gun comes loose. My dad's gun. And suddenly it's up, sailing through the air. And the freddie goes for it. We both go for it. And I'm fighting him, punching him, trying to get to the gun. And my dad is shouting. Everybody's shouting." Calvin hesitates, startled by the remembered noise, by the harsh and angry clamor of it, and embarrassed at the hint of a sob still quivering in his voice.

"You must have been scared."

He swallows. "Jesus God. I bet you'd have been plenty scared."

"I bet you're right," says Book gently. "And what about your eyes?"

It's his first time telling the story. He's never really straightened it out in his mind. There's been no time to think. But now it's right there, everything that happened. The darkness is like a movie screen, and there's no place to hide.

The freddie hurls himself at the Bear, and the gun comes loose. He makes his own leap, and his hands are filled with the struggling man, both of them sprawling over the trestle, scrabbling, scratching for the gun. And the Bear is coming forward, and he's in a rage. He's got a surprise for him, for this stupid freddie. A little jar in his pocket. He always says it's his trademark. People remember him, he says, after a tussle. And the freddie is still going for the gun. And the Bear shouts, Look out, Pisser. And Calvin doesn't know what he means. He looks up. He thinks that's what he wants. He thinks he wants him to look. And the freddie shoots. He sees the Bear twist, sees the glass jar jerk in his hand. And in the moonlight a curtain of droplets is hanging there like a wave taking shape. Then the whole world explodes. His eyes are on fire. And he stumbles; he's at the edge. And the Bear is screaming. And he can't see a goddam thing. But he can hear it all. And the scream goes over, and then down and down. And Calvin is clinging to the tracks, to the edge of the trestle, hanging on like crazy. But it's like the scream is reaching up and trying to drag him down.

Then he feels Book lifting the pistol from his clenched fist. His heart is pounding. "That goddam freddie," he whispers. "If only he'd left us alone." He feels half a chocolate bar pressed into his hand and he chews it slowly. He used to think he could never get enough candy, but now he barely tastes it.

"So what's the plan?" asks Book.

"Hole up somewhere, I guess. Till I get my eyes back. Then I find the freddie."

"How?"

"I'll find him."

"Did you get a good look?"

"Oh, yeah. I'll remember him. That's not someone I'm going to forget."

They sit in silence, rocking to the motion of the train. After a while he reaches over for a handful of Book's coat. "You still there?"

"Still here."

"You want another candy bar?"

"I'm good."

"There's jerky."

"You go ahead."

"I'm good," he says.

Book reads aloud from *Huckleberry Finn* until it's finished, then Calvin sits in silence, letting the words all settle. "Its good," he says. "But it goes all storybook at the end."

"Maybe a little."

"Why do they do that? Ruin it like that?"

"People like a happy ending."

"It's not real, though. Not like a real ending."

"I used to think it was," says Book.

"Nah. You want to read it again?"

The first time they have to put drops in his eyes he can't imagine opening them. They are raw and burning and fastened shut, sticky and cemented with sand.

"Do you want to be blind for the rest of your life?"

Calvin lies flat with his head on the surprising comfort of the man's lap and feels cautious fingers working the bandage loose. "Not yet," he says breathlessly.

"Slow as can be."

His palms are slick. His breath is gone. He feels the two gauze pads peeled away. "Oh, God." Then a single raindrop on the hot, pinched seam of his lid. Then another and another. The drops sting as they seep beneath the edge, but he feels them loosening their grip, freeing them, so that his eyes open without command. It is much too bright. The afternoon sun is like a knife. But Book holds his eyelids open for the time it takes to daub the ointment in, and then he's pillowed once again in the comforting dark.

The first few times they re-wind the hospital bandage around his head, but it soon grows dirty and ragged. At the next stop they steal a bandana from a Cum'n'Go and tie that in its place. "You look like a man about to be shot," says Book. Calvin hears the word *man* and feels a glow in his chest.

Somewhere in the middle he rises out of a fitful sleep and, feeling for the reassuring grip of Book's sleeve, brushes against the hard shell of a bottle. They've picked it up somewhere along the way, and Calvin catches the sour hint of it beneath the smells of cattle and train. Book's knees are tucked up and for a moment Calvin thinks he is reading. He feels a quick, panicky resentment that he has gone on without him, but then he hears the scratching of the pen.

At first there is something comforting in the sound, but after a while it begins to make him uneasy: the steady, unceasing urgency of it. He can feel the man beside him, bent and huddled in a knot of concentration. "Book?" But there is no reply. "What are you writing?"

"A letter."

The pen scratches along determinedly, and Calvin can hear how hard he's pressing down, as if cutting his way through the paper.

"What does it say?"

What he means is: don't leave me here alone. But he feels foolish. Like a child. Might as well just say: Tell me a story.

And then he does, Book does. The low voice rises. And it sounds for a second just like *Huckleberry Finn*. But it's not. Calvin can tell how much he's been drinking. The scratch of the pen hurries through the darkness, and the low voice murmurs along behind, as if the whole headlong story is coming unwound and

Book is just trying to catch up. It is bitter, poisonously angry. Made somehow more terrible by the low, startled voice, as if Book, himself, is surprised at every line—the fury, the wretchedness, the ease with which she left, the simple cowardice of abandoning him, the sudden emptiness of his days. The letter goes on and on.

Then stops. A quick rip and crumpling of the page, and a silence as if, even now, Book is not sure what to do.

"Just throw it away," whispers Calvin.

He feels the crumpled paper thrust into his hand, and he leans over to shove it out through the slats of the wall. But he stops and, for no reason he can say, stuffs it into the bag with the candy. "Tell me another. Tell me a different one."

But there's only one story. A fairy tale that starts in whatever way it can, and always ends the same. Each page, torn and crumpled.

He is writing letters to a woman.

In the weeks ahead, when his eyes are mended and the bandage comes off and Clean begins to squint his way through the world, when anything too bright hurts his head and he can live comfortably only by limiting how much of each day he lets in with every glance, he will come upon the pages, unrolling each tightly crumpled ball and poring over them in secret. He will be shocked by the wild variety of them: some so loving they are a form of desperation; others so furious and ugly they burn his cheeks.

But now he is innocent of any such thing. It's only a story now. Emerging in fragments over the long course of the ride. It starts and stops, repeats and moves on, veering from expressions of wonder into the darkest spite as if drawn off course by the pull of some relentless fate. And he finds himself guiding Book back, coaxing him, bending him toward a happy ending. He tries and tries again, as if it's his story to get right.

And finally he does. The couple walks through a deepening

twilight over the gentle slope of a park. It is a walled garden, untraveled, preserved by stillness. Book has come here before, that afternoon, but he doesn't tell her that. They enter by climbing the low bough of a tree and dropping into the middle of a dream. They stop beneath a wide stone bridge. There is no water. It hangs suspended over a river of grass. She wonders at the needlessness, but there is always a bridge, he tells her. You can't have enchantment without a bridge.

And nothing could be more enchanted. The pale gleam of a table and two white chairs. The plates and silverware. The brand new champagne flutes. He draws from the pocket of his jacket a lighter and sparks a pair of candles. The white table glows.

"It's magic," she whispers.

"Magic is sinister and slippery," he says. "Enchantment is the work of love."

Even as he listens Calvin cannot imagine anyone speaking like this. But he welcomes it into the cradle of his belief. For what is this rocking, manure-smelling voyage but a kind of enchantment? He doesn't even need to close his eyes; they are closed already. He can picture the glowing table, alone in the night. The candlelight, the heavy darkness of the bridge. There is wine, there is an apple, a piece of cheese, a loaf of bread, all carried there with the furniture in a series of back-breaking trips; endless journeys by cab to arrange things just so. In the light of the candles all effort is forgotten. And as if to mark this as true, one by one the fireflies appear, floating in the darkened air, slowly gathering until, when the couple look up, they are at the center of a moving, blinking constellation, reduced and aligned for this moment alone.

When the story finally comes to an end, he can hear Book holding the page, smoothing it on an upraised knee as if this, at last, might be worth preserving. But Calvin is unsurprised when he crumples it like the others. By this time he understands you cannot pick and choose among the pieces. Even an enchantment as strong as this is bounded by rules of iron. The past is a single curling line; to cut it is to lose it all.

Book says he'll write a letter for him, but with a sinking feeling he knows he has no one out there. The only one he can think of is Peach, and what is there to say to him?

"They don't have to be alive," says Book. "Do you want to write to your father?"

He thinks of those last moments. "Look out, Pisser!" Then the shot and his burning eyes. He shakes his head.

"Your mother?"

"I can't picture her."

But there is someone he does remember. In that moment on the trestle—still struggling with the freddie, straining after the gun —he glanced over the man's shoulder and there was a woman. It's no one he knows. A dream, perhaps, if only he'd been asleep. She stands frozen on the trestle dressed in yellow, clear as an angel, and her hands are reaching out to him as if she could pluck something crucial out of the air. It's an instant and gone. A clear and perfect moment. And then the burning in his eyes and all the darkness in the world. He doesn't know her name. He doesn't know anything about her. But she was the last clear thing he would ever see.

"Just tell her a story," Book whispers. "About yourself. She'll know it's for her."

But the only story that comes to his mind is the one he's in the middle of right now.

"We're on a train," he says, "and we're heading west. It smells of cows and chocolate. And every so often a breeze blows through and it smells of grass." He hesitates, waiting for Book to laugh or interrupt, but there is only the thin scrawling of the pen. So he tells her about Book. About how he's writing this letter for him. And over time, over the long hours of the trip, as he spins out the thread of his story, starting and stopping, fingers moving over the fine, warm curve of the ring, which Book lets him hold, which becomes a kind of key to his own remembered tale, he tells her all he can remember of his life on the road, all the fragments of memory stitched together by the scratching of the pen.

He wants this ride to last forever. But every time the train slows he feels the low dread of its inevitable end. He waits for Book to gather up their things, to announce that they've arrived wherever it is they are going. And every time when the men come and go, voices rising and falling through the slats of the car, and the train jerks itself back into motion, he starts to breath again.

"Where are you headed?" Book asks in the cool of the night, the question rising up out of nothing that came before.

"Nowhere. What about you?"

"I thought you had a grandmother in Cleveland."

"No. She's just a house."

"You're going to need someone to take care of you, just until you get back on your feet."

And he feels a stab of grief, lightning fast, before he can push it away. "I don't need anyone."

"There's no rush," says Book.

"Where are you headed?'

Book hesitates. "Still thinking about Chicago."

"I could go to Chicago."

But Book says nothing. The train carries them along.

And then in the middle of *Huckleberry Finn*, their third time through, he feels the buck and shudder of the brakes as the train begins to slow. They lie beneath the straw in the unaccustomed stillness of an unmoving floor and hear the muffled voices of the workmen. There's a clang of metal that travels up the train, the deep, offended lowing of cattle. And then, perhaps because it is the very last thing he wants to hear, there rises a sudden clarity of sound amid the muffled conversations of the roustabouts. Someone muttering to someone else, a story he's telling, directions he's giving. *Cleveland,* the man says. And Calvin lies still, hoping Book hasn't heard. Hoping they can just continue on.

But in the end it doesn't matter. With a sudden calamity of sound the ramp is dragged out from beneath the floor, and he hears the men swing aboard. The cows clamor. With yells and slaps they are driven from the car, and the two huddled figures are abandoned in the now deepening silence, broken only by a startled voice, "What the hell are you doing here?"

10.

It takes an effort to get to their feet. Their muscles are stiff, the dust from the straw is in their throats. He clings to Book's arm as they totter down the ramp and stand on ground that is unaccustomedly still. "What do you see?" he whispers.

"Early evening. It's chilly."

"No joke. What's it look like?"

"It's a world of fog. It's like walking through smoke."

"Let's not get lost."

"We're already lost," says Book. "What can it hurt?"

They stroll now, prospecting, waiting for the eddy or current that might make their direction clear. The faint creak-and-concussion of the train yard falls behind.

"There's a bit of a crowd ahead."

He is aware of other footsteps. He can smell the crowd. They become part of a staggered procession, stepping through a doorway into the echo of a room.

"Where are we?" he whispers.

"Our Lady of Sorrows."

"Doesn't sound so great."

At a rickety table they eat something tasteless and warm. It might be porridge and bread; a hard-boiled egg. There is powdered milk to drink. After all the candy the food is welcome, but eating is like a joke he suffers through over and over. Find the bowl, find the porridge, find the mouth. Where did he put the glass? He moves slowly, determined not to spill. The difficulty of every movement is the only answer to his rising panic. His fingers find the egg and discover Book has already peeled it. There is a long sermon, but he's too tired to follow—something about fishing or bushels of grain. It seems to end on the note it began.

Someone puts a broom in his hand. It steadies him. Everybody works to tidy up. He hears the clatter of chairs folding away before him. Half-drowsing he feels a touch on his shoulder. Book lifts the broom away. Then they're walking down a hallway and into a crowded room alive with the rattle of cages. Not cages. Bed springs. The room is already packed. Every bed is filled: a rough boot, a shove, a thick smell of unwashed skin. The hand on his shoulder is his only comfort. "Here you go. I'm just a few beds down."

"You're not next to me?" It bubbles out before he can stop it.

"Just three away. Wait." Book has one of his hands. He ties a loop of twine around it, and he can feel the tension as the length of it is drawn away. "Just give it a tug. One for good, two for bad."

He can't help it; he tugs it twice.

"That's it," Book says kindly. "Just like that." And he eases him down, settles him on the bed, draws up the thin blanket. "Sleep tight."

"Can it, asshole!"

"Pipe down!"

"Shut it, Nancy!"

It's only the click that tells him when the lights go out. He feels a gentle tug on his wrist and gives one tug in reply.

He's asleep and then he's not. The thick stench of sweat is like a cloth over his mouth. A hand. A sudden weight drives the breath from his lungs. There's a voice in his ear, a terrible puff of awful air. "You're pretty, aren't you? Such a pretty boy in the dark." He must be asleep. It has to be a dream. Otherwise he'd be able to move. The weight is immense. He's pinned under the man. The hard lump of the gun is in his pocket, but he can't move his arms. He jerks at the twine around his wrist, jerks again, but it comes loose. There's nothing at all on the other end. He is twisting, struggling. A cry would save him, but as in the worst of dreams he cannot speak. And then with a roar and a tumble the weight is gone. The man is gone. And he's breathing again. The sounds are no less nightmarish, grunting and crashing, the scrape of beds and the wet-solid thud of punches landing, but distant now. Voices rising in a hubbub of complaints. He doesn't hear the lights come on.

There isn't much to gather up. Under the glowering silence of the nun, for whom all sins have a cause and blame enough to go round, they lace on their shoes. Book is panting as if he'll never recover his breath. His own voice, freed now, is running over with a muttering flow of curses and fright. They trundle along, the two of them, until they are free of the building. The rain has begun.

When they step out into the night air it feels better than anything he could say. Much later, long after he and Book have parted, he will read more and more, poring over all the possible stories of what one human being can do to another. And always he will come back to that moment of rising out of sleep into the terrible grip. And then the moment of breaking free. And in his mind he will test it against all the scenes of rescue and relief, finding nothing that will do it justice until he comes to the story of Odysseus in the underworld and imagines with perfect clarity that final emergence into the light.

"Are you okay?"

"What a jerk! What a piece of dirt!"

"Did he hurt you?"

"I was going to bite him but he smelled so bad."

"Did he hurt you?"

"No! I woke up and that smelly hand over my mouth. Did you hit him?"

"I did. I hit him in the face. With your shoe."

"Oh, that's got to hurt." His laughter is a little wild. "How many times?"

"I don't know. Over and over. I didn't count."

"Good. That's good." He twists his hand in the fabric of

Book's sleeve, burying his knuckles in the grip of it. His breath won't settle in his lungs. "You sound funny."

"My nose is a little puffy."

"He hit you?"

"Couple times."

"How much did you hit him?"

"Over and over."

"Good. That's good."

They stand together in the rain. He is listening, already straining his ears for all the places where someone could lurk. In the distance a train etches its mournful whistle on the night. They begin to walk. Not hurrying. The train is too far away; they don't want to get their hopes up. So they're just strolling. When the whistle comes again they walk a little faster. "Step down," says Book. "Careful. Down again. And the curb. Now duck." He hears the rattle of a fence held aside.

Is there a difference between illusion and opportunity? They're walking faster now. The sidewalk turns to gravel under his feet. But now they hear the whistle again, farther off. Definitely farther. Disappearing.

"Too late?" In spite of himself he feels bereft.

"One door closes, another opens."

"I'm too tired for poetry."

But in the next moment he smells it, too. The perfume of frying potatoes, heavy and fragrant with grease. His mouth begins to water as if a switch has been thrown.

In the days ahead he will see Rodney's Diner for the first time, when the bandana comes off for his eye drops and he sneaks a peak around. He'll see a low ceiling, linoleum floors, the lollipop surprise of red stools at the counter. There is always an early morning crowd, eating with the kind of workmanlike fortitude that marks their day at the yard or the welding barn or the host of smoky, clamorous sheds that keep the trains rolling clear. Rodney is a balding man in a black t-shirt and apron. He cooks and serves and carries as if the whole point of his labors is not to feed the people but to fill the great sinkful of soapy water that seems always on the verge of overflowing.

But that first day he sees none of it. Book leads them around to the alley and together they stand at the open back door in a warm cloud of vegetable steam and coffee. Rodney clatters into the kitchen. There is a muffled landslide as he dumps a stack of plates into the water, but no sooner do the sounds of washing begin than there are shouts from the front. Someone bangs a coffee mug on the counter. A ripple of laughter rises. Soon it sounds like a prison riot.

From the doorway Book's voice carries an air of coincidental interest. "My friend and I are professional dishwashers by trade."

The boy straightens up and tries to look respectable in the weighing silence.

"Couple aprons over there. For God's sake, wash your hands. And don't let anyone see you."

Calvin sits on an overturned bucket, listening to the sound of dishes being washed. Afterwards, in the late-morning lull, they sit at the lunch counter eating eggs and leftover pancakes. Rodney makes a point of not mentioning the bandana over his eyes. "Gets busy at breakfast, then lunch. We close at three. When the sun's out, there's a park about a block away. It's not much. But nobody minds if you close your eyes there."

It is paradise. Bellies full, they lie for an hour under the fragrant whisper of a pine tree before returning for the second rush. This time he stands at a long counter, sorting the newly clean dishes into piles, distributing silverware among the wide trays. His fingers creep across the unfamiliar landscape, learning the shape of each piece, listening for the reassuring clink of one dish on another or the low, wrinkling sound of silverware settling into place. When the counter grows crowded, Book carries dishes out to the front room, ready for their next life, and as the door opens the hubbub of voices pours in.

In the afternoon they clean the kitchen, clearing high shelves and sponging them down, organizing canned goods, pushing a mop into corners that haven't known one in years. It is more than they need to do, but the satisfaction of an orderly task, the high and momentary pleasures of cleanliness, keep them at it longer than required. When Rodney returns, his surprise is clear. Calvin feels the mop lifted from his hands and replaced with a ponderous sandwich, turkey and lettuce and cheese. He doesn't even bother to sit down. "You got a name, kid?"

He goes through the list his father has given him: boy, squirt, pisser, bug, moron, jack-off. "Clean," says Book. "What else could it be?"

He has always lived small. Now the darkness makes it smaller. A corner in a storeroom with a mattress and a pile of ancient blankets. But here's the thing. Everyone looks out for him. Book, of course. But Rodney, too. Some of the regulars. They tease him, shout suggestions, tell him he's getting warm or cold. They leave him teetering piles of coins that spill when he wipes the counter. In a loud voice Rodney marvels at the way he navigates the cluttered kitchen, "But put a bag of garbage out for the dumpster and that thing'll sit there all day."

And it's true. Clean hesitates before the wide, uncertain blankness of the alley. But slowly he learns his way, counting steps, constructing first with Book's help and then on his own, the pattern of dumpster, doorway, fences, street. There is the park close at hand. There is a grocery store of narrow aisles and lively voices tumbling through a language that sounds like singing. He trundles along like a wagon, guided here and there, and at the end of each shift he lies beneath the rough-skinned pine tree on a stretch of grass that smells faintly of cats, and listens to whatever book they're reading at the moment.

His eyes are healing, they no longer burn. The pain is reduced to a rough sandy feeling under the lids and a mask of permanent sunburn across the bridge of his face. But still Book thinks its better if he keeps them covered, and in truth he doesn't mind. He's afraid of what it will mean when he can move on his own. The threat of his grandmother lies always in the background; the half-heard *Cleveland* like the echo of a bell that can't be unrung.

But one time, as they're putting in the ointment, Rodney drops a pan of freshly sliced potatoes, and the noise is shocking. His eyes burst open against all intention, and he finds himself staring up into Book's face. Before he sees anything else, the expression catches him. Startled. Dismayed. Book hangs there with the bandana in his hands as if his only thought is to cover the eyes again before any further damage can be done. But he stops, sags a little, like a man who knows it's too late, and Clean peers up with a squinting, hesitant smile. "Hey, Book. Nice to see you."

He isn't sure how he imagined his face. Something in line with the voice: big and heavy with kindness. Instead it's thin with a long jaw and dark eyes glinting behind bent wire-rimmed glasses. He's badly bruised: cheeks, chin, a thick purple necklace clasping his throat. And Clean thinks of the shelter dormitory, the heavy man dragged abruptly away and the long, muffled struggle of punches and grunts.

"God, Book. You're a mess."

"Like you're some thing of beauty." And it's odd to hear that familiar voice emerging from this stranger's mouth.

"I didn't mean it. I like your face."

"What a nice thing to say. How do you feel?"

"Good. Are all those bruises from the shelter?"

"Most of them."

"Not all? Someone else been choking you, Book? You been getting into fights?"

"Nothing I can't handle."

"You just point 'em out to me," he says. "I'll protect you."

"Close your eyes. That's better."

And it is. The drops are cooling, the ointment turns him back into a fish moving smoothly through a realm of moisture.

But he remembers that look on Book's face. It unnerved him at first, a look of such sudden dismay. But the more he thinks about it the more it warms his heart: that there is someone who worries about so insignificant a thing as his comfort.

Every day he leaves the bandana off a little longer. Book won't let him near a mirror, and even on an overcast day the sun is too bright, so they sit in chairs and look around the kitchen. Familiar objects of touch and smell take on new identities in the realms of sight. He learns the world over again.

Book has borrowed from one of the diner's drawers an atlas of the fifty states, and occasionally, when he thinks no one is looking, he'll pore over it. In the past he's simply left it out, but now he makes a point of putting it away. Clean imagines the street map of Cleveland, imagines Book identifying Lakewood, searching through all the fine lines for the street where the old woman is waiting.

"I'm not going," he says one morning.

"Family is family."

"She's nothing to me."

And Book just shrugs.

He tries to ignore it, to go about his business. But occasionally he can't help it. He drifts over to the drawer. And there's Ohio, there's Cleveland. He can't keep from looking. But once, when he bends low to squint down at the map, he finds it open to the state of Illinois and the city of Chicago laid out in all its confusion.

The comfort of routine sneaks up on him. The sound of pots banging and the smell of coffee. In the early morning he wakes to a dark world growing lighter, a pleasure he could not have put a name to before.

He drinks coffee with lots of milk and sugar as he washes and stacks the plates. He has been promoted, and he is surprised by the comfort of working through a morning's dirty dishes as

Book turns a surprisingly deft hand to the bacon, the bubbling oatmeal, the great landslide of potatoes. After the rush Rodney brings him a bacon and egg sandwich, warm and slick with grease, and he wolfs it down at the sink, then dips his fingers clean.

After breakfast they get ready for lunch; after lunch they clean. Then in the sunny afternoons—and in the memory of later years every afternoon is sunny—they stroll to the corner park. There is no library around, but the tired men on the early shifts often bring the company of a stained and battered paperback, read and then abandoned, and Clean finds himself led by that familiar voice through a shifting terrain of spy thrillers, murder mysteries, and the occasional Harlequin Romance.

When there is food left over on any given day—a spilling pile of pancakes, a mountain of drying home fries and toast—they move a steel table out into the alley with a clutter of mismatched chairs, and Rodney hangs a lank red pennant from the fire escape on the corner. Within moments, men start arriving, wandering in as if by accident. Gradually they fill the table.

Clean stays in the kitchen, setting out plates and spoons and cups. The hubbub makes him nervous, the rough and raspy voices, so he peers out through the half-open door as the men arrive. He watches with a strange, proprietary satisfaction as Book and Rodney move among them. It puts him in mind of Huck sitting in his comfortable room at the widow's house. And he's thinking maybe Huck shouldn't have struggled so much; should have maybe enjoyed it more.

And then he hears the voice.

It's odd the way a sound can come to you—not simply from the next room but from weeks or months before—slipping out of its tight-locked cupboard with a single word. One moment he is picking up a heavy pitcher of milk, ready to pass it outside, and the next an angry voice rumbles clearly through the open door, "What the hell is this!"

The sound freezes his heart. And there it is again: the hand on his mouth, the sour breath in his face. He creeps to the door. The daylight is caustic, but he strains to see, squinting into the glare.

The man is a dragon, a grizzly bear, fiercely hunched and terrible. A huge blur of a thing with close-cropped hair and a week's growth of beard. He shifts to look around the alley as if waking from hibernation. His face is mottled dark with bruises or dirt. There are wide scratches under one eye, as if he is weeping blood. He prods at the potatoes with his spoon, then raises his head. Clean ducks back, but it's too late. A moment's recognition. A slow grinding laugh. "Well, isn't this something. Here I was thinking I smelled something nice. A little something tasty and tight."

Clean can't move. He thinks wildly of the gun, but it's tucked away in his bag. If he closes the heavy door he will be safe, but his muscles won't work. His legs are cold. He holds the pitcher of milk as if it will protect him. The man is easing back from the table, huge and grinning. He's in no hurry. *Help,* he thinks. *Help me,* but his voice is gone. He feels his knees turn to sand. The heavy steel pitcher has no weight; it's rising from his hands.

And almost briskly Book is striding toward the table. Skinny Book. Bruised and battered. He's a twig beside the man, a scarecrow. He steps up as if about to help him from his chair and there is a splash, an arc of milk against the sky, and the pitcher comes down with a sound like concrete hitting a thick side of beef. It isn't a fight. With the first blow the whole, enormous mass of the man sinks down with the grace of a dirigible into its dock. And then the measured repetition of the pitcher coming down and down. Again and again. Clean thinks it will never stop. And when it does the alley is silent except for the ragged sound of Book's panting.

"Well isn't that something."

The second voice rises from the silence. And it marks the

extremity of his feelings that such a familiar voice should take so long to find its way to Clean's ear. He draws back. Peach slouches in his chair at the long, battered table and gazes with something like appreciation at Book, who is leaning now, breathless against the alley wall. The other men are climbing to their feet, making their departure in ones and twos.

But Peach picks up a stale pancake and takes an enormous bite. "Isn't this nice?" he says around the mouthful. The dead man sits slumped across the table. Peach swallows and nods. "You got some nice rage going there."

Through the window, even squinting past the cobwebs in his eyes, he can see Peach is unchanged: the knit cap slipping back from the high forehead, the boneless chin, the nose like Gibraltar above the thick blonde mustache. He is eating with one hand; the other waits in his pocket with the patience of something sharp.

It's not exactly that he fears Peach—though he has seen him slash a man across the face with a look of wild good cheer. It's that he can suddenly imagine a life free of him. He wants to whisper to Book, to get him back inside. Don't say a thing. Don't speak.

And now Rodney has come out. He is standing in the doorway, pale and sagging under the weight of all that greets him. "Christ's sake!"

"We've had a little accident, boss." It's Peach talking. Book seems unable to get his voice to work. "I think my friend here tripped and fell."

"Christ's sake." It's all Rodney can manage.

"I know what you're thinking." Peach gives him a smile. "You're thinking we got ourselves a problem here. A disposal problem. Ain't that right? I can always tell what a man's thinking. And you know? I could maybe help you with that." He reaches for another pancake.

"What kind of help?" says Book.

The pancake stops at his mouth. "Say that again."

No, no, Clean is thinking. Don't talk. Don't talk.

"Say what?"

"Anything," says Peach. "Mary had a little lamb, it's fleece was brown as shit."

"What kind of help?" Book demands again.

"That's nice." Peach is nodding now, admiring. "That's real nice. You're that book, ain't you? From all that time ago. The book at the flop in the woods over Hartford way. Fucking *Huckleberry Finn*. Well, I'll tell you, mister book. This is the kind of help that costs ten dollars."

Clean holds his breath. He wants to tell him Peach isn't stupid, no matter how he looks. He wants to tell him about the cheerful smile when he cut the man under the bridge in Merriam. But instead he hovers at the corner of the window like someone trapped under a house with his nose pressed up for air.

"Ten dollars," Rodney agrees. "We get him away from my diner."

Peach stuffs the last of the pancake into his mouth and climbs to his feet. "Never one to shirk a task," come the muffled words. He takes one arm, Book the other, and they drag the body into motion. There is no one around to see them haul it up the street and lay it, slumped and boneless, at the edge of an intersection.

Afterwards, as Rodney scrubs the table, Peach settles back into his chair with the satisfaction of a job well done. "This is nice," he says again, taking in the alley, the table, the bowls of cold food. "I'm thinking maybe a few more potatoes, some of those eggs there. And I'm thinking maybe that ten bucks comes with a cup of coffee."

As Rodney reaches glumly into his pocket Book comes inside. He pours a mug of coffee. Clean hurries over, his voice an anxious whisper. "What's he doing? Don't make him mad. Don't let him come in."

"It's fine," says Book.

"What does he want?"

"He's just here to eat."

"How did he find me? How did he know?" He can feel himself shaking.

"I've got this. Just stay quiet. Stay inside."

Clean is amazed at his calm. There is blood on his sleeve, a little ribbon of drops. There is blood on the hand that pats him lightly on his shoulder.

He picks up the coffee and carries it outside. "You're a long way from the campfire," he says.

"Not as far as I meant to be. Fact is, I barely got out ahead of the noise. Been nothing but cops and stops ever since."

"Didn't you have a boy with you?"

Clean's grip tightens on the window frame, his whole body stiff with listening.

Peach laughs around a mouthful of eggs. "That Pisser. Talk about bad luck. First he gets himself blinded. Dragging around my neck like a bag of rocks. Then the chimps come crawling out."

"Sounds rough."

"It was," Peach agrees. "But that's the thing about bad luck. It's got to stick to someone. It just don't have to be me. Kid's okay. They ain't gonna hurt him. He's a kid. A blind kid. Jesus, they'll probably adopt him. Make him the chimp mascot. Let him sit on the sergeant's desk and play with the hats."

"So, you're what?" says Book. "Just passing through?"

"You know what they say. Places to go, people to see." He nods with some approval at his half-finished meal. "Though this is not such a bad gig. How often you put out the food?"

"Not me. It's the owner. Not very often."

"And you're like, what? His busboy?"

Peach pushes his empty mug along the table. "How about a little more coffee, then?" In the silence he follows Book's glance to the empty milk pitcher, bent and toppled on its side. "Unless you're out."

"That was the last of it," Book agrees.

Peach nods again. "Funny thing about that kid, though. Pisser. Son of a friend of mine, or used to be. We're like family. I went back, looking for him. No sign. No word. No little stories around the chimp shop about some cute little mascot. Only word, some little blind kid catching a cow car heading west. Running along beside it, jumping on. Wouldn't that be something to see? Little blind kid jumping on a rolling freight? It's like a circus act."

"Sounds impressive."

"Doesn't it? I love stories like that. Warm your heart. Thing is," says Peach, "kid's like family. You got any family?"

"No."

"Well. Thing about family is all those close ties. All those family secrets and shit. Makes you tight. You look out for each other."

"That's really sweet," says Book.

"Yeah. Well. You'd know, wouldn't you? You're the big reader." Peach is peering up at him now, raising that nose and mustache as if testing the air. "Thing is, you look familiar to me."

Book picks up the battered pitcher, weighs it in his hand. "I'm not an expert," he says, "but maybe it's because we met."

"Nah. I remember your voice. But it's more than that. Something else. Where you from? You a Connecticut man?"

"I'm a citizen of the world."

"No shit. Ever been in Florida for the picking?"

"Never have."

"San Fernando?"

"Nope."

"For a citizen of the world, you don't get around much, do you." He's peering closely at Book now, as if maybe there is something in his clothing, in the way he stands. Then he turns back to his plate. "Don't suppose you got any more potatoes?"

"Sorry."

"No coffee, no potatoes. Still," says Peach. "Tomorrow's another day."

Book carries the pitcher inside and washes it carefully at the sink. He sets it down on the counter, but it won't stand up so he lays it on its side. Clean's afraid he's going to be hard to convince. But he goes straight to the mattress in the corner and begins packing up their things. Rodney has their wages ready. Clean tucks them away. He is sorry to leave, but it's a comfort that Book would rather go than give him up to Peach. It gives him a warm feeling that lasts through the wrapping up of leftovers and the final tidy of the kitchen, a sentimental gesture they perform without a word. It lasts, in fact, until they ease out the back door and down the empty alley, heading through the darkness toward the glow of the train yard; until Book, head down, striding along, hand tucked firmly under his arm, says, "We're going to get you to your grandma."

"What? No!"

"It's the only thing. He can't touch you there. She'll take you. You were headed there anyway."

"What about you? Are you coming?"

"I'm going to keep going."

"Where?"

"There are places. I can think of places."

"What places?"

But Book just shakes his head.

"I'll come with you."

"No."

"Why not?"

The answer is slow in coming. "I just killed a man. You think that's not going to get ugly?"

"I don't care. No one knows it's you."

"Your friend there does."

"Then let's just keep going. I'm coming with you."

But the train yard is before them, and Book comes to a stop.

He is silent, standing there. Waiting and waiting. Clean can feel his life tipping away from all he has come to hope. Cleveland. Who needs Cleveland? They can just keep going. Just stay on the road. "Yes," he says. "Right? You're thinking yes, aren't you? That's it, that's the answer. Come on, Book. What are you thinking?"

But it doesn't look good. The familiar face is drawn, the expression bleak. They are at a side gate of the train yard, all but deserted at this time of day, and Book is staring at it, as if it's the gate that's important. As if that's what's going to part them.

But it's not the gate. Not the gate, not the trains, not the thought of goddam Cleveland. It's the sign. He's staring at the sign beside the gate. And when Clean turns to look, leaning closer, squinting to make out the words, he sees there is only one. Chicago.

CLEAN

11.

Clean stands awash in relief: Cleveland long passed, the unknown grandmother miles behind. Even the prospect of Peach can't undo him. They can hit the road right now, slide out of town. They can leave everything—Peach, Chicago, even the terrible thud of that heavy steel pitcher. He is concentrating on his eyes: sharpening them, focusing them, trying to ready himself for the train, for the leap and the grab. In the distance he hears a freighter sighing into readiness for another long pull. And still Book is motionless, as if there is more to read in the seven letters of the sign than he can possibly absorb.

"Book? You okay?" And Clean wonders if he's hearing it too, the pitcher, the awful echoing sound of it. "It's okay. It's behind us." He glances back over his shoulder. The street is starting to wake up now. Starting to fill. "Time to slide. We'll just leave it behind."

"You think?"

Book is smiling, but it's not a smile he's seen before. Thin and crooked, like something left behind when everything happier blew town. Clean wants to shake him, to drag him into motion. He thinks of the body lying in the street. "Can't stay here, Book. Where to? What's the plan?" He feels just like the rumbling freighter, straining against the stillness. But Book turns, gazing over the dark streets of warehouses and sagging storefronts. A distant patter on the sidewalk, and Clean feels the rain begin.

They find a highway overpass with a good slope up from the road, and they wedge themselves in for sleep. It's early, but there's no light to read by. They could sit in a diner; they have the money from Rodney. But Book seems reluctant to leave the vicinity. He glances out through the rattling rain as if just the sight of the sign is something.

Gradually other men appear, shaking off the wet. Two arrive dragging a steel barrel like an awkward piece of luggage, and soon they have a fire going. Cautiously Clean edges closer. "Something for the pot." He holds up a bag of Rodney's leftovers. The men look down at the fire as if gauging whether the heat can be divided two more ways, but they say nothing. Clean taps Book on the shoulder, and they settle closer to the warmth. They pass around cold potatoes and scrambled eggs, stale pancakes. Clean wraps himself in his blanket, but even as he slips off into sleep he's aware of Book lying brightly awake like a glowing coal in the night.

In the morning he is gone.

Clean searches, but his eyes are too shallow for the depth of the world. He walks up and down streets, peering at huddled figures, looking into the occasional gleam of a window. His path grows wider, more desperate. Movement is hope. Cautiously he sidles past Rodney's. No police. No Peach. He sees the crowded counter and the warm people, readying themselves for the day. He slips around back, but the door is locked. Five minutes of pounding, and Rodney peers out, irritable and aggrieved. But there is no sign. Even their pallet in the corner is cleared away. He goes to the little park, but in the overcast chill it is empty and bleak.

He can think of no other place to look, so like a lost sailor he clings to the broken remains of where he started. He is huddled under the overpass in the last of the daylight when Book emerges from the blur of it all. A yellow cab swings up, the only color in the dreary rain. A figure climbs out—out of a cab!—and grows suddenly familiar.

"Where were you?"

Even as he asks it, Clean is startled by the question, trapped by it, embarrassed. He remembers how angry his father would get if he ever asked such a thing. But Book pats him on the shoulder, tired and unsmiling "Just stretching my legs." He goes to sleep early, wan-faced and distant in the grey bundle of his blanket.

In the morning they wake together and wander through the day. Find food, stay warm. Somewhere out of the wet if it rains, and then somewhere to sleep that doesn't smell too much of cat piss or garbage. Clean understands the pattern and pace. And though he misses the comfort of Rodney's diner, he slips without much effort into the shortened horizon of one meal and then the next, one night's sleep and then the next. How to look, how to move, how to pick your way through a restaurant dumpster for the remains of something choice. But even as they find their way back into motion, he is conscious of Book beside him, hesitant, uncertain, his mind on other things, as if suddenly it's all new to him, as if he's never done this before.

And during all this time he is aware of Peach lurking somewhere in that vast, blurred city. He listens carefully. Prepares himself. He needs to protect them both because, tough as he is, Book is no match for Peach. And with every night Clean dreams of some new trap or terror where Book is cut down, dragged away, fallen to his death. Every childhood terror returns now in his sleep, and he finds himself again and again on the trestle in the woods, in the darkest night of his life with the deep, boundless open air beneath him. And Book is there, too, and Clean tries to save him. But he never does. Sometimes he slips. Sometimes there's a bear. Sometimes Peach steps smiling from the darkness and with the delicacy of a magician's wand draws the blade of a razor across Book's throat. Because that's the other thing. In all his dreams Clean is never the one in danger, though he is the only one afraid.

But even as his fears grow ever more vivid, his life turns unsure. He starts losing Book again. He would tie a string around their wrists if he could; one tug for good, two for bad. But instead he'll glance around in the middle of the most ordinary task and realize he's gone. And though, each time, there is a pang of something like dread, Book always returns, showing up at the end of the day as if nothing had happened.

He starts to follow.

It isn't easy. He mustn't get too close. His eyes are getting better, but still, at a distance, Book is nothing more than one dark blur among many, and Clean must anchor his gaze on that single shape and not let go. The effort makes his head ache; the sunlight is a needle in his brain. It's a long, long walk. But always the same.

It ends in a park. More beautiful than the one they used to visit together, but still, why go so far just to sit beneath a tree and read? That's all Book does. He chooses a sycamore and settles down. And Clean feels a pang at the thought that he would come all this way to be alone. But gradually, day by day, he sees that reading is not the point.

The park faces a row of modest houses, tidy but small, on the edge of a much grander neighborhood. Book watches them, watches one in particular. When a car pulls into the driveway or out, when a pair of voices, two women, mother and daughter, emerge from the house or enter, he lowers his book, stares across the wide street as if he could close the distance by wanting.

Clean hears their voices clearly. The older one, bossy, demanding, disappointed; the younger one quiet. She sounds, he thinks, dispirited, but how could that constant badgering voice not wear anyone down? On the days when she comes out alone Book is sharp as a wolf. Usually she walks to the car and drives away, but one day she turns at the sidewalk and heads down the street. Book follows, hidden among the trees and then out on the city sidewalks, moving slowly, hanging back. Clean watches with an ache in his chest.

The next morning when he walks away, Clean goes alone to the other park, the small and scruffy place they had once gone to read. He sits in a picnic shelter and presses flat upon the table the crumpled and rustling sheets of paper he gathered together all those months ago on the train. He has glanced through them from time to time, but more to remind himself of that first trip than to remember what they said. Now he reads as if it's for the first time.

An evening before the fireplace in an empty college room. A mattress they have dragged in from somewhere else. They watch the fire carefully, not wanting the light to spill out the windows, not wanting to draw attention. They are naked. They warm their food at the edge of the fire, but neither of them is hungry. They have cheese, crackers, an apple. They laugh over the apple, passing it back and forth, bright in the firelight: a single spot of red against the fire-washed gold of their skin. Carefully he rolls the apple up her thigh and across her stomach, as if it were the earth rotating through its days. He traces the curve of her breast, moving the fruit more slowly now—the very earth slowing down for them—up to her throat, her cheek. He presses it to her lips. She bites.

Reading makes his cheeks burn. It makes his throat dry with longing. Once his father had found some sagging, abandoned shack on the outskirts of Bridgeport and they had weathered the worst of a winter there. It smelled of mice and ancient food, and the floors creaked beneath them with every step. The windows were cracked, the walls were water-stained. His father thought they might stay there forever; he imagined himself a house-holder, a man of property. But with the spring thaw the smell drove them out.

Clean can find no connection between those abandoned rooms and the one in Book's letter, and the realization makes him queasy. He feels the gulf opening between them, between the facts of their lives.

But it's the other letters, the ugly ones, the angry ones, that he returns to. This, after all, he doesn't have to imagine. No story, no candlelight. These are the ones that give Clean a kind of strength. He can almost hear the words, half muttered under Book's breath as he scratched them down. *How could you abandon me? After all that we had meant to each other. After all we had promised. You have killed me, and now I return the favor. You are dead to me. And every memory of you is dead.* Clean holds the letters tightly.

It's not that he thinks it through. It's not exactly a plan. He is helping Book, preserving him. Saving him from his own despair.

He steals a box of envelopes from a Seven-Eleven and throws away all but one. He steals a pen. He chooses the worst of the letters. It is unsigned. And because he can't match the handwriting, he cannot focus his eyes enough for that, he scrawls just the first initial to seal the angry words. A single B at the bottom, like that last drop of something that binds the spell. He writes the address on the front, and then he hesitates at her name. Bonnie? Could it be Bonnie? Buzzy? Barbie? He couldn't quite make out the mother's words. Another B, then. To B from B.

That evening he outwaits Book in the park under his sycamore tree. He sees him finally stand up and head back to the overpass. And under the gaze of the now abandoned tree Clean hurries across the street, keeping to the shadows. He creeps up to the front door and slips the envelope through the mail slot before turning and running away.

The next afternoon he follows him, and the next, and the next. The mother appears and disappears, drives off in her car and returns. Visitors come and go. Repairmen. A week passes. Another. There is no sign of the daughter. Each day under the sycamore tree Book sinks further and further into the earth.

Early one morning a van arrives. People move in and out. In the backyard, just beyond the corner of the house, Clean can see the edge of a tent going up. Book watches as if committing every moment to memory. A second van pulls up, and tables are carried. Armloads of folded chairs. In the early afternoon a long black car pulls into the driveway, so gleaming and smooth it becomes automatically the center of things. A woman climbs out. Even Clean can make out how beautiful she is. He has seen pictures of wedding gowns. This one is not so much sleek as snug. She is plumper than he's expected, her body rounded and filling out in ways that even Clean can recognize.

The people go inside. The music and laughter rise from the tented back yard. Book waits, so Clean waits. The bride and groom leave at six. When they climb into the big black car Book rises as if he's going to follow. But when it's gone he only stands there.

Hesitantly Clean approaches. Book seems unsurprised to find him there; lost to anything so ordinary as that. He peers bleakly for a moment, then gropes for his canvas bag. He pulls out a little bundle, a handkerchief, mud-stained and crumpled. Unfolded, it holds a ring. He picks it up carefully, thumb and forefinger, then lets it go as if half-expecting it to flutter away. Instead it falls to the grass. Book watches it for another moment as if, even now, it might be transformed. "Isn't that something?" he murmurs.

He turns away.

Clean knows he should leave it. Just leave it there. But he plucks it up, squeezing it, feeling the hard seed of the stone bite into his palm. It slips, light as a dream, into his pocket.

Gently he takes Book's arm. He has expected sadness and anger and resolve, but there is something frightening now. Something in the slow gathering together of his thoughts. "Well," he says, "that's it for me. I'm done."

And Clean thinks, it's okay. It's okay. He's just talking. He's just talking to himself. But then Book turns and fastens the words onto his heart. "I've got nothing left."

"That's not true."

"Go to your grandmother."

"No."

"She'll take you."

"No! Come on, Book. Snap out of it!"

And it's that smile again, that terrible smile. "I have," he says. "I'm going home."

"Good. That's good. What home? Where? We going back to Rodney's? Hartford? Somewhere else?"

But with all this talk of going, he seems to have no strength to move. "I'll see you, kid."

"No."

"Take care of yourself. You'll be fine."

"Shut up, Book! Don't say that. We're pals."

And he seems to consider that for a moment, listening to the sound of it as if from far away.

"Say it! Say it, Book. We're pals. You and me. Say it."

His knees give way. Clean follows him down, taking his arm, sitting with him, keeping him upright with the fierceness of his grip. But Book just shakes his head. His voice is almost lost in the low rush of traffic. "For heaven's sakes. Who'd have thought it?"

They make it back to the overpass. Book sleeps for two days straight, and Clean worries that he's sinking away, into the grip of better times. But after all the sleep he finally wakes. He buys a bottle and sits in the sunshine like an infant taking in all that looks so strange. They hang the first freight they can catch. They're on the road for three more years.

CLEAN

12.

They go west at first, just to open the distance between Book and his heartbreak. He drinks and reads with a fearsome lack of moderation, whole days passing in the shadow of a tree or beneath the leaky comfort of an overpass. They work when they're hungry or when the weather is bad, for wages and a warm place to stay. For two such dusty men, they clean ferociously, as if it were a joke they continued to play.

They are drawn to cities with good libraries even though it means they have to wash their clothes. Clean objects at first—a lot of bother and expense—but for Book each new library is a first date. They hoard their quarters and then sit in the laundromat wrapped in their coats, emerging wrinkled but clean. They are quiet and devoted readers. Whenever they find a book they like, one or the other will drop it out the men's room window for retrieval later that day. They'll return it to the next library they see. Clean likes to imagine them as a pair of old time outlaws on the run, always skipping town just ahead of an angry middle-aged woman in a bun, but the truth is they are seldom noticed.

They develop a new set of comforts. There is the pleasure of being dry for several days straight—each new day not so much an extension of the last as a whole new level of satisfaction. The pleasure on a cold day of layers of clothing, all warm from the dryer. The pleasure of sitting out a storm, of hot food on a winter morning, the inexpressible luxury of good coffee on those unexpected days—rare as sapphires—when some stranger buys you a four-dollar Kona because he sees you sitting on the sidewalk in a little nest of your possessions, so absorbed in *David Copperfield* that you only notice when he sets the pair of cups beside you.

They keep themselves clean. They comb their long hair back behind their ears. They wear suits drawn from the bins at homeless shelters or the racks of the Salvation Army—jacket, vest, pants—like a pair of bankers fallen on bad times.

They read aloud for tips: a more rigorous form of panhandling. They take turns sitting on a corner sidewalk, reading from one of their purloined books with a hat upended before them. They refine the technique. You can't look comfortable. You can't sound cheerful. You can't seem too self-sufficient. This is Clean's problem, at first. He becomes involved in the book, eyes inches from the page, and even though he continues to read aloud, he is so clearly uninterested in the freddies walking by that they rarely give him a thing.

Book is better. When he reads, the freddies gather hesitantly, uncertain about the little knot of interest and determined to move past. But Clean is sitting there, despondent and thin-faced, his eyes wrapped in a bandana, with a cardboard sign on his lap that says "Will Read for Food," while beside him Book sits like an old vaudevillian, slightly comic in his formality, reading from Dickens or Robert Louis Stevenson. The freddies wonder, at first. Is it a joke? Some kind of street theater? They look around for cameras. But almost always they listen. A word or two, and then a sentence. The hat starts with a dollar and a small handful of change; they are careful not to let it seem too full. But at the end of a good day they might have thirty dollars to their names.

Book becomes a collector. Small metal items of use and beauty. Tin cans, discarded flatware, broken ornaments and scraps. In the quiet moments of the day he assembles them. His back against a tree, a pile of broken, rusting bits beside him. He looks crazy, like a watchmaker gone round the bend. Or like Twisted Pearly, who collects pinecones in a sack and who, when he comes to a fresh one on the floor of the woods, lays out his whole store on the close-packed earth to decide which one will now have to be thrown away. They have bought a pair of tin-snips and Book spends time slowly piecing things together, trying one shape with another. He'll slice a tin can lengthwise and flatten it carefully under his boot and then, for the detailed work, spend an hour tapping it out between a big rock and a small one.

It embarrasses Clean, all this crazy fussing. He'll go for a slouch somewhere, maybe the new pizza place where the ovens have been misbehaving. And when he returns, a pair of blackened calzones wrapped in newspaper, he'll find Book sitting beside a small, ragged toad, assembled from delicate pieces of tin fastened together with silver spots of solder. It is untoadlike in its skinniness: long legs, long arms, a surprisingly thoughtful face. It is lounging beside Book with its knees up and its back against the same oak tree. There is a volume open on both their laps. Clean bends down, squinting closely, afraid to touch it. He can see a small pair of wire-rimmed glasses drooping on the toad's thoughtful face.

"Oh, man. Can I be a toad?"

"I'm not sure about a toad." He hesitates. Then he reaches into his bag and sets a second little figure in the dirt beside the first. It's even smaller.

"Can I pick it up?"

"Careful."

He lifts it to his eyes. Ears, nose, short fluffy tail.

"So I'm a rabbit?"

"If you like."

Clean laughs. "How about that."

They become sensitive to the reading of portents. Three different librarians tell them in one afternoon to take their feet off the table. Clean is nabbed in a hardware store stealing needle-nose pliers. A stranger steps into the firelight carrying a few old vegetables for the pot and shaking his head over some story he's heard about a crazy man somewhere, attacking people with a milk pitcher.

They move along at a moment's notice. Gradually they refine their criteria until the process of deciding becomes its own branch of superstition. If the library is closed more than three days in a row; if the local pizza parlor makes only thick crust pies; if the local police cars have green or purple in their colors. They live cautious lives, and almost anything can turn into a reason for leaving.

But that's the thing about caution. A little can be more than you need, and too much isn't always enough. Their first plan is to go west and south until they feel like stopping, until the train deposits them somewhere so different there is no chance of bumping up against their older selves. But once they begin to respond to the leanings of the world they find themselves moving gradually back over ground they have covered, through places they have already passed. They are drawn north again, not exactly against their wills but against their first intentions, back to familiar places. And the very signs they notice and follow become the long, twisting tail of the signs they are leaving behind.

They begin making friends. A nod of the head, a familiar figure easing down beside you in the firelight. A few words, a name. A piece of jerky handed over, an apple tossed. He begins to look forward to the flop at the end of the day. Clean has been on the scrounge his whole life. This is nothing like that. Around the campfire there is an odd but steady formality. The decorum of cats: touchy, suspicious, easily embarrassed. But it lends itself to a kind of grace. Everybody takes care. Everyone moves slowly. There is a comfort in moving slowly. He used to be afraid all the time: of thunder, darkness, heights. But now he jokes with men who grudgingly nod. He takes his turn reading when Book is tired. He looks forward to sleeping and, when the weather is fine or they have shelter from the cold and the wind and the rain, to waking up.

But then a stranger arrives. He comes to the flop one night, emerging out of the dark. It's early spring, when the warm days turn you soft and the cold nights strike an anxious note. They hear his footsteps long before he shows. He glares around at the faces. His jacket is too thin for the night. He wraps himself in his arms, head down as if looking out from under a shelf. "Cold night," he says. "Is that something hot?" He eyes the blackened pot on the fire as if about to make a grab for it. "You're a quiet bunch."

There is a moment when the man can just walk away. The circle regards him without a word. His hands are hidden; his stance is tense. Clean glances over, but Book's expression is bland; his open hand rests lightly on a rock the size of his fist.

"You don't mind if I help myself?"

There is no sound, but Raggedy Bob reaches down and picks up Smooth Bob, a short length of galvanized pipe that travels everywhere he does. The man gives them a look of cranky disgust, as if he's fed up with exactly this sort of thing, and when he unwinds his arms one hand is holding a gun. He grins as if it's a trick he's been practicing. No one stops him as he strolls almost jauntily to the fire and squats down by the pot.

It turns dark where he obscures the fire. A wide shadow draped over the ground. Clean doesn't see who hits him first, though Smooth Bob is there second. The man sprawls, half-lit, half-smothered in darkness. No one touches him, except to remove the gun. "Too bad," says Raggedy Bob to no one in particular. "I like this flop." And he starts to assemble his possessions, though no one will leave until morning.

Clean tries to eat. He gnaws his way through a week-old bagel but his eyes keep wandering to the sprawled figure on the ground. Book pulls out *Kidnapped* and begins to read. Clean tries to fasten onto the story, to let the weight of the words settle him down, but then he hears the scuff of a footstep in the outer dark. When the second man steps into the firelight he sees the slouching walk, the long knit cap, the mustache like a blonde mouse under a monumental nose.

"Well, I'll be," says Peach in an easy voice, as if any tension has died with his friend, as if the dead man lying in the dancing light is just a misunderstanding. "If that ain't just the smoothest thing I've heard. Been a while, mister book. But you still sound good." He starts forward, and there is a general stirring. "It's okay. Ain't no problem here. Me and the Book are old friends."

Clean makes himself small, hunching back into the thick darkness, shrinking beneath the brim of his hat. He watches Peach as if from a hilltop.

In the moment just before, he would have been prepared to say that nothing on the trestle had ever really happened. That it was all just a terrible dream that had long since been mended and soothed. He could almost swear that he had always been ranging with Book and that their daily eventlessness and small occasional comforts had always been the sum and texture of his life. Over time he had almost forgotten the gun in his bag. It had ceased to be a curse or a promise. It had turned into a stone, a rock, a small weight he could throw away any time and be made lighter by it. There was no stranger out there whose death was required.

And in this moment he sees that this can still be true. If he just believes strongly enough. If he can just succeed in not recognizing Peach, then he won't have to go with him, and the past can stay where it is.

He sits there unmoving, wanting more than anything to believe that this is one of those moments when a person can choose. When you can make yourself into a river and not a chain. And even as he sits in the shadows wishing it to be true, he knows that everything depends on him. On his transformation. If he is a different boy now, he will go unnoticed. He will be invisible. If he has embraced this new life properly, if he has become the new person that Book has made him, if he has put aside all the darkest moments of his past, then he will vanish from Peach's eye.

He sits there, watching. And he sees that it's going to work. Peach glances down at the body, and offers a nudge with the toe of his boot. "He's nothing to me." His hands are hanging loosely by his pockets. "I'm just looking for a warm place."

"Anything for the pot?" says Raggedy Bob.

"Couple potatoes. Cheese sandwich. Piece of cornbread from the shelter."

"Potatoes'd be a friendly gesture. Pot on the left is still cooking."

With a too-cheerful grin Peach unfolds a straight razor and slices the potatoes into the pot. Then he wipes it carefully and folds it away. Clean's eyes can't leave the pocket now. Peach turns back to Book. "Don't stop on my account. I'm all about a story."

He steps over the body and walks toward where Clean is sitting, invisible, invisible, invisible. "Don't mind, do you?" He sits down on the other side of Book in the warmth of the fire and pulls a sandwich out of his pocket. Clean longs for Book to start reading. Once the story begins he'll be all right. Once time starts again. He is sitting, pushing on the silence, willing it into motion.

"So how you been?" Peach asks, his mouth full of sandwich, his eyes drifting back to the body by the fire. "Had yourself some exciting times."

Book says nothing. Clean has never admired him more. Silent, careless of the razor in the pocket, he opens *Kidnapped* and begins to read. Clean feels himself start to relax. He feels the long freight train of minutes creaking into motion. Everyone will sleep soon, and they can slip away. Never see him again.

And Peach leans forward, elbows on his knees, and looks right at him. "Pisser? Is that you? Well, damn. If that don't beat all."

Peach is grinning at him now, flecks of bread still clinging to his teeth, his sandwich all but forgotten in his hand. He leans over in front of Book and gives Clean a rough, companionable shove. "I didn't know what'd become of you. Look at the size. You been growing, boy. How you been getting by? Shit, let me look at you."

He shifts over to a rock by the fire, so he has the light behind him, so he's leaning forward over his knees, gazing at Clean as if he is words on a page and Peach is slowly sounding them out. But then his eyes drift over to Book. And back. And then again. And they settle somehow between the two.

"Well, fuck me," he murmurs. "All these years. If that don't beat the shit."

And Clean thinks of the razor in the pocket, because that's the worst thing he can imagine now, in this moment, before everything he has come to count on suddenly washes away. He stares at Peach, as if, between them, he and Book can somehow keep him at bay. At his elbow he hears a shift of movement, a scuff of shoes, and he turns back to Book, ready to fight, ready to run, ready to back whatever play he makes. But in the flickering glow of the firelight the seat is empty, and Book, like every good thing in his life, has suddenly vanished.

CLEAN

13.

Years pass.

Some stories continue; some begin again. Tonight he can't be sure which is which. He is seventeen years old and once more he is standing in a park, as if it is part of his destiny that every great change in his life will occur among trees. The sky through the branches turns indigo deep, but the darkness doesn't matter. He has grown to depend on more than sight, and there is nothing about the man on the bench that he wouldn't recognize.

He sees him straighten, hears the familiar breath of a laugh—half startled, half rueful. He was always a smart one, Book. He must have known it was bound to happen—no warning but the scuff of a boot, the sudden sound of the past drawing near. And there is part of Clean that feels a little glow of old affection.

Though another part, the part that's been thinking about this moment so often over the last few years that he would sometimes wake up uncertain, in those first vague moments of the day, whether he had already done it or not—whether it was all finally over or he had only imagined it. That part of him would like to see Book sweat.

"And here you are," says Book.

He's been reading by the light of a streetlamp. His eyes have always been sharp, as if between them circumstances are determined to balance, and what he took from Clean he kept for himself. Now he closes the book, slips it into his canvas bag. There is a little scrap of cardboard left behind.

"You don't want to mark your place?"

"Do I need to?"

"No."

"I thought as much."

Book gazes up at him. "You've gotten so tall. I didn't recognize you at first."

"Not you. All this time, and you're exactly the same."

He can hear the smile. "*Plus ca change, plus c'est le meme chose.*"

"I don't know what that means," says Clean, though he is surprised how little it bothers him. He is prepared to be angry. He's had five years to practice.

"I wondered about you," Book says. "How you were doing."

"Doing fine."

"I thought you might show up years ago. I hoped you would. Then, after a while, not so much."

"And here I am. Doesn't that just go to show?"

He sits down beside him, shoulders touching; the companionable closeness of lowered voices. "I brought you something."

"Did you?"

"You don't sound curious. Look. It's a present."

He draws it out. The old gun is heavy in his hand. It used to surprise him with its weight, all those years ago. But lately, he's been taking it out at night, as if the heft, itself, will give him a feel for what he has to do.

"I remember it being bigger," says Book. He shifts, and just for an instant Clean thinks he's going to make grab, but instead he just reaches out, pats him on the knee. "So tell me. Are you still a drinking man?"

"Not since I was twelve."

"I think we need to find ourselves a bottle."

"I don't think so."

"On a night like tonight?"

"I don't think we'll have time."

"How can we not? There's always time for a drink between friends."

And like that he's on his feet—up and on his way—so suddenly in motion there is nothing to do but clamber after him, stuffing the gun back into his bag, picking up the pace.

There are lots of ways to walk. Peach is a lurcher, a hurrier: impatient and fretful. He makes every mile longer and every choice a hard one. But Book is easy as cream. And whether it's temperament or just that they learned their pace together, they have always walked well. In spite of everything, in spite of all that's happened, Clean settles naturally into step.

They cross the park, they're at the corner now, where the row of big houses stand guard against all comers. But Book pays no attention. Despite the bright windows, the neat lawns and porches—all that suburban candy just waiting for a chance to bite—down the sidewalk he goes, sweet as you please, as if they're just another pair of freddies out for an evening stroll.

But that's Book. That's always been the blade of him. That cheerful disregard for all the cake, all the unprotected plenty, laid out across the suburbs like so much pastry on a window-sill—with no good news except to avoid it and never wonder how it might taste.

So with Clean alert to every noise, they stroll through the darkness like sightseers on a sunny day. "What do you feel like drinking?" says Book.

"It's okay. I'm good."

"And who among us can say such a thing? I was thinking a little whiskey. Something smoky and strong."

Deliberately Clean tries to harden his voice. "Better find it fast."

But it's no good. Book just smiles. "Your wish is my command." And he turns past the ramparts of a lilac bush and into one of the narrow lanes running behind the houses.

Clean follows with a breath of relief; nothing safer than an alley. Out of the light, out of the view. But his comfort lasts only a moment. Book is slowing down. "Wait! Don't. What are you doing?"

"Prospecting."

"Not here."

He turns, all injured innocence. "I thought you said to hurry."

"What did you tell me? Over and over? What did you used to say? People in nice houses? What do they love?"

Book smiles. "I didn't know you were listening."

"What do they love, Book?"

"Big dogs and shiny police cars."

"That's right."

They stop in the darkest portion of the alley. "So, you choose."

"What? No!"

"Pick a house. Any house."

"Absolutely not."

"That one? How about that one over there?"

But even as he stands squinting nervously from choice to choice, straining through the dark gossamer of his damaged eyes, Book reaches out and unlatches a gate.

"Will you stop it!"

"You have to keep your voice down."

"This is bad," he mutters. "This is monkey bad."

"Quiet as mice," comes the whisper, and Book leads the way through.

The house is dark, the windows blank and staring. But on either side, beyond hedges and trees, houses show their share of light. And the sound of a television shivers on the air as if to mark how close the nearest shout might be. But Book is a creature of unconcern. He creeps up the narrow walk, past the canopy of an elderly tree gnarled and thick with blossoms, past a corner shed, past a little patio table with two chairs. Someone sits in those chairs, Clean thinks. Someone looks at that tree. They've gone to bed now, but their mind is in the garden. Their thoughts are an instant away. They could be watching now, they could be peering out a window.

But there's part of him shining with pride for the sheer, unbounded nerve of the man.

Book steps to the door. A clean, spare kitchen shows through the mullioned windows. For an instant Clean wonders if he's going to smash one. Just like that. He seems ready for anything. But instead he bows over the doorknob as if praying to the gods of home security, and when he raises his head the door opens.

This is badder than bad; this is crunchy bad. This is jail time bad, all wrapped and waiting. Clean can feel it walking up his spine and he knows he should run. Every man for himself. But he's a boy again, that stupid kid from all those years ago, and his nerves are humming. He's stepping forward. As Book slips inside, he's right there behind him, and with the fear like a bare wire sparking in his chest, he's just a breath away from smiling.

He snuffs the inside air. It smells of soap and herbs, not so much sweet as clean. It turns the whole house strange. He stares hard into the shadows, as if by strain alone he can see. But Book is untroubled, strolling like a cat across the open floor. The cupboards are pale, the hinges silent. He tries one and then another. Clean almost laughs. Is there nothing he won't do? The third one opens on a crowd of bottles. He draws out one, two. They bump; they clink. And Clean recoils, backing away, nudging with his hip an unexpected chair. To the chime of glass is added the sudden scrape of wood on floor. The two men turn to stone.

A woman's voice, sleepy and thin, floats down the stairs. "James? Is that you? What are you doing?"

His mouth goes dry; his throat closes for business. But Book is in motion, shutting the cupboard, dragging him along, out through the closing door and down the garden path sweet as you please. A firm hold on Clean's arm to keep him in check—running at night is like a shout for attention: as easy a ticket to the deep dark as you'll find—and off they go. Out the gate and down the lane, strolling as if it were all theirs for the taking.

He cannot stop grinning. When Book passes him a bottle

he drinks without thinking, and the burn in his throat is a siren call from childhood. He takes a second drink to put out the first. His pulse is skipping, his voice shining with admiration. "Oh, you're a Possum, Book. You are Mister Possum. You're a Puss in Boots. Quiet as quiet could be. Why didn't you just answer the lady? 'Be right there, honey. Just getting myself a drink.' Oh, Mister Possum! Oh, man!"

And Book is smiling as he leads them along the alley, strolling this way and that, taking the path as he finds it. "That does get the blood moving," he says, and Clean laughs. Though the pleasure fades as he remembers. Where he is. What's coming.

Book doesn't seem to notice. "So what are you reading these days?"

"Nothing. Not now."

"That's no good. Hardest days of my life, when I was between books. We need to get you one."

"I'm okay."

"No such thing. Remember: there's no friend as loyal as a book."

And the knife of this catches Clean under the ribs, where there's still a part that's soft, even after all these years.

They head downtown. Staying off the roads, staying off the sidewalks. The alleys change around them, gravel giving way to concrete giving way to asphalt. Medieval passages thick with all that life can spill. In the darkness nothing vanishes; it's all transformed into smell. This isn't a big city, but it's old, and nowhere is it older than here: ancient brick walls buckled and patched, the concrete stained with years. They walk for a while, passing the bottle back and forth, and when they stop it's beside a dumpster in a little cul-de-sac of shadow. Book takes a long drink, gazing up at the implacable face of a high brick wall. "So what do you think?"

Clean almost smiles. It's a joke, of course. He's not a climbing guy, and who knows that better than Book? How does it go?

It's not the falling, but the landing? Except it isn't; not for him. It's the falling. It really is. Just the thought is enough, the memory.

But Book is smiling as if he's forgotten, as if this is just another of their old games. Fifteen feet overhead a rickety fire escape clings to the wall, the short, teasing stub of a ladder hanging down. Book turns and slips the bottle into Clean's rucksack. It clinks against the gun. "Better use both hands," he says and jumps and catches hold.

With nothing more than that he is suddenly perched on the dumpster, reaching out across the wide brick wall. And partly it's the unaccustomed whiskey, partly it's his eyes, but Clean somehow misses every step so that Book is magically hanging from the fire escape, climbing, swarming up the ladder, and he is standing on the roof, looking down, before Clean can even catch his breath.

"Nothing to it," he calls, and vanishes.

He's been tricked, of course. Smooth as smooth can be. Book is flying across the rooftops, now. Vanishing without a trace. And Clean is left standing there: stupid, stupid, stupid.

The anger is enough to start him climbing. The dumpster's slippery, but there are places to grab. He gets balanced on the rim. The bottom of the ladder is over his head and way beyond his reach. His knees are wobbling, starting to shake. Even this is higher than he likes. He tries to remember what Book had done. His hands, his boots.

There's a drainpipe, flimsy as a piece of foil. But he wedges his foot against one narrow bracket and wraps his hand around. His jaw is tight but nothing like his chest. Swing out. Swing out now. He grabs for the end of the ladder, hand waving, whole body lurching through the air, and with a grunt he fastens on to the bottom rung. It promptly gives way. For an instant he's falling. But his left hand grips in spite of itself and, dangling from that bottom rung, he clanks and settles, ratcheting down on frozen gears, until his feet touch ground, sweet as you please. As if this is something he has practiced. As if it's something he does all the time.

Climbing is easy after that.

The rooftop is a broad, gravel patio before the rising brownstone of the upper floors. All around him the lights of the city. He cannot get enough air. In the exhilaration of not having fallen he makes the mistake of looking down. The dizziness hits him. The empty air opens beneath. His hands are nothing but slick, and he feels the scream like a pennant unfurling in his chest.

Until Book's grip fastens onto his arm. It hauls him off the ladder and away from the edge until he's standing on legs that have lost their feeling, arms too heavy to lift.

"Is that it, Book?" His breath is scraping in his throat. "Is that why we're here? You going to throw me off, for old time's sake?"

"Deep breaths."

"You think I'll just get dizzy and burst into tears? You think I'll tip and fall?"

"Look up. Just up. Look at the stars."

"I can't see the stars!"

"Then look at me."

"I'm not scared, Book. I'm not a kid anymore."

"I know. I know you're not."

They sink together onto the rooftop, their backs against the comfort of the brownstone wall. And maybe it's the height, or the whiskey, maybe it's just the memory that's never far away, but the sound of his father's scream comes to him again, that long last unfurling cry. He shakes his head wearily. "Why were you even there, you and that girl? What were you even doing there?"

Book's smile is wistful. "It was love. We were running away from our lives."

"And you pick a fight? Why didn't you just keep running?"

"We should have. I was scared enough."

"Goddam right. He was Frank the Bear. And you went crashing into him."

"I thought it was a fairy tale. You never win your heart's desire by running away."

"Your heart's desire! For God's sake. A skinny college kid. Flailing around. And he was just wailing on you. I couldn't believe it. Down you go. And up again. Down and then up. You just didn't know when you were beat."

"My strength was the strength of ten because my heart was pure. How was I to know there'd be a gun?"

Clean shakes his head. "Fucking Peach. He's always carrying. And the Bear tries to snatch it away, and there it goes. Flying out over the tracks. A clatter and a bounce. And Peach is yelling, Get the gun! Get the goddam gun! But it was miles away."

"I didn't see it," says Book. "But I was turning, and suddenly there was someone all over me. Grabbing, punching, choking. All elbows and knees and fingers. He weighed about ten pounds, but he was a crazy man."

Clean almost laughs. "Did I hurt you?"

"Not too bad." He hesitates. "How about you? Does it still hurt?"

Clean tries to brace himself against the tenderness, but it's more than he can resist. "Sometimes. When the water's too hot, or I get too much sun. It's like my face is on fire." And as if that one bit of honesty has unleashed more, his voice catches in his throat, "You remember the way he screamed. All the way down? And the rocks?"

"No."

"I do."

And the terror. The edge of the trestle right there under his shoulder, and all that empty space below. And the struggle and the shouting and the gun nowhere to be found. "Hey, Pisser!" And the shot. And his eyes on fire. Though it's the Bear who is screaming.

"Jesus, Book. You could have been miles away. You could have been anyplace at all."

"I know," he says. "It was just bad luck."

"My father? Was that bad luck? My eyes?"

"That was the worst luck of all. But it wasn't me."

"None if it, Book? None of it was you? Not the fighting? Not the gun?"

"I didn't have the gun."

"You're a liar, Book."

"No."

"You shot him."

"I didn't."

"I saw you. Christ! You and that girl! I remember her."

"Do you?"

"What was her name? Rhonda? Robbie?"

"Bunny."

"Jesus. That's right. 'Come on, Bunny! Let's go, Bunny!' I remember all the yelling. Was that you?"

"No. Someone else. Her fiancé. He followed us there. He wasn't part of my plan. Who brings a fiancé to a fairy tale?"

"She was beautiful." Clean's voice is almost reluctant, as if this is the last thing he wants to remember. But he thinks about her, the girl on the bridge. The moonlight girl. It's a frozen moment for him. A touchstone. He doesn't even know how much of it is real. His memory has held it for so long, elaborating, expanding, touching that darkest of nights with the pale yellow glow of her dress. And somehow over the years it has grown clearer. He's held onto it through all that's happened: a bright angel of his darkest moment, the last clear thing there can be. "Were you laughing all the time?" he asks. "On the road. Were you thinking what a joke it was that I never knew? Poor little handicapped kid?"

"No. Of course not."

"All those years?"

"No." And there is a long moment's hesitation. "How have

you been?"

"Me? Are you kidding? Life of Riley. You know that grandmother? My mother's old lady. You probably don't remember."

"I remember."

"Turns out she wasn't all that excited to see me. So I tried foster care. That's a sweet gig. Three squares a day. Soft bed. One set of parents after another. Many as you need. But everything comes to an end. They let you out at eighteen. For good behavior."

"You're not eighteen."

"No, see. That's the good part. What Peach calls my window of opportunity."

"Is that right?"

"Just a little joke we're having, me and Peach. Turns out I'm a juvenile until suddenly I'm a genuine adult. Responsible for all my crimes. Isn't that something?"

He takes a drink, and then another. The whiskey doesn't burn any more. It warms him in places he didn't even realize were cold.

"Can you stand up?" says Book after a while.

"What? Suddenly you're in a hurry?"

"We've got things to do."

He is wobbly on his feet, but Book helps him up. Behind them the building is dark. There is a low pile of bricks. Above them a window which, on closer examination, is not quite closed. Book touches his arm. "Quiet as a dream," he whispers.

They squirm like lizards up over the windowsill into the porcelain stillness of a men's room, urinals lined up like voting booths in the shadowy light. Step out into the dark hallway and it feels like magic: a building that was empty, now isn't. They prowl amid the cozy library smell of dust and old paper. "We don't want to disturb anybody." It's impossible to tell if he's joking.

From his bag Book draws a small miner's lamp and slips

it over his head. The room is full of shelves. He finally finds the one he wants. But it isn't long before a thin voice, dry as old newsprint, rustles the darkness beside them. "Is that you Book? You're here early."

Clean almost jumps out of his boots, but Book merely pauses in his search, politely turns off the lamp. "Beatrix?"

"You're not alone."

"This is Clean. He's an old friend of mine."

He can see nothing, barely a twitch in the fabric of the darkness, but on the air there is a sudden scent of dusty, unopened closets and, even more unlikely, canned ham. "He doesn't look old. And not that friendly. There's hotpot down in the basement."

"I don't think we can tonight. But thank you."

"Another time, then. Happy hunting. And, boy? Stop back any time. Any friend of Book's can read here for free."

Clean holds his breath to listen. A light tread on the stairs. The headlamp comes back on, and Book is smiling now in its scattered light.

"Am I an old friend?" Clean asks

"Of course you are. Aren't you? And here's another." He draws a battered volume from the shelf.

Squinting close over the cover, Clean can make it out. *Huckleberry Finn*. "I've read it."

"Lately?"

"Not lately."

The light goes out. He feels the suddenly familiar weight of the book slipping into his bag.

As they move back through the dark Clean cannot stop thinking about the ladder to come. The starkness of the open air. If climbing up was hard, climbing down is nothing but a long, long drop. His hands have turned damp with the prospect, and he cannot wrestle his mind away from the all but inevitable fall. Book seems not to notice. But once on the roof he leads them to an unlocked door, a narrow stair, and when he pushes through a heavy fire-door, they are outside, and all Clean's knotted fears are untangling like snakes.

"That's it? That's all? We could have come in here."

"Didn't you see the sign? Exit only."

Clean is almost giddy with relief. They walk and stop and walk some more. Sometimes they drink. There are houses and streets, and the occasional narrow stretch of alley that comes as a note of comfort, a little sigh of familiarity amid the dreamy darkness. One bottle goes into a garbage can. "Whoops a daisy," Clean murmurs.

"Broken glass is nobody's friend."

But there's a fresh one now. "Are you drunk, Book?"

"I believe I am."

"Me, too." It's a comfort to be able to confide even that much. "I've missed you."

"Me, too, boy."

"I'm sorry I have to kill you. It breaks my heart."

"I know," says Book. "Let's not think about it now."

Their route grows uncertain; Clean can't keep track of it all. But he finds himself on a sidewalk, then they are strolling through a stone gate and onto the softest grass he has ever felt. "Oh, Book. It's a secret garden."

"I knew you were the right person to bring. Come on. I want to show you something."

The darkness hides all but what he can feel under his feet and catch in the mixed fragrance of a summer evening. They descend into a little valley, and over their heads a shadow blocks out the faint blur of starlight. And then, as Book's headlamp comes on again, Clean sees in the reflected glow an ancient stone bridge hanging overhead. Immediately he looks down, expecting to discover they've wandered into a stream without noticing, but there is only a river of grass beneath their feet.

Clean kneels down to feel the softness of it. He only realizes he's been asleep when he jerks awake. It gives him a terrible moment. It is the worst of his dreams. He is curled beneath a highway overpass, alone and lost and miles from anywhere he's meant to be. Though in this case someone has draped a black suit jacket over his shoulders like a narrow blanket, and there is a small bottle of water beside him.

When he climbs to his feet he discovers Book, sitting against a tree. He is reading by the gleam of his headlamp as if nothing untoward has happened. The sight comes to him like a weight on his heart. "I thought you'd run away."

"Tell me," says Book. "Do you really think killing me will make you feel better?"

For five years Clean has thought exactly that. His anger at the man has been building without limit. But now. "It doesn't matter what I think. There's no getting around it now."

Clean waits for something, some twisty bit of argument, but all he says is, "Come over here. I need your help."

In the light of the headlamp he draws a handful of scraps from his pocket, thin, oddly shaped pieces of copper and tin, not exactly random, but unrelated at first. "The tricky part is to hold them in place. You'll need these." He hands him a pair of pliers that have seen better days.

Clean is still very drunk. "I'm not really following."

"You just have to hold them together while I solder."

It is ridiculous, of course. But the whole business pleases him, the two of them, working together, bending over some perfectly useless task. Drunk as he is, Book's actions are precise. He draws out a small roll of wire and a butane lighter. As Clean presses two scraps together Book carefully lays a bead of melted silver along the edge. As the minutes pass a flower takes shape from the oddly cut pieces. A tall, graceful construction of petals and leaves and a short, dividing stem. And then a second and a third. They have come all this way to build a little bunch of daffodils and plant it in a park.

But even that pleases Clean. "Is there a toad, too? Is there a rabbit?"

"Not yet. This will have to do."

"I'm the rabbit, aren't I, Book?"

"Of course you are."

Then they're walking again. And then the train yard is before them, stretching away in the moonlight and the glare of security lights. It's a lonely place. On the center track a long freight is rumbling, diesels turning over for an early departure. They sit on a bench at the very edge, hidden by darkness.

Clean had never put any great hopes in his father. They had simply been joined beyond the possibility of parting. His death did nothing more than transform a bond into a weight. "It's on you," Peach used to say, and he supposes that's true. More than true, it's now. There is a rustle in the shadow behind them, and Peach emerges.

His appearance always sparks a note of doubt. Where the Bear was enormous, Peach is pinched, with eyes bulging eagerly under the pressure of his frantic thoughts. And in place of the Bear's expansive beard Peach has focused all effort on a mustache that rides his lip like a plump blonde mouse. Now he peers down at them seated on the bench, his eyes are bright. "What are you doing? You out on a date? Where's the gun? Why aren't his hands tied? Jesus, Pisser, are you drunk?"

"I've got the gun," says Clean.

"Well, get it out!"

Book is gazing up at the man, the second bottle cradled in his lap. "I know you," he says.

"You surely do. It's been a long time."

It seems to take some effort to consider this—a whole night of drinking finally coming home to roost—but in the end Book says, "That is one hell of a mustache."

"Glad you like it. It's gonna be the last thing you see."

Book pats the bottle absently. "I didn't say I like it."

Peach's smile sours. "Here's the trick. That freighter's leaving in ten minutes. Pisser and me are gonna be on it. Worst luck. You won't."

Book unscrews the bottle, takes a sip. He fumbles with the cap.

"What?" says Peach, all sugar now. "Ain't you going to share?"

Book wipes at the mouth of the bottle, weighing the possibilities of saying no. "Careful. It's strong."

"I'll chance it." Peach snatches it up and tilts the bottle, working at it now, swallowing hard. Like everything else, thinks Clean, he's making an uphill job of it. But when he lowers it to catch his breath, the bottle comes down empty. His grin is loose. "Hope you didn't want any more." He starts to toss it away into the weeds.

"Broken glass is nobody's friend," says Book.

Clean almost smiles at that.

"Suit yourself." Peach drops it in his lap. He's nodding now, snapping his fingers in time to some eager rhythm. The scotch is humming in his head. Around the train the scattered maintenance men are packing it in, drifting away. The engine takes it up a notch.

Book cradles the empty forlornly as if all his hopes have leaked away. "Body in a train yard's easy to find," he says.

"What? What'd you say?"

"I mean, there it is. Just lying there." He's frowning at the ground in disapproval as if the future is already plain. "Who's going to be able to miss it?"

Peach laughs. "How much has he had to drink?" But he doesn't wait for an answer. "Here's the thing. What do we care? We'll be gone."

"You'll be gone. Chimps probably won't. All I'm saying is, you throw it from a train instead, that's a different thing altogether. Could take weeks to find. Maybe years."

Clean marvels at the thoughtful tone, the layers of calm, when he himself is knotted and frayed. But Peach is alight with the idea. "Aren't you too smart for everyone's good. On your feet. Let's have the gun, Pisser."

They are moving, creeping along the length of cattle cars. Clean's memory sparks at the sight of them, all those years ago. And now this. The cars are empty, the gates unlocked. It takes only a moment and they are sitting on the crusty, straw-covered floor as the train jerks into motion. Then they are moving through the darkness, the rocking, clacking rhythm picking up speed. An occasional street light slips past in the darkness; the sudden glimpse of a parking lot, a row of moonlit houses. Then the darkness of trees and fields. Clean's heart is pounding, lurching in his chest. He tries to keep his mind on his father's scream. Tries to focus on the scalding of his eyes. Peach leans against one wall with the gun in his hands, his eyes on Book, his head nodding with the movement as if counting off the time.

"This'll do," says Peach finally. "How about it, mister book? You happy with this spot?"

Clean waits for him to speak. Just the sound of his voice would be something. But he's sitting, dull and silent. He's had more than a quart of whiskey in the last five hours, and now he's cradling the empty like a doll in his lap.

Peach can't keep the smile from his face. "You got any last words?"

Book shrugs. "There are some woods up ahead. Might be a better place."

"Such a smart guy." He glances at Clean. "It was your old man. You want to do it?"

And Clean supposes he should. Isn't that the way it works? Every balance added up in the end, every figure coming due? But he shakes his head, and Peach doesn't seem displeased. He opens the gate, dragging it wide. He has picked up the motion of the train now, and he's rocking in the doorway. They're moving fast. The rush of trees is like dark velvet, the hard ground spinning past.

"You just know that's gotta hurt," says Peach. "Good news is, you won't feel a thing. Bring him over."

Clean bends down and helps Book to his feet. The man is still hugging the empty like a comforter. He wants to say he's sorry, but what's the point? And if he once starts talking he's afraid he won't stop. Peach is standing by the open door, breathing the air. His eyes are bright. He grips the gun firmly, though it seems to weigh more than he expects. "You got any last words?"

"You already said that."

"What?"

"Any last words. You already said that part." Book's voice is unexpectedly clear.

"What are you? Funny?" But Peach is having trouble with the gun, he's having trouble standing. The handful of Benadryl slipped into the scotch has been working for a while now. Clean watches with something brighter than surprise as Book swings the empty bottle and catches Peach sharply behind the right ear. The falling man is like a pinwheel, arms spinning for balance, but Book reaches out and plucks the gun from his hand as he tumbles out into the rush of air with barely a cry.

And now Book is standing lightly in the doorway, swaying with the movement of the train. He peers out, looking ahead down the tracks, the gun held lightly in his left hand, the bottle, cracked but solid, in his right. Clean is dry-mouthed and silent. "Another few miles," says Book. "The train curves around the back of the woods. Slows to a crawl. It's a piece of cake."

He flips open the gun and shakes the bullets out into the night. Then he reaches out and tucks it into Clean's shoulder bag. From his own he pulls out something, a little box of black plastic, and slips it into Clean's pocket. "You remember how to do this? Tuck your chin, elbows close…"

"…springy knees," says Clean. "I remember."

"Straight south. Don't linger in the woods. There's nothing nice that lives in the woods." He moves him firmly into the doorway. The air is cold; it's rushing past faster than ever. But then the train begins to slow. He can feel it turning under their feet, leaning away from the curve.

"I'll see you again, Book." It sounds like a threat. But even Clean isn't sure what he means.

"I don't think so."

A hand rests lightly on the boy's shoulder, just a moment's benediction, then the gentlest of shoves. Chin tucked, elbows in, springy knees. He hits the ground and rolls. When he climbs to his feet the train is receding, but in the moonlight he can make out Book, leaning in the doorway, watching, not waving, until it slips around the long, slow bend of the forest. Clean reaches into his pocket and draws out the cool plastic case of the compass.

He goes straight south, as much as the land allows. The night is the longest he's ever known. He has never been so frightened. There are sounds in the darkness, sometimes far away, sometimes close, howls or screams, he can't tell which. The daylight is better, but not much. He reaches the river, then the trestle. He knows his way from there.

He wakes in a little grove of willows beside a pond just down the hill from the park bench where it all began. It's mid-morning, and he opens his eyes to the sight of a girl with corkscrew brown hair. She is standing beside the water pointing the parabolic dish of a microphone toward the brightening sky as if reaching out to her distant people to please, please come and rescue her from this wild and unknown place.

14.

He thinks it's just a dream. Sitting under the willow in the grey light of morning with his muscles aching and the strangeness of the night holding him like a fading echo, he watches the girl by the edge of the pond. There is no rule, he tells himself, that says you have to wake up.

His past is calling, his purpose. He needs to stand. He needs to walk back to the train yard and out along the track. Find Peach where he's lying, bruised and spitting in fury. Dust him off, take him to the shelter quack, or just go get him drunk. Then together they catch another freight, follow the trail, track him down, get their fingers around his throat. That's what they've done for five years now, with the on-again off-again fury that Peach brings to any task.

But five years is a long time, and he thinks maybe he has earned a dream.

If it had been more real, it would have turned to nothing. A frightened girl, a sudden stranger in the park. But somehow she doesn't run away. She is wary but not frightened. And then the stories begin: the ones he tells her, halting, fragmentary; the ones she offers back.

Afterwards he'll realize it isn't the stories that entangle him. Not even the low bounce and flutter of her voice. It's how she offers his own life back to him in a shape he's never seen. The dreariness of it emboldened, burnished into fable. Wood sprites and dryads and witches and trolls. He's heard of them, of course, in the long ago stories that Book read aloud, but he's never thought they might be even a little bit true. Now she gathers up the frayed threads of his life and weaves them into something he cannot recognize but, after only one long morning of talk, cannot imagine doing without.

"I'm Del," she says.

And she comes back. She brings him food. They seem to make each day from scratch. He notices how clean her skin is, how smooth her cheeks. As they walk he bumps against her, shoulder to shoulder, hand to hand, each time as if by chance. They look everywhere but at each other. And the scent of her—he asks her what it is; peppermint soap, she tells him shyly. It makes her skin smell like summer.

He has walked before; he has walked all his life. But now it feels like something new. And at night, beneath the willow—returning there as a kind of charm against the ending of this dream—he imagines how her hair would feel, the softness of it, the sense of all that possibility threaded into every long and spiraling strand.

She brings sandwiches and little boxes of juice like the ones he's found crushed and empty in the dumpsters. Her face alight with the hesitant pleasure of being watched, she demonstrates how to pry off the straw and pop it through the foil seal. The first time, she mimes sipping from the straw as if he might never have imagined such a thing.

Each day lasts forever. On the second night, when they are walking and his hand again brushes her knuckles, she takes it. Just reaches out and intertwines their fingers. As if it were nothing in the world. As if it were the most natural thing.

For years afterward he remembers that moment. When he is lying at night in the undying twilight of his bunk in juvie, it remains like a little box he can open. A dream of hands brushing and bumping; fingers holding tight. It is all about hands until one night she takes him to the golf course—I'm going to show you Wyldwood, she says, her eyes alight in the streetlamps—and then it becomes about lips.

Her life is full. She is helping her mother, her father. He

imagines a whole family of people just like her. But in the evening she is free. She sneaks away and comes to him, and they move along the calm and manicured streets. Del sticks close, as if they are moving through the wildest of landscapes, but even to his wounded eyes the place is lit by its own prosperity. They come to a street lined by high hedges, a wall of evergreen. She touches a finger to her lips and, dropping down, burrows through, emerging from low branches onto a pristine, perfect lawn.

The grass is the smoothest he has ever felt, trimmed to the nap of a carpet and rolling like an ocean beneath the night sky. The moon is a lantern for them alone.

"If I run," she whispers, "will you chase me?"

"I can't run," he says. "My eyes. There's too much to run into."

"Not here."

And wonder of wonders. In every direction there is space.

He is slow at first, uncertain. Del skips away out of his reach, laughing, teasing, spritely as a colt. But gradually constraint gives way before the wide enticement of the moonlit lawn. A few steps, a jog, as if testing the limits of his luck. And by the end they are running with an uncontained effort he cannot ever remember. His foot catches. He sprawls. But the grass is a cushion, and Del is laughing. Sometimes he trips just for the pleasure of falling. And once, sprawled on the grass, he pulls her down, and they lie there, laughing and then silent. And this is another thing he has never felt before. The softness of her lips beyond describing.

A tiny flagpole rises a few feet away. The number fifteen is plain on the pennant. "That's my birthday flag," she says. "Five days from today. Will you wish me a happy birthday?"

And he feels a note of panic, a flutter of the heart. To count on even that much, makes him afraid. Five whole days. He remembers all that should be pulling him away. He thinks of Peach. He thinks of his dead father. He thinks of Book, waiting somewhere down the line for his fate to catch up.

"It's bad luck," he says, "to wish before it happens."

She snuggles close, her breath against his neck. "Will you be my birthday friend?" she whispers.

"I will." Though he knows it is a terrible risk, putting your happiness into even such words as these.

At night, when Del is gone, he dreams of Book. Not even about his father anymore, the nightmare of falling, that long, trailing scream. He remembers instead that last moment in the freight car. It is one of those dreams where he cannot move, his feet are fastened to the floor. And there is nothing he can do but watch as Peach raises the gun, and the disaster Clean has worked toward all these years is suddenly upon him.

But then up comes the empty bottle, jaunty in its swing, and it frees them from all they've had to do. And now he can only imagine where the train is going. He doesn't want to know. He just wants to picture it, rolling out along the endless track into a distance growing vaster and more untraceable.

During this week he stays away from the train yard, from the downtown alleys, from every familiar place. Once, stretching his legs, he hears voices rising from some darker spot up ahead, and he quickly turns away. He won't risk meeting anyone he knows. He sticks to the park, the willow tree, the open moonlight of Wyldwood. Each night after walking Del home, he returns there and runs, breathing deep, lying down on the manicured grass as if it is their bed.

Time slips past. He barely sleeps. She visits when she can, but her mother keeps her busy. Her parents are fighting again, and her mother comforts herself with endless birthday plans. In the morning Del brings food, and he can barely swallow with distraction. Even with her sitting right beside him, he is already imagining her return, so that even their time together is turned into waiting and postponement. But the evening is theirs. Together they walk with the microphone cradled in her hands and the earphones shared between them. The sounds of the birds and the insects and the rustling leaves come to them both in the same instant, so that every noise they hear binds them together.

The first time, Del slips the earphones on his head and starts to aim the microphone. "How's that? Are you getting anything?" But her voice comes to him muffled and strange. He doesn't like it; he's about to take them off. Then she swings the cone past a song sparrow's tree, and the five pure notes, startled out of the twilight, drop sweetly into place. "Wow," he murmurs. "Isn't that something."

They learn the streets by sight and then by sound, as if the very landscape is growing more complicated because of them. And in the darkness, when their eyes fail them and the birds have gone silent, they learn all they need to know by touch.

He has started to look for signs of the future, small tasks and accomplishments that can be taken as proof. They reach the base of a tree before the hawk in its branches flies away. They cross a road at night without a pair of headlights in sight, or turn a corner to find two small quail, a bird that usually travels in coveys of six or more. Each sighting offers its own tentative proof. Each evening ends the same. Clean walks her home, though not all the way. She doesn't want to risk her mother finding out.

But tomorrow is her birthday, and they can't bring themselves to part. They walk to the end of her street, then to the mouth of the alley. Then, as if they are toying with the risk, he starts up the alley with her hand still locked in his. It feels like a triumph, like some proof, as if the closer they get to her home, the more real they become.

As they approach the lighted yard, its boundary marked by the billows of lilac above a low picket fence, they hear the sound of voices, muffled by the windows but clamoring out from the house. He feels Del sag beside him, sees her face go pinched and sad as she draws them to a halt amid the shelter of the lilac. The scent fills his nose. The warmth of her hand is a comfort. And there is something in the way she steps back, closer to him—drawing together against the noise—that lays a reassuring hand on his heart.

"My parents," she murmurs. "It's just sometimes." And she glances up worriedly, as if he might misunderstand, as if he's never heard people shouting. A woman's voice rises, sharp and furious. And he hears her father's low, dispirited reply, threading its way through the clamor. The night is quiet. The voice carries clearly.

"It's nothing," she says. "It's just the way they are. My mother says it's just how some people communicate." But she's peering up at him now. He doesn't know what she sees in his face, but now she's tugging on his hand, dragging him away. "Let's go. Let's go back to the park."

They come to a stop under a tree. "I'm sorry you had to hear that." But he just stands there, as if he can hear the voices still. "It doesn't matter," says Del. "It doesn't change anything." She tugs at his hand. "Kiss me."

And he does. It's as if he hasn't kissed her before, as if he wants to do nothing but kiss her for the rest of his life. Shyly she smiles. "Will you wish me happy birthday?" It has already become a game they play.

"Not yet."

"Tomorrow, then? You promise? Tomorrow in Wyldwood? At my birthday flag?"

He will never forget those words.

The next day is busy. Her mother is obsessed with her birthday, and they spend the day shopping, lunching, strolling around department stores. Del is impatient, but not displeased. Her mother is at her best on family occasions, and the whole day seems like a long and pleasant prelude to the evening to come.

He sits beneath the willow tree or on the park bench, or he walks, retracing all the different paths and routes they've made their own. But in the daylight the residential streets have no help to offer, and as the evening approaches he wonders what he is supposed to do. It's surprising how familiar a voice can be, how certain, even when it's the last thing in the world you expect. So that, hearing it, Clean has realized that this whole week, which seemed so much like the sudden new center of his life, has always been only a fairy tale. It will end the way all fairy tales do: with something dreadful and dark and unavoidable.

And he sees that he is not the hero, not even the villain of the story. He is an inconsequential turn of the plot. He's the wood sprite, come to wreak havoc on the pleasant, bright, comfortable cottage of the innocent and beautiful maiden. And it is almost without meaning to that his hand slips into his pocket and wraps itself around the heavy weight of the gun, freshly loaded and waiting.

With the evening he readies himself. Walking up the alley he hesitates by the low picket gate, recognizing it now, of course. Seeing it clearly. That first stop on his long night with Book; the house they broke into for whiskey. It makes him feel like a child, foolish and cheated. The sudden anger takes his breath. He sees the house, so neat and tidy, so solidly comfortable and permanent. And through the windows, within the low, golden light, he sees the man, Del's father, standing alone in the clean and perfect kitchen.

Perhaps he has in mind that charade of Book's, when he bent so craftily over the lock and then eased it open. Perhaps it's just the rage. With the pistol he smashes a pane of glass. And then, given the shock of noise, he is startled at the silence that greets him, the man standing flat-footed in the bright and sweet-smelling room.

"How did you find me?"

"Did you think I wouldn't? Did you think you could hide?"

"I wasn't hiding."

"You should be long gone," says Clean. "You should be a

hundred miles away."

"And where would I go?"

He feels his hand tighten on the gun. The image of Del comes to him. He pictures her waiting on the fifteenth green, smiling up at her birthday flag, knowing he'll be coming. And he wants so much to be there. But the anger is sudden and hot. Maybe it's the smile. Maybe it's the house, so clean and solid. So heavy and neat with every luxury and comfort. And it's Book himself, looking cleaner than he ever has. So freshly washed and pressed—clean clothes, clean hair—as if the dirt was only a kind of camouflage all these years. And Clean can see that he looks tired. Older than he remembers, older than he'd realized the other night when, in the darkness, his voice was as springy as ever.

He tries to feel angry, reaching for that note of fury. "You threw me off a moving train."

"It wasn't moving very fast. Did you keep your knees loose?"

"I landed fine."

"How was the forest?"

"It was fine."

And Book nods, as if that's that.

Clean finds himself filled with a luminous rage. "Is that funny, Book? You think that's funny? You think, after all these years of chasing you down, I'm not going to shoot you dead in your own goddam house?"

There is part of him that is amazed. The gun—after all these years it doesn't seem so heavy now, though it's shaking as if trying to take flight. As if the fury were an electric current running from his heart all the way down to his fingers.

And Book notices the change, as well. No joking now. He says, "I don't think you want to."

"But I do. Don't you see? You were right when we were out there. On the train, on the roof of that goddam library. I couldn't have shot you then. Not good old Book. But now I'm thinking maybe I should. I'm thinking maybe I ought to put you out of your goddam misery. I mean look at this!" He almost snarls at the bright cheerfulness of the room. Half his life spent picturing him dead. And now to find him here? Living like this? A rush of something so hot it roars right through him.

"Jesus, Book! Who the hell are you? All these years? This is yours? You've got a fucking house? A fucking family? I thought you were on the scrounge. I though you were a rough rider, Book. I thought you were a ranger. But look at you! You're a freddie! For God's sake! You're a fucking freddie! You've got a kitchen, Book. You've got a fucking kitchen! Bedrooms. Furniture."

He's almost crying now, fierce tears clinging to his eyes. "What's in the refrigerator, Book? What's in the fucking cupboards, huh? And what about me? All these years? Do you know what foster care is like? One dump after another? One set of freddies after another? You run away and they catch you. Run away and they fucking catch you. And all this time, you're living like this? Without me? God damn it, Book! Without me! We were pals! You said we were pals. You said we were partners."

"Clean...."

"Shut up!" He squeezes the trigger. The gun bucks in his hand, and a framed print on the wall shatters.

"Look out! Be careful!"

"Oh, was that yours, Book?" he sneers. "I'm so sorry.

"Put the gun down, Clean"

"Are you scared, Book? Is that it?"

"Please--."

And the gun bucks again. There's another explosion. And this time a scream, louder than the gunshot, piercing through the humming and the ringing in his ears. A woman screaming.

And it bursts the rising bubble of his rage. Leaves him shocked and staring. A woman standing on the stairway in a bright pink bathrobe. Her hand pressed to her mouth, her eyes wide. Her hair, all short and mussed from sleep, is flared about her head.

"Luanne," says Book. "Go back upstairs." Even now, in the middle of everything, his voice is soothing and calm. And that's something else to admire.

"He shot you!"

"He didn't shoot me."

"He's got a gun!"

"It's all right. Go back to bed. It's going to be fine."

But of course, it isn't. Nothing's going to be fine again. Everything is coming undone. Because in the hand pressed convulsively to her mouth the woman holds a phone, gripped as if it might save her life. And in that long moment when they all stand balanced around the cozy, golden-lit room, Clean hears the sound of sirens rising. Through the windows he sees the alley fill with flashing lights. He sees the chimps edging cautiously past the picket fence. He hears the crackle of a radio. And he thinks of Del, waiting for him under her birthday flag.

Book has him by the arm. He snatches the gun. "How old are you?"

"What? Seventeen."

"Remember that. There was no gun. You get it? You were looking for food. It was just a scrounge. You hear me?"

"What?"

"Say it!"

"A scrounge."

"That's it. You're underage. It's just a scrounge."

And the police come through the door, cautious at first and then faster. They grab him, jerk his arms around. And Clean is thinking back, another memory floating up and bursting like a bubble. All those years ago. *Just go soft. You're a kid. They'll go easy on you.*

And in his mind he can picture them all as, one by one, they abandon him: first Peach and then Book and then Del. They all just float away. Except the police. They're here to stay. They take him and they lock him up, and for a while it seems they will never let him go.

CLEAN

15.

And then they do.

All those years of juvie over. All those years of waiting. And he's out: an old man of twenty-five. And everything he's ever been is behind him.

He sits on a bench at the edge of the train yard, the long, repeating runnels of track already sinking into twilight. He takes off his sunglasses—the ones Bunny had noticed, the ones that had turned him, just for an instant, into a thoughtful businessman lost in his book. He doesn't suppose it's true he can see better at night, but it's always such a relief to open his eyes without pain that when he peers into the darkness it seems he can see every shadow, every corner and detail. Or maybe it's just that he doesn't expect too much. Other people stumble along, always wanting it to be brighter, clearer. Wanting the darkness to be something it can never be. But Clean understands the night. It just wants to be left alone. It wants you to go about your business, find what you need to find. And mostly, it just wants you to leave each other alone.

He thinks of Book, gone without a trace, vanished months ago. He takes a Hershey bar out of his pocket, peels it, breaks it in half. The larger piece he throws as far as he can, out into the middle of the tracks. He doesn't hear it land. The rest he chews slowly. Though chocolate isn't really the proper offering. After that first long train ride, Book never really had a taste for chocolate anymore.

He can feel the ring on its little cord around his neck. A little bit of the past transformed: part hope, part desperation. He is aware that this is something like happiness he is feeling. Another escape. Another reprieve. After all, he can't kill Book if he can't find him. Both of them off the hook.

Then he lets himself think about Del. The sight of her in her garden, in the laundromat. So close they could have touched. Older, transformed, but somehow still the same. The way *he* is still the same.

Or no. Not *still*. Again. They are again the same. The two of them. As if they've been redeemed.

From the darkness comes the scuff and crunch of gravel. He could turn to look, but there's no need. Even eight years in juvie couldn't make Peach a stranger. The one recurring figure in his life. If we could choose the ghosts that haunt us, he would not have chosen Peach.

And Clean realizes he has half-expected him to disappear, to vanish in a puff of smoke like some attendant spirit whose task is done. It seems somehow ridiculous that he should show up here, as if he doesn't recognize how much has changed. How little there is between them now.

Peach settles onto the bench with the exaggerated effort of a man who hates to be ignored. "What a night, eh? Isn't it something. Isn't it a hell of a something. Like spring. It's like spring is in the air. Must be nice to breathe free air, eh Pisser? You been away a long time. I thought you were beginning to like it there."

And it's true. Who goes away to juvie like that? Goes in at seventeen and then, what? Just forgets to come out? Usually they keep you till you're twenty-one, until you're an adult, then you're somebody else's problem. But if you fight, if you argue, if you tussle and talk back, it turns out they'll keep you there as long as you want, with no choices to make, no fate to avoid. Keep you as long as you can stand it. "Are you drunk?" he says.

"Hell, no. Just a few high spirits. Not that I mind sharing with family." Peach holds up a pint bottle, tilting it enticingly.

"No. Thanks."

"Go on. A little something. Do you good. You know, you can be one dreary so-and-so, Pisser. Come on. It's a hell of a night."

And that's true enough. He unscrews the cap, takes a sip, hands it back. The burning almost makes him smile. *Are you a drinking man?*

"Never mind. Keep it a while," says Peach. "Let the magic do its work. I tell you, Pisser, I'm high on life. That's what it is. Happy just to be alive." He pats his own knees as if he's proud of them. "Something about the air. Puts a little pepper in your step."

Clean says nothing.

"I tell you this much, Pisser. Your dad'd be proud of you. Growed up good."

"Is that right?"

"You remember him?"

"Course I do."

"Cause I'm wondering a bit. All this time."

"I remember."

"And do you remember what we decided to do to him? That son of a bitch? All our plans? Broken bottle in the face. Tire iron to the knees. Smash him down to a little stain. You remember? You remember what we said? How long we been waiting?"

And Clean almost smiles. He takes another sip. He can't quite bring himself to say the words. As if, like all that he has felt for Book but been unable to say, the knowledge of his vanishing is something best preserved in silence. But tonight silence is beyond him. "He's gone."

"What?"

"Disappeared. Vanished without a trace."

"Is that right?"

Clean thinks of the lawyer's office, the photographs. Trying for something to make it stick. Something for that skeptical glint in Peach's eye. "You ever seen anyone hit by a train?"

The man considers for a moment, as if it's a pleasure to be conjured up. "You mean hit, like in a car? Or you mean squashed? Sliced and squirting on the tracks?"

Clean tries to let the words slide off, but the image sticks.

And he has the sudden fear that, in conjuring up the story, he might somehow make it real. "I've seen the pictures. It's nothing you walk away from."

"Jesus," says Peach. "You'd have to be pretty damn drunk not to get out of the way. Or maybe pass out on the track. Wouldn't that be something? Hear all that noise, that whole creaking, roaring weight coming down on you. And you open your eyes and see it. Just like that. You got about a second before it cuts you in half. What are you thinking about then, do you suppose?" He laughs, a wheezy, rusty sound. "Like a fly, I guess, right before you squash him. Or maybe you're just thinking, Boy. I wish I had another bottle." And that carries him further into wheezing amusement.

"Yeah," says Clean. "Whatever."

"Oh, man. Wouldn't that be something. The Book doing the big squirt. Boom! Squish! Like a bug on the tracks. But no. Oh, no. No, no, no. That's just too easy. That'd be way too good for him."

"Forget it," says Clean. He climbs to his feet, hands back the bottle. "Thanks for the drink."

"Wait a second! We're talking here. We're remembering your old man."

"And now I'm going to forget him."

"And then what? What about that damned Book? You going to forget about him, too?"

"He's gone. He's not our problem any more." Clean starts to turn away.

"Hold on."

"I'm leaving."

"Not just yet. Oh man oh man, Pisser. You are going to love this."

The woods are deeper than he remembers. A darkness even he can't like. The Thousand Acre Wood they used to call it on those old colony maps, when it would have been a good deal more than a thousand acres. A whole rolling swath of rough and gullied land that was too inhospitable to plow and, with its wolves and bears and Indians, too forbidding for anything else. He had seen a map in the library years ago, framed on a wall. It looked old and stained, but somehow quaint, as if it could reduce the whole frightening blankness into a cute, fairy tale kingdom. The Thousand Acre Wood. It sounds like Winnie the Pooh, but isn't.

Huge trees rising like crooked dreams. Grasping branches and cruel imagined faces in the bark. The Wood isn't a place for regular folk. It's for sticks and twigs, for sprites and mutts and teeth. Clean was always afraid of it as a child, and he's afraid of it now.

"Don't dawdle, Pisser. I got other things to do."

But it seems to take forever in the darkness. And then, there they are. Nowhere special. A clearing in the middle of the towering oaks. And there is Book, lying in the moonlight, hunched against a tree.

"Jesus Christ." Clean's voice is a whisper. "What have you done? Is he dead?"

"Just about," says Peach cheerfully.

"He disappeared."

"I thought he was hit by a train."

"He left town months ago."

"I'm thinking maybe not."

Peach has tied him there, looking worse than anything Clean can remember. Filthy clothes, long brown hair. Even in the darkness his face is awful. Peach has been busy. It's hard to tell the shadows from the blood. A shovel lies beside him, smeared and darkened.

"I had a few things I wanted to say to him, but he's still breathing. I knew you'd want to finish him off." Peach leans low over the battered figure, turning the head almost tenderly. "Guess you'd better hurry. I don't know my own strength."

"What did you do?"

"What you should have done. What your dad would have done. You think he didn't deserve it?"

But Clean can only stare. Book is moaning through a broken mouth, breathing up little bubbles of blood. The sound is awful. The crooked sprawl of his legs.

"Come on, Pisser. This is how it goes. This is what it's all been about, all those years. I've done the hard part. One bullet to finish him, that's all. Where's the gun?"

The gun. All those years he carried it, and then it was gone. He was free of it. Book had freed him even of that. "I lost it. Years ago."

"Well, never mind. Shovel works good." He picks it up, hefts it cheerfully. "Step it up. He's not going to last. If you want to do it, you got to do it now."

He holds it out, but Clean can't take it. His arm is too heavy. His hand doesn't work.

"What do you want? A rock? You got a rock you like? That's fine. It's all the same to this guy. All these years? You gonna just stand there?"

And Peach is squatting over the body again. "Fuck's sake! You stupid bastard." He is pressing the throat, feeling for a pulse. And Clean is thinking, at least this. At least let him be dead. But Peach punches him furiously in the chest, and there is a murmur, a shifting groan. He punches him again. "Hurry!" he snaps, climbing to this feet. "Hit him, for crissake!"

Clean tries to run, but his legs don't work. He tries to turn and flee. Book is moaning. Peach is smiling down at the sounds. There's still time. He can pick up the shovel, swing it at Peach. He isn't expecting it. Knock him out; there'd still be time. Cut the ropes, carry him out. Get him to the emergency room. And even as he thinks it, Clean is certain it'll work. There is the symmetry of it, the fatedness: the same emergency room Book had taken him to all those years ago. He'd take him in. They'd fix him up. They'd be even: pain for pain, rescue for rescue. The sound of his breathing is awful. The weak scrabble of his hands.

"Oh, for God's sake!" snaps Peach. "Just hit him! Hit him! It's not a game. Jesus Christ!" And Peach is staring down at the silent body. "No, no, no. Don't do that! You son of a bitch! Don't you dare! Come on!"

And then Peach is there like some twisted Little League coach, wrapping Clean's numb fingers around the handle of the shovel. Swing through, damn it! Swing it! And he's too numb to resist. There's a swing, a blow, muffled and clumsy. The shovel connects with a sound he'll never forget. And he's dead.

They bury the body in the worst place Clean can imagine. Right there in the shadow of the trestle. Serves him right, says Peach; put him in the ground where he started it all. Clean digs while Peach goes through the pockets of the filthy clothes. An envelope, a few scraps of paper go into the hole. The entirety of a life. They cover it with dirt. Then Peach claps him on the shoulder. "Pisser, aren't you one sorry piece of work." And he turns and strolls away, shovel on his shoulder, like a workman home to his well-earned rest, leaving Clean alone in the silence.

And that is that.

Part Four

Delilah

DELILAH

16.

For Del each shift at Café Ion is an ongoing emergency, clattering through the orders on a humming tide of steam and espresso until her heart is beating like a sparrow's and her eyes dart from cup to cup, table to table, keeping every need balanced like a juggler with her plates. Afterwards her spirits sag.

Today she is saved by the unlikely sight of a yellow taxi chugging like a barge down the narrow channel of the alley behind her house. It draws to a halt just outside the picket fence. She half expects the driver to emerge and ask for directions, but instead Colette steps out as if expecting to find a red carpet beneath her elegant shoes. She pays the driver and lets herself in through the picket gate.

"Have you come to rescue me?" says Del.

The bright orange dress, the black wig, the pale, pale face. She's like a long lost friend. And if it surprises her that Bunny is still wearing Luanne's clothes, that she's still dressed and accessorized for make believe, Del tries not to wonder.

"I've just been driving around," says Bunny. "Seeing if anything looked familiar. Trying to shake out some of the cobwebs. And then I thought, what if there's an angel somewhere waiting for me with a cup of coffee?"

"Did the angel say anything about coffee cake? Or gingerbread?"

"I've always thought heaven would smell of gingerbread."

Despite a whole morning of coffee, Del bustles into the kitchen, boiling water, measuring, setting out the mugs. When she steps outside Bunny has seated herself at the little table with a look of such determined cheerfulness it almost breaks Del's heart.

"You don't have to smile, Bunny."

But at the gentle tone the woman seems to deflate before her eyes. "Oh, what did I think I was doing?"

"It was fun. We had fun."

"What could that man have thought?"

"Bertie? He had a wonderful time. You just know he's never been out with two girls at once."

"Oh, Delilah. I think I'm losing my mind."

Without a word Del wraps her in a hug. Luanne was fragile, too, but not like this: avian-boned and flightless, drooping under the weight of disappointment. Del feels sturdy beside her, and when Bunny glances up, teary-eyed and sheepish, she offers her a gentle shake. "You're not.
You just need a little coffee. Maybe some gingerbread. Your body's just depleted by all the fun you had."

"Do you think?"

"No question." But then she can't help herself. "You're still in that dress?"

Bunny looks down as if she might have forgotten just how bright it is. "The other night I felt just a little closer to being myself. I thought I might try to hold onto it a little longer."

"Well, you look like a dreamboat."

"Wouldn't that be nice."

Del bustles about, setting out napkins, plates. She smiles as she pours the coffee, slices the gingerbread, adds a piece of coffee cake. If the day is a series of pillows, she arranges them around her. "I ran into your guardian angel the other day. At the laundromat."

"You don't use a laundromat, dear?"

"All the best people do. He just about finished my brownies." She hesitates. The overbright eyes, the thin gleam of moisture at the temples. "Is there something you should be taking now?"

"Did Clean tell you to say that?" Her smile takes a little stitch in Del's heart. "Ruth used to say it to me when she was young. Well, not quite that way. Take a chill pill, mom. She hasn't said it lately. The thing is, I'm trying to stay clear-headed." Bunny glances up at the thin blue sky. "What do you suppose it's doing in Grand Cayman now?"

"Raining. Definitely. All day every day."

"I think so, too. I can almost picture it." Bunny sips her coffee as if this alone might mend her. "My daughter ran away from me."

"I'm sure she didn't. You know how it is. The relationship with your mother can be tricky."

"She couldn't wait to go away to school. Couldn't wait to get married."

"Maybe she just wanted to try something new."

"She went to Roger's old school. Does that sound like something new? A chip off the old block. It's here. Just a few blocks away." Her tone goes rueful. "Does that sound like fate, Delilah? What did we decide about that?"

"We don't believe in fate."

"He's proud of her as can be. I think that's his one redeeming feature."

"Does she like it? The school?"

"And then to get married like that. Everyone running away. Sometimes I wonder," Bunny says, "if I got sick for a reason. If I did it deliberately, somehow. I felt so desperate. It's like they were choosing sides. What did I think? That Ruth would have to choose me? I mean," and her tone is wistful, "what's more irresistible than a woman with cancer?"

"You didn't decide to get sick."

"No. But sometimes I wonder. All the choices I've made. I came out here thinking... I don't know what. If I just had another chance. A new start. An old start. But Ruth is gone, Roger's gone. Everybody's gone. So now what do I do?"

"What do you want?"

"I want a do-over." She offers up a wistful smile. "But how does that work? A gal's got to do what a gal's got to do. And what I've got to do is go home."

"Not yet," says Del with a sudden pang. "Not right away."

"Soon. But before I do, there's somewhere I'd like to go."

"Grand Cayman?"

"Somewhere closer."

"Is it a quest?"

"I'm not sure I'd go that far. But I wouldn't mind a little company.

The cab drops them in front of a wide stone gate. St. Augustine's Academy. Bunny climbs out warily and stands, holding firmly onto Del's hand. "Did you like high school?"

"It was nothing like this," says Del.

"That's the spirit."

There are wide lawns and garden beds and a few ancient trees. The term is over for the summer, though the school is never empty. This week there are middle-aged men and women in maroon vests glancing through glossy pamphlets or walking toward an auditorium in the shape of a granite chateau.

"Do you know where we're going?" Del asks.

"I suppose we could ask."

Instead they sit on a bench. Across wide lawns is a row of buildings whose varied architectural styles are all joined beneath the reassuring uniformity of the same grey stone. "Roger always loved this place. Pride and suffering, he used to say. That's what they teach you here. Though I'd be surprised if it was anything more than a little light discomfort. He brought me once, early on when we were dating." She glances over ruefully. "Do young people still date these days?"

"I'm not a good person to ask."

"My parents used to ask me, How's your love life? As if there was some way I would know." With a sigh she draws their two clasped hands onto her lap. Del goes very still at the tenderness of the gesture. "Do you even believe in a love life, Delilah

Belle? Do you suppose that's even possible? I mean literally? A life devoted to love?"

Del says nothing, and as if taking that for a reply Bunny nods. "You might not think it, but Roger was quite a catch. His family was quite a catch. And if it wasn't *love* love. Well, I wasn't going to let that stand in my way. Then I took a course in my final semester."

She falls silent. Del gives her hand a squeeze. "You took a course on love?"

Her smile is grateful. "Love poetry. Which, I suppose, isn't quite the same thing. I was twenty years old. Going on forty. And now I'm almost forty, going on eighty. And every so often I can still catch a glimpse of what it felt like to be in love."

"You don't look eighty."

Her laugh is like a little breath. "It's never what you think. All that poetry of unrequited passion. We used to laugh about it later, Bill and I. Well," she amended, "not exactly laugh."

"So there's someone named Bill."

"Aren't you a dear. Didn't I mention him? He sat down beside me on the first day of class. How can it not make you wonder? He came in late, and it was the one empty seat. I was saving it for Karen Trachtenberg, but he sat down instead. He picked my scarf up off the seat and handed it to me. He said, Sometimes you have to be ruthless in love. Can you imagine? The whole class had been Karen's idea, and she hadn't even showed up. I was so annoyed I almost left."

"But you didn't?"

"No." She glances up again at all the solid, grand, grey buildings. "Have I told you about Ruth?"

"Not much."

"She's a lovely girl. Almost eighteen. A little flinty. A little set in her ways." The timer in her phone gives a small reverberating ding. She reaches into her purse and reluctantly takes out a plastic vial of pills and a small water bottle. She shakes a little avalanche of color into her palm and holds it out. "Would you mind? One of the blue ones and—yes, why not—a little yellow one, as well."

She pours the remainder back and swallows the pills. "Please let me know, won't you dear? If I become a little odd?"

Del pats her hand. The dress, the wig. Bunny sits as if listening to some distant note. "You were talking about Ruth?" says Del.

"I don't know why. I've always had trouble seeing her clearly. Don't you find that? Everything is always so much more what it *was* than what it *is*." She gazes around. "What does it say about me? That they both love this place, and it only makes me tired?"

Eventually Del helps her to her feet, but instead of heading back to the main gate they turn without a word and follow the stone walkway in among the trees. The gentle slope of the hillside draws them down. "Isn't this nice?" breathes Bunny. "You can't even tell where we are."

The shape of the world is changing, and Del has the sudden sense of moving through one of her mother's self-healing exercises. Clearing a Path to Your Best Self. She can almost hear the comforting voice: *from the grey granite heaviness of loss and responsibility to the cool, shaded hillside of contentment.* They stroll past a dark-stained maintenance shed. A few men in work clothes move about their quiet business with wheel barrows and shovels, as if the landscape needs constant shoring up against the weight of all that granite and privilege.

One man wheeling past with a load of compost passes through a drift of sunlight, and the name on his jacket brightens and fades. *Lawnkeepers Grass and Grounds.* An odd moment. The smell of earth and effort seems to come straight from Del's childhood. She imagines her father here all those years ago, moving with the slow, inscrutable air of work to be done, and she tries to imagine the place as these men see it. No pile of dirt without the need to move it; no hillside without the knowledge of how long it will take to mow. She turns to say something of this and sees Bunny poised and uncertain.

"Is something wrong?"

"Not wrong," she says. "Lets go further."

They descend under the spreading trees and emerge on a grassy slope that rises and falls like an ocean of green to the distant limits of an encircling wall. It was the original corner of the school, now reduced to an ancient stone foundation like some Roman ruin. Stones calling to stones across the long-blanketing grass and, for no reason at all, an old stone bridge spanning the gentle dip between one hill and the next.

Bunny gazes at the scene. "Would I know if I were crazy, do you think? Is that something I would be able to tell?"

And Del can hear another of Luanne's voices now. Not the strong, confident narration but the other one, the low, worried, fretful one. She steps closer. "Absolutely not."

"Really? Are you sure?"

"Trust me. You wouldn't have a clue. Crazy people don't think they're crazy. You have to be sane for that. It only makes sense."

"Then, do you think maybe it's you, Delilah Belle?"

"No," she says firmly. "I don't think it's anything. Maybe the pills. Maybe you're just tired."

Bunny smiles. "That's not what I mean. I mean, maybe it's you who's doing this. I think maybe you're my fate. I think you were sent to me."

Del's heart is beating fast. She takes Bunny's arm gently as if it were a bird that could be soothed. "Now that sounds much more like it to me."

"The cherry tree in your back yard."

"It was a crabapple."

"The art museum. And now this. I've been here before."

"Of course you have. Ruth, Roger."

"Not the school. That's a completely different place."

Del's heart is sinking. "I don't know what that means."

"I remember that bridge. Of course I do. But it doesn't have anything to do with Roger. That's the whole point."

"Maybe it just *looks* familiar."

"No. Don't you see?" Her voice is eager, pleading. "We were walking. It was all we did, at first. I was engaged. Leaving in three weeks. And we knew about unrequited love. We'd been reading about it for months. And there was part of us that felt if we just locked ourselves within our own narrow restraint, it would all be somehow possible. We thought we could be innocent and passionate and pure. Is there any chance in the world that you understand?"

Del grips her hand, but what can she say?

"We were walking. We couldn't sit in public, of course. Oh, I suppose we could. We weren't actually doing anything. But it felt as if we were. So we walked and walked, as far as we could. Turning this way and that as if we were following every single road I'd never had the nerve to choose." Her voice is almost breathless with remembering.

They would stop at a little park or sit on a bench at the corner of a street. Just sit and talk. That's all. With their hands locked together. Cut loose, in that moment, from all that their lives required. And on the fourth day—"Oh, dear. It sounds so biblical, doesn't it?"—they walked through the twilight and into the evening, and the ordinary houses and lawns and windows gave way to something wonderful.

Out of nowhere, for no reason at all, a high stone wall rose up, solid and mysterious. It changed the feeling of the night like a boundary they had crossed. They stopped, aware of the high branches visible over the wall, the confined and untamed mysteries within. And Bill said, *Look, there's a tree.* It had grown inside the wall, but a thick branch extended over and drooped down above the sidewalk.

"It was like a stairway out of a fairy tale." She is hugging Del's arm. "I'm not a tree climber. So it tells you something about that evening that we climbed it without a thought."

Up and over. Into a magic garden with sloping lawns and a bridge that took them from one magic hillside to another and then down into the sheltered stillness beneath. They came upon a small white table and chairs, laid with a tablecloth and set with wine glasses and small white plates. A picnic basket nestled on the grass beside it.

"Can you imagine?" Bunny whispers. "Coming upon it like that? What it would have been like?"

"What did you do?"

Bunny's smile is a benediction. "We sat down. There was wine. There was cheese, bread, and fruit. And as we were eating, one by one the fireflies came out, floating around us, glowing, until we could look up through our own constellation into the wider stars above."

"How beautiful," Del breathes. And there is part of her trying to imagine the sounds that would have accompanied it, trying to hear the whole story in the lingering echo of her mother's voice.

"It was. He had carried it all there that afternoon. In a cab. I don't know how many trips. All the way around through the gate. Is it any wonder I kissed him?"

It's a story Del wants to believe. Though as she gazes around there is no tree to be seen, no hint of the sudden oak ladder reaching up and over. The wall runs straight, untouched and alone, as far as she can see.

And as if Bunny has somehow glimpsed this in her mind, her smile turns wistful. "Do you suppose there's any chance it could be true?"

"We can make it true," says Del. "We can just decide."

Bunny gazes around as if searching for threads to gather up. Slipping into motion, she follows the curve of the hillside down. "We couldn't leave that night unmarked. We kissed and kissed, lying on the grass. Then we buried a little treasure to make it real." She is standing under the bridge now, peering down at the grass where a little cluster of daffodils has seen better days.

"What did you bury?"

"A poem. A sad poem. A watch. And a ring. His father's pocket watch. My mother's ring." She runs the tip of her tongue over dry lips. "Do you think they could be there still?"

A beautiful story, Del thinks. Shouldn't that be enough? It's how she feels when she listens to one of her mother's old recordings. Knowing it will end, knowing she'll have to turn it off. Just another moment, please. Just another turn in the story.

"We could look," says Bunny.

"Or we could just leave it."

"I don't think I can."

Reluctantly Del climbs up the hillside. The men are resting in the shadow of the maintenance shed. Del sees a trowel in a basket of small tools. "May I borrow this? Just for a moment?"

They say not a word. She turns and hurries down. The breath catches in her throat. "Where?"

"We laid our blanket here, I think. We knelt down over here." Two steps and Bunny sinks onto grass, bright orange dress, black wig and all. But once down she turns motionless. Perhaps the sudden fact of being on her knees has tricked her into inadvertent prayer, or maybe the prospect of testing all that has come to mean so much is simply too impossible. Del kneels beside her.

"This isn't crazy, is it?" Bunny whispers. "You would tell me if it's crazy?"

"What if you leave it?" Del says. "We can go home. You could just remember."

But Bunny is gazing down at the little patch of daffodils, wilted into stiff and darkened versions of themselves. "You're an adventure artist. What about the story where the unhappy princess digs up the treasure and it answers all her oldest prayers? Doesn't anyone tell that story anymore?"

The ground is hard. The lawn is thick and impenetrable. Del grips the trowel and presses the point into the grass. "Here?"

"I don't know. Over a little? Maybe beside those flowers?"

Del shifts. And when she does she sees there's something funny about the daffodils. They are stiff and bent and rusted brown. There are thin silver seams. Del reaches out a finger and flicks at one. It vibrates like a muffled bell. "It's metal. They're made of metal."

Bunny's eyes are shining. Del has seen it before. Her mother's eyes. And she knows that hope is always there, furled and ready, even for a moment like this. "Do you think it's a sign?" Bunny whispers.

Isn't there always a sign? A tree will point the way, or the rising moon, or a silent possum ambling along its solitary way. "It might just be a prank."

"I think we should dig."

"I'll do it," says Del.

"No. I will."

Bunny leans forward. The earth is softer here, as if it's been recently disturbed. She digs quickly, opening a tiny hole that grows wider and deeper as Del sits poised on a little pinnacle of hope. The trowel seems to snag on something, and Bunny reaches in, drawing out a muffled bundle. It might have been white once: a handkerchief mottled brown by the soil and wrapped into a shape no broader than her palm. "Oh, Delilah," she breaths.

The very existence of it has taken Del's voice. She had been ready to dig and dig and then to comfort Bunny in the knowledge of all the other places her dreams might yet be buried. But finding something, so solid and filthy and smelling of dirt.

And perhaps Bunny feels the same. She lets it lie on her palm, the edges easing apart as if determined to unwrap itself. "What was it you'd buried?" Del asks.

"My mother's ring, his father's pocket watch, a poem. All wrapped in his handkerchief."

"Do you want me to open it?"

But Bunny's fingers are already plucking at the cloth. She spreads it open across her hand. There are two items. The twisted little bundle of a plastic watch, bound up in its own wristband, and a small jeweler's box, scuffed and time-worn. Del isn't breathing as Bunny snaps it open. There is a narrow, pale circlet—not quite a ring. A band of stiff white cardboard rolled around itself and sealed with tape.

Bunny is staring. "I don't understand."

But Del is beginning to. It was a mistake to dig it up. She thinks of her mother in the front seat of her car, with so little hope of escape that she has closed the garage door tightly behind her. A woman with no place left to go but away. Even in the warm sunlight it's not hard to imagine a woman so battered by grief and illness that she has nothing left to call upon but what she can pretend. Life is a story we tell ourselves before we tell it to each other. That doesn't make it crazy. Where's the life that doesn't need improving? So she buries something—yesterday, the day before. Not for the chance to dig it up, but for the comfort of imagining it there, letting it be transformed by all your hopes and all the passing time.

"It's okay Bunny. The magic hasn't had time to work yet, that's all. We can just bury it again. That's the best thing. Bury it and let the magic work."

But Bunny is twisting the cardboard ring on her finger. "Oh, Delilah."

The tone slips smoothly into Del's heart. "It's okay. Let's go home. We'll go home and lie down. Everything will be better."

She lifts the watch gently from Bunny's grasp. She weighs it in her hand. There is almost nothing to it, just a little piece of the imagined past. A square black, digital face with small white words inscribed across the top. GPS Golf-a-matic. She regards it for a moment. Then turns it over, straightens it out. And there on the back, drawn with white paint in childish, uneven letters: *This belongs to Del.*

DELILAH

17.

There was a game her father used to play, after she had followed him out into the dusk. He offered it as a sort of consolation prize, and for a while it had consoled her. It began as a note waiting on the kitchen table: a small scrap of paper with a pair of long decimal numbers written in her father's neat, block hand. That was all. No explanation. No clue except itself. Del tried to puzzle it out. She took it online, searched everywhere. Her father sent another and another. She began to collect them, poring over them, rearranging the order, constructing elaborate webs of understanding that amounted to nothing. Even when he stopped by he refused to explain. You'll figure them out, he said. And then, when she had collected nearly a dozen, the package arrived, the Golf-a-matic, and she was so delighted with the sudden insight she put her name on it immediately.

She wore it as a watch, she wore it as a lucky charm. She went out in the twilight, all over the neighborhood, tracking the one hidden spot where the GPS numbers aligned. And there she would find, under a rock or in a garden bed, a small treasure wrapped in plastic against the dew. There were hairclips and bracelets and charms and little pewter animals that she arranged in even rows on the top shelf of her bookcase.

She loved the game at first, as if she were walking out with him each evening, tracking him down, getting closer with every discovery. But one night she saw them all, the little prizes, crowded on her shelf, and felt suddenly nothing but foolish. The watch and all the treasures went into the drawer behind *The Anatomy of Melancholy*. She hadn't thought of them in years.

But now. What it means that Bunny must have found it, that she must have taken it and buried it, Del doesn't understand.

To have something so crucial and forgotten buried with the rest of someone else's fantasy—she doesn't quite know how to feel. Unsettled. Protective. Angry. That Bunny should have uncovered such a long ago treasure and buried it as her own.

As if overhearing her thoughts Bunny says, "I would remember if I put them there, wouldn't I?"

"Do you?"

"It's not the same watch," says Bunny.

"No." Del takes her gently by the arm. "I don't think it can be."

"You're not playing a joke on me, Delilah?"

"No," she says. "Of course I'm not."

Forlornly Bunny gazes at the watch. "It must mean something, don't you think?"

Del takes her home. Together they go up to the guest bedroom and she helps Bunny out of the dress and wig. Enfolded in Del's pajamas she looks thin and fragile, wide-eyed as she climbs into the bed. Del is half-startled to find her mother's words on her own lips: "There's nothing wrong that a little nap won't help."

She starts to clean the house, though it isn't her day. She wipes counters, cleans drawers, runs a dusting cloth over the furniture. She would like to vacuum, but worries about the noise, so instead she wraps a t-shirt around the head of a broom and runs it over the floors, pausing to untie and shake it out the back door in the slowly gathering dusk. At one point, flapping it briskly through the air, she recognizes the shirt she'd been wearing when Russell last came over. It had been among her favorites until then, but now it looks like something abandoned: limp and filthy. She can feel her life disappearing. Is love even a thing anymore?

She is reaching down to rewrap the broom when she sees a now familiar figure letting himself in through the gate. She is surprised how much of a comfort it is.

He nods at the t-shirt. "You look like a castaway signaling for help."

"At least my desert island is clean."

It sounds reproachful, but the fact is he's looking more presentable than she remembers. His suit, though not yet unrumpled from the washer, is impressively fresh—thin lines of color running through the darker weave of the tweed—and his face, where it is unobscured by braided hair and beard, is pale and well-scrubbed. Too well scrubbed, it seems. The skin looks pink across the cheekbones and eyes, as if he'd used a nailbrush to get out the more stubborn grime.

"Do you want anything?" she asks. "I have gingerbread. And there's some coffee cake."

"You bake a lot of sweets."

"Is that a yes?"

"Is there coffee?"

As she steps behind the kitchen counter Del marvels at what an effortless host she has become, who used to have no guests at all. Clean hovers for a moment; perhaps he's hesitating in the face of so much bright tidiness. Then he settles into one of the chairs.

"Bunny's upstairs," she says. "Do you think there's a line between crazy and not?"

"What did she do?"

Del sets the coffee before him and a plate of gingerbread. "How long have you known her?"

He seems to need some time to consider. "A while," he says. "Off and on. It's more like we keep meeting for the first time over and over. I used to think it meant something."

"Do you like her?"

"How could I not?"

Del imagines the woman asleep upstairs. A low vibration of expectancy seems to jump like a spark from Bunny's life to her own. "Do you believe in love?"

"I like this gingerbread," he says.

"I used to think it was waiting out in the world somewhere. Lurking. I used to think love was lurking. And that it would find you, no matter what you did."

"But now?"

"It doesn't seem likely."

"It doesn't have to be love to be lurking."

She considers this. "My boyfriend is kind of a jerk, but still..."

"You have a boyfriend?"

"I'm thinking of going out. Could you stay with Bunny? In case she wakes up. I don't want her to feel disoriented."

"I'm not sure I'll be a lot of help with that. Where are you going?"

"I'm going to be surprising."

"Is there more coffee?"

"In the pot. There's food in the fridge. Some frozen burgers in the freezer."

"Imagine that," he says.

She climbs the stairs to her mother's closet. Bunny is fast asleep in the bed. Del moves silently, drawing back the louvered doors.

She has always dressed for escape, for a kind of bright and clashing deniability. She has done it from childhood, and what child wouldn't look foolish in these clothes? But now she remembers the afternoon at the museum.

She takes out the green dress, but this time when she tugs it down over her hips she notices the thin pinched line of her underwear, the way her bra shows through. Frowning, she turns off the closet light, standing in the glow from the hallway. But having seen it once, she sees it again. The narrow ridge around her hips, the outline of the bra. Too fat. Too fat and too ordinary. Hurriedly she peels it off, drops it on the floor.

There is a low knock at the door.

"Don't come in!" she hisses.

"Why are you standing in the dark?"

"I'm getting dressed."

"You were already dressed. Is Bunny in there?"

"She's asleep."

"I've got her purse here. I thought she might want it when she wakes up. It's got her pills."

"Hold on."

Del wraps herself heavily in a bathrobe and steps to the door. She opens it a crack. In the light of the hall she sees the crazily bearded face, eyes directed politely away, the purse held dutifully before him.

"I don't suppose she has any pills for embarrassment?"

"I'm not sure. Can you be more precise about the symptoms?"

"Never mind."

But he has the purse open now, delving through. After a moment his hand slips past the door, a tiny yellow pill in his palm. "She says these are a little bit of heaven."

If I were a story, Del thinks, what would I do? She swallows the pill.

Clean waits at the door.

"Don't look."

"I'll need some descriptions, then."

"Fat."

"No."

"Depressingly solid?"

"What color are you thinking?"

"I don't know. Orange?"

"No."

Her hand, half-reaching for a hanger, draws back. "Do you know anything about women's fashions?"

"Do you have anything yellow? A yellow dress in the moonlight can catch the eye."

There is no yellow dress. But there is a pink one, a red one, a wild lilac print. As the pill dissolves in her blood, self-consciousness melts like early snow. She tries them all in turn, opening the door a little wider each time for a moment's consultation. Every dress looks better than the last, though Clean remains noncommittal. She tries to find in his wooly face some signal of appreciation or intrigue. "What do you think?"

"How about the green?" he says in the end.

"Too small. I tried it. It doesn't work."

He eyes it where it lies crumpled on the floor. "You might try it again."

She picks it up, reconsidering. The original Dauphine. "Don't look."

It takes a moment to get it on—her balance has shifted a little off-compass. And there it is, the little pucker of her underwear. But the yellow pill has given her a solution. She skins the panties down, then smooths the dress back into place. It's magic. The yellow pill is magic, the dress is magic. Clean himself is probably magic.

"How does it look?" he asks.

"Hold on!" The red wig is on its stand. She pulls it snugly into place, then steps to the door. "Okay."

And now the two of them are standing before the mirror. A fairy tale pairing: Beauty and the Beast, Snow White and a very tall dwarf. Del is smiling at the sight. "I look nice."

"You do."

"Do I have to give you three wishes now?"

He says nothing.

"Any last advice?"

Her fingers flutter at the air miming accessories: scarf, gloves, purse? Clean is blank-faced. From *The Anatomy of Melancholy* she plucks a joint and with an eye in the mirror she tucks it down the snug front of her dress. The vision makes her smile. She tries to stand perfectly still, striking a languid pose, but her blood is humming.

"Are you going to fly?" asks Clean. "Or should we call a

cab?"

When she climbs out onto the sidewalk in front of Russell's house her first thought is that a lesser woman would be nervous. A woman without her advantages. She touches the joint in her bra and straightens her shoulders. The dress is squeezing energy into her.

Del has never been to Russell's house. He has never suggested it, and she has shied away from the prospect. It's a small brick bungalow in among evergreens. It looks nothing like him. He answers the door wearing jeans and an old flannel shirt. She supposes he looks the same, though tonight she notices the tight reddish curl in his hair, as if he's set it earlier in the evening, and the little squinty lines as he takes in the sight of her with an uneasy frown. It's not that he doesn't recognize her, though it does seem to take him a moment. "Well, hi," he says.

"Dauphine."

"Is that right?"

And now with the first shock over, a glint of something shows in his eyes. Anticipation, maybe. Maybe something else as well. "And what is Dauphine doing here?"

"I thought you might be getting tired of Delilah. She can be so ordinary."

"Can she?"

"I thought you might think so."

"Well," he says. "I can see there's nothing ordinary about you."

He escorts her in with a new degree of care which, Del perceives, is not entirely ironic. She is expecting books, student papers, a spare if not actually barren air of rumpled and amused disorder. Instead the house is bright with color. The walls are crowded with art. Paintings, prints, elaborate constructions of wood and cardboard and plastic—dolls and models airplanes and little plastic shoes—that sit on shelves or hang on walls like twisty dioramas.

It occurs to Del that he is merely squatting here, living in someone else's house. And in that instant she imagines a whole life for him, a vagabond's life, moving from friend to friend, sofa to sofa: migrant, unsettled, and lonely. She sees him as a kind of fellow spirit, unsettled in his life—a view that almost instantly disintegrates. "So now you've seen my house, too."

"Is all this art yours?"

"No. A friend of mine."

"Is he an artist?"

"She," he says reluctantly. "Goofy stuff. But she likes it."

Del likes it, too. There is an arrangement of fresh fruit in a bowl: bright bananas, a pink grapefruit, and a large plastic potato with bright eyes and a jaunty sombrero. It is only at this moment she wonders if it was a mistake to come.

Russell takes her hand. He leads her down a hallway, through a door, and into his study. It is austerely untidy. Bookshelves line the walls, a wide desk stands in the middle of the room. And though it is exactly what she originally expected, it now looks dull and self-serious.

But now, as if sheltered from the rest of the house, Russell begins to relax. He turns to the stereo on the bookshelves. The music is already cued, something slow and sweet. As his eyes drift over the dress with a considering glint he says, "So tell me about yourself, Dauphine."

Bunny's yellow pill is losing a little of its magic. She is aware of that first edge of self-consciousness like a storm front approaching. She wishes Bunny were here. She wonders what she would advise.

Her two fingers dip into the front of her dress and draw out the joint. Though in the same moment she thinks, Can this possibly be a good idea?

"Well, what have we here?" says Russell.

She has the sudden image of herself as a ballerina, tiptoeing out on a narrowing limb. Nothing keeping her up but her smile. She lights the joint, holds it out. He helps himself, concentrating as if suddenly aware he might do it wrong.

That makes her smile. Without a word of warning Dauphine says, "Let's dance."

"Is that right?"

Del is only a bathtub crooner, a closet dancer, but clearly Dauphine has more confidence. As she steps close, Russell seems to forget his amusement. In its place is a sudden intentness, a glimmer of unease. And she sees why. He is a terrible dancer. His hips ignore his feet; his shoulders are aloof.

Del laughs and slips a little something into the sway of Dauphine's hips. "You're a very good dancer," she purrs. Who knew Dauphine could purr? "What did you say your name was?" She presses a kiss onto his lips. She should have worn lipstick. She's sure Bunny would have.

Russell smiles, but his eyes twitch toward the windows beyond the desk. "Someone just went by on a bicycle."

"Is that right?" There is something to this purring business. Del wonders if Dauphine is the kind to call a man 'doll'.

"Again. He just went by again."

Del glances over, but there's no sign of anyone. The road, lit by streetlamps, is a vacant silvery wash. "I think someone's a little jumpy."

"Just let me close the curtains."

He draws them tight. The room's muffled glow seems to reassure him. And the fact that they are no longer dancing. He offers her a more practiced smile. "So, what is Dauphine's story?"

"She doesn't tell me much. I don't think she's a confider."

"How would she feel about a little adventure?"

His hands are on her waist now, smoothing the already smooth fabric. They bump up against the desk. And before she can reply, before she quite realizes what is happening, he is corralling her, turning her. Kissing her neck as if that might distract her. And there is something faintly ridiculous about it. The memory of the bathtub comes back to her, the sharp smell of cleanser right under her nose. She tries to recall it as exciting, but instead thinks of the fruit bowl and the bright cheerful surprise of Mr. Potato Head. She thinks of the quirky art on the walls. And she is aware of having come all this way into another woman's house.

His hand is on her back now, bending her forward over the desk. Bunny's pill and the joint, which between them have done so much, are now only slowing her down. She tries to picture Russell again as he'd been when they first met: handsome, assured, appealing; but now she's left wondering if any of it was true. And as much as she suddenly wants to leave, she is embarrassed by her changeability. It seems foolish, childish. And he has always admired her for what she is willing to try. She wonders about Dauphine. Maybe she's the sort of woman who can appreciate the hungry look in Russell's eye. So she concentrates on that, on how much he clearly wants her, and she reminds herself that life is experience and this is something she might as well try.

One hand is on her back. His other fingers slip beneath the lifted hem of her dress and discover nothing but skin. "My goodness. What have we here?"

The tone makes her cringe.

And then abruptly there comes a sharp tap on the window, brisk and sudden, even through the curtains.

Russell jumps. "Jesus!"

"It's the window."

"I know it's the window!"

He switches off the lamp. Light creeps in from the hallway. Cautiously he slips to the window's edge and peers out. "There's nobody there."

"Maybe it's a burglar," Del says helpfully. She's tugging her dress down, straightening herself. The leftover joint goes back into her bra.

"I suppose it might have been a bird," he mutters. "Sometimes they fly into the window."

"And then they rob the house?"

"What?"

From the direction of the front door comes a hard peremptory knock.

"Jesus!"

"Maybe the bird has friends."

"You stay here."

But as he moves toward the hallway Del follows. She finds him standing uncertainly before the door, peering out through the peephole. "What do they want?" she asks.

"There's no one there."

The sharp knock—rat-a-tat-tat—makes them both jump, but Del is the only one to laugh. It's the laugh that does it. Russell wrenches open the door, revealing a perfect corridor of empty air from the front step all the way to the quiet, tree-lined street.

"Trick or treat," whispers Del.

"Jesus Christ. Goddam kids."

He stands uncertainly for a moment, then turns back to her, but she steps briskly past and stands gazing up and down the street. She is buoyed by relief, riding on the loft and swell of it.

Behind her Russell frowns. His fingers play a little rhythm on the doorknob. He seems about to speak, but even Russell knows when there is nothing more to say.

"What a beautiful night," says Del. "I think it's calling my name. Tell your friend how much I like her art." And she sets off without a backward glance.

She has never ventured out alone in her mother's clothes, never taken her imagination for a walk in quite this way. No need for a cab. The evening air swims coolly against bare legs. Between the yellow pill and the smoke and what Del is already thinking of as her rescue, she is aware of the night in a way she hasn't been in years. The possibilities are in the air, and already she is testing them, imagining the voyage she might make.

She smiles at the memory of Russell going all twitchy at

the most ordinary of sounds. He thinks everything is pointed at him, but for Del the magic is just the reverse—every lighted window is another person's life. She thinks of Calvin: their wandering walks, the moonlight over Wyldwood. She doesn't know why he should come to mind now, except that he was the start of it all. The first trembling knowledge that there is nothing ordinary about the night.

Though just then there is the whisper of tires on the road, the thin, ratcheting glide of a bicycle. It's nothing. Probably nothing. But with a faint brush of uneasiness she picks up the pace, not wandering now but heading straight home. Up the street and then over; a few blocks, that's all.

Under the glow of a distant streetlight she sees a dark figure pedal past, into the light and out. The sound fades, then grows louder. The tick-tick-tick as it circles back. Del keeps walking, straight as can be. Shoulders set, head high, sternly ignoring all possibilities. But she is aware of how short the dress is, how bare her skin. She can run if she has to. How far is it now? Two blocks. Three. Tires whisper behind her, gliding alongside.

She forces herself to glance over, and there are the long braids like dreadlocks and the quivery, patchy beard. The long coat is unbuttoned to allow him to pedal, and beneath it the rumpled suit hangs with a kind of schoolmasterly dignity as Clean carefully dismounts to wheel the bike along beside her.

It takes a moment to catch her breath. "Is that my bike?"

"I didn't think you'd mind."

"Where's Bunny?"

"She's fine. I didn't make you nervous, did I?"

"No."

The darkness begins to re-settle into its familiar shape. The clicking wheel is a comfort. Despite the wild silhouette of hair and beard, the figure beside her is strangely reassuring. For no reason they stop in the middle of an intersection; tree-lined streets lead away in every direction. He raises his face as if to sample the breeze, but it is the single, unaccompanied filigree of birdsong—five notes as perfect as a teardrop—that comes to them. The sound of serenity. The moment before everything goes wrong. "Well," he says. "Isn't that something?"

It comes to Del just like the birdsong—out of nowhere but slipping without struggle or doubt back into its waiting shape. Something in his stance, the quizzical tilting of his head.

"So, there you are," she says.

He doesn't smile, but he nods his agreement. "What did you do to your hair?" he says.

"It's a wig."

"I mean your real hair."

"I cut it off."

"I liked it."

"I cut it off when you left. I burned it and buried the ashes under the willow tree."

"I thought I felt something."

"And what about you? That hair? That beard? You look like a crazy person."

And finally he smiles, though it looks a little wistful. "That sounds about right."

DELILAH

18.

It is like that long ago birthday in reverse. They return together down the alley to the waiting gate and the yard, but this time all the widely gathered fragments of her life are in tow. As if it has taken all these years for that one night to come to an end.

"So, did he like the dress?" His voice is warm in the darkness. She doesn't look over, just listens and walks, letting the sound of him grow familiar.

"Russell? I'm not sure," she says.

"He must have liked it."

"He didn't really say."

"Didn't he seem a little jumpy at the end? I thought he seemed jumpy."

"I think a bird flew against the window."

"That would explain it," he agrees.

She feels a little bubble of stubborn anger. All these years. "I didn't need protecting."

"I know."

"You don't get to protect me. Not after all this time."

"I know."

They step in through the gate. Up ahead the kitchen windows are glowing warmly, the light falling over the little table and chairs. The whole world might be asleep, with this one small spot reserved for them. She feels a sudden flutter of nervousness that melts away the years, and she is fourteen again, returning from their walk. They used to kiss at the gate, with all the breathing darkness around them. Then she'd sneak into bed, so breathlessly full of all that her life now contained she would lie in bed for hours remembering.

Beside her now, Clean is hesitant, a study in courtesy. "I

have wine," she says. "Fruit juice. I think there's liquor in the cabinet."

He smiles at this, and Del can feel herself blush. "It's not mine," she says.

"I know."

Does he think she's putting on airs? Playing the hostess?

He says, "I wouldn't say no to coffee."

"I can do that." And suddenly hesitant, "Wait here."

Nothing could be more ordinary than the smell of coffee. It is the marker of her working day. But as she fills the pot and sets it to brew, it isn't the repeated hubbub of Café Ion that comes to her, but the first taste of it—the first she'd ever tried—sitting on the green at Wyldwood, sipping strong black coffee from a thermos as if it were a magic elixir, as if the taste of all that was to come and all that was to vanish were the same. He had asked for it then, too, and she had brought it as a kind of wild assertion of all that she was feeling. Not juice boxes or little cartons of milk. Something strange and adult and bitter tasting that made her nerves race and her heart pound.

When she steps back to the open door, mugs in hand, he is still there. She has wondered, for an instant, if he is something she has just imagined, but the night is beautiful, and now that he has turned back into himself, he seems a part of it. "I put in a ton of sugar," she says.

"Just enough."

"I have gingerbread. And coffee cake." He is waiting patiently. "Won't you please sit down?" she says.

They take their seats at the little table. He is oddly dignified in his suit, the wrinkles smoothing out in the dark. Del sits up straight in her dress. The wig lends its own snug formality; the primly crossed legs might belong to someone else. He sips the coffee slowly.

"I bought special underwear," she says. "For that night."

He might not have heard, he is sitting so still.

She doesn't tell him she threw it away years ago. It is enough that she remembers now. Little pink bows printed on white. A bra and underpants together. It had been a nightmare of embarrassment to buy, but she had imagined what he would say when he saw. She bathed and powdered and dressed and crept out and made her way through the softly singing night to the fifteenth green. And on the close-cut grass, soft as a carpet, she had waited until sunrise. When she returned, alone and woebegone, it had been to find her household in an uproar. Luanne was furious to see her, then weeping, than unable to let her go. Clinging to Del she couldn't stop murmuring, "What have I done to deserve this?"

That evening was the end of everything she knew. Her mother never released her grip on all that outrage and despair, and the stronger it grew, the more she seemed to weaken and fray. The anger carried her for three full days, and then it carried her away. And only Del, with her heart already shaken to pieces, was there to find her.

"Where were you?" she asks. But what does she want the answer to be?

In the days that followed she had wondered if maybe he was dead; and then she began to hope for it. Because only if he'd been killed, only that would explain it. But then her mother really did die, and Del knew there was no comfort in death.

"Away," he says.

She shakes her head impatiently.

"No. Away," he repeats. "Put away. Far away. Chimp time. County time. I was in jail. In juvie."

"You deserve it," she says promptly.

"You don't know what I did."

"I don't know anything about you." She grips her mug as if someone might take that away from her, too. "How long? How much time?"

"All of it."

"What? Seven years?"

"Chimps arrested me that night. Got out a couple of weeks ago."

"What were you thinking? How could you get arrested on a such an important night?"

"It isn't what I planned."

"Doing what? What was the charge?"

He hesitates for just a moment. "Burglary."

"You broke into someone's house? What did you steal?"

"It wasn't like that."

"I was waiting."

"I know."

"I was sitting under my birthday flag."

But he has no answer for that.

She is looking at him now, peering into his face, but that's no help. The voice is familiar, but the hair and beard look crazy bad, and with every word spoken she realizes how little they actually had together. She has saved it all, all the memories. Hoarded them. Woven every scrap into something huge. But now she sees that, even after all these years of remembering, he is nobody she knows.

"Don't look like that," he says.

"Like what?"

But he just shakes his head. "Was it bad?" she asks.

"Worse than foster care, but not much. I got the hang of it, after a while."

"I waited all night."

"Did you?" He is wistful. "For a long, long time, every chance I had, I imagined you there. The grass and the breeze. It was a full moon that night. Did you notice?"

"Yes."

"I saw it through the window of the police car. I hoped you were seeing it, too."

She nods. But what can she do with this now, after all these years? Every twilight walk, each imagined adventure, every Voyage of Del has been working its way toward this. But now she sees it was all an illusion. All those years of shaping the past. Because sitting here before her is the actual fact of it all. The point of all the sadness and the longing. And it's a shock to see it in the shape of something so foreign and strange.

"Look at you," she whispers. "I don't know you."

"Yes, you do."

But for a moment even the familiar voice is no match for all they have become. Then she reaches out and pinches one of the little braids of his beard. "Don't come in," she says.

"I won't."

She climbs the stairs in the tight green dress, aware of his gaze through the windows. She checks on Bunny, drowned in sleep and cast up against her pillow. Then she undresses quickly, sets the red wig on its stand, pulls on jeans and sweatshirt like a superhero in reverse, taking off her costume to prepare for an adventure. When she comes out again she has the electric clippers and a bowl of water; shaving brush, soap, and a razor. She arranges them on the table. He might be smiling; she can't tell. He sits up a little straighter.

His hair is thick and filthy; the braids are like cables. But she moves the clippers slowly, easing under each matted knot, watching the hair fall like clumps of rope. The low buzz is like a field of cicadas.

"Did you ever think about calling me? Writing me?" She is almost shy now. It feels like a question she's been asking her whole life.

"No."

She tugs a braid ungently. "You shouldn't lie to your barber."

"All the time. Every day. Day after day," he says. "But I couldn't. You were everything I had."

The shape of his head emerges. She sets to work on his jaw. The beard drops away in pieces. From the bowl she takes the shaving brush, working it over the bar of soap. He sits like a child posing for a photograph, chin raised, waiting for the flash.

She has only ever shaved her legs and now she is overly cautious. She nicks him once on the throat, but he doesn't flinch. Again on the jaw. There's a trickle of blood. "Oh!"

"Don't lose your nerve now."

She finishes slowly. Wipes his face with a towel. She runs her fingers over his cheeks, over the bristly smoothness of his head.

"Now we're twins," she says.

Bending down to press a kiss lightly on his lips, she tries to remember if it's the same; she tries to recall their kisses. There weren't so many. And this is not that shy and smooth-lipped boy. Even so. She kisses him again, feels his lips bloom.

"I'm all alone," she whispers.

"No, you're not."

"I killed my mother. I drove my father away."

"No, you didn't."

"You don't know. You don't know how it feels."

As they slip inside, the house turns strange. She has been a child living alone for too long, and now everything feels on the verge. She thinks, if only they could be in bed together, suddenly and without choice or movement, everything would be fine. It would all find its way. But he is ready to flee; she can feel it. Tense and trembling.

Maybe it's her. Now that he's seen her in the light of day, after all these years. Maybe he doesn't want her. Not that way. She doesn't know what to expect. It's only been Russell, her experience with him, that tells her there must be something more, something different. Something that fashions out of all the awkwardness and embarrassment a single thrilling moment. She used to think there was a well of passion waiting to transform her.

But now, standing here, she is only what she's always been. She catches a glimpse of herself in the glass of the kitchen cupboards. Broad, solid, unsuited to anything so high flown as romance. She has thought for so long, if he would only return, that everything would be made whole. And now he is here.

Slowly she moves closer, hoping he will touch her, hoping he will kiss her again. She plucks at his jacket. Her voice is low. "I wonder if you'd like to take a shower with me. Upstairs. We could take a shower together. Wouldn't that be nice?"

He seems to have forgotten all language but the touch of her hand. "I'm not very clean," he whispers.

"That's okay. I have soap." She is blushing. But she has latched her fingers in his, and now she is leading them up the stairs.

Del marvels at how calmly she moves. She draws the shower curtain, turns on the water. In the mirror, as the steam licks at the margins, she sees her face, a smooth mask of concentration. There are candles in the corners, on the shelves. In the past she would light them and lie in her bath alone, but now they paint the two of them with gold. She turns. Her heart is wild. She reaches up for his coat and jacket together, presses them back off his shoulders. She unbuttons his shirt. There is a second shirt beneath, and then a t-shirt. He is layered in clothes. She tugs them up out of his pants, pulls them off. He doesn't help. There is something around his neck, a woman's ring hanging from a piece of cord.

She feels a cold finger brush her heart. "Whose is that?" she asks.

"It's mine."

"From a girl?"

"Nothing like that. I've had it forever." A moment's hesitation, then he lifts it over his head and holds it out. "It's my whole life on a string."

"I'll put it over here for safe-keeping."

She sets it down beside the sink, then bends to unlace his shoes. She pulls them off. She unbuckles his belt. He is a mannequin whose only telltale life is in the rough metronome of his breathing. She unbuttons his pants. Not one, not two, but three pairs of boxers dragged as one down the length of long pale legs. He is very thin. A rivulet of dark hair trickles down his stomach and widens into a little forest within which his penis, not exactly surprising but imbued now with its own singular presence, is the only creature in the room unquelled by the moment. Hesitantly she reaches out, a little brush of greeting, as if, like a strange animal, it needed only to catch her scent to be friends.

"Wait," he says. "Now you."

She cannot distinguish dread from excitement. The warmth of the steam, the candlelight. As she draws the sweatshirt up over her head he holds his hands before her, hovering in the air, as if defining the shape of what she will become. The jeans skin down. Balanced on one foot then the next, a ballerina of grace, she pulls the legs free. He breathes a word she doesn't catch, but the look is enough. Steam coaxes her body, warms her skin. When she straightens up he still hasn't moved. His flesh is taut, his whole body straining in place.

"There's something I need to tell you," he says.

Her nervousness has vanished. His hesitancy has set her free. "Do you need to tell me now?"

"Yes."

She draws back the curtain, steps over the rim of the tub. "Tell me in here."

He is shaking, though he can't be cold. His fingers are on her hips, waist, ribs, smoothing her skin where the water has made her smooth already. She touches his chest, his belly. She takes in her hand the hard, imploring flesh. She is teasing now; who'd have thought she could tease? "What is it you want to say?"

"Oh, Del."

It catches at her, the ragged something in his voice. "What is it?"

"I can't."

"What? What do you mean?" Her hand slips away. "Why not? You like me, don't you? Calvin? You like the way I feel?"

She reaches down and lifts his hands, guiding them over her stomach, her breasts, willing him to feel how good it feels. She can sense the need in his hands, the demanding eagerness. "We're here," she whispers. "We're here together."

"I can't."

"All we have to do is touch. That's all. Nothing else. You touch me, and I'll touch you."

"You don't understand." His voice is low. "You don't know what I've done."

"It doesn't matter." She is soothing him now. Hands on his skin, stroking, smoothing. His own hands come to rest on her hips, hesitant, uncertain, but with all the weight of wanting. "It's just a shower," she whispers. "We're just taking a shower. Here." She fits a bar of soap into his fingers and, cradling his hand in hers, she moves it over her body, slowly circling her breasts, her stomach, slowly stirring into foam the dark V of her hair. Then she turns under his hand, leaning back against him. He has relinquished the soap but his hands are still slippery. They have gathered up the modest weight of her breasts. "That's nice," she murmurs. "Isn't that nice?"

And he is pressed against her, nestled in the crease of her bottom. And she reaches behind, feeling for him, touching him. His breath is panting in her ears, "Oh, Del. Oh Del," rough as sobbing. He is sobbing. Oh my God, she thinks. But his arms are wrapped around her tight. And he is weeping, weeping as if his heart will break.

DELILAH

19.

Del wakes from a dream, and though she cannot remember details, the lingering air of sadness is preserved in the dawning realization that she is alone. She lies there, listening to the silent house.

"Just sleep," she had told him. "I won't try anything funny." Fighting to keep the smile on her face; pleading with a smile.

But he lay down without touching her, uneasy in his dreams. The occasional moan or muttered cry. Once he jerked awake, wide-eyed and embarrassed. "I'm not very good at this." When he slipped out of bed it was like a piece coming loose in her chest.

Now she belts her robe and descends the stairs, tiptoes to the sofa. She peers down at the long, mysterious body cramped and tangled in its blankets. He wears a dark t-shirt and dark socks, surprisingly clean and unholed, and all the boxer shorts, three pairs, layered in little puckers of competing plaid. A warm scent rises from him, peppery and surprising.

What does it say about her that he would rather sleep like this, uncomfortable and alone? She steps behind the kitchen counter and begins to assemble the coffee, glancing at him, taking note of the parts she can see: the fragile wrist, the chapped point of the elbow. And Del thinks maybe she just doesn't understand. Maybe that's the only problem. Getting used to love, learning how it works.

She tries to imagine herself baking in the afternoon while he naps on the sofa, or busily cleaning the house around him, lifting his feet to run the vacuum over the carpet like some character from a TV show. She imagines walking home from work knowing he'll be waiting, unwrapping with each step the tiny parcel of her expectation.

When he finally stirs and turns, Del has a moment's indecision. Where should she be standing? How to look? And then he's smiling woozily up at her, blanket shyly gathered to his neck. "You're up."

"There's coffee."

He nods. He runs his tongue over sleep-dried lips. "I'll be right back." Swaddled in the blanket he stands and picks up his clothes. "Bathroom?"

She points. "Do you want some breakfast?"

"Oh, yes."

They cook eggs, toast, fried potatoes. "You have so many pots," he says. And this is better; they work easily together. But shyly she keeps glancing over, looking for some answering sign: nervousness or the prickle of excitement. Their shoulders rub. Their fingers bump and touch. They laugh. He slips a fragment of over-crisp potato between her lips. "This is what a morning on the road tastes like." He smears a little butter on the back of her thumb and licks it.

But after breakfast, when they've washed and dried the dishes and put them away, they stand uncertain. Her only point of comparison is Russell, but nothing she remembers about him seems to fit. She wishes she hadn't made the bed. Would it seem more accidental? More natural? Oh look, here we are? But she can't quite bring herself to speak.

"Do you have anything to read?" he finally asks.

The afternoon stretches on. Clean prowls the bookshelves, takes down a battered copy of *Great Expectations*. "That's my father's," she says, and then at the expression on his face, "I'm sure he won't mind. I'd like him to meet you. I'm sure you'd like each other."

But he puts the book back. Del finds herself wondering when Bunny will wake up. What does it say that they need the company? She tries to think of what to do. He glances an anxious smile; he touches her hand. He's going to leave her, she can tell.

Then there is a creak on the stairs. They both look up. Bunny stands in pajamas and Luanne's pink chenille robe, an old knit cap of Del's on her naked head. "Oh, Delilah. I'm having the strangest dream."

She is wearing the cardboard ring on her finger, the plain, plastic watch on her wrist. She carries something clutched in her hand. And Del's heart gives a little lurch. The pink chenille, the air of a lost child: it is her mother all over again. It takes a moment to see her clearly. And she realizes how dark the house has grown with the slow encroachment of dusk. "It's almost evening, Bunny. You've been sleeping a while. Can I make you some tea? Are you hungry?"

"There's coffee cake," says Clean.

Bunny turns at that. She is startled, hesitant. She's about to introduce herself to the strange young man when familiarity registers, and she regards with new interest the thin face, naked and young. "My goodness. I thought you were someone else. Oh, I'm so glad you're here."

And Del can't help it; she feels a little pang at the note of welcome in her voice, the sudden lively tone.

"I was dreaming about him. About Bill. He said he needed me. He needed me to find him. But he couldn't say where he was. I think something's happened."

Her attention is all on Clean, but he stands wordlessly, unable to shape an answer. It is left to Del to say, "It's all right. It was just a dream."

"That's what I thought. I woke up and I thought it was just my mind playing tricks. But then I found this." She opens her clenched fist and there on the palm is Clean's childhood ring on its puddled loop of twine.

And now Del is at a loss. She tries to think of what to say. What would Luanne have wanted to hear at a time like this?

Where would the comfort lie? "It's a beautiful ring," she says finally.

"Yes. But don't you see? It can't be here. It's my mother's ring. It's the one I was telling you about." Her eyes are back on Clean. "It's Bill's. It's mine. It's the ring I buried. It's gone forever. Don't you see? Touch it." He tries to pull his hand away but she presses it into his palm. "Can you feel it?"

"Yes."

"Oh, please. I don't want to be crazy."

"You're not," says Del soothingly. "You're not crazy." And she waits for Clean to explain. Waits for him to tell her the truth about his childhood ring. But he says not a word.

Now Bunny is turning it in the morning light. She is looking unsure. She tries to slip it on her finger but the twine gets in the way.

"It's been so long," says Del. "I don't see how it's possible."

"But it has to mean something, doesn't it? The ring, the watch?"

Del speaks as gently as she can. "They're not the same. It's not the same watch."

"But don't you see? The watch that isn't the watch. The ring that isn't the ring. He was there in my dreams. He was calling for help. How can it not mean something?"

And now Clean is the one who takes her hands, anchoring her in the insistence of his touch. "Remember, Bunny? The lawyer? The photographs? You have to believe him, Bunny. He's gone. I'm sorry, but he's dead."

"No! He's not! Don't say that! You know he's not. He's waiting somewhere. He needs my help. It's a test. Don't you see? He's testing me. He wants to see if I'll let him down again. I ran away once. But I thought he would forgive me. I thought he would come. But he sent me the most awful letter. He dropped it through the slot. No postage. Do you understand? He came all that way, walked right up to my door, and then he walked away again. But now he's giving me another chance. It's a test of love.

Don't you see? It has to be. After all this time it would be too cruel if it were anything else."

And Clean is lost at that, his inspiration run dry. He stands there, bleak and helpless under her gaze.

And Del feels a little spasm of grief. As if Bunny has forgotten her completely. As if she's moved on. And it startles her, after so long, to feel that again. To feel like a child again, left out and abandoned.

But Bunny's eyes are fixed on Clean, a guardian angel who can't quite meet her eyes. "You remember, dear. What the lawyer said. The shelter. He would go there sometimes, when he was feeling low."

"What shelter?" says Del. "What are you talking about?

"He's not there, Bunny. He can't be there."

"He might."

"He's not. It's nowhere you want to go."

"Yes," she says. "It is."

And Del thinks, *Please. Don't leave me. Don't leave me behind.*

They are walking, and it's as if every moment has conspired to wipe away all she has tried to preserve. Out at night again, together, after all these years. And it feels nothing like it should. There is the pale, blooming crown of the crabapple and the fragrant air holding out its welcoming hands. And Bunny is alive to every moment, and Clean is lean and steady. And it's only Del who is out of place. Who is afraid of the dark. Who is nervous at every sound.

They have dressed for it. Clean's dark suit and Del's voyaging clothes. Bunny has no dark clothes of her own, so she buckles herself into Del's, cinching the jeans tight, swimming in the dark hoodie. They walk out the gate, down the alley. Del tries to atune herself to the moonlight, but all the world is strange. Every corner is a new choice. Clean leads the way. Under their feet the alley peters out into cracked and crumbly asphalt, and trees give way to weeds and then the sudden high brick walls of the city.

Of course it's the sounds she notices first. The scuff of their steps off the high brick walls. The distant murmur of voices. And then, as if rising out of the muffled noise, the smell of rotting food comes to her. And urine and worse. It seems not so much gradually to fill the air as to transform it: a whole story of unhappiness and despair that only her nose can read.

"Is this right?" says Del. "Are you sure this is the way?"

"We're just walking. There's nothing to it. People walk all the time. Just don't look. Don't make eye contact."

"What? What do you mean?"

Though out of the corner of her eye she sees Bunny nod to herself, as if recognizing the requirements of an adventure. "What else?" she asks.

"Don't stop walking."

"Is it dangerous?" asks Del.

"Can't you feel it?"

"Are you making fun of us?" She reaches out impulsively to clutch his sleeve.

"Don't touch," he warns.

She snatches back her hand.

"Don't touch. Don't put your hands in your pockets. Don't make any sudden moves."

And then she notices, in the darkness around them, the alley is growing crowded. An inventory of debris: cinder blocks, dumpsters, rolls of ancient plastic, leaning walls of cardboard, and amid them all the shadows of huddled figures, hunched and sleeping. She tells herself there is nothing to fear, but Clean is murmuring now under his breath, raising his hands in little gestures of greeting. And Del sees the figures shifting, climbing to their feet.

There isn't enough room. She tries to give them space, but they surge slowly forward into their path. Then Clean is dipping into his pocket, drawing out small chocolates wrapped in foil, gleaming even in the darkness. The men snatch them gently, whisking them out of his grip. They take whatever he offers and back away. One brushes at the air as if Del is a mosquito he is trying to repell.

"Keep moving."

Clean is nodding, showing his hands again, empty now. They are moving past. Bunny hesitates, and a few of the figures start forward again. "Don't stop. Don't look."

They are at the end of the alley, opening onto a street, poised on the edge of emptiness. The whole broad stretch of Elm Street without a car in sight. Del feels exposed under the sudden glow of the streetlamps, but it's nothing, an ordinary street. And as they slip across and back into an alley, into the narrowing darkness, she feels an odd, distorted shape to the world, as if they must squeeze their bodies to fit.

The smells change. The mixture of competing odors like a canine world of scents and trails. There are, she notices, more men here, lurking at the edges, nestled into the corners. Del feels a kind of hollow wonder. "Is this where you live?"

"Me? No. This is all rags and paws."

She glances up, as if he might be joking. "Rags and what?"

She wishes he were smiling. Instead he looks as if it takes him a moment to remember who she is. "Everybody's different. Folks divide up. Freddies are all the cake and candy people, all the lawns and shiny rooms. Then there's everybody else. Rags and roadies, sticks and rollers. Thumbs, boots, scrags, cartmen, trainmen, paws, jobbers, rats, and feelies."

"It takes a lot of folk to make a world," Bunny murmurs.

"Who would come here?" Del asks. "Who would live here?"

"Not here," says Clean. "Up ahead. Our Lady of the Sorrows."

"Is that what it's called?" asks Bunny.

"It's what they're all called."

Though, in fact, the shelter doesn't seem to have a name. Del's heart sinks at the sight of it. She wants to protect Bunny from all that they're seeing, but Bunny doesn't seem to need her protection. It's a grim storefront with a pair of wide windows soaped into murky swirls. A few figures gather outside, little knots of inaction. A hunched and bleakly expectant man stands at the open door with a black coat and the vaguely disappointed air of a maître d'.

"All souls welcome. Come and ease your burdens." He gives Clean barely a glance, though he peers a little vaguely at Del as she slips past.

Inside it's narrow and grim. The air smells stale, like a sick-room during mealtime. Rickety chairs and tables cluster before a ramshackle serving station with baskets of bread and crackers, crockpots of soup, pitchers of reconstituted milk. There is a rough kitchen, pieced together from steel racks and tables, and a charred, ancient stove that might have been dragged from the wreckage of one too many restaurant fires.

Clean glances back at her. "Never pass up a meal." She can't tell if he's joking, even when he plucks a slice of orange cheese from a tray on his way past.

Del stays close, peering around. The men are sitting at tables, bent low over their food—a collection of ragged coats and scarves and hats. Then one of the men turns, mouth open, chewing earnestly, and just for a second—for no reason she can imagine—Del thinks of her father. She remembers the dirt stiff on his clothes, his hands, the fatigue that bent his shoulders at the end of the day when he didn't realize she was watching. And suddenly all the divisions are gone between what is possible and what is not. It is, she realizes, very loud. The creak of chairs, the scrape of bowls and spoons, the churning murmur of voices. She is buffeted by the noise.

There is a grip on her hand. Bunny is beside her. "I don't see him. He's not here."

Clean nods, as if he has expected as much. He's nibbling a piece of bread without any sign of enjoyment. Del feels a sudden, panicky breathlessness at the sight of him, fitting so smoothly into this terrible scene. She doesn't remember everything from their first week together, though she has held onto the quiet, the peace, the low building excitement as they walked and talked through the empty suburban streets. But now.

"Let's not do this any more," she says. "Let's go home."

"We can't just give up." Bunny's grip is still fierce. "He needs us. He's waiting for us."

Clean touches the sleeve of one of the men overseeing the food. He turns, and just for a moment Del half expects to recognize him. But he's just a thin and bearded man. "One of our guests?" he says, and there is no trace of a smile, as if the language of hospitality has already been crushed under the weight of all that's true.

"Bill." says Bunny. "His name is Bill."

And it seems absurd now, hopeless. Del wants nothing but to leave. To run away.

"Could he have mentioned me? My name is Bunny."

And the man smiles. It is the nature of the world that there are moments, hidden points, on which the slightest breath of weight will bear and open wide the secret doors. "Bunny? He said you might come by."

"He's here?"

"Not now. We haven't seen him for a while."

"But he's all right?"

"He was. I can't say fairer than that."

"Wait," says Del. "Just wait. He lives here?"

"No. He stops by, helps out. He sweeps and cleans. Sometimes he helps cook. Sometimes he reads."

"Did he leave me a message?" Bunny asks.

"Not a message. Let me see." He goes out through a doorway and emerges again, carrying a little bundle. "This is all he left."

"For me?"

"I couldn't say for sure."

Bunny takes it eagerly, sets it on a table and hurriedly begins unfolding. It is a work shirt, dirty and stained, wrapped around nothing at all. She stands over it, startled and unsure.

"What does it mean? I thought there would be something more."

But Del has seen this shirt before. Faded and stained, it hasn't been new in years. She turns it over. Printed across the back, creased and flaking: *Lawnkeepers Grass and Grounds.* She had always hated the name.

DELILAH

20.

Del tries to remember the last time she's seen her father. The last time he stopped by to sit with her in the yard. She tries to count off the days: not last week, or the week before, or the week before that. And she realizes with a sinking heart that she hasn't thought about him for such a long time. Even more than that, she has no idea at all who he is.

She gazes bleakly at Bunny. "Let's not do this any more. Let's just go home."

"We can't give up," says Bunny. "He needs us."

Clean hesitates. And that, at least, is a kind of comfort, thinks Del. He's as left out as I am.

"Where else would he go?" Bunny demands.

"Nowhere," says Clean.

"He's got to be somewhere. You're thinking somewhere. I can tell."

"He's not going to be there."

"We have to try."

"You can't get your hopes up."

"Is it like this?" Del asks.

"No," he says. "Not exactly."

The alleys seem almost familiar now. After the noise and crowding of the shelter the way stands open and clear. Clean is silent as he walks, hovering on the verge of speech.

"What's the matter?" says Del.

"Nothing."

"How far is it?"

"Almost there."

Another intersection. Not a street this time, but a widening of the alley—a clearing in the crowded pressure of concrete and brick. Before them rises the back of a dark stone mansion, adapted now to more pedestrian times. A low brick annex has been added on: a two-story afterthought.

Clean eyes the building as if it were a problem he had hoped to avoid. The upper windows are dark. The wall is sheer. "I'll be back," he says. "Don't get arrested."

And then he is clambering up the stained bulk of a dumpster, hoisting himself to the lip and standing shakily. "Is that safe?" whispers Del.

He doesn't reply. He is reaching across the sheer wall to the thin plumb line of a drainpipe. Then he steps into the middle of the air and grabs the short stub of a ladder hanging down from the fire escape. With a clatter it ratchets down, depositing him awkwardly on the sidewalk.

"That's a nice trick," she says.

"I had a good teacher."

"I'm afraid," says Bunny, "my best days in the circus are behind me."

"I'll just be a minute."

Up he scrambles out of sight. Time passes. The silence of the alley gives way to the distant sounds of traffic. Del is wondering how she could ever have thought she was made for adventure, when a blank-faced door opens beside the dumpster and Clean emerges. It's like a magic trick.

He leads them up the narrow stairs and across the gravel roof, circling the dark mass of an air conditioner, edging toward the brownstone rising above them. Del has queasy visions of a second drainpipe or the narrow fingerholds between blocks of stone, but he just strolls to a window. The sill is too high, but instead of looking up he bends down. There are loose bricks scattered. He draws them into an unsteady pile.

"Isn't that lucky," Bunny whispers.

The window lifts smoothly with barely a sound. Then he's up, a too-sudden leap, toppling all the bricks and squirming over the sill, vanishing with a last flutter of feet like a swimmer kicking for bottom.

Moments pass. That seems to be the end of the trick. "I think we need more bricks," says Bunny.

But Clean is leaning out the window, a heavy janitor's bucket hanging from his hand. Del upends it on the roof. "Anything else?"

After a moment he's at the window again. A steel wastebasket, a plastic storage box, and finally, as if the point of the exercise is only gradually becoming clear, a folding step-stool three treads high. They ascend like royalty through the window.

Tiled walls catch the gleam of moonlight, arrays of plumbing. "Is this a bathroom?" Del whispers.

"We have to be quiet."

"I don't suppose we have a plan?"

The building is silent and cloaked in shadow. The air smells of dust and another scent, familiar but unnamed until they see, by the faint glow of distant windows, the high shelves of books crowded beneath low ceilings. Understanding is like a sunrise. "My father used to bring me here."

"Me, too," says Clean.

"Your father brought you here?"

"More or less. A long time ago."

"Let's go to the library, Calvin? That sort of thing?"

"I thought it was so he could push me off the roof."

They are moving slowly; Clean leads the way. They skirt a wide stone staircase and arrive at a pair of heavy oak doors. Stepping through they enter a room made huge by the darkness. High windows let in a grey glow of moonlight. Low shelves edge the walls. In the middle a shadowy circle of broad leather armchairs hunch like boulders in the gloom.

Clean hesitates, then he leads the way into the center of the circle and stops with an air of quiet formality. "I'm Clean," he says softly. "Do you remember me?"

There is a long silence. Then a muffled click. A narrow light comes on, shining from the depths of a leather chair. It plays over his squinting face, over the dark coat, the wrinkled suit, then it turns blindingly on Del, picking her out too brightly in the darkness. Just as suddenly, it's off, and the room is darker than before.

"Strangers," snaps a voice, pettish and irritable. "I say we kill them and bury them in Biography."

"What?" gasps Del, but Clean finds her hand in the darkness as other voices rise.

"You've never liked Biography."

"I like it fine."

"Digital resources. Now that's a waste hole."

"We could bury them there."

"Don't be silly. It's the first place anyone would look."

"That's enough," said another voice. "I think you're frightening them." And more soothingly now, "There's no cause for alarm. We haven't had to kill anyone for such a long time. And if we did, I'm sure we wouldn't bury them in Biography. I think that's just one of Langston's little jokes. Though last year there was that unpleasant man who broke in during the winter storm. He was perfectly awful. He wanted to use the books to start a fire. Can you imagine? In a library? Well, of course, he had to go. But it does make you wonder about people, doesn't it? Besides, that's Clean. We know Clean."

"I don't know him."

"Of course you do."

A second flashlight clicks on and steadies; then a third and a fourth. Clean stands calmly, eyes closed against the glare. The light paints his newly shorn hair like a fine mist. The skin around his eyes is red and raw. "See? You remember him."

There is a grudging murmur. "Maybe."

Two of the lights shift and settle on Del. She braces against them. "I don't know this one. I say we kill him. And his friend." As if marking their agreement, all the lights switch off.

"Hey!" says Del. "I'm not a him. I'm a girl!"

"You know me," says Clean, "and they're with me. You know me, so you know them."

In the darkness there is a low grumble of debate, then the flashlights come on again. In the spilling glare Del can make out the figures. They look tiny in the overstuffed chairs, neatly polished shoes hanging well short of the floor. And though they are all dressed in mismatched clothing, the effect is an oddly dapper one. They wear sweaters, ties, scarves, pocket handkerchiefs—a host of decorations that have nothing to do with warmth. And they smell of dust. The dust of books, of unswept shelves, of paper left to disintegrate under the weight of years. Each has a light, some as tiny as pencils, some strapped like miner's lamps to their foreheads. They sit easily in the silence like trout in the current, but when they speak it is with a bark of irritation that seems to have been years building. "What is it they want?"

"They can't just come in here."

"Clean was just a boy. That's not a boy."

"That one's a boy."

"I'm a girl!"

"And who's the third?"

"She's a girl, too."

"We've brought presents," says Clean.

As one, the figures lean forward in sudden interest, and Del sees that what she has taken for small, lumpish men are women. Hair cut short and every shade from grey to white, feathering out in the glow of the lamps. Their faces are hawk-like, lined and fierce, and they all wear glasses or have them close at hand, peaking out of pockets or hanging from chains around their necks.

"Well, this one has manners at least," someone mutters gruffly. "That's not the worst thing."

Clean's hand dips into his pocket, and hesitates. When he draws it out there is a single remaining Hershey's Kiss. Del can feel the temperature of the audience drop.

"That's it?"

"Well, push your heart back in."

"What are we supposed to do with that?"

But now she is reaching into her own pockets for the snacks she has inevitably packed. Carefully wrapped brownies and slices of cake and some pieces of the new gingerbread. "I have them," says Del. "He asked me to carry them. He reminded me not to leave them behind."

She turns toward the grumpiest voice, but too fast. There's a startled breath, and all the lights go out. Del freezes. "Sorry," she murmurs. "I'm sorry."

The silence fills with a low muttering like a ruffled flock of hens, and then one by one the lights come back. Now Del can see, along with the glasses and the ties and the scarves, each lap is decorated with a thin gleam of steel, casually resting on a trouser leg or folded in the old hands: letter openers, scissors, and in one lap, startlingly out of place, an old carving knife.

"Excuse me," says Del. And carefully she holds out the gingerbread to a fierce little woman in a red bowtie, who plucks it from her fingers, brisk as a bird, and settles back in her chair.

"Well, she has nice manners."

"Not so nice. Didn't she bring one for me?"

"I don't think we like her."

"I don't know why she came. I wish she'd leave."

"I don't see why we can't kill her. No one ever looks in Biography."

But Del is hurrying now, distributing the treats. "This is gingerbread. I just baked this. And that's a brownie. There's some pound cake, but it's a couple of days old."

"I often think it's better that way," says a woman graciously.

"All right. I've change my mind. He might be nice."

"It's a girl."

"Doesn't mean he can't be nice."

"That Clean is nothing."

"He's with Book. And Book was nice. You know he was."

"Oh, Ivy. You always had a little crush on him, I think."

"It wasn't a crush! We were just being polite."

And Del realizes that, of course, they are talking about her father. "Wait," she says.

"Presents are always appreciated. My mother used to keep a whole bureau crowded with presents, just in case one was needed."

"Please...." Her voice is a whisper.

"My mother had a whole closet of wrapping paper and ribbon, ready at a moment's notice."

"Please!" says Del. "You said *was*."

"What?"

"He *was* nice. Has something happened?"

There is an instant's hesitation, then the flashlights click raggedly off, and they are standing in darkness again.

"Oh, good, Fish," one says bitterly.

"How was I to know?"

"It's not as if we decided to tell them."

"You knew my father?" says Del. "When? How?"

She gets no reply. But the library ladies are alive on the subject.

"Father? Oh, that can't be right."

"Is this the one? The girl?"

"Oh, the poor thing."

"It could be."

"We should ask her."

"Maybe just her name."

"We could start with that."

"Delilah," she says. "Delilah Belle."

"No. That's not right."

"That's not the name."

"Didn't he say sweet pea?"

"I think that was just a joke."

"Delphinium."

"Del," she says. "My name is Del."

"Well, that could be right."

"And this is Bunny," says Del.

And every voice stops. The lights click back on.

"That can't be Bunny."

"That's not Bunny."

"She's nothing but a boy."

"That isn't how I thought she'd look."

"We heard you were dying."

"Not quite," says Bunny. "Not just yet."

"We heard you were getting married."

"My daughter. Ruth."

"That's right. He said her name was Ruth."

"He said you might come looking for him."

Bunny takes a moment to answer. "Did he?"

"He said you might."

And Del feels herself slipping, coming unanchored. "Wait," she says. "I don't understand."

"What don't you understand?"

"What's happening?"

"Well, what has Clean told you?"

"Clean?"

"He must have explained."

"Surely he has."

"No. How? How would he know?" Del turns to face him in the dim light. "How?"

Clean swallows. His mouth opens, but he can't make the words come out.

"Oh, heavens," the ladies cluck. "Everybody knows."

"Book and Clean. They go way back."

"Here and there."

"Miles and miles between them."

"Friends forever. That's what Book said."

"Like a son to him."

Clean's voice catches now, rusty with effort. "He said that?"

"Like family, he said."

"They had a falling out."

"What family doesn't?"

"I don't understand," whispers Del.

"Oh, my dear."

But her eyes are on Clean. "You knew my father?"

"It was a long time ago."

"You knew him?"

"Oh, Del."

"I think," says the gentlest voice, "a little food will do us good. And Bunny needs to get off her feet." As if on signal the room goes dark. Del feels a small hand on her arm, urging her into motion. "You'll join us for a bite, won't you, dear? My name is Ivy, by the way."

"Ivy?"

"Compton-Burnett. She's always been one of my favorites."

They are led out of the room. Emerging into the main hallway, far from the windows, the flashlights come on again, guiding them over the marble floors.

"The secret of a quiet life," says Ivy. "I think we'd all prefer candles. They're so much nicer. And books are such old-fashioned things. But the smell of smoke. Someone's bound to notice. And an open flame among all this paper. Just imagine. No. We can't always have things just the way we want." She pats her hand. "Though I think everyone here appreciates the microwave."

Down in the basement the small group seems to disintegrate, lights dispersing, bobbing away through archways, around corners, leaving Del and Bunny and Clean alone with their guide.

"Where is everyone going?" asks Del.

"They've gone to dress. We don't have many chances to wear our nicest things. And Beatrix has been saving a plum cake for as long as I can remember."

It had been a storeroom once, when the library was new, but as the need for book space was gradually replaced by the need for anything but, it was converted into a snack room. White plaster walls and ceiling; tables and chairs to match. The only color comes from the imposing bank of vending machines lined up against one wall.

"They're really just a tease," says Ivy. "Langston figured out almost immediately how to open them, but they're quite obsessive about keeping track. If they suddenly started losing Snickers bars, even the slowheads are bound to wonder."

They gather at a round white table. Someone sets out a lantern, and the glow turns the whole room into a bubble of light. They have unpacked an array of delicacies: cookies, crackers, fruit rollups, canned peaches, the tail end of a loaf of bread; cans of deviled ham, sardines, and peanuts; a bag of raisins, a tube of powdered donuts, and three cans of microwave beef stew, open and steaming. Before each woman is a tea cup and saucer, each different, each delicately glinting. An enormous china teapot claims the center, painted with ferns and woodland creatures, a pert porcelain chipmunk clinging to the spout. The women bustle cheerfully, directing each other to take a little more or a little less. "Once we open it, we have to eat it all."

The scent of chamomile fills the room.

"Isn't it nice to have guests," says Margery. She wears an ancient hat of felt and flowers with the crushed and rehabilitated air of something stored too often in a space too small. "I'm only sorry Book couldn't be here to enjoy his delicious stew."

"These are his cookies, as well."

Langston frowns. "The Fig Newtons are mine. Though of course he'd be welcome to them."

Del's mind is slow and reeling. Her throat is tight. "Thank you for your hospitality."

"You're very welcome, dear. Book was like family."

"Yes," she says. "I need to ask about that, too."

"We should tell her."

"I don't know. It's not a pretty thing," says Margery.

"And we can't be sure."

"We heard there are some people," Ivy says. "That's all. That might be all. Over in the woods. New people. Looking for someone."

"Police?" says Clean.

"Nobody nice. They broke the Padre's fingers."

Del shakes her head. The low light, the stuffy room. It all seems to fall just short of sense. "But what does this have to do with anything?"

"And then there's the stew."

"I think so. Yes."

"Book always stops by. Every few days. Brings us treats."

"He mentioned some bakery cookies," Langston says wistfully. "From that shiny place over on Clement."

"But last time he returned his books. All of them. It was a month ago."

"And he brought stew. Three cans of it."

"He told us to save it for you."

Del stares in surprise. "For me?"

"For all of you. He said you'd be hungry. And nervous. And maybe a little frightened."

"He knew we were coming?"

"He said to feed you. Try to comfort you."

Sitting in the lamplight Bunny looks almost unsurprised. Her face is pale and calm. "What else did he say?"

"He said to tell you it was okay."

"What was okay?" says Del. "What's happened?"

"He's dead," whispers Clean.

"What?"

"I don't believe that," says Bunny.

"I know," says Ivy. "But here's the thing. He had something on his mind. Something bad. Someone was coming. Someone he knew. Someone was coming for him. He said his past was catching up."

Clean leans forward. "He said that? From his past?"

Bunny's eyes are bleak in the too-bright light. "Did he say

who?"

"He said he needed to lay low. He said he had to get away. But it's not an easy thing to hide from your past. And it's been a while. We've had no word. We're beginning to think the past has come and gone."

"What are you saying?" Del demands. "That doesn't make any sense."

"I'm sorry, Delphinium.

"But it can't be true. I don't believe it."

"I know, dear."

Bunny's voice is barely a whisper. "I don't think I can bear it."

"No, dear. I know."

"But what are we supposed to do?" says Del.

Ivy pats her hand gently. "He said you should talk to the Padre."

"At the Chapel. Near the Backbone."

Del shakes her head despairingly "What if we don't know what that is?"

"And he told us to give you the nine rules."

"Why?" says Clean bitterly. "Did he think I'd forget?"

But the women ignore him and each in turn chimes in, adding her part to the spell.

"Don't hurry."

"Don't dawdle."

"Don't touch."

"Don't get lost."

"Don't be stupid."

But it's too late. Del is already lost, already stupid. Though Bunny is nodding as if this is exactly what she has expected. It is a dream, after all. Every dream has its rules.

"Don't whine."

"Don't get close."

"Don't fall behind."

Each rule locks itself into place. "That's only eight," says

Del.

"Don't go into the woods. That's the last one. That's the one you always have to keep in mind."

"And one more thing," says Ivy. "He told us to give you this. If it looks bad."

She reaches into the darkness at her feet and lays something on the table before them. It's an old, illustrated edition of *Huckleberry Finn*. The cover has gone brown with all the miles. There's an old string tied around it twice and knotted to keep it closed. Del can only stare. "My father left us this?"

"If things got bad."

It makes no sense. But when she glances up at Clean his expression is pinched and anguished. He cannot bring himself to touch the book, so Del reaches out. She brushes her fingers across the cover, cautiously draws on the string. The knot pulls free.

"Page twenty-six," says Ivy.

She turns the pages, opens the volume wide. Nestled there, where someone has painstakingly cut a vacancy into the heart of the book, lies a dark, short-nosed revolver.

"Jesus." Clean's breath is a whisper.

"What? What does it mean?"

"He said you'd know," says Ivy. "He said Clean would know."

Del turns. His face is a mask of sadness, disbelief. His hands are clenched on his lap, as far from the gun as they can be. "What is it?" she repeats.

He doesn't reply. But after a moment he reaches out and lifts it heavily from the book. There's a cold knot now beneath her ribs. And there is something in the solid heft of it, the incontrovertible weight— the way he cannot take his eyes from it—that sinks the cold certainty into her heart. "What have you done?" she whispers. "What have you done? Is he dead? Did you shoot him?"

He grasps at that. "No."

"Is that yours?"

And it looks as though he might have spoken if only his voice had worked, if only his throat hadn't sealed itself shut. But it is Bunny who answers. Who gazes sadly at the gun and says, "Never mind, dear. It's mine."

Part Five

Bunny

BUNNY

21.

They return to the house. Impossible as it seems they fall asleep. Everybody dreams. In her bed Delilah tosses and moans. On the sofa Clean tangles himself in a knot of blankets.

In the comfort of cool sheets Bunny goes on a journey. There is a landscape that is almost familiar. A voice urging her to move, to play, to be strong, to pay attention. There is a feeling of excitement that seems to inhabit every moment. When she wakes it's with a certainty that she has recovered something, something important, though she is unable to recall exactly what it is.

But, the Padre. She remembers the Padre. That, at least, is real. That has been a gift to her.

She smiles as she climbs out of bed, smiles at the black jeans and sweatshirt draped over a chair, the orange, well-worn dress. She is surrounded by other people's clothes. If she is going to meet her past, she needs to look like herself. There is the grey silk dress, of course, but it has lived through better days. Still. It will get her where she needs to go. She slips it on, snugs down the silver wig.

Down the stairs she goes, light as can be. Past the sprawled figure on the sofa, clutching at the pillows as if his dreams are trying to wrestle them away. She writes a quick note: *Gone to get my things.* She starts to write *See you soon,* or *Let's have lunch together,* but that seems too ordinary for all that she is feeling. Instead she ends with: *I can see the future, and we'll all be in it.* She slips out the door with a smile. Back in no time, she thinks. Back before you're awake.

She calls a cab.

All those years ago no one had mentioned the Nine Rules.

They had gone into the forest, the two of them, and the forest had welcomed them. A whole new world—far from anything that shaped their ordinary lives. And they had met the Padre, just like that. As much a part of the forest as they were. We should get married, Bill said. A May wedding can be beautiful. Bunny remembers the excitement but not the place. The wonder of it. The hope. No, not hope. It was a game they were playing. But the sense of possibility! How many of the most crucial moments in our lives are founded on the strange and unconnected? How often do we find our way only because we're not afraid to be lost?

It was, perhaps, the one time in her life that she was unafraid. Perhaps that's what it means to find the best of yourself. She had broken free for a moment, a week, three weeks. It seems incredible now: a lifetime of freedom squandered in such a short time. Is it really so beyond the realm of possibility that some portion of that might remain?

She feels it now; she feels the way the universe is sending out little threads of connection. Delilah, Clean. The house, the tree, the moments of illumination that seem to promise a fuller understanding.

How is it that it's sometimes the most fragile moments that survive?

The cab pulls up in front of the hotel. Bunny climbs out. Around her people come and go, calm and well dressed, unruffled by possibility. The rich softness of the lobby carpet makes her smile. Her room key is somehow still in her purse—its own little miracle. It feels like ages since she's been here. Gather up her suitcase, pay her bill. The feeling of hope is like wings.

But her room startles her. It's a shambles. The bed is rumpled, the cushions of the sofa tumbled off. Pillows are scattered on the floor. It gives her a bad moment, a little flutter of panic. In her mind it was pristine, but now she wonders what it says about her that she could leave it this way. That she could walk away from such a mess and reconstruct it in her mind.

So when she walks in and sees Bertie Clutter sitting calmly in the corner her first response is embarrassment. "Oh, Bertie. I'm so sorry that you should see it like this. This isn't like me at all." Though even as she says it, she wonders if it's true.

But Bertie is smiling. Kind and gentlemanly Bertie. Trim in his grey suit. Pale-crowned and tidy. He would never leave a room like this. "Welcome, Bunny. How nice to see you. Please come in. I hope you don't mind. I asked the desk to let me know when you arrived."

Bunny smiles. She feels a little flush of affection. And something else. Her life has not prepared her for this. There has been a marked absence of gentleman callers, and Roger has never required much delicacy of handling. She will have to be gentle. Still, it's nice to be thought of.

"I'm not really dressed for company."

"It is unexpected, I know. But I'm not sure how much longer I'll be in town. And we had such a nice time the other night." His expression is shining behind the heavy, black spectacles. His bald head gleams earnestly. "I'm making us some coffee. And I thought you might like some cookies."

"How did you get in?"

He offers her a little smile of triumph. "I'll tell you over coffee." And rising from the chair he steps into the little kitchenette.

The coffee does smell wonderful. And she's going to need a little pick-me-up to help her let him down gently. She steps in, searching for something playful to say about the time of day or the gallery or the mess in the hotel room, something to get them off on the right foot.

He has put an apron on over his suit. It is blue and white. Unexpectedly frilly. He gestures jauntily with what she recognizes, after a moment, is a pancake spatula. "Please sit down. I'm so glad we have a moment alone. I had no idea you'd be so busy." But before she can speak he says, "Let me get these cookies out and then we can talk."

"This is very sweet, Bertie. But I'm in a bit of a rush. Why don't we just meet for coffee tomorrow?"

"Not a bit of it." He is leaning cheerfully over the small oven, and with a clatter draws out the baking pan and sets it on top. "I wonder if I should have made tea. I didn't think to ask. But coffee is so much better for you. And it's soothing. Especially for a woman in your delicate condition."

A pair of stools offer the comforts of a romantic *tête-à-tête*. Bunny perches a little awkwardly, balancing against the counter. His fussy, distracted air makes her smile: the too-bright, uncomfortable setting he's chosen for his romantic confession. She hopes he isn't a man whose feelings can be hurt.

He scoops cookies onto a plate. There is a blue and white coffeepot Bunny has never before seen. As she watches, he bends to a dark nylon satchel on the floor and retrieves from it two matching cups and saucers, a sugar bowl, and a small pitcher which he sets on a tray. Then he turns to open the little fridge. "Hmmm. I thought as much. I wasn't sure if you'd have time to shop." He takes from the satchel a small carton of milk and fills the pitcher. "In my line of work I find it's such a satisfaction to be prepared."

"I'm sure that's true. You work with Roger? I've never really been sure what Roger does. Are you a lawyer, as well?"

"In a sense." He is pleased with her interest, slipping into the cheerful pedantic tone of one rarely asked about himself. "I deal with lawyers, certainly. But arbitration is really my field. Nowadays there are so many different things to do with the law. So many sources of conflict. Litigation is so expensive and unreliable. Increasingly businesses are moving into the sort of behind-the-scenes work that I've made my own."

It occurs to Bunny to wonder if she's dreaming. If this is one of those complicated illusions of waking, where everything moves by its own separate logic. She's aware of something strange about the light; that little chemical dip. But if this is a dream, it's not one she's had before. And certainly the smell of the cookies is real if anything is. Besides, if she's dreaming him now, wouldn't that mean she had dreamt him at the museum? And Del was there, so either he was real, or Delilah had dreamt him, too. Or, and this is even more troubling, Bunny has dreamt them both. Dreamt everything.

But then she realizes it's merely time for her pills. The knowledge is reassuring. The dry mouth, light-headedness. Everything has an explanation. Everything is fine. She starts to climb from the stool.

"Please don't," says Bertie. He holds up a hand. "I need your attention."

"I just have to get a pill."

"This won't take long."

So she concentrates on being interested, to see if that will help, to see what happens next. He places a cup of coffee beside her. "Milk and sugar?"

"Just sugar please."

His forehead creases a little in disappointment. "I brought milk. But I should have known. I suppose I should have double-checked. But there's a sense of companionability, a sense of discovery that you lose, if you're too prepared. Don't you think so? It's nice to be surprised. I mean, by the little things. I'm not really one for big surprises. Are you?"

Bunny hesitates. "I suppose it depends."

"And I think sometimes two people are so fated to meet, that there's something substantial to even their earliest connection. Don't you think that?"

"I think that's very sweet," she says. "But I'm a little tired, Bertie. Do you think we could continue this tomorrow?"

"It will just take a moment. And I have to say," he smiles, "I'm a little nervous. A moment like this. So much depends…," he hesitates. "On so much, really. You're not what I expected."

"Aren't I?"

"Is that a terrible thing to say? It makes it sound as if you're being judged, doesn't it? No one likes that. Though it's true, isn't it? More often than we like to think. We're always being judged. Always being considered. I spend so much of my working day considering. It's really my only skill."

Bunny sips her coffee. It's very good. She is hoping it will somehow make sense of things. "Considering what?" she asks.

His eyes gleam appreciatively. "That's always the question, isn't it? Isn't that always the point? You're thin, of course. And a little wan. Peaked, my mother would have said. Overall, a little frail. That's to be expected, given all you've been through. But your prognosis is good. That must be a comfort. Your doctor said they had a healthy margin around the edges. He's confident they got it all. That must be reassuring. These," he says, as he sets the cookies on the counter between them, "are an old family recipe. Nothing more comforting than freshly baked."

He makes no move to try one but gazes down at the plate. "I have a problem, Bunny. And in the way of the world, that means that you have a problem."

"I'm sorry, Bertie. I don't understand."

"Oh, Bunny." Behind the heavy glasses his eyes looked hurt. "Let's not go that way. There's no need to go that way. Look. We have coffee, we have cookies. This could be so friendly. We can drink our coffee, and go our separate ways, pleasant as can be."

Bunny licks her lips. The coffee is no substitute for those little white pills. "You don't think there's been some kind of mistake?"

"I think there has, yes. And that's exactly why I'm here. I'm here to put everything back the way it was. But it needn't be awkward. Here we are, Bertie and Bunny. We sound like friends already. And they're such perfect names. They just make you smile. You can't be afraid of a Bertie, can you? It's such a friendly name. Just to say it is to think, Oh, this is all going to work out well. You can't help but be cheerful, talking to a Bertie. Just as you can't be angry with a Bunny. Not angry. You can be a little short, perhaps. Annoyed. But not angry. You want to take care of a Bunny. You want to bake her cookies, make her coffee. You want to sit down and talk things over reasonably so that everything works out just as it should. Smooth as can be. So that nobody has to regret anything. Isn't that right? Don't you feel that, too?"

"Who are you?"

He looks a little wounded at that. "Bunny. Is this the illness talking? Or all that medication? I was a little surprised to learn all that you're taking. That can't be easy. I imagine it can leave you at a loss. I do understand. So let's just say I'm a friend of your husband. Or really, more a friend of a friend."

"Whose friend?"

"You're right. To be perfectly honest, I work for a friend of a friend. A good friend. At least he thought so. They were working closely together. But we never know, do we? We can never be sure. It's all about the circumstances, isn't it?"

"What does he want?" demanded Bunny.

"My friend?"

"Roger."

"Oh, I don't know what Roger wants," Bertie says. "I mean, I can guess. Given the circumstances. But you'd know better than I. The ties of matrimony. So many years together. Even when all those bonds break they leave a lasting connection. At least I always imagine they do." His smile is almost proprietary. He looks her over as if he has dressed her himself. "That is a beautiful dress. I'm glad you wore it. I like a woman to look elegant. So perfectly put together. Though I'm sorry about your hair. Still, your skin is beautiful. Youthful, really. Are you ready for more coffee? Because it's ready for you." He shakes his head wistfully. "That's what my mother used to say, God bless her. Are you ready for school tomorrow, because it's ready for you. It's funny what we remember. What stays with us."

Bunny's throat is dry. Her voice, when it emerges, is thin and wispy. "I think maybe you should leave."

He regards her benignly. "I will. I certainly will. We just need to take care of a few things first. Would you mind?" He leaves the kitchen, and Bunny half expects the sounds of plumbing, a toilet flushing, the rush of a faucet. But after a moment he returns dragging the enormous pink weight of her suitcase. He opens it on the floor and straightens with satisfaction.

"Names can be a sad burden. But listen to you. Bunny Bingham. It's a skip and jump. It's fun to say. Bunny and Bertie. Listen to that. It sounds like a dance team. Or perhaps we juggle. Can you juggle, Bunny?"

She says nothing.

"Magic tricks? Have you ever done magic? Pulled a rabbit out of a hat? Made something disappear?"

"Never." Though now she thinks of the envelope on Roger's desk, the pamphlets, the money. Now she wishes she had left it alone.

"I have a magic trick for you." He bends to the suitcase.

She hadn't known what to pack. In the end it had been such a rush she had thrown in clothing almost at random. The dress he draws out, rose silk, is much too formal for daily wear. It embodies hopes for her trip that she can no longer even imagine. "A beautiful dress," says Bertie. Then, starting at the top, he draws his hand down, and there is a tearing, splitting sound.

"What are you doing!" Bunny tries to stand up, but her legs won't obey.

He looks hurt. "It's a magic trick. I thought I'd show you mine, and then we could talk about yours." He has, she realizes, a knife in his hand. A small-bladed utility knife that might be used to trim carpet or open a box. He shreds the dress before her eyes into long, even strips.

Her voice has dried up to a whisper. "Stop it."

He picks up another.

"What are you doing? What do you want? I don't have the money."

"Ah," he says. "See what we're doing now? We're communicating." He cuts the second dress into strips with frowning efficiency, then reaches for another and another. Bunny can do nothing but sit. He drops the last of them; the case is overflowing with bright rags.

Bertie sighs. Then he turns and helps himself from the plate. "A good cookie is a real treat, don't you think? And a challenge each time. I've made this recipe hundreds of times, and each time it's different. That's the nature of challenges, isn't it? There are so many different kinds. There's the challenge of doing something new. And there's the challenge of doing something familiar. And we're drawn to them at different times, under different circumstances. Sometimes we just really want to try something new, to branch out. To take a chance. And there's a pleasure in that. I know there is. But there's a pleasure in the familiar, which—and I may be biased here—can be, it seems to me, just as challenging and rewarding. Though it's true," he concedes as if generously, "you and I are at different points in our lives."

He slides the plate of cookies toward her on the counter. "I think you should have one. In your condition I think it's important to maintain your blood sugar. And don't let your coffee get cold. It's really best when it's hot."

Obediently Bunny takes a sip. It is strong and smooth, but cooling quickly. The cookie is hard to swallow.

"That's better." He regards her for a moment. "You see so many different things in a person in your position."

"My position?"

"I've seen a number of them." He smiles deprecatingly. "It's like the cookies. A familiar recipe. But still there are surprises. I thought you'd be more desperate. More frightened, frankly. And foolish. I thought you must be foolish. It's always foolish to take what doesn't belong to you. But you're not, are you?"

"Aren't I?"

"I think you and I can have a simple and easy conversation, and solve everything just like that. Wouldn't that be nice?"

He reaches out to her now, takes her hand in his. "I like you, Bunny. I like your name. And I like that you're not stupid. You may have simply thought you were getting even with

Roger. I've met him. I certainly understand how you could feel that. And I understand how you might think it makes a perfect kind of sense. A kind of poetic justice. And when he told us that you had been in his apartment, that you had helped yourself to what wasn't yours, my friends and their friends thought it was a simple matter. But now look at you. You made the money disappear. And now you've made Roger disappear. And now it's all become much more complicated. And so much more serious."

"What? What are you talking about? Roger's in Grand Cayman. At my daughter's wedding."

"That would be easy, wouldn't it. And so convenient. But that's the thing about magic, isn't it, Bunny? If it were obvious, anyone could do it. Roger's not a stupid man. He's not just going to walk off with it. Carry it around in a duffle bag. People would notice. Better to make it disappear. Then the only question becomes: where is it going to reappear? Don't you see?"

"I don't know what you're talking about."

"I thought it might be Patrick. Of course I did. Good old Patrick. He's always so helpful. And practically a member of the family. But he turned out to be no help at all. And there I was, at my wit's end. But then, wonder of wonders, you show up. You check into their hotel. You make yourself at home. You start wandering around, here and there. Obviously looking for something. How foolish would I have to be?" He helps himself to another cookie. "What are you doing here, Bunny? Suddenly. Out of the blue. A bus from Chicago? Since when do you take the bus, Bunny? Are you a regular patron of sticky seats and mass transit?"

"I'm not supposed to fly. I'm taking medication."

"Are you meeting him here? Is that what this is? A reconciliation? Is it all just a plan?"

"It was my daughter's wedding."

"I know. That is so sweet. I got an invitation. Well, I didn't. The friend of a friend. I'm sure you got one, too. I've seen it somewhere. But Grand Cayman. Who goes to the Caribbean in the summer? It seems an odd time to take a trip. Don't you think?"

"I don't know," she says. "Roger does what Roger wants."

"Exactly." He is nodding now, smiling. "And that's exactly my question. What does Roger want? And where is it?"

Her mouth is dry. "Hand me my purse."

He fetches it cheerfully. With shaking hands she holds out the thick envelope of cash. He looks surprised. With his knife he slices it open, leafing through the packed bills with interest that soon cools to annoyance.

"Now you're just teasing me," he says.

"Please tell me what you want."

"A great deal more than this. So much more, it isn't even money any longer. A swipe card, a letter, a few numbers in a row. What have you done with it?"

"I don't know what you're talking about."

His fingers encircle her wrist. His grip is stronger than she would have expected. He easily draws her hand down to the counter. And suddenly he has a loop of plastic, slipping it around the wrist, cinching it tight to the handle of a drawer. She has to lean forward. The ache in her shoulder. The hollow, lightness in her head. The room is too bright. Every second feels untrue.

Bertie reaches into his pocket and brings out the knife again. It is yellow and new, with a small triangular blade like a bird's beak that is suddenly at the center of the room. "This is the part of the recipe that can vary each time." His voice hasn't changed, though now he isn't smiling. "I know I don't have to tell you all the things that can happen. Fingers, ears, the tip of a nose. I took a man's eyelids once, just to make a point."

Bunny sits very still. Her free hand is clutching at the bound wrist, tugging at it desperately, trying to keep her fingers clenched, as if they can hide themselves.

He holds the knife before her eyes, then reaches up. She feels the pressure of his hand on her forehead, holding her steady. She feels the point on her scalp, pressing down; she hears the delicate sound of tissue giving way. There's no pain. She is shocked by that. She waits for it to come. He slices again, and again, and when he releases his grip, she feels an unaccustomed looseness, and with a limp and slippery sensation the wig falls in pieces from her head.

Almost gently, he takes her free hand. His grip is like stone. He turns the hand over, opening the fingers as if he were going to read the future in her palm. "The fingertips are so sensitive. All those nerve endings there. Think about all the things we do with our fingers. How delicate they are." She is straining at the grip, but he only smiles. "They say it's our thumb that makes us what we are. We take it so for granted." Gently he places the tip of the knife against the base of her thumb. The tiny, razor point presses into her skin. "Can you imagine a life without it. You'd be like a dog. A little puppy. All you could do is paw at your food. Wouldn't that be adorable."

Her breath is gone. Her throat is dry. "Please," she whispers.

"Oh, Bunny." He presses on the knife. She feels the sharp tang of pain. She sees the blood well up, a teardrop of deep crimson. He moves the blade around the base of the thumb. But he's just tracing his way now, barely scratching the skin, leaving a bright, stinging line like one of those marks on a dress pattern where a seam will go.

He releases her hand, but she can't seem to move. She has turned hollow, weightless.

Now he is searching through her purse. One by one he sets the amber prescription vials in a line on the counter. "Queasiness. Muscle pain. Anxiety." He shakes his head. "Medication is so interesting, don't you think? Take too many, take too few. It's hard to find just the right balance." As he talks he opens each vial and pours its contents down the sink. From the last he shakes four yellow pills into his hand, then adds two more. "These are particularly strong, don't you think? I'm a little surprised your doctor was so casual. Pills like this, you've got to be careful." He drops them into her coffee and stirs. "All of it, please. Straight down. That's a good girl."

The coffee is bitter. The pills are bitter. But after a moment the ache in her muscles starts to fade. Comfort rises like a loaf of bread. And rises and rises and rises.

"They say the prospect of death sharpens the mind. Please be sharp, Bunny. There's no reason in the world we shouldn't help each other. Roger's a bum. You know he is. But Bertie and Bunny. We were made to help each other." He cuts the plastic binding from her wrist. "See? I help you, and you help me. What could be nicer?"

22.

She wakes slowly to a voice in her ear, its whispered advice and insights taking her on a vaguely guided tour. She can't always make out the words, but the tone is clear: firm, directing, sometimes chiding. In her dreams she has been moving through a world of trees. There could be something crucial hidden beneath each one, but she has no time to dig. The landscape opens like a curtain, and a castle appears, wildly crenulated, sweeping and grand. And she thinks, of course. The castle. How could she have forgotten that?

It doesn't matter that it's impossible. She follows the voice. A whispering river runs nearby. That's not quite right, she thinks, but she gets the idea. Now the ground beneath her shifts and folds, hemming her in, shaping all the beauty of her dream into a single enormous cave, glinting with diamond light and cloaked in moon-glow. And it looks so impossibly beautiful that when everything fractures and falls away—when she is left behind, dull and immoveable, mired in the weight of her body—she knows she is waking up. But she doesn't want to open her eyes. She doesn't know what she'll find.

She is lying on the bed in the hotel suite, alone. There is nothing as it should be: the too-brightness of the light, the lurking instability that seems to invest every color and shape. Through the muffled softness of it all she feels a small knot of terror pulsing, pulsing somewhere out of sight. Six yellow pills, she thinks. The trick is to be calm. The trick is not to be afraid. She should call the police. And tell them what? Even now it seems like a dream.

She climbs out of bed. Her head is bare; she finds a scarf in her suitcase. There is nothing but scarves: all her dresses reduced to scarves. Except one. Her grey dress is merely rumpled; she pulls it on, straightens what she can. Everything is a little spongy: her legs, her lips, the handle of the door. She is careful in the hallway, in the elevator.

She needs to get away, though she has that feeling, familiar from any nightmare, that you can never run when you need to. Her senses are unreliable; she understands that. Just be careful, she thinks. No sudden moves.

Unsteadily she sets off down the sidewalk and is immediately reminded of learning to ride a bicycle. Motion is balance. Slow down and you'll tip. Her heart is pounding, but that seems unrelated to the lightness in her head. She pictures Del's house, the comfort waiting for her—Del will know what to do; Clean will help her—but it is the Art Museum she sees suddenly before her, and it's with a little murmur of welcome that she enters.

She has hoped to feel a connection, to feel anchored by the safety of the past, but stepping through the glass doors, even the smell is unfamiliar. Or rather, it only reminds her now of the previous visit: the wine, the art, the gentle hubbub, Bertie looming pale and ghoulish in her memory. All the deeper associations are lost. There is the dusty air, the faint tread of her own shoes. Nothing more.

She forces herself to walk the galleries, but every painting is like a bricked up hallway. It might have led somewhere once. Standing before *The Night Café* she is unable even to pretend. But she has found the ring. That, at least, is true. She wears it now around her neck on Clean's old, tattered string. And the watch... though even she can see how ridiculous it is. The cheap plastic band, the dark face of the Golf-o-matic. Crazy as she sometimes feels, she isn't foolish. It has nothing to do with her. But still. She turns it over in her hands, she grips it tight.

It's always a beautiful day for golf, a tiny voice erupts.

Bunny stands unmoving. Her mouth is dry. Already there is so little difference between dreaming and not. She squeezes again. A thin voice rises from a tiny hole in the molded plastic:

The power is in the shoulders, but the grace is in the wrists. It's not a game, it's a gift.

She regards the watch. There are two tiny buttons on the face below the digital time display. She presses the left one. *Unbelievable. Are you playing with a bag on your head? Your last shot has travelled a total of... zero ...yards. You are now… 16,256 …yards from the first pin. Two hundred and twenty six strokes over par.*

She presses it again. *That was terrible. You make me want to weep. Your last shot has travelled a total of ... zero ...yards. You are now… 16,256 …yards from the first pin. Two hundred and twenty-seven strokes over par.*

She tries the other button. It is nothing but considerate, though the voice has a strained and tinny quality, as if it's been present at more than its share of disasters. *Bad luck. Maybe it was the wind. This is a challenging course of three holes with a combined distance of 12,643 yards. There is a water hazard running through it, and a number of trees that could prove difficult if you can't stay out of the rough. There are no sand traps but the ground is uneven and you will need to consider the slope and lie of your ball in planning your shots. But remember, the most important part of the game is played on the real estate between your ears.*

She touches the wide, cardboard ring on her finger. There is comfort in the smallest things. When she walks to the main door she sees the clouds have opened and they are emptying themselves onto the earth, popping on the sidewalks, coursing down the edges of the street. But there is a smile on her lips. She presses the watch.

Now you're playing. Your last shot has travelled a total of…twenty-two… yards. You are now… 16,234 …yards from the first pin. Two hundred and twenty-eight strokes over par.

There is a coat rack by the door, a low basket for umbrellas. It's almost empty; no one has foreseen the storm. But there is one—a slim, dove-grey number—leaning jauntily against the rim. Everything is a sign.

She steps out through the door and opens the umbrella,

feeling the sharp patter of drops, hearing the sound as if she has heard it only once before. Where did they go that day, stepping out of the museum together all those years ago? She sets off down the street. At the corner she turns in among the high dark buildings of the university.

The light is different here, turning the whole scene reminiscent. It is the pills, of course. She knows that. But still.

He had brought an umbrella on that first afternoon. He held it over them with a young, proprietary air. But it wasn't large enough, and she had to take his arm to make sure it covered them both. "Where shall we go?"

"It's a beautiful day," he had said. The rain was pounding down. "Why don't we just walk."

She remembers it now: the breathlessness, every bump of their shoulders as they walk. They hadn't even kissed yet, hadn't made love, but this was the beginning. For if making love is new each time, and kissing can continue to surprise, the sudden awareness of the two of you alone—that you can feel only once.

The smell of damp pavement blends with the sudden earthy scent of a flower bed. You never know what will bring it back. She crosses a street to the low shush of tires and the romance of headlights slipping by.

Her past is somehow before her, as if she's taken some hidden turning in the rain. She smiles at the thought. There is no place to go but back.

Gradually she becomes aware that there is a figure walking beside her. He is dressed in grey, an overcoat and hat, and he seems unbothered by the rain. It's only misting now, but still, the water seems barely to touch his coat. It doesn't trouble her. In fact she feels a little proud at how calmly she responds. It isn't what she had expected, what she was half-hoping for—once you embrace the possibilities of hallucination there is always the chance of running into an old friend. But here she is, walking this old familiar route with the all-but-solid embodiment of her all-but-ex husband. It's oddly companionable.

"Hi, Bunny."

She thinks about ignoring him. It seems healthier somehow, but more childish. He is, after all, one of her oldest friends. If friend is exactly the word. And certainly he is not the only one at fault. "Hello, Roger. How's Pilates? I expected you to be thinner."

"I've lost ten pounds," he says. "This coat's a little big on me."

As if that's going to last, she thinks. But then she chides herself. No need to be bitter, even now. And she finds herself wondering why this is the Roger that has come to her. This kindly-voiced, comforting Roger from so long ago. Not the resentful husband from the first years of their marriage, or the callous, indifferent stranger he became.

Not even the angry, frightened, harried young man who had followed her that night, afraid of the fighting, afraid of the gun. Dragging her away in the face of all that sudden chaos. Saving her, he said, from all that was about to happen. And then holding it against her for all the years it took until there was neither a chance that she would leave him nor a chance that she would ever love him again. But oh, those first months were awful. Three months, four. Those long weeks of doubt stretching through the summer into fall. A moment of truth that seemed unable to end, until it did.

Poor Roger. When he'd gotten her home he must have thought that would be that. Put it all behind them. Everything back to normal. But she held him off, she waited. She needed time to think. (And surely that was true.) But just as true: like any princess in a fairy tale she was waiting to be rescued. Waiting for her prince to come and break the spell. And finally he came, his letter came. That terrible letter. And the spell was broken.

But maybe the truth is she didn't deserve to be rescued. Maybe it just comes down to that.

Bunny tries to remember those moments on the trestle—for so long, she had tried to forget them. She'd been so afraid. Suspended out over that terrible darkness with the rush of the river below. That awful figure rising suddenly out of nothing. The shouting, the fight. One moment spiraling out of another, always already out of control.

If only they had run. Both of them. Bill and she. If only they had fled together, she wouldn't have had to flee alone. Or what? If she had stayed? And this, of course, is what played through her mind every night for all those early months. If she had stayed, despite the shock, the danger, despite the terrible fact of murder, she would have been bound to it all, the way Bill was bound. They would have been bound to each other.

But she was too afraid for that. Her frantic heart knocking like a fist on a door. Let me out, let me out. And then a gunshot, thin as a fire cracker, and the struggle roiling up in the middle of the bridge. And the little dark shape, like a rock but not a rock, bouncing and skittering over the tracks, and coming to rest at her feet. She had picked it up. No hesitation. Her heart was racing.

What are you doing? Roger had shouted. Don't be stupid. Put that down! Let's get the hell out of here!

But Bill was in a tangle on the tracks and the huge man was leaning over him. And he was shouting something. And his arm came up. And her whole mind just tightened around the gun until it went off in her hands with the smallest of bangs. And the man jerked back. He toppled and fell. And the only thing that tied him back to her was the scream.

Say what you will about Roger: in that moment he knew what she wanted, even if she didn't. To be gone. To be away. To be suddenly anywhere else. So when he snatched her into motion, she went. Because that was the truth about her. That was the nature of destiny. For all your moments of bravery, it's the instant of fear that defines you.

Now she turns to Roger, this Roger—this calm and smiling version she has conjured up out of everything she has forgotten—and she says, "What in the world are you doing here?"

"The thing is." And he looks a little uncomfortable, poor dear. "I'm not really here right now. If you know what I mean."

"Thank you, Roger. I think I get the picture. I'm hallucinating, not insane."

"You're not happy to see me?"

"It's a little unexpected."

"Well, what about you? I thought you were still in the hospital."

"No, you didn't."

"Well, you didn't tell me you were coming."

And she can smile at that, so like him. And *this* is a surprise—she finds it doesn't hurt to talk to this Roger. She can say all she would have liked to say, and that's a kind of comfort, isn't it? "How could you think I'd want to miss our daughter's wedding?"

"I sent you an invitation."

"Please, Roger."

"I did. Didn't you get it?"

"You don't have to be here if you're going to be like that."

"It was a little late," he concedes. "That's all. Are you sure it didn't arrive? Patrick was carrying it. I don't suppose you've seen him. He was supposed to be here ahead of me, but he never showed up, and now I'm starting to get a little worried."

"Stop it," says Bunny. "Don't you see? That's the worst of it. Not the babysitter, or the school teacher, or even the Pilates instructor. The fact that you could have the wedding without me. That you could be so cruel."

"Janine," he says with a reminiscent smile.

"What?"

"The babysitter. I'd forgotten."

She shakes her head. They have come, all but unnoticed, to a little brick park at the intersection of several narrow streets. There is a concrete fountain, a pair of benches. Bunny sees it with a rising sense that might be recognition. "I think I'll sit down."

He vanishes. When she sees him again he has joined her on the bench. The weather is letting up, though there is still a thin drizzle. She keeps the umbrella over her head. Roger is, of course, untroubled by the rain. She considers, for a moment, the familiar landscape of her aches and nausea, emerging now from the woolly softness of her brain. All her pills are gone. But she draws from her pocket the remains of Del's joint, nearly forgotten.

"What are you doing? You can't just light that here."

"Don't be such a scaredy-cat." She draws the smoke into her lungs. Just the roughness of it is a comfort. After a moment the nausea recedes. Even the hollow lightness of her mind takes on a smooth, more cheerful cast.

"Is that a new ring?"

She touches the little cardboard circle. "Don't you like it?"

"What happened to your watch?"

This she ignores. "Do you know this place?"

He glances around. "Should I?"

"Maybe it's just me, then."

"This is one of your secret hideaways?"

"I don't remember," she says. "I guess that's why they're secret. You never told me about your friend Bertie."

Roger looks suddenly wary. "You met him?"

"I did." She touches the scratch around the base of her thumb.

"He's not really a friend. More a business associate. I wouldn't see him again, if I were you. I don't think he's right for you."

Bunny almost smiles. She is touched that this imagined Roger should worry about her. But then, she has never talked to him as easily as this. "Just for you, I'll never see him again. But he mentioned something about money?"

"Yes. The money. He didn't mention our passports, did he?"

"What?"

"It was just a thought. I wondered if you had taken them."

"Not everything is my fault, Roger."

"No. Sorry. It's just that we're a little stuck without them, Ruth and I."

Bunny glances around. "She's not here? Tell me you didn't bring her."

"No. Not here," he concedes. "She's safe. She's waiting at the school. But we need to get out of here."

"For Heaven's sake, Roger! You've already left."

"Not without the passports."

She shakes her head wistfully. What does it say about her that even her hallucinations don't really listen? "Sometimes I wonder, in my little moments. I wonder if it might have worked. With Bill, I mean. Do you think we could have been happy?"

He frowns. "I'm not the person to ask. I never liked him."

"I'm just talking to myself. But it makes it easier if you answer. It doesn't sound as if I'm making everything up."

"Three weeks, Bunny. That's all it was."

"Sometimes it just takes a moment, a glance, and you're done for."

"This isn't poetry."

"But don't you think it could have been? Such things do exist. And a girl's got to have something to wonder about."

"If he walked up right now, would you still love him, Bunny? Would you even recognize him?"

She gazes around at the little brick park, so dreary in the rain. "We walked everywhere. In the daytime, the afternoon. But evening was always the best. We had a world of places. And I don't remember any of them. Well, that's not true. One of them. Who knew it was next to that horrid school. But still, that's got to be progress, doesn't it?"

"Now you're just wandering."

"Reminiscing. About old friends."

"He's no friend of mine. I'm not going to be your bridge to Bill."

She smiles again. "No, dear. Thank you. I found the bridge. That lovely Del helped me. Turns out it wasn't the tree, at all. Just the bridge and that beautiful park. Do you think you can dream a thing over and over until it becomes real?"

"Now I'm really not a good person to ask," he says drily.

"No," she agrees. "But do you remember the rest?" And it almost feels true to her. "A castle. A beautiful castle. High turrets and towers. A huge hall filled with candlelight. As far as the eye could see. We were going to celebrate our marriage there."

"Yours and mine?"

"Don't be silly. Bill said the king was out of town. He wouldn't mind if we used his castle." She laughs. "Isn't that sweet? Trust Bill to know a king."

"Trust him to know when he's out of town."

"Don't be like that. He had flowers for me. And we had my mother's ring. He proposed. It was so beautiful. How could I say no?"

"Because you were already engaged?"

"It was a dream. There are different rules in a dream. We walked along the path toward the castle, but the Padre met us. He led us to the chapel instead. Wasn't that amazing?"

"A chapel?"

"Cloaked in candlelight."

"What's the cost of candles in your dreams?"

"Stop it. You don't have to stay." But he doesn't move. "He married us there. Isn't that sweet? A forest wedding."

"It certainly sounds unusual. I wonder if it's legally binding."

"We were going to spend our wedding night in a magic grotto."

"Of course you were. How could you not? And then live happily ever after?"

"That was the plan. He was fixing up a house for us. An enchanted cottage in the woods."

"Oh, please."

"Magic is dangerous, he said, but enchantment is a product of love. We were on our way there that last night."

"So you never saw them? The castle or the grotto or that magic cottage?"

"I never did."

It makes her sad to remember. The sadness is all that's left. Maybe that's why she stopped trying to recall it, all those years ago.

"The Padre said it was a spell. That's what he said at the wedding. Instead of a blessing. A wedding spell. But spells always come in threes, he said. To seal it. To make it last. The chapel, the grotto, the enchanted cottage. Wouldn't that have been beautiful? If we'd been able to seal the spell?"

Roger's voice is gentle, but it draws even the faint thread of hope out of her heart. "I'm sorry, Bunny, but don't you think you're going off the tracks here? None of it is real. It's all in your head."

And that's a little unfair, she thinks, coming from an hallucination. But still. Just having it in her head is something. Besides. "What if it's not?" she says.

"You need to go home. This isn't good for you. This isn't going to help." And it's the voice of her conscience, clearly. The voice of reason. He has always been able to offer that, though she has seldom felt less grateful. Isn't it like her to bring out the worst in herself? "I've got to go, Bunny. Are you going to be all right?"

"I'll be fine."

"Will you be able to find your way back?"

She doesn't even bother to answer. But when she looks up, he is gone. *Don't you think you're going off the tracks?*

She wonders about that. If it's really as easy as that.

She presses the face of the watch. *Great swing! Now that's what I call golf! Your last shot has travelled a total of…seven hundred and thirty-two… yards. You are now… 15,502… yards from the first pin. Two hundred and twenty-nine strokes over par. Remember: when you're in the weeds, you have to hold your head high.*

Part Six

The Woods

BUNNY

23.

The rain has stopped, though the mist still hangs heavily on the air, protecting her from the intrusion of anything less mysterious. Under the grey umbrella she follows the railroad tracks. From time to time she consults the watch. The voice is encouraging. Her game is strong.

How could she not have thought of this before? The trestle is fixed in her memory, however unreal it's become. And where there is a railroad bridge, there must be tracks. Sooner or later the present will run directly into her past. And the fog is a gift. It doesn't matter that this is nothing she remembers; she is on a path even a blind man could follow.

Bunny waits for the route to swerve into the familiar, for the memory to draw her in. But instead the single track splits; it widens and divides; it divides again. And then the whole visible world becomes the flat, repeating pattern of a train yard. There are voices, emphatic gestures from distant men, but she clings to the central track. And in response to her resolve, the multiplying paths recombine again until there is only one, and Bunny finds herself alone and curving around the shoulder of a hillside within the solid grey cloud of the world.

She walks. There is a moment's excitement when the fog finally thins and she sees the unending stretch of trees on either side. Surely that's good. Something is beginning. But the trees prove as regular and unyielding as the track, and by the end of an hour she is exhausted and hungry. Her joints ache. She is dreaming of food. She turns back.

In the brightening sunlight everything becomes clear. Trees, track, the gravel bed. She is undone by the ordinary. And as she enters the long curve around the hillside that marks the only recognizeable moment in her journey, she feels the last of her strength ebbing away. All this for nothing.

Then she sees the chair. A folding aluminum lawn chair on the hillside beneath a copse of trees. When everything is a sign, surely this is a sign, as well. Bunny settles into the creaking web of the chair. It is late afternoon. Amid the trees to her right there is a shape of deeper darkness: a black and ancient train car abandoned on a siding. Before her a scuffed and threadbare slope falls away to the distant, grey drudgery of Long Island Sound and the industrial clutter of the port. It is nothing she remembers, but still, it blesses her into sleep.

She wakes to early twilight and the rich aroma of cooking food. Everything ordinary has vanished: the water, the shabbiness. She opens her eyes on the lights of the harbor, glowing like a constellation in the deepening blue of the air.

"Oh, my," she murmurs and breathes in the fragrant air.

She sees that someone has draped a blanket over her lap against the encroaching chill. She touches the watch. The thin, companionable voice. *It's always a beautiful day for golf.*

Bunny climbs out of the chair. The abandoned train car—an ancient caboose—is now alive with light. A glow of red neon against the black front. *The Cab'. Eat now!* The low sound of a radio emerges from within.

She climbs the iron steps, feeling on the verge of almost anything, and steps into a narrow room: walls paneled in old wood and lined with booths, a thin scattering of diners, already hunched and exhausted from the day. At the end of the room the proprietor sits with a pile of yesterday's tickets before him and an ancient adding machine. He is the thinnest man she has ever seen, with a narrow face, cheeks dark with stubble, and a high forehead that is made to seem oddly exposed by the narrow paper cook's hat sitting upright on the table beside him.

He regards her with a complete lack of interest which is, itself, somehow reassuring. If this were only a dream, he'd have long since invited her to sit down.

But then, after a moment, he does. "Take a load off, why don't you?"

She sinks into the chair across from him, purse cradled in her lap. "I'm Bunny," she says.

He seems unsurprised. "All I got now is coffee. Everything else is still cooking."

"I don't suppose you remember me."

"Depends. You ever been here before?"

"I'm thinking maybe I have."

"Your name really Bunny?"

"Barbara Jean."

"You want some coffee, Barbara Jean?"

He goes to the counter and returns with a heavy china mug, scuffed and time-worn, which he sets before her along with a tiny steel bowl. "You look like a woman takes sugar."

"Two, please."

He considers that for a long moment, as if it's a rule he never breaks, but then he spoons the sugar in and stirs it with a little flourish. "Anything else, madam?"

"I had a dream that your name was Stan."

He contemplates his own cup for a moment. "Is this a recent dream?"

"I don't know. It's hard to tell with dreams."

He nods at the evident truth of that. "If I was to ask you what you were looking for, Barbara Jean, what would you say?"

She sips her coffee. She feels it trickle down into the puzzle of aches and pains, warming a little path, giving her something to concentrate on besides the general, unsettling awareness of coming undone. "I'm a maiden looking for a castle," she says.

"A castle."

"It's beautiful, mysterious, hidden away. At the end of a long, long path."

"I think I've heard this one before."

"It's in among the trees, I think. Though I might have added that. It was all drenched in candlelight. Hundreds of candles." She hesitates. "Though that doesn't sound likely, either."

"And this was all a dream?"

She offers him a wistful smile. "It couldn't all have been, could it?" But Stan says nothing. "Maybe I could settle for the Padre."

"And what exactly do you want from me?"

"I was told not to go into the woods."

Almost reluctantly he smiles. "That was you, was it? Grandma tell you that?"

"I have money, if that makes a difference."

He considers that for a moment. "How much are we talking?"

Bunny reaches into her purse and lays the thick manila envelope on the table. With a glance at the nearly empty room he cautiously reaches out, riffles the edge of the thick pile of bills. "I don't think it'll cost this much." He pinches at a few bills and draws them out. "I'm thinking maybe a finder's fee? Does that sound fair?" Then he notices something at the bottom of the pile and draws out two stiff blue folders. "Last time I heard, you don't need a passport to go into the woods."

"They aren't mine." She leafs through them. Roger, looking formal and stern, and Ruth. Even her passport photo is beautiful, though so grownup. "Poor Roger," she murmurs. He had made such a convincing hallucination. "Better not lose these." She hands them back. Stan tucks them into the envelope.

"Does that mean you'll help me?" she asks.

He looks at the five twenties in his hand and then at the remaining pile, as if performing a rough calculation. In the end he takes the whole envelope and tucks it into the pocket of his apron. "I think maybe I should hold onto this for you. Just till you get back."

She regards him gravely. "You're not teasing me, are you, Stan?"

"Scout's honor." He turns in his chair. "Hey, Raggedy."

Bunny sees a pair of men slumped at a table. One is thin, tidy, with a large nose and a mustache like a blonde mouse perched beneath it. The other is lumpy and dazed. He gives his head an irritable shake, as if there's a buzzing at his ears.

"No, Raggedy. It's me." And Stan gives her a glance. "It'll just take a sec."

Raggedy climbs to his feet and makes his way over with a hesitant air as if he hadn't expected to be moving so early in the day. He is whispering to himself, and when he reaches the table he begins whispering to Stan instead, as if it were all one continuous conversation.

Bunny sits in her chair. Roger, she knows, would already be out the door, pulling her along, dragging her into flight. And maybe that's part of why she stays. But it's something else, as well. There is no danger that's not already here. Without the pills she imagines the ongoing destruction of her cells, little bodies breaking apart, poisons slowly leaking into her blood. She considers the string of mistakes that already comprise her life. To be afraid of danger is to be afraid of all there is.

"This is Raggedy Bob," says Stan. "He knows the way. It's not that far."

"The way where?" says Bob.

"She needs to talk to the Padre."

The round face screws into a frown. "I was eatin' here."

"It's just a quick-and-back. Twenty bucks," says Stan.

"I don't even like the Padre."

"And there's a castle," Bunny reminds him.

Raggedy eyes her nervously. "What's she saying?"

"She dreamed about a castle. Out in the woods."

"I don't know any castle. If there was a castle, don't you think I'd know it?"

"She *dreamed* it," Stan says patiently.

The man is shaking his head. "I gotta say...."

"She just needs a little help. Just take her to the Padre."

"Is he even around?"

"Isn't he?"

"I haven't seen him lately."

"Well, she wants to look," says Stan.

Raggedy lowers his voice. "Well, jeeze, Stan. What's that she's wearin'?"

"It's just a dress."

Bunny brushes self-consciously at the rumpled grey silk.

"But what if someone sees? What are they gonna say? She looks like a damn starlet."

Bunny feels a little flush of pleasure. "That is so sweet."

His eyes go wide. "Oh no. I don't want her talking to me."

"Thirty bucks," says Stan. "You just have to walk her to the backbone."

"She's not going to the backbone looking like that?"

"Forty bucks, Bob. When did you last see forty bucks?"

"It's a fucking dress."

"Fifty."

"Now wait a minute," says Bunny. "That's all I've got."

Stan turns and regards her for a moment without expression. Then he glances at Raggedy Bob. "You heard the lady. Straight there, straight back. I'll hold the money." He considers for a moment then glances at Bunny. "And anything else you got that's shiny." She passes him her purse.

"It's a walk, Bob. A quick-and-back."

"I just hope nobody sees."

24.

They walk along the tracks. The first indigo of early evening seeps across the sky. Without the mist everything is dreary: the gravel bed splashed with oil, the warm air smelling sometimes of creosote, sometimes of urine. Raggedy Bob doesn't try to get too close. He walks ahead as if alone, though there is something in the worried tilt of his head, the half-flutter of his hands, as if he is drawing her along in a little eddy of fretfulness.

Past the shoulder of the hill and they are in among the trees. Small saplings and sumac and the rising clutter of weeds. Nothing like the big trees in her dream. The whole landscape seems inadvertent. And as if in proof, Raggedy Bob remains staunchly oblivious to any and all that they see, moving forward at an undistractable ramble that forces Bunny to keep up.

The watch keeps her company. *Try not to rush your pace. Open your shoulders as you swing through. Your last shot has traveled a total of ...minus two hundred twenty-six...yards. You are now... 2,476 ...yards from the first pin. Two hundred thirty nine over par.* In all her life she has rarely considered the value of a guide. In her life with Roger none was ever needed; they never went far afield. But now she recalls the excitement of all those years ago, the mystery of it, as one new thing after another spread its arms in welcome. Since then nothing has felt the same. She cannot remember the last time she actually wanted something. No. That's not true. Life is full of wanting. But she cannot remember the last time she wanted things to be precisely as they are. *Open your eyes. Remember, the rough is not there to trap you; it's there for you to soar over. Your last shot has traveled a total of ...minus four hundred thirty-seven ...yards. You are now... 2,913 ...yards from the first pin. Two hundred forty over par.*

"Raggedy?" she calls. "Mr. Bob? We're going the wrong way. Can we stop for a moment?"

Peevishly he glances back, but he must see something in her face. "I guess we could sit."

"That would be nice."

His gaze settles on a fallen tree trunk that has lodged itself beside the tracks. He bends low and for an instant she wonders if he is going to pick it up, hoist it hugely over his head. But instead he settles both hands gently upon it as if it's a horse he's calming, then he pats it once. "This looks good."

Bunny eases down. The queasiness is like a shadow keeping pace. Her dress, stained now beyond all saving, is turning a little raggedy itself. "Are you sure this is right? This direction?"

"All shiny," he says. "Backbone's just there."

The evening is growing warmer. There's no air moving among the trees. Bunny feels an air of hopelessness rising on the heat. "I'd offer you a pill," she says, "but I'm afraid I'm all out."

"That's okay. Me and Smooth Bob, we're more of a drinking man."

The scarf is tight around her temples; on impulse she strips it off. The air against her scalp is lovely. He regards her uncertainly, as if this were an offering that requires something in return. He says, "I kind of wish there was a castle. It'd be a beautiful day for it."

"Listen." Bunny presses the watch. *Are you playing with your head in a bag?*

"Sorry," she murmurs, and finds the other button. *Your last shot has traveled a total of ...minus fifteen...yards. You are currently... 1,928 ...yards from the first pin. Two hundred forty-one over par.* "See?" she says "I'm getting close."

Bob eyes the watch uneasily. "It's not supposed to be talking, is it?"

"I think so. Yes." The woods are quiet. She weighs the passing moments, the slow gathering of dusk. "Isn't this pretty."

He peers around, as if he's never considered it in just that way before. "It's okay. But you don't want to go too far."

"I was told to stay out of the woods."

"Good advice. The Padre's harmless enough. Bit of a loon. But the backbone's chancy, and past the river it's all claws and teeth."

She feels the last of the yellow pills dissolving away. Now the poisons planted near her lymph nodes are stirring, opening their eyes. She feels it in the way the colors grow deeper, brighter as the twilight approaches. There's a slow pressure building in the shape of things. "Are we almost there?" she asks.

"That depends. How far is 'almost'?"

"Have you lived around here long?"

He looks a little offended. "I don't live here. It's a flop, that's all. I'm sliding through."

"But you know the area?"

"Not sure there's much to know." Though he seems prepared to give the matter more thought.

"And the castle?" she asks. "The chapel? Does that ring a bell? A moonlit grotto? An enchanted cottage in the woods?"

"Sorry," he says. "Sounds pretty, though."

Your last shot has traveled a total of ...zero...yards. You are currently... 1,928 ...yards from the first pin. Two hundred forty-two over par.

She touches the watch again.

Smooth and effortless power, isn't that what we all seek? Open your shoulders. Put your mind in your hands.

"It shouldn't be talking," mutters Bob. "What does it want?"

Bunny climbs to her feet. "I think we need to go that way."

"Padre's over there."

"This is the way," she says.

Your body is the engine. Pivot smoothly to release the power. The whole secret is in the wrist.

Raggedy eyes it warily. "I don't think Smooth Bob likes this."

"It's just a little further."

"I don't think we should be listening to a watch."

"It just wants to help."

In the distance she can see an opening in the trees. As they approach it opens into a trail like a narrow service road, cut through the bushes and trees. It's made of a fine, golden gravel that glows even in the fading light. It makes her smiles. "Have you read the Wizard of Oz?" she asks.

"What?"

"This will take us somewhere."

"That's not the right way."

Nice hit! Your last shot has travelled a total of …127… yards. You are currently… 1,801 …yards from the first pin.

"How can you argue with that?" she says.

They move slowly along the trail. "It's getting dark," Bob frets, but he's wrong. The air is opening up, turning cool. The underbrush is thinning out, the trees easing apart. They are taller now. Grander. The canopy is high over their heads. It's as if she is slipping smoothly into her dream. She rubs her fingers over the watch but doesn't press. She doesn't want the voice intruding. And when she begins to see the suggestion of a shape, a building in the distance, she doesn't hurry. It emerges like an ocean-liner from the darkness, a big block of a building. The same color as the path, as if it had gathered itself out of the dust and gravel with the force of her need.

It's not a castle. Not exactly. An old factory, square and abandoned in the wide expanse of the forest. It looks shabby, overgrown, as if every year has drawn from it a little more of its hope. They come to a fence, a sudden chainlink intrusion into the scene. It stretches across the path, carving out a moat of space around the unkempt building. The gate is chained shut and has been for years. There is a sign, weather-worn and grafittied. *Hilliard Quarry and Stone. Keep Out*. Someone has added in krylon years ago: *This Means You!*

But there are no rules in a dream.

Bob is uneasy. The sign is shouting at him in particular. "We need to go," he says. But one corner of the gate has been sprung, and the fence is curling up.

Now that was magic! Your last shot has travelled a total of …1,622… yards. You are currently… 179 …yards from the first pin.

Bunny bends and slips through the gap. Bob hesitates, clutching the fence. "You don't want to do that."

"Yes, I do."

"We should leave."

"You go," she says. "I'll find my way home."

"You'll get hurt. You'll get lost."

"How can I get lost? It's my dream."

The forest surrounds her, holding the building like a jewel in a ring. There is a low plaza of stone before the main door. She climbs the steps and stands before the entrance. It is square and workmanlike. There's nothing fluted or crenellated or marvelous about it. Nothing like a castle. There are rusted cans, shreds of plastic bags and papers trodden into the ground. She feels the dreariness of it like a weight on her shoulders. *Congratulations. Two-hundred and forty-seven over par. But remember, golf isn't a number, it's a state of mind. Press both buttons firmly to begin the second hole.*

She had been certain somehow that the path would end with a glimmer of recognition. But the chains on the heavy doors, the rusted locks. They are nothing she remembers.

"Scoot! Go away! Scoot! Scoot!"

The voice leaps out of the twilight. Bunny jumps, turning, the breath catching in her throat.

"What are you doing?" the voice demands. "What do you think you're doing?"

"I'm supposed to be here," she says.

"I doubt it! I doubt it very much!"

The man before her is dressed entirely in moss. No, not moss. Not exactly. An ancient robe, belted at the waist, fringed in tatters. It isn't so much stained with dirt. It is dirt, as if he's swept up all the forest floor and hung it from his narrow shoulders. His face is grizzled with whiskers, a tight black cap sits low on his head. He flicks and darts like an outraged squirrel, one moment closer, then edging away. "What are you doing? Here, I mean. What are you doing here?"

Bunny hesitates. She owes something to the strangeness of it all, something to his obvious timidity. "Hello, padre. Do you remember me?"

"Remember?"

"I'm returning to the scene of a dream."

"Is that right? Is that what you're saying? But that's the question, isn't it? Isn't that the question. Have you brought the key? Do you have it?"

"I didn't think it would be locked."

"Of course it's locked. Dreams are always locked."

But something in the moment seems to quiet him. He stops pacing, slowly subsides. She thinks he is praying at first, but then she sees one hand is roughly bandaged and cradled in the other. He peers at her in renewed concern. "Aren't you too old for dreams?"

Her hand rises hesitantly to touch the silver down at her temple. "I'm younger than I look," she says. "But older than I was. It's Bunny, Padre. Bunny Bingham. Bunny and Bill?"

And now it's his turn to sink into wonder. "Has it really been so long?"

She steps forward, gently takes his wounded hand. "I'm very glad to find you in my dream."

"Yes," he says. "Yes. It's good to see you again. After all this time." He offers an uneasy glance around at the trees. "But we must always keep in mind: there are limits even to our dreams."

"I don't suppose you have the key?"

"You were supposed to bring it. That's the whole point of this. We carry our own keys."

She nods. "I was afraid it would be something like that. I

don't suppose you could lend me one?"

"It's nothing you can lend," he says. "But under the circumstances I think it might be suitable to share."

Together they turn back to the square, blunt-faced building. The night is almost upon them. The grim walls seem to sag in the darkness. She feels the wash of disappointment. "It doesn't really look like a castle."

"A castle? No. It's a granite quarry. Well, not this part. This part is the opposite of a quarry. But at the other end of the track it's the surface of the moon. They dug a big hole. And then here they piled it up. Cut it, smoothed it, shipped it out."

"Why here?"

"Well. It turns out, like so many things of this world, good stone is where you find it. And it has to be carried. They built the track, the trestle, the building. But nothing is as solid as it seems. After a while, when the price of granite fell, they woke from their enchantment. They took all their money and put it somewhere else, and a hundred years of peace settled on the land."

"It looks a little dreary."

"Dreary is as dreary does," the padre murmurs primly. "Please be careful of the hand."

He leads her away from the wide front door, down the steps, around the corner to where, even in the darkening twilight she can make out a narrow doorway, arched like a little mousehole in the stone. "Did you bring other clothes?" he asks. "Food, water? A tent? A sleeping bag?"

"This is all I thought I'd need."

He gives her shoulder a gentle pat. "Grey is nice. But bright colors are often better in a dream."

He unlocks the door, and they move inside. The padre takes a candle from his pocket and lights it. "Watch your step." They start down a narrow corridor. It seems only a few feet long, but then the padre touches his flame to a waiting sconce, and they are standing in a bubble of light. A few steps further, and there is another. They make their way slowly, a new candle lit every few steps until they are walking at the head of a long lighted tail. If Bunny hadn't already known it was a dream, she could tell now.

He pauses, darkness before them and the line of candlelight behind. "I think this is the moment when I should offer you advice. I think this is the time. Sometimes," he says, "the thing to do, is just to believe that everything is going to be all right."

"Really?" she asks. "Do you think it will?"

He raises the candle. A heavy wooden door, unwreathes itself from the darkness. He reaches for the handle. "God knows."

It is an enormous room. She can tell that by the sound and by the faint smudge of moonlight coming in through high windows. It is crowded with dark shapes, hunched and waiting—she thinks of the library ladies, she thinks of the sharp objects cradled in their laps. "Don't move," the padre murmurs, and he floats away into the darkness, his candle a flickering beacon that touches here and there, igniting one flame and then another, weaving together a slow accumulation of light. An earthbound constellation, it turns the ceiling to utter darkness and casts a wonderland of firelight onto a whole building's worth of tables and chairs, bookshelves and desks, all piled together and abandoned in one great room, as if a meeting had been called, from which everybody fled.

There is barely space to move. Bunny finds her way to where the padre stands in a little clearing at the center. There is a table laid with a white dustcloth and its own bright candle among the rest.

Bunny starts to cry.

"What's the matter?" he says. "Isn't it a beautiful dream?"

"How can this be life?" she asks. "Everything you go through, and by the time you find your way back, you're too weak and old and foolish for any of it to be real."

Gently the padre draws back a chair. "You're not old, Bunny. Are you hungry?"

"No," she says. "I don't know." She sits.

He places on the table a bottle of wine, a round loaf of bread. The bottle is open. There is only one glass. "You're not going to join me padre?"

"It's your dream, my dear."

He stoops and picks up a blanket, drapes it around her shoulders. She sees there is a pallet on the floor, a pillow, more blankets. And she notices that someone has draped across the makeshift bed a yellow sun dress the color of moonlight. There is a pale cardigan and, more unexpectedly, a pair of Converse Allstars. "I don't remember bringing those."

"You dress for the dream you want."

"I was hoping for someone else," she murmurs.

He cradles his bandaged hand as if protecting it from the news. "There might have been some trouble. We're hearing some disturbing rumors."

"The library ladies told me. I don't suppose he could be all right?"

"Let's, both of us, just imagine that he is."

Bunny notices, by the bottle of wine, a small jewelry box. She opens it. A second wide cardboard ring, the mate of the first. She slips it onto a finger.

"Whom God has joined together, let no man put asunder," murmurs the padre.

"That's such a nice thought."

She isn't hungry. The growing ache in her muscles has drawn her appetite away. She thinks the wine might help, but a sip tells her no. "I don't think I can do this justice."

"I understand. Your spirits are a little dashed."

"And the rest of me, as well."

"Let me see what we have."

From another pocket he draws a small First Aid tin. It seems to be full of dirt, but as he sets it under the candle's glow Bunny sees that there are mushrooms, small and large, little umbrellas and blunt, shapeless lumps with a texture of dusty cork. "What would you say are your symptoms?"

"I'm very sad," she says, "and I feel like death."

"I have just the thing."

He chooses one of the corky shapes. "These are for pain." He pops it into his mouth, carefully chews. "They're a little gritty." He pinches a cluster of the little dried parasols. "And these are excellent for raising your spirits." He puts them like a tiny bouquet into his mouth. After a moment he offers a little nod of benediction. "The rest are for you."

At the center of the vast glow of candlelight she chews slowly, as if this part of her dream has to be enjoyed at its proper tempo. After a while she notices the padre has left. He has turned back the blankets on the bed. She sits in her chair, attending to the rising comfort in her blood. She has the yellow dress. That seems right. And of course she has the gun.

After a while she lies down on the pallet beneath the blanket and the vast glow of candles, smiling as one by one they flicker and go out, so that the chamber slowly sinks from dusk into darkness, as gentle as gentle can be.

25.

In the morning Del knocks lightly on the guestroom door. There is no answer. She eases in. The bed is made; the room is tidy. Downstairs she finds the note: *Gone to get my things. I can see the future, and we'll all be in it.* It makes her smile, though it's hard to imagine a single future that will contain them all.

Clean is sitting up, reading on the sofa. He lowers his book, but when he stands to greet her, they kiss like strangers, fingers tentative, lips dry. The memory of him with the gun in his hand weighs her down. Every thought seems to weigh her down.

She brews a pot of coffee. Together they make breakfast, though this time the rubbing of shoulders is gone, the bumping of hands. It's an ordinary breakfast. Nothing burns. Nothing has much flavor.

With Calvin there had always been so many things to ask but, where before she didn't know the questions, now she is wary of the answers.

"How long did you know my father?"

"All my life. All the part that was any good."

"You didn't think to mention it?"

"No."

"Who's the padre?" Del asks.

"I have no idea."

"You think he's dead, don't you? You think it's true."

"Yes."

"You think someone came and killed him?"

"Yes."

"Will you help me find out who?"

"If I can."

"I don't want him to be dead."

"I know."

The silence isn't uncomfortable. It leaves her with an ache in her heart. So many things she thought would get better have only come apart.

"What do you want to do?" he asks. "We could take a walk."

"No."

"I could read to you."

"No."

They go grocery shopping. He is wide-eyed and murmuring as they roll up and down the crowded aisles. He is pushing the cart. "Raggedy Bob used to have one like this."

"Big shopper was he?"

"He'd like this."

He is amazed by everything she buys, startled by the ease with which she chooses each new item, just plucks it off the shelves. He marvels at the weight of the bags, arranges them in the basket of her bike. It should be like a date, walking home, wheeling the bicycle along, talking about the dinner they'll prepare.

And she thinks, maybe this is just what it's like. Every moment its own kind of effort. You say one thing, he says another. What's important is not what's lost in the back and forth, but what slender threads of understanding weave the moment into something you can keep. She thinks of those long afternoons with her father, sitting and reading, barely speaking. She remembers that blend of hurt and satisfaction with which she watched him stroll away. How could that be the last she's seen of him? And part of what turns her so bleak inside is that she can imagine it. She can imagine never seeing him again. It's the experience of her life with him, but longer.

What is the difference between away and simply gone? Is it something that could go unnoticed? How would she know if he just stopped being alive? What is the difference between waiting for a man who won't come home and waiting for one who can't?

The doorbell is a blessing. Clean hesitates at the sound, but Del hurries over to find Bertie Clutter, shiny and bashful, elegantly groomed and smooth. He stands in his grey suit and glasses, a nylon satchel in his hand. His appearance is like a little sigh of relief. His open face slips into an easy smile. "Dauphine. I hope I'm not intruding."

And just the name is enough to make her blush. The tight dress, the wig, the faulty French. It seems like another season. Nothing but a t-shirt and shorts now, but she can't stop smiling. "Just Del," she says. "Dauphine is my stage name."

He laughs. He steps inside. "I'm here on a mission of mercy. At least, it's a mercy for me. I'm looking for Bunny. We were supposed to have dinner together, and I'm not sure where she is. I was getting concerned, and then I thought of you."

Del feels a prick of something almost like jealousy. He is so smooth, so easy. She remembers him at the museum, all his little efforts. She imagines a dinner without fraught silences or long discomforts, a dinner made almost suave by his eager care and attention. And she wonders what he and Bunny have been up to in their private moments. "She's not here. She said was going back to her hotel."

"I found her there," he says cheerfully, "but then I lost her again. They say she's checked out, and I'm not sure where she's gone. We said we'd meet up later, but we never decided where. I think she might have turned off her phone."

"I'm sure she's all right," says Del. "Sometimes she just forgets."

"I'm sure that's it. You don't have any idea where she might be?"

"Sorry." Del glances back at Clean who is standing at the kitchen counter. There is something in his stance, his slight hold on the counter. As if his grip might be loosened by any stiff breeze. As if he might drift away at any moment. "We were just about to make dinner," says Del. And when Clean makes not the slightest move to agree or disagree, she says, "Would you like to stay. Bunny might come back any moment."

With a grateful smile he settles on the sofa. Del steps behind the counter, drawing Clean along side her. It is, she imagines, a chance to be together in company, to act out their feelings before a friendly audience of one. But Clean only grows more silent.

Del opens wine, distributes glasses. She tries to imagine what Bunny would do in her place. "Why don't you chop the carrots?" she suggests, but he complies as if breaking stones on a prison road crew.

And yet with every moment Bertie grows more festive. He tells jokes, he admires the artwork, the simple arrangement of the house. He asks questions about her mother's work, about her father. Del is planning a stew, but even as she begins, it is clear she has badly miscalculated. It's a comfort meal, easy and simple, but it will take hours to cook, and in the end it will look anything but elegant. She is feeling foolish, unpracticed, uncertain how to proceed when Bertie comes strolling into the kitchen.

"This looks delicious," he says. "But what if we make it into a stir fry? That might be fun. And it would be so much easier. Do you have coriander? Maybe a touch of ginger?"

She doesn't need to check her spice shelf.

"No matter," he says. "Let me see what I have." He bends to his satchel and from it draws a blue and white apron, a little frillier than she might have expected. The sight of him protectively garbed over the sleek elegance of his suit makes her smile. He pores through the contents of the little bag and straightens up with a chef's knife, a bottle of wine, and a cluster of spice bottles.

"You just carry them around?"

"I try to be prepared. I was a boy scout once. You never know what you'll need." He arranges them on the counter and turns his attention to the vegetables. They are a pile of chipped and irregular fragments, much too big. His hands move lightly. He juliennes everything, slicing the vegetables thinly, lining them up in little regiments of color as if the whole dinner were on parade. Del watches at his elbow, laughing at the skill, and topping up his wine, glancing back at Clean who seems determined not to have any fun. "Come on," she says. "You have to see this. Bertie's like an artist with that knife."

The scent arising from the pan is bright and exotic. Coriander, turmeric, cumin, shaken onto the hot pan and instantly transformed. It's like a trick unfolding before her eyes. Del couldn't help but compare it to the awkward breakfast this morning, to her old evenings with Russell where nothing could be further from this careless flair.

Bertie plates the food, pours the wine, arranges their seats around the table. They eat by candlelight. The evening has turned effortless. Except for Clean. He sits down, shy in the presence of so much food. He eats when she does, but slowly, assembling every bite. She suggests another bottle of wine. Clean shakes his head. But their host is up, bending over his satchel, drawing from it a bottle. He opens it gracefully.

"This is delicious, Bertie." And something in his smile, the extra brightness in his glance, makes her wonder. He's here for Bunny; of course he is. But she remembers the pleasure of being fussed over at the museum, the low electric charge of being flirted with. When he looks at her, his eyes seem sharper than they had, as if with every sip of wine he is reconsidering his feelings. The old Del would have blushed, would have gone quiet, but now she turns to Clean, tries to bring him into the conversation, tries to rub off some of the gentle charge on him. Do you see, she wants to say. Even this is something we could have. An elegant dinner, an elegant evening.

Which is why it is so undoing—when she is already casting ahead in her mind to when the dinner is done and Bertie has left and the dishes are washed, to when she is carefully lighting the candles around her bed, turning the darkness into a dream of light—that he stands up from the table and picks up his coat. "I'm going to take a walk," he says.

"What? Now? Where are you going?"

"Just around. I'm just going to get some air. Stretch my legs."

Abruptly she is a child again, the panicky feeling in her chest, half-remembered, half-brand new. "You're leaving? Just like that?"

"Just for a while."

"Can I come?"

"It's raining," he says, and it is. Beyond the windows the night is misty, the rain falls with a sound that only now comes to her.

"I don't mind."

"I'll just be a little while."

"I'll wait up," she says.

When she kisses him he looks startled, as if it's nothing he would have thought of himself, but he smiles and nods. He runs a hand lightly over the short, soft brush of her hair. "For luck," he says and steps out through the door.

Del stands for a moment uncertain, then finds her way back to her chair. The table feels different now, larger. And it seems larger still when, after a moment, Bertie gets up and clears away Clean's plate and silverware.

"You don't have to do that."

"This way it will feel like just the two of us."

Del glances back at the windows, but the darkness shows only the reflections of candlelight. What should she have done? Is it so wrong to want to have some fun? It comes to her with a kind of quick inevitability how easily people can leave her. But she's not a child now. That has to be a comfort. Is he out there waiting? Watching? She sips her wine, and then glances down at her t-shirt and shorts "Do you mind if I put a dress on?"

It's a sundress, floral and bright, something from her mother's garden party phase. Too small, of course, but she doesn't think Bertie will mind. She decides against a wig. Dauphine has already had her chance.

"And what are you doing here in town, Bertie?"

"You mean," he says, "besides have a series of dinners with beautiful women?"

It's not like a real compliment, she knows, but it warms her anyway. "That's quite a bag of tricks you have. If you needed a tuxedo, would you just pull it out?"

"Of course. A man in my line of work should always be prepared." He smiles. "That is a beautiful dress."

Candlelight is kind to Bertie. The wine is kind. There is a little knot of anger in Del's chest that the wine isn't quite reaching. But almost. She wonders if Clean is watching now, if he can see them. She smiles. "And what is your line of work?"

"Arbitration," he says. "I try to see everybody's point of view and help them all to see mine."

"It sounds very smooth." She doesn't know why she says it, except that he looks so smooth, his cheeks, his scalp. After all that roughly braided hair and beard. Though with that thought she remembers the skin of Clean's back, the feel of his bottom under the running water, smooth as smooth could be. She tries not to blush. That's right, she thinks. A woman of the world.

"The fact is," says Bertie, "I work for some of the same people Roger works for. Bunny's husband."

"I've never met him," says Del, "but he sounds like a jerk."

"He's an easy man not to like," Bertie concedes. "He's taken a great deal of money that doesn't belong to him."

"That can't be good."

"No. And I've been asked to get it back."

He smiles again. A smooth smile. Smooth cheeks. She takes another sip of her wine. "That sounds exciting."

"It doesn't have to be. I've been talking to a number of people. Just asking here and there. That's mostly what I do. Just talk. And do you know what I've learned? Apparently all that money, two hundred million dollars, has been turned into a series of numbers, twenty of them, written across the bottom of a card.

A wedding invitation. Isn't that something? All that money on a scrap of paper. And you'll never guess who the invitation was addressed to."

"Could I have a little more wine before you tell me?"

He looks startled, but he picks up the bottle and refills her glass.

"This is delicious." Del finds herself drinking with slightly exaggerated movements, smiling more than she needs, leaving forward to show her interest. It should be easy to see from outside, but she remembers his eyes aren't good, and the rain is smearing the windows. Look how much fun I'm having. See what an adult evening looks like? "You're such a good host, Bertie."

"The invitation?" he says.

"Oh, yes. I'm sorry."

"It was addressed to Bunny. Does that surprise you?"

"Is this her daughter's wedding?"

"Yes."

"Poor Bunny," says Del. "They left her out of it completely, didn't they? Isn't that awful?"

"Not completely. They sent her an invitation."

"I wonder if she got it. I'll bet it would have made her feel better"

"I think we can assume she did," Bertie says drily.

"I don't know. She didn't mention it. Letters get lost."

"You don't lose two hundred million dollars," he says. "Though I suppose you might hide it. And then you can just turn those numbers back into a pile of money."

"It's like the frog and the prince," says Del. Her glass is empty. She waits a moment, then pours herself some more. She's grateful that Bertie's not handsome. Men like Russell make her nervous. But after three glasses of wine Del is thinking she might be one of the nicest things that's ever happened to Bertie Clutter. "Does it have to be kissed by a fairy princess?"

"I don't know. Did you have a princess in mind?"

He's smiling again, eyeing her with something a little brighter than affection. Not everybody just gets up and walks away, thinks Del. Some people are actually interested. "How about me?" she says.

"Or Bunny?"

"I suppose."

"There are banks in the Caribbean that specialize in such things. One magic kiss and you're wealthy again. But here's what you need."

"You need good lips."

"And you need to have that number."

"So get the invitation, and I'll kiss it for you."

"That's the problem," says Bertie.

She knows they're just playing, but still, this hurts a little. "Well, Bunny doesn't have it."

"No. But I'm thinking Roger might be interesting to talk to."

"I thought he was gone. I thought they all eloped somewhere."

"Maybe not. You haven't seen him, have you?"

"I don't even know what he looks like."

"Tall, blonde. Running a little to fat."

"Sorry. I'll keep my eyes open at the café."

"And Bunny hasn't seen him?"

"Oh," says Del. "I'm sure she'd have told us."

Bertie eyes his plate thoughtfully. With his knife he is delicately separating the individual strands of green and red pepper, lining them up carefully, turning it into a kind of absent-minded dissection. He has beautiful hands, Del notes, but there is something in his movements that unnerves her a little. "That's something I wanted to ask you," he says. "Does she seem alright to you? Does she seem all there?"

"Well, she's ill," says Del. "She's a little distracted."

"She seems to be looking for something."

"Oh, that."

"She hasn't said anything about the money?"

"It's nothing like that. It's love. Lost love. Like all the rest of us, it's passed her by."

"Not Roger."

"No. Can you keep a secret? It's my father. My stepfather. Bunny's long lost love. And here's the part that makes it so sad. All those times he ran away from me, all those times he just wanted to be alone? Well now he is. He's dead. He could have killed himself for all I know, just like my mother. Isn't that terrible? It wasn't enough that he ran away. He had to go even further. And Bunny can look for him all she wants; she won't have any better luck that I did."

Maybe the wine wasn't such a good idea. It has turned all the candlelight sad. Even her anger has gone droopy and soft and no use to anyone.

Bertie sits motionless, his smooth face bent into a frown. "And where is she looking, exactly?"

"I have no idea. The padre, whoever the hell he is. The backbone, wherever that may be. People are always giving me directions and then not telling me what they mean."

"I see," he says. "Well. I'm so glad we talked."

"What?" She looks up, startled. He is straightening his napkin. He tidies his knife and fork. "You're not going?"

"I'm afraid I have to."

"No you don't. You could stay. I put on a dress."

"You look lovely." He's on his feet now, clearing the table, busily stacking the dishes in the sink as he speaks. "I'm sorry. But really, this is much better. I wasn't sure what kind of a talk we were going to have. This went very well, don't you think?"

And she wonders if she should have worn the wig after all. If maybe Dauphine was who he wanted. But he seems untroubled by the loss. He is whistling under his breath as he washes all the dishes, all the glassware, until everything is spotless. He wipes the counter and table with a flourish. "Good as new."

"Wait," she whispers. She could get the wig. There's still

time. "I'll be right back."

"I'm sorry, dear. I really do need to go."

She follows him to the door. "But Bertie. Don't you like me?"

"Of course I do."

"Don't you want to kiss me?"

He smiles. "How could I not?" And with the touch of dry lips he is out the door.

DELILAH

26.

She reads on the sofa, makes herself a cup of tea; she wanders idly around the house straightening what's out of place. She remakes the bed with fresh sheets, fetches the candles from the bathroom, sets them out around the room. An hour passes. An hour and a half. She steps outside. It's warm. The rain has settled into a drizzle. She opens the umbrella over her head but then all she can do is stand there. He could be anywhere. The whole empty night is spread out wide before her, empty and unfathomable, as if that's simply a part of who she will always be.

And then she notices, as her eyes grow accustomed to the dark, the door of the shed is ajar. She rarely keeps it locked these days, and already she is wondering what she will do when she finds him sleeping on the cold floor among the tools and the lawnmower. She wonders what it says about her that a man would rather sleep out here than join her in her bed, though even as she wonders, it's already clear. The ease with which people leave her is the one definite thing she knows.

Del opens the door. The spill of light from the house doesn't reach very far, but it's enough to see by. The shed is mostly corners, all tools and equipment. There is no room to lay a blanket. The lawn mower fills the center, to be wheeled in and out as needed. The rest is all but rusted into place. A wheelbarrow. Rakes and shovels. A wall of small tools hung on nails: wrenches, pliers, pruning shears. They're old and stiffened with disuse.

Del doesn't know whether she's relieved or not. If he's not here, where is he? What is there to do? Walk the streets till morning? She turns to leave.

In the corner there is a faint line of golden light, running down the edge of one wall. The familiar stretch of rough pine boards, braced and studded and solid as her childhood, is now askew in the darkness.

She suddenly feels as if her balance is shifting, the thin line of light turning everything strange. Her father built the shed when she was eight. She has looked at it every day of her life. Now she pushes, and the panel gives way on hidden hinges.

It's a tiny space, a hidey hole. Just beyond is the outer wall—the real outer wall. A space perhaps four feet deep. It disappoints her. What has she expected? A door into another world? An entire Narnia beyond?

But there is, she realizes, candlelight.

She steps in and, after a moment's hesitation, swings the wall back into place, careful not to latch it. The hidey hole expands into a narrow room. She breathes in the scent of old lumber and something warmer, achingly familiar: a mingled scent of wood smoke, earth, and unwashed work clothes that summons up her childhood in an instant. But though the air is tinged with years of living, it isn't stuffy. She sees the vents here and there on the wall and high on the roof, slatted and muffled against the light, but open to the air. The wood walls are warmly lit. They catch the golden play of an oil lamp burning in the corner.

As her eyes grow accustomed, the room expands; it stretches across the width of the shed and down along its length, an L-shaped echo, pressed between the cluttered room of tools and the night outside. There are hooks on the wall for clothes, though all that remains is a heavy wool coat, too warm for the weather. There is a low table with another oil lamp, now unlit, and a shelf for books, now empty. There is a futon neatly made and piled with blankets, and sitting on the end, in a daze of wonder, is Clean, who looks up hesitantly, as if there is no room left in him for anything but surprise. He says, "How long have I been here?"

"We stayed in our share of sheds over the years. Falling

down, rotting, barely a roof over our heads. Nothing half as nice as this."

But Del is thinking about all the nights her father didn't come home. All her life she has pictured him walking all night, or sleeping on a park bench, or, in her worst of moments, tucked into another home with another wife and daughter. And she is trying to decide if it is better or worse that he was this close all the time. That he would walk all this way from whatever place he had wandered and stop just short of coming home.

"I hate him," she whispers.

"You don't mean that."

"I'm glad he's dead. Why would he do this?"

Clean looks around as if the shadows, the snug, golden light, has something special to tell him. "Maybe he was hiding."

"From what? What was there to hide from? All these years?"

"Maybe someone was after him. Maybe he was afraid."

"From me," whispers Del. "He was hiding from me."

"No."

"Who else? There was no one else to get away from."

"That's not true."

"It is."

Hesitantly he whispers, "Come here. Lie down with me."

She feels a sudden spark of anger. "No! Not now. Not here." Always too little, always too late.

"Just lie down," he says. "That's all. I want to show you something."

Reluctantly she sinks onto the end of the bed. Clean is lying back now, his head on a pile of pillows. She crawls up beside him, and he takes her hand. The mattress is firm but not uncomfortable. The small space is snug around them. "Look at this," he whispers.

He reaches back behind their heads. A vent in the wall. It's closed up tight. As he levers it open a new fall of silver light enters the gold. He peers out, and after a moment Del puts her head beside his. She can see the house framed in her vision.

The lights of the kitchen and, upstairs, the lonely square of her bedroom window glowing in the night. "He put this here to see you," Clean murmurs. "He was watching over you."

"What good is that? What does that do?"

But she can imagine it now. Her father watching over his house and daughter without her slightest awareness. I keep an eye on you, Delphinium. And he couldn't just come in? "What good is that?" she mutters again. But there is something peaceful in the view, something comforting. The high, lighted lantern of the house sailing silently on through the night. "Sometimes, after he'd been away, my father would walk in and he'd barely be able to speak. He'd sit at the table, silent and happy. There'd be something about him so peaceful."

"It's the warmth," says Clean.

She turns at the certainty in his voice. "Is that right?"

"And the quiet. And the smell of food cooking."

"What if I didn't have anything cooking?"

"Or baking."

"What else?" she asks. "What else was he thinking?"

"I don't know. Book was always thinking."

"What was he feeling, then?"

Clean closes his eyes. He inhales the warmth of the little room, the air of coziness and comfort. "Home is the sailor, home from the sea, and the hunter home from the hill."

She is looking at him longingly; it's like a hunger. "Did he say that?"

"There's something about it; the air moves differently inside. Comfort has a different feeling than anything else. A good chair. A table. The chill of the night behind you."

It takes her a moment to ask. "Was he happy, do you think? When you knew him?"

"I don't know. Sometimes. Happiness is tricky at the best of times. Out on the scrounge it comes in little pieces, little moments that find you. And always in degrees. Happier than before. Less happy. Happier than you realized at the time."

"But was he happy to be home?"

"How could he not be?"

"I always made him scrambled eggs and coffee."

Clean smiles. Head on the pillow he closes his eyes. "What else?"

"Toast. Fried potatoes."

"Butter on the toast?"

"Yes."

"You have to say it."

"Buttered toast. Hot, with the butter melting into it. And strong, hot coffee."

"Four sugars?"

"More, if you like."

"Oh, my."

They lie still for a moment, fingers interlaced.

"There's one other thing," says Clean.

He reaches over to the low table and retrieves what looks like a pad of ancient paper, stained and creased. It's very thin. Not a pad, but a book. The remains of a book, looking as if it has come through the wars. The covers have been lost in some earlier adventure, though the spine is intact. And as she leafs though, Del can see it is old, though not as old as it pretends. *Shake-speares Sonnets. Never before imprinted. At London By G. Eld for TT. 1609. A Facsimile edition 1829.* And the inside pages, square blocks of heavy text, are like puzzles that even in brighter light would be hard to decipher. Clean reaches over and sparks a lighter. The oil lamp cups the flame.

It seems sad to Del that her father would let something he loved get so battered and worn. But as she turns the heavy pages, naked without their cover, pliant under her hands, she feels a pang of jealousy.

"It had a cover way back when. Brown with gold letters. He carried it everywhere. I mean, he carried everything everywhere. But this, it was always in the bottom of his bag. He tried reading it to me, but I don't think I got it. And in the end we settled on stories. I feel bad now. I think he would have liked to read it aloud."

"He never read it to me," says Del.

"Maybe he didn't think you needed it."

She hands him the book. It relaxes in his hands. He begins where it falls open. *"Shall I compare thee to a Summers' day? Thou art more lovely and more temperate."*

"See?" she murmurs. "Is that so hard?"

"Rough winds do shake the darling buds of Maie, and Sommer's lease hath all too short a date."

She presses against him, hugging his arm is if he were walking her across a busy street.

"Sometimes too hot the eye of heauen shines, and often is his gold complexion dimm'd, and euery faire from faire some-time declines, by chance, or natures changing course vntrimmed."

"You're reading me poetry," she whispers.

"It's not the most you deserve."

"Don't stop."

He reads as if he is making up every word just for her. *"But thy eternal Sommer shall not fade, Nor loose possession of that faire thou ow'st, Nor shall death brag thou wandr'st in his shade, When in eternal lines to time thou grow'st, So long as men can breath or eyes can see, So long liues this, and this giues life to thee."*

It is as if everything in this room has been laid out for them; as if it's been waiting for them all this time. "What's the name of that one?"

"Eighteen."

"Really? That's the best he could do? Read me the part about more lovely."

"You are."

"You have to say it."

He presses a kiss onto her temple. And now he is leafing through the pages. She closes her eyes, listening to the sound. She whispers, "Bunny said they were going to bury a poem at every spot. I wouldn't have the heart."

"They were going to dig them up again."

"Too late," she says. "Think of all those beautiful words buried in the ground."

"Do you want me to read another?"

"What do you think?"

"Since brasse nor stone nor earth nor boundlesse sea, But sad mortalitie ore-swaies their powere. How with this rage shall beautie holde a plea, Whose action is no stronger than a flower?"

She is floating on the ebb and flow of it, smiling like a queen. "Do you think it matters that I don't understand a word?"

"Del."

Her voice sinks to a murmur. "I was thinking," she says, "about a hot bath. Water up to our chins. I have lavender bath beads. Candles. We could lie there for as long as we want, and then climb into my nice soft bed. What do you think of that? Doesn't that sound like a poem to you?"

"Del," he whispers. "Look."

She opens her eyes. He is squinting up at the wall where the lamplight dips and rises, washing it in gold. Patterns in the wood mark the passage of years, swirls and smudges and stains of time; she sees nothing more at first. But then her eyes grow sharp. It's almost dreamlike how it comes into focus. A penciled sketch, a landscape, glowing and fading in the shifting light. A fairy tale traced on the bare wood the way a carpenter might lay out measurements and plans. Not a map, exactly. Or if it is, it's the map of a dream. In a roughly ordered circle, floating in the light, there is a high stone bridge above a field, an elaborately crenulated castle, a chapel with curved stone ceilings, a grotto, and what is clearly an enchanted cottage, all set amid trees and the narrow, winding passage of a stream. A dotted path like a curving arrow ties them all together. It's like the atlas at the beginning of a child's adventure, where all the wild imaginings are given places and names. To follow it you have to step into the pages of the book.

"It's old," says Clean, his voice a whisper, as if there is

something in the drawing that mustn't be disturbed. As if the slightest sound will make it disappear.

Del picks up the lamp and holds it higher. Each picture has a label, a little pennant drawn beneath, and in each label where a name should be, there is a number. 18. 116. 73. 142. 65. No apparent order. But an odd sort of precision, as if each number anchored a spot in the sprawling fantasy of the sketch. "What's this thing with numbers?" she says. "Doesn't anyone use names any more?"

"Look at these."

The shelf beneath the drawing isn't quite empty. There is a row of tiny objects, dark and rusted. Little puddles of shadow until she raises the lamp.

They peer down together at the clusters of wire and flattened metal, flakes of rust and tin, the silver beading of solder. Each one shaped into something it isn't. There is an ancient circlet of wire, twisted and joined like a wedding ring. A cluster of metal shavings formed into a bouquet of flowers. There is the sculpture of a key too delicate to turn, a tiny candlestick in its stand, and at the end of the row a small book cut and folded out of metal pages foxed and well-thumbed.

"Where did he find them?" Del whispers.

"He made them."

"He did?"

Clean reaches for the book. It is intractable in his fingers. He turns it over, searching for some meaning beyond the simple shape of it, but there is none. He starts to set it down.

"Wait."

In the spot where it is supposed to go, a smudge of pencil catches the light. He lowers his eyes almost to the board. Scratched onto the wood with the same pencil that has drawn the map, a single number. 142.

Del brushes at the mark with a fingertip. He sets the book back down in place. Carefully they lift each of the others: ring, flowers, key, candle. Each is anchored beneath its position by a penciled mark. 18. 116. 73. 65.

"What are these numbers?" Del mutters, but she is already turning back to the bed, picking up the battered book of poems.

Shall I compare thee to a summer's day? Just the sound of it now lays a hand on her heart. She sees that her father, too, has marked this as one of his favorites. There is a star in the corner of the page, and the number of the sonnet is circled. She reads the poem through to the end: fourteen lines and a world of hope condensed into the smudged black print. *So long as men can breathe, or eyes can see, so long lives this, and this gives life to thee.* Around the page there are little marks, the tracks of her father's sojourn: doodles, flowers, little figures living in the margins of the poem. The quick sketch of a rabbit. A frog. Little notes written in a familiar, tidy hand. *Beware a life reduced by hope.*

"What do you suppose?" Clean asks.

But she's already turning the pages. "What's the next number?"

"Seventy-three."

She tilts the book to the lamplight. Drawings, sketches of the little sculptures, marks and figures, all that might have been tumbling through her father's mind.

Clean is at her shoulder. "What was he thinking?"

"Every poem to a place, every place to a poem. This is all their time together."

She glances at the map, every image floating free of the world. She imagines her father standing here, in all the years after Bunny had left, tracing their path on those long ago weeks, recalling every spot, every evening, every hope, making a kind of fairy tale of the too-brief times, as if memory alone could draw them back together. And she feels a new pang of loneliness for her stepfather, who with all his shortcomings, with all his desires to be free of the family he had seemed to love, was clearly a voyager like her.

"And what's that?" Clean asks. "That's kind of weird."

She is stung by that. "I think it's sweet."

"Not the drawings. That bit there. That number. What's that number?"

There, in the bottom corner of the page, a number has been written in the same clear hand. 41.38329. It looks narrow, exact: all that precision in counterpoint to the sprawling emotion of the poem.

"I don't know."

But now that she has seen it, she sees more. In the lower left hand corner, beneath a little sketch of the rusted candlestick, a second number. 72.91368

"What was he doing?" Clean murmurs.

But Del can see. "What's the next number? The next place." She glances up at the wall. "The Chapel. What's the number for the Chapel?"

"Sixty-five."

She riffles to the page. *"Since brasse nor stone nor earth nor boundlesse sea, But sad mortalitie ore-swaies their powere. How with this rage shall beautie holde a plea, Whose action is no stronger than a flower?"*

There at the left hand corner was a drawing of the tiny bouquet, and beneath it another number. 73.03287. And over at the right, balancing the page, 41.69327.

Clean is squinting close. "What is it with all the numbers?"

"It's not a number," says Del. "It's a scavenger hunt."

BUNNY

27.

Bunny opens her eyes. The ache and longing of her dreams make way for the hesitant acceptance of another day. The hall is less impressive in the grey morning light. The chairs and desks, which in the darkness were light as floating stars, look crowded now, sluggish as if, like her, they're slowly coming back to themselves on the cool, dusty comfort of an abandoned floor. She is braced for the deep-set ache, the low, oceanic roll of nausea, but today she wakes only to a bitter loamy flavor in her mouth and a realization that the bright yellow dress has proven to be the most durable part of her dreams. It hangs there still, across a chair

She traces the tiny scratch on her thumb over and over, as if the thin, scabby line might transport her like Aladdin's lamp back to a time when everything made sense. She is barely in control; she feels that. She feels the places in her blood where the pills should be. Her mind is still her mind, but now the world has become a dream. She understands this. And though it's not a precise calibration of the growing distance between what she should be experiencing and what she is, it provides a reassuring shorthand.

Her life, as she has lived it, is no help. It has long since given way. But her hopes remain. And if all she can find is a true glimpse of her life as it once was--a chance to hold that close again, to make it real--that will be enough.

Her problem, in a sense, is that she is too clear-headed. Too prickly and self-aware. Every thought is suspect. But she is on the trail, aligned now with her younger self. She need only remember who she was, and she will know where she should go. And if she is uncertain what she'll find, if she recognizes that the events she is retracing have vanished too many years ago, she still feels in them a lurking importance, an understanding that will be hers only when she has broken the spell.

She stops herself at that. Be careful. There is no witch, there is no spell. Though it comforts her to think that Del would understand. She is looking for what was once real. But it has left a trail that can only be followed through her dreams.

So much of where we are is in our heads. She can piece together the fragments of her memory, however wild and unreliable, but only so long as she is careful to believe in them with all her heart. *When my love swears that she is made of truth I do believe her, though I know she lies.* The line of poetry comes back to her. Bunny smiles. Oh, Billy Bill. I knew you wouldn't desert me.

She makes her way back along the corridor and out through the little door to find the day is overcast, a wash of grey light and clouds. All the stillness of the surrounding forest is centered on a small blackened barbecue grill, like a campfire in a little steel bin. The padre is sitting on a rock, humming under his breath, a serious, tumble-down figure bowed beneath the silence.

"I've decided to treat it all as a dream," she says.

"Wise idea. At least you're dressed for it. I'm making you tea."

"I suppose even that might help."

"I've been gathering our daily bread. The lord's bounty is without limit. Did you know that you could live on acorns and sumac, if you guess right about the sumac. All those little twigs and bits of bark that most people walk right by? You could make a feast."

Bunny's reply is timid. "And have you?"

"Lord, yes."

He reaches beside him and sets upon his lap a large brown paper bag crowded with food and already darkening with grease. "If you catch Stan when he's shutting down the grill, he'll give you everything he was planning to throw away. Of course, you have to pick and choose. Sit down and have some tea."

"I just have to excuse myself for a moment."

When she returns from the woods, reminded of her girl scout days and somehow reassured that there is this familiar side to things—the body is the body, after all—the padre has arranged breakfast on a bent enameled plate: two darkened hot dogs, a hamburger patty like a thin scouring pad, a wedge of blackened meatloaf still gelid with gravy, and a pile of French fries that look, against all possibility, as golden and fresh as if they'd just come from the pan. "There's also a little turkey and an apple, if it comes to that. As John Wayne says, you need something for the trail."

She sits down and delicately takes a fry. Her hunger proves as evanescent as her dreams, but it tastes good, and there is always something comforting in the texture of a fried potato. "And there is a trail?"

"Isn't that why you're here?" From a steaming pan he fills a metal mug, and using his ragged sleeve as a pot holder, sets it down on the rock beside her. "Let it cool."

She lowers her face to the steam. "It smells awful."

"In an old burgundy they would call that aroma 'barnyard.' It's highly prized." And then murmuring, he trickles the rest of the pot into a battered tin canteen. "This is my blood which I shed for thee. Do this as often as ye shall drink it in remembrance of me."

Hesitantly she takes a sip. She tries to think mushroom consommé, though there's a tang there, a faintly chemical fillip to the earthy tones. "Why am I drinking this, padre?"

"Give it a minute."

The grey light brightens, as if the sun has broken free above the clouds. The edge of anxiety dulls. "I see." She takes another sip. "So what do I do now, Padre?"

"It's a pilgrimage. Only you can know."

She sits uncertainly, with all the world before her. Then

half-apologetically she touches the watch. "I have to consult a friend."

The second hole is a dog-leg to the west, 3,276 yards, par three. There's a water hazard that you'll need to cross and a considerable journey through the rough. This looks like a job for your longest driver.

"Well," she murmurs. "That's less helpful than I thought."

The padre is looking nervous. "It's very loud, isn't it? And a little optimistic about the par three."

"When I was first married, all those years ago," Bunny says, "I used to keep a dream journal. It was something my friends told me about. Jung was having a little revival, I think, and people were trying to get to know themselves better. I wasn't interested in that. At that point I knew myself better than I liked. But I wanted to get in touch with the other me, the one that might have been. So I wrote down all my dreams. I filled journals with the descriptions. But that's the thing about remembering. It's hard not to confuse what you hoped for with what you actually dreamed. I would write them all down, but when I read them back it was just a story. So now I'm thinking—now that nothing seems real—I'm wondering if it isn't some kind of a gift. Not a dream, exactly. But like that moment as you're rising out of sleep. When you can gather up the threads of your dreams and tie them to everything that you really want." She hesitates for a moment, as if hearing the words for the first time. "I don't suppose you understand."

The padre considers. "It could be the tea."

She takes another sip. "So what do we do?"

"There are some rules: Don't dawdle. Don't touch. Don't get lost...."

"No, dear," Bunny interrupts. "That's the point. We need to get lost. That's the whole secret."

"Oh," he says, as if startled to find himself the sensible one. "So, how do we know if we're lost?"

"I knew in my dream. I'll know again."

"And you're dreaming now?"

"It only needs to be half a dream." She takes three steps up the trail. *And we're off. Your last shot has travelled a total of...2... yards. You are now... 3,2762 ...yards from the second pin. Two under par.*

"Well," says the padre. "Begin as you mean to go on, and go on as you began, and let the Lord be all in all to you." He pours water over the fire and upends the empty pan on the grill. Then he tucks the bag of food under his arm. "I think we can leave the rest for the maid."

A new set of railroad tracks begins improbably at the base of the castle. They head off into the woods.

"For transporting the granite."

It's a path the watch seems to approve of. As they walk the padre nibbles on the French fries. "Breakfast?"

"I don't think so. Thank you."

He takes a bite, drops the rest on the ground. After they've walked a ways he does the same: half a bite and drops the rest.

"Should you be doing that?" says Bunny.

"Have to. How else will the good luck find us if we don't give it a chance?"

Bunny thinks about that, about the chance of luck finding them. She says, "Think of all the dreams we have, all stored up over the years. Think of all our wishes. All our fondest desires. We think about them so vividly. We dwell on them. We carry them with us to bed at night. How can they not be real? It's like a whole country we build for ourselves. A whole world, made up of all the places we haven't been, all the things we have wanted so much to do. It must have substance. It must have its own weight. So I wonder if, when we sleep, we visit that place. We build it slowly over the years, and then we carry it with us. And at night we can stroll along those paths that we thought we'd forgotten. Eat the bread and cheese. Drink the wine. Eat the apple. Surely all that can't simply have vanished."

"And where do you go in your dreams?"

"Here," she says. "That's what I'm trying to say."

And there before them the rounded riverbank gives way to a wide expanse of empty space. The grey sky opens over their heads, and the low rushing sound of the river rises to greet them. Like the weight of her dreams, the heavy, dark, slab of the trestle lies open before them.

In her memory it was a path, a challenge, a single terrifying moment that forced her whole new life to a stop and turned it back on itself. But now she marvels that an idea so wild and frightening could have such an ordinary daylight shape. The sight of it, the feeling of standing again in that shadowed moment, opens a spring of memory.

She feels the tears in her eyes, though when the padre looks over she can only smile. "He brought me here at the very end. He had such plans. I couldn't stop thinking about our plans. They had become so real. He had planned our honeymoon. He had prepared a magic grotto for our wedding night, a cave of moonlight and magic, and then we would move on, gathering our happiness as we went, to a far cottage, where we could live, untroubled by all the shortcomings of our forgotten lives. Wasn't that sweet?"

"You were running away together?"

"We were escaping into a dream."

"How far did you get?"

"Just there." Bunny glances up at the wide rusted expanse of steel and track. "Which I suppose is farther than most people get."

One step and then another. The gravel of the train bed gives way to the ancient, muffled thud of steel plates, gapped and rusted with age. The padre follows at her elbow, as though he might need someone to hold onto at a moment's notice. The ground falls away on either side, the great columns of the trees. And then she is standing high in the air, at the pivot of her life.

She had turned back, all those years ago. Turned and fled.

But now it's clear this moment has been calling her all this time. She listens to the low sound of the rapids beneath them. It has the churning rush of something deep in her mind.

She had been so terrified. She remembers the fear, the certainty of falling, the whisper of gravity clutching at her body. But more than that. The sudden shock of other people in a dream she believed was theirs alone. Voices shouting. And in the moonlight the cluster of men driven together in the narrow center of the bridge. Shouts, curses.

Even that would have been all right. But Roger had come, had followed them through the woods. He was all bluster and anger at first. What are you doing? Don't be ridiculous! Come back with me this instant!

And her first thought had been, don't you see? I'm not that woman any more. I'm not like you. But they had both stared with the same panicky shock when the fighting began, the thin dry crack of a gun. And even in moonlight as bright as her dreams, all she could see was the tangle of bodies as Bill and the smaller man seemed to launch themselves back over the trestle, tumbling, grappling, struggling, it seemed, toward her. And then she heard the bounce and skitter of something heavy, something hard, and there at her feet lay the gun, spinning slowly like the counter of some game show. Who's turn will it be? Who's turn?

Hers. It had been hers.

And now, standing in that place again, she feels the ghost of the old panic wrap around her heart, binding her tight.

"Are you all right? It's very solid," the padre says. "They made it for trains remember. It won't collapse."

"No."

"Watch out for the holes, though."

She feels his hand on her arm. He urges her gently into motion. In the middle of the span, she sidles to the edge.

"What are you doing, Bunny? Don't do that."

The low stub-wall, a foot high, no more, confronts the empty air. She forces herself to peer down into the pale froth of the rapids. Fifty feet is nothing, but her heart seizes for an instant. The hand touches her again. "I think we should probably keep moving."

When she steps onto solid earth her strength vanishes, and there is only the firm grip on her arm. Dear padre. Who'd have thought he could get himself across, much less her as well. "You should rest," he says

She is struck now by the strangeness of it all. She has stepped into her past now and out the other side. The tracks continue on through the trees, straight and certain, but the forest, itself, is blank, pathless, and inscrutable.

"Do you want to go back?"

"Not for anything."

The padre helps her off the tracks and down the gravel bed. He leads her along the riverbank and settles her at the base of an enormous oak. When she peers up at the branches, they seem to support the sky. The ground is cool. It feels good to sit. Her eyes won't stay open. She feels the weight of his blanket settling over her.

"You sleep," he murmurs. "I'll be back. I have just a few things to arrange." He sets the bag of food beside her. "In case you get hungry."

Her voice is heavy with sleep. "How will you find your way back without the French fries?"

"Maybe I'll take just a few."

DELILAH

28.

In the late afternoon Del dresses in voyaging clothes: shirt, sweatshirt, jeans, all black. They protect her. They make her secret and fleet. "How do I look?" she whispers.

"Very clean."

The gps compass is a small black box with a digital arrow and two blinking numbers. He presses it into her hand. "Your father gave me that just before he threw me off a train."

"He gave me one, too. But then he gave it to Bunny instead."

"You carry it."

"Don't you want it?"

"I have something better." He reaches into his bag and comes up with a fist-sized piece of pink stone, smooth as a cobble. Someone has drawn a smiley face on it with black magic marker. "That was Raggedy Bob. He thought it needed something."

Del hefts it in her hand. "It's nice."

"I call it Delilah because it's so hard."

She considers that for a moment. "It's smooth, though, too," she says. "It's pretty. It's not just hard."

"No."

She reaches over and gently touches the rock to his skull just above the ear. "What happened before? In the shower?"

"We have to talk about that."

"Are we going to talk about it now?"

"Not now. For now let's just walk."

She has forgotten how finicky the gps is. It takes some getting used to. She tries to remember how to navigate with just the numbers on the screen. It's like moving yourself by fits and starts. They are always off course, always correcting. No longer making their own way through the world, here every step is approximate. One street leads to another. They turn at the corners. Del wonders if they can walk all the way back into their childhood. There is the sound of a lawnmower trying to hurry its way through the last of the light. Is this so bad, she thinks, to be walking together on ordinary streets?

And there in a driveway just ahead a handsome couple, wrapped in the easy familiarity of a long marriage, are unloading groceries from their car. Their voices weave around each other, little teasing jokes and half-considered comments, the languid rise and fall of a story. The man hoists a crowded bag in both hands, grunting exaggeratedly with the effort, and the woman shakes her head, not so much amused as accustomed to be. The man glances up and catches Del's eye, and of course it's Russell. Of course it is.

Del walks on, allowing herself now, when it's too late, to be steered by the light hand on her elbow.

"Don't say anything," she says.

"What would I say?"

"Did you bring us here on purpose?"

"No. Of course not."

And Del sees, even in this, how little of her life has escaped the ordinary. "From now on I don't want to go anywhere I've already gone."

"Good," he says. "That's good."

Roads turn to alleys, alleys to cracked and weedy asphalt beneath the cavernous roar of the interstate. They slip through a curling gap in a high chain link fence, skitter down a short dusty hillside to come to rest on a single line of tracks running like a rusted river down the center of its broad gravel bed.

"Who doesn't love a train," he says.

The tracks curve away, moving past distant warehouses, over a narrow, sluggish stream with rusted cans like river rocks and the ancient beached remains of a sodden bedspring. They come to a flat stretch, and without warning the single track splits and splits again. Two becomes four becomes eight, and Del can see stretched out before them a wide, rusting delta of track.

Just for a moment, in the bright sunlight, it looks like one of those model train sets where every figure, every car and bench, stands toy-like and unmoving. Clean's hand, light on her arm, slows her pace, and they stand together, in the shadow of a catalpa tree, contemplating the ambling movements of a few distant orange-clad men. "They can be a little touchy about trespassers."

They sit on a bench beneath the tree, and Del's mind goes to the track, the moving trains. "What was he like?" she asks after a while.

She's grateful when he understands. "He's your father. You tell me."

"You must have known him better than I did."

From his bag Clean draws out a Hershey bar. He unwraps it and breaks off a piece. "For a while, when I was a kid, just the sight of chocolate would make me queasy." He cocks his arm and throws it as far as he can out into the middle of the yard. He watches for a moment as if something else might happen. Then he breaks the remainder in half and holds out a piece. She takes it.

The air is warm, the chocolate already starting to melt. Del gazes around at the yard but she can find no setting for what she can barely imagine. "Whatever he did, whatever happened, do you think it was an accident?"

He hesitates. "I think it was bad luck."

"So you don't think he did it on purpose?" And she realizes even now how much better it would be, if only her father wasn't trying to leave her.

Clean swallows, gathering his thoughts. He is searching, she knows, for something that might help her. "I don't believe for a second that he wanted to die."

She drops the chocolate bar on the ground and starts to wipe her hands on her pants, but he draws a bandana from his pocket. "It's better not to smell of food." When her hand is clean she makes no move to take it back.

They climb to their feet, eyes on the orange-clad figures. "Are they going to mind us?"

"We're just strolling. Minding our own business. Nothing more harmless than a couple of love-struck freddies."

She glances at him. "So you're love-struck now?"

"It's just a figure of speech."

And perhaps there is something in the moment, something completed by the holding of hands like any good magic spell, because they stroll down the track within twenty feet of the working men, and with the merest glance or two they are ignored. Once beyond the train yard Del expects him to draw away, but the spell clearly works under all conditions. Their fingers squeeze together, the warmth of the grip glowing between them.

"I used to dream about your hair," he says. "I used to try to imagine what it felt like."

"You know what it felt like."

He smiles. "I used to hold tight to my own hand at night until it went numb. Then it's like kissing someone else's fingers."

"You are such a liar," she says.

She watches as he drops a kiss, light as a snowflake, on the knuckle of her hand. "How is it?" she whispers. He kisses the knuckle again, pressing warm lips against it. Then he turns the hand over, opening the fingers, pressing his lips against her palm.

"One night, in Wyldwood, I remember touching your breast through your shirt. When we were kissing. When you thought I brushed it accidentally."

"I never thought that," she murmurs. "You can touch my hair now if you want."

"I don't think it will be the same."

He says it with a smile, but the lilt of sadness in his voice is real, and for the first time since she cut it off, since she plugged in the clippers and sheared off her childhood like shearing a sheep, Del feels a pang of loss. She has forgotten what the long hair felt like, forgotten the weight of it, the unnoticed movement against her cheek and shoulders. "Please?"

He reaches out and runs his hand over the short brush of hair. "It feels soft, doesn't it?" she says

"It does."

Del reaches up, as if her hand is the hand of a stranger, as if she has squeezed it tight until it's lost all feeling. She lifts his hand, as if shielding it from both harm and escape, and slips it beneath the placket of her sweatshirt, pressing it to the shallow warmth of her breast. He steps closer, but he doesn't take her in his arms. He doesn't sweep her into a kiss. Del isn't sure what she has expected after all these years, but somehow to stand perfectly still, with the beating of her heart cupped gently in their shared hands might have been exactly what the night had been promising all these years.

29.

He steps away, the warmth of her breast still glowing on his hand. It is crazy. Of course it's crazy. If she knew what he had done, she would run away crying. If she could picture it. The blow of the shovel. The terrible sound. She would hate him until the day he died. He should tell her everything. But he is alight with hope. To have this much, to be holding her. Del is smiling now, happy, and he cannot risk anything that would mar that smile.

"Don't go into the woods," she says. "Isn't that one of the rules?"

"It didn't say 'This means you'."

They step off the tracks and in among the trees. On the scale of western parkland the woods are modest, and along the very edges, frayed and well-travelled. They have become so ordinary a sight on the maps of the area, glimpsed from the highway or from the pass between the low hills heading out of town, that they have blurred into the mass of other, lesser trees that line the residential streets or muffle the park around the glacial base of Willow Rock. The city takes them for granted. The residents ignore them. But they are enormous. This is one of only three stretches of first growth forest in New England south of Maine, and the trees look as if they have been there from the beginning. Trunks like pillars rising into a canopy of green light. High branches arching wide, indifferent to the earth. It's all green shade except where a fallen trunk, moldering and massive, lets in a spill of sunlight.

Clean has never liked the woods. It is the place where all the worst has happened. But as they walk he realizes he has never entered the woods in daylight. The thin, cool glow is gentle on his eyes, the lurking silence opens as wide as the world. Every tree stands as if there is some secret it's willing to tell.

"Have you ever been here?" Del whispers.

And he starts to say, yes, of course. This is the last place he ever saw clearly. It is the end of his childhood. It's been at the center of his life for longer than he can actually remember. But now he gazes around at the obvious strangeness of it all, and he feels a sense of relief, of possibility. There is something about the quiet, the gentle sunlight, the cushion of the earth. In the distance there is an occasional sound, the faint rustle of movement that calls up the whole range of small burrowing and rustling animals that make the forest their home. All go about their business. The forest has forgotten him.

"Just a walk in the woods," he says.

"That's it? You weren't planning anything else? No funny business out here? All alone? No one to hear my screams?"

And the light tone, the carelessness, makes him laugh. He draws her close without thought or hesitation. They are alone. Freed from all the weight of their lives. "We should live in the woods. I think we should live here and never go back."

"This is how it starts," Del says wisely. "Wandering along, minding our own business. And then the little cottage made of gingerbread, the old woman with long teeth and a hot oven. It all ends in tears."

He kisses her. He's never been so aware of lips before.

Del presses close. "You think we're lost. That's what you're saying."

"You can't be lost if you don't know where you're going."

"Do you have another chocolate bar?"

"Are you hungry?"

"I'm always hungry."

"I have beef jerky."

"Who brings beef jerky on a date?"

And he laughs because he had never before realized that

it was possible to feel so light. Del dips a thumb and forefinger into the open neck of her shirt and draws out a joint. "If I give you some of this, will you promise not to take advantage of me?"

"I promise."

She sparks her lighter. He is aware of her lips pursed, the smooth column of her neck. He draws a finger lightly down and traces the boundary of her bra. She rises on tiptoe to press a kiss onto his lips, breathing smoke into his mouth. It catches him by surprise. He pulls away coughing.

"You are so lame. It's supposed to be romantic."

"I wasn't ready."

"You do it."

He takes the joint carefully, draws in a tiny lungful, fearful he will disgrace himself again. Then he leans down. She breathes him in without a flaw. "Where did you learn to do that?"

"You stick with me," she says. "I'll teach you everything I know."

The smoke casts its glow on the forest. The silence grows velvety. Del stubs the joint out against her shoe and tucks it back in her bra.

"I have water," he says, and feels foolish. His mouth is dry; his thoughts bump together like freight cars. He peers around at the trees, and realizes she is looking at him expectantly. With a little start he draws the bottle out of his bag.

When she tips her head back to drink he has to make an effort not to touch her.

"Can I feel your hair again?"

"Is that what you want?"

He swallows hard. He reaches out and gently brushes his fingertips over the smooth skin at the base of her throat.

"Don't do anything," she whispers. "Okay?" He nods. And hesitantly she unzips her sweatshirt and draws up the t-shirt's black hem. Her bra is grey cotton. "Do you want to kiss me?"

He can't think of the words so he just nods.

"Not yet," she says.

She reaches down and slides the bra up. Her shallow breasts spill out, pale cream and rosy-tipped. He has never wished harder for eyes that were sharp and clear. He leans down as if she were the pages of a book, and when he is inches away, she is as clear as a revelation. The pale skin roughening into goose bumps, the rosy nipple hunching delicately against the chill. "One kiss," she says. And he drops it, light as a butterfly, before Del, flushed and smiling, pulls down the bra and draws the thin, black curtain of her t-shirt.

"It's an adventure," he whispers.

They move deeper into the woods.

"There's a path," says Del.

"We don't need a path."

"And yet," she whispers, "here it is."

More like a deer track, all those delicate hooves cutting a narrow scuffed trail through the trees. But something about the path bothers him. Not memory exactly.

"What?"

"Nothing," he says.

They creep among the tall trees, a pair of mice at the feet of a gathered crowd. When they cross the occasional patch of dried leaves or twigs, the rustle and snap are too loud against his ears. The ground grows uneven. It starts to rise. Expanses of bare rock have pushed their way up in a series of curving mounds as if a tremendous granite serpent is swimming beneath the soil, breaking the surface and then sliding beneath. Up ahead the light through the trees is doing something strange. It's turning bright and powdery, hovering in the air. And just for a moment it feels as if he is coming unbalanced. But then he realizes they are climbing. A jagged ridge emerges like a granite spine. And as they reach the top of the ridge the ground before them opens up, and the solid roll of the forest drops away to a river bank and the fall of empty space.

"Yikes." Del's hand tightens in his. He is grateful for the grip.

Sunlight falling through the open air lights up the narrow gorge. He waits for the first wave of fear, the wash of vertigo. It is startling to see the river here, tied as it is to all his earliest fears. But in the darkness of that long ago night the river was just a sound, the rush of water and the certainty of falling. Now the sunlight makes it almost unremarkable. Walls of rock the color of dirt and at the bottom a moderate stretch of sluggish water the color of dirt as well. He tells himself there is nothing terrifying in the sight of muddy water. He anchors himself to Del's hand

"Isn't this something," says Del. "I've lived nearby all my life and I've never seen this." She is smiling, casting her eyes around in the brighter sunlight.

But he is looking only for the safest way down. Then it comes to him, the faintest hint. Just a tickle on the breeze. "Let's get down. Come on. Let's go," he says.

"But isn't this great?"

"Shhh! Not so loud!"

She turns, smile fading, as if only now realizing his discomfort. "I'm sorry. I wasn't thinking."

"Come down," he whispers. "Don't stand up there."

"It's okay. I'm steady as can be. I'm a mountain goat. I'm the queen of the forest."

"You need to come down."

He sniffs again. It's there. Paco Rabanne. He'd like to run away, to leap down into the forest and flee, but it's too late for that. Where is it coming from? They need to get out of sight. He grits his teeth and starts down the rocky incline toward the river. He tries to put the empty fall out of his mind. "Be careful," he says. "Hurry."

His hands are damp. He tries to move quickly, but it's such a long way down. Then he is standing on a narrow path at the edge of the cliff, pressing himself against the granite ridge, turning all his attention away from the steepness of the fall. He grabs Del's hand and draws her close, so his lips are nestled against her ear.

"I need you to be quiet," he whispers.

"Are you all right?"

"Shhhh."

She drops her voice to a placating whisper. "I'm quiet."

"I need you to be very brave."

"I'm okay," she says. "I'm okay with heights."

He shakes his head. "Do you smell that?"

And now she looks worried. "We can just leave. Let's go back."

"You don't smell it?"

She sniffs. "No. Nothing. What is it?"

"Paco Rabanne."

"What?"

"It might not be new. It might just be left over."

She is caught between surprise and a little hiccup of laughter. "Will you stop it? You had me going there."

"Shhh. Quiet."

And now she is staring at him, wide-eyed, uncertain. They sit, crouched together, arms inter-tangled. The silence grows. After a long moment he climbs to his feet, helping her up beside him. "No noise." And he picks his way carefully along the path. Del follows, but she is more troubled by his nervousness that by the danger. She seems drawn to the edge, to the broad, empty fall of sunlight hanging still and deep beside them.

"Nice place you've got here."

"Be careful." His heart is lurching against his ribs. She presses her mouth against his. "I'm a night ranger," she says.

"It's daytime."

"I'm a day ranger, too."

He is beginning to think it is nothing. The narrowing path gives them one way to go. They make their way along with Del now in the lead. Rocks and fragments, freed by years of frost, lie scattered across the path. "It's all just a mental thing," she says. "You know you're not going to fall, so there's nothing to be afraid of."

He is concentrating on his footing. The sunlight cuts shadows into the sloping face of the granite. Then up ahead he sees Del skirt a small outcropping and then a broad shadow reaches out and draws her in.

"Stop!" he hisses. "Del?"

He hurries forward, aware of the scrape and catch of his shoes against the path. "Del?" He eases around the outcropping. It's like he is hanging out over the drop. Then he draws himself back to the cliff face and feels it curving away, deepening into darkest shadow. There is a shallow cave that draws him in away from the edge, giving him room to breathe again. A sudden spark of light catches in the blackness. Del is lighting the stub of a candle, and the light fills the shallow cave.

30.

They peer around at the narrow space, black and shadowed against the late light of day. There is an old bronze cross standing on a table. It is the only peaceful thing in the room. The rough walls are painted with images, black-smeared and fierce. Little figures creeping through the trees, running in fear, huddled awkwardly around a single man. His hands are raised; a sooty cross is smeared upon his chest. The rest of the space is monsters. Huge and terrifying. Wild abstractions of claws and teeth. Bears, wolves, dragons, and some things in between. Amalgamations of terror and imagination.

They give her the creeps. Standing before the walls Del can feel the strangeness roughening her nerves. She fights the urge to run. And then, beneath the sooty smell of the candle she picks out the sweet, sharp scent of something new. Perfume? Cologne? Drifting in the cramped air.

"Douse the light."

But before she can move Clean has blown out the flame.

The sudden darkness blinds her. She reaches for the rough granite wall and touches Clean instead. She latches on. "Be very quiet," he whispers.

But it's too late. Because isn't that the thing about fairy tales? It's always already too late.

At the scrape of a boot on the ledge outside they turn and see, silhouetted in the dimming sunlight, a slender and raggedy looking man with a nose like a cockatoo's. His pale face seems to gleam. He has a thick mustache, its curling ends twisted up like tiny lariats. Beneath it the thin, wet curve of a grin. "This is so sweet. Oh, you're holding hands. You're going to make me cry. Come out into the sunlight kiddies. It's time to play."

Releasing her hand, Clean has slipped in front. "What do you want, Peach?"

"Why do I always have to want something? I want to see you, boy. Come on out into the light."

Clean hesitates.

"Oh, come on. You're not afraid of a little sunlight, are you? Vampires? Is that it? Oh." He makes a production of noticing the drop off just a foot away, the crumbling edge of the path with nothing beyond. "It's the heights, ain't it? That's gotta be tough in a place like this."

"What do you want?" he says again. Del hears the tightness in his voice.

"Both of you. Come on. Let me get a look at you."

One hand on the granite wall, Clean steps out reluctantly, and as she follows, the man's smile broadens. "That's better."

The sunlight is less than she expected; twilight has snuck up on them. In the deepening gloom the three of them make a crowd on the narrow path. The edge is too close. The man's cologne is overpowering.

"That is one terrible little cave. Did you see it? That Padre's got some scary thoughts. Wouldn't want to meet him on a dark night. But, hey. That's probably what he's saying about me. And now he's gone. Doesn't seem very friendly. And you, Pisser. I'm a little surprised to see you here." He glances at her. "And company. Ain't that nice? Got a friend now, Pisser? Partnering up again? Cause that worked out so well, didn't it?"

"Just met," says Clean. He glances at Del. "Jeff. This is Peach."

"Jeff, eh? You're a little bulky, ain't you, Jeff? A little big in the butt."

"Not everyone has your girlish figure," says Clean.

"I don't know, Pisser." And quicker than thinking he steps forward, too fast for the dimming light and the narrow ledge. Del tries to back away, but there's no room. He leans close and sniffs. "Doesn't smell like a Jeff. You're not trying to fool me, are you, Pisser?" He's walking around her now on the narrow ledge, that huge nose almost brushing Del's cheek, the smell of Paco Rabanne so strong on his clothes and skin it seems impossible he could smell anything else. "I'd say, maybe Gloria. Or Barbara. You smell like a Barbara. Don't you, Jeff? Or a Betsy. Is he a Betsy, Pisser? You get your hands on a genuine Betsy?"

"Cut it out, Peach!" Clean is tensed, but there's no room to move.

"And so clean! Oh man. I could smell you for hours."

Clean makes a grab for Del, but too late. The stranger snatches up a fistful of her shirt, yanking her close, jerking her toward the cliff. "You going to push me, Pisser? Is that right?"

"Stop it!" He fastens onto the man's jacket. "Don't move!"

"You going to send me over? Whooeee! It's a long way down. Just look at that. It's a long scream, ain't it? Takes a long, long time to get it out of your ears."

"Let her go!"

"You want to dance? Is that it?" They're bunched together, too close for steady footing, rocking slightly, swaying together. And all Del can see is the empty space opening wide just over the thin man's shoulder. The gorge is deeper now in the gloom; the twilight turns it bottomless. And Peach is panting, his mouth a wet grin, peering from face to face, just inches away. He is teasing now, taking a series of little steps toward the edge and away. "We're dancing. Can't you feel it?"

"Let her go!"

"And what? You and me? You want to dance, Pisser? We go over together?"

Clean's face is white. His jaw is clenched tight. Del's heart is pounding. "I'm letting go," says Clean. It takes him a moment. Slowly he releases his grip, though his hand still hovers. And behind her back she feels his other hand locking onto the hem of her shirt.

Peach is grinning still. "Getting a little slow there, Pisser."

"Now you. Let her go."

He steps back slowly, empty hands ostentatious in the air. "I think you're losing a step. Maybe all this domesticity is slowing you down."

"What are you doing here, Peach?"

"Maybe nothing. Maybe we're just playing a little. Maybe we're just going for an afternoon stroll."

"We?"

"See? You almost made me forget. Grief!" he shouts. "Grief! Goddammit!"

"Let's not get excited," says Clean.

"Bring 'em on down!" And he is all smiles again. "You know Grief? Doesn't matter. Just a guy. Big guy. Gives me a hand with the tourists. What was I supposed to do? Couldn't find you."

She can hear a rising murmur, the crunch of footsteps on loose rock. "Got something?" calls a voice.

"Company!"

There is a scrabbling on the rocks above them, and a large figure clambers down. "What's the party?" Behind him two other men make there way more slowly.

"She's not here," says Peach.

"Well, what the hell. If you're just here for a clinch don't call me. I'm heading back."

"This is Pisser. I told you about him. The Bear's boy."

"Yeah? And who's the Barb?"

"I guess it's love."

Del is breathing hard, trying to empty the fear from her lungs. She's got a handful of Clean's jacket and a hand on the granite, but still she can barely move. With the careful scuff of footsteps two men appear. One is tall and blonde, in a camel coat much the worse for wear. He favors a hand whose fingers are heavily bandaged. And behind him....

"Bertie!"

She is almost foolish with relief. "Bertie, what are you doing here?"

He looks out of place, but exactly the same; a sleek grey suit, heavy glasses, manicured fringe of black hair. He is chewing slowly on something, a French fry. He has a little pile of them in one hand. And he is frowning at her. "It's Del," she says. "Dauphine. Don't you remember?"

He smiles. But the smile isn't much of a comfort. "How nice to see you again. I don't suppose Bunny's with you."

She hesitates. The man called Peach is grinning now, for no reason she can see. "No. We don't know where she is."

"Of course not. And where is it you're going?"

"Just walking," says Clean.

"A little romantic getaway?"

"That's right."

"Sounds like just the sort of thing Bunny would like. You're sure she's not here?"

And Del sees that what she had taken for a raincoat hanging over his arm is a grey dress, torn and stained. "Is that Bunny's?"

He takes another bite of French fry. "I fear so. Yes. I'm afraid something may have happened to her."

"Where is she?"

"Out here somewhere. We're trying to find her, before it's too late. Do you know where she's gone?" His smile is not winning. His eyes are cold.

Del thinks of the map on the wall of the shed: the chapel, the castle, the grotto. And at the end of the trail the fairy tale hope of an enchanted cottage. "I thought she was back at her hotel."

"No. Not our Bunny. She's on the run. But not to worry. We'll save her." He picks up another French fry, and examines it as if for dirt, then drops it back in his hand. "The padre and I have an understanding. It shouldn't be a problem. But, still. Many hands make light work." He glances at Peach. "I think we'd better bring them along."

"What?" says Del. "No. It's late. It's dark. We should get home."

But Peach just laughs. "Why did I know you'd say that?"

They make their way along the narrow path, walking carefully until the backbone subsides back into the earth and the path widens to include all the forest to their left. Twilight changes everything. All the reassurances of daylight have disappeared. The trees, themselves, are turning strange.

To their right the sound of the river rises, a rush of water. Far above, the sky holds onto the light, but up ahead she can make out what she has, at first, taken for the dark, distant bank of the river, but which now, she sees, is the heavy bulk of a railroad trestle stretching across the wide expanse, steel beams open to the sky beyond.

Clean grows still beside her. She can feel the fierceness of his grip, but he says nothing.

Peach glances back, his voice jaunty. "A walk down memory lane, eh, Pisser? Returning to the scene of the crime?"

"What does he mean?" she whispers. Ahead of them, on the bank an entire hillside is turning into something else. The foundations of the trestle, a great rising shoulder of concrete that seems to start deep in the earth and then bend itself out over empty space. "Where are we?"

But Clean can't bring himself to answer. It is Peach's voice that rises from in front. "Well, whoops-a-daisy. What do we have here?"

It's a world of shadows. Up ahead flashlights snick on, and the evening darkens to midnight. In the play of light Del sees the cracked concrete, wide streaks of rust staining the wall. She sees the earth, a lumpy pile of dirt, and darkness.

"For God's sake," Bertie snaps. "Is this a joke? You think this is funny?"

Peach is laughing. "It wasn't me."

"What did I tell you to do?"

"It wasn't me!"

The scattered lights are concentrating now, cutting through

the darkness at the base of the foundation. She becomes aware of something, a scent, a smell that's creeping out from under the heavy cologne. It might just be the rising mud from below, sour and decayed, but the way Clean grips her hand turns it into something worse. She has smelled it before, in the park, coming on the stiffened body of some torn and long-dead squirrel. But stronger now. Much stronger.

His grip is painful. "It's okay," she whispers. Which is foolish, of course. Which is stupid. The smell is getting worse, hanging thick on the air, clinging, it seems, to this one sheltered spot.

Up ahead Bertie is shaking his head. "It's just sloppy. You think that's funny?"

Peach is glancing back. "I think it's kind of sweet. I see the family resemblance."

"I'm sorry," Clean whispers. "I am so sorry."

"What are you saying? What are you talking about?"

But Grief is behind them, herding them forward. In the glare of the light there is something slumped and broken. A log. A pile of discarded clothes, dark against the dark earth. Her eyes swim and sharpen. And she sees what she has probably seen from the very first: the body of a man, his clothes caked with dirt. It sits slouched in a shallow hole with its stiff and muddy fingers wrapped around the handle of a shovel. It is hunched against the edge as if exhausted by the effort of digging itself out. And there is something darker than the dirt on the battered face. It smears down, caked on the stained, pale shirt.

"Oh."

Del can feel the breath caught in her too-tight chest. There is no reason that it should be him. No way it could be. They are miles from anywhere her father would be. But something in the way they stand, all the men, glancing back as if inviting her to read her future in the huddled figure. "Who is it?" But she knows.

"Don't look."

Clean's grip is on her hand, dragging her into motion, hurrying her past, but she can't take her eyes off the body. She sees the face, darkened and battered. And even now a low and terrible familiarity is trying to make itself felt. The hair is long and dirty, but someone has almost lovingly brushed it back from the forehead. There is a pair of wire-rimmed glasses, smashed and twisted, but almost daintily arranged. And there is something in the posture, some easy, cheerful, self-possession that seems to reach beyond death.

"We don't have time for this." Bertie kicks a clod of dirt into the hole. "Bury it," he snaps to Grief. "Deeper this time." And without another glance he clambers past and up the slope and onto the tracks.

"Come on. Don't look." Clean draws her into motion.

As they step onto the tracks she can hear the big man behind them kicking dirt into the hole. Her voice is a whisper. "Who was that?"

"Oh, Del."

"We should call the police. We should get help."

But he doesn't reply, and in the silence she turns. He is stiff beside her, as if he has taken root. The hand in hers is damp and slick. Before them the flat steel bed of the trestle stretches away, ancient and rusted. Gaps between wooden ties, gaps between ancient beams, a narrow path of steel down either side right up against the edge. It is hard to tell the shadows from the empty space. The man named Peach is grinning at them, standing carelessly out over the gorge. "I gotta say, Pisser. You are always good for a laugh."

"Is this a problem?" Bertie is standing there impatiently.

Peach laughs. "My boy's not good with heights."

"But this is the guy, right? Your little helper."

"Oh, yeah. Pisser and me go way back."

"Jesus wept. Why does this need to be so difficult? Bingham, Grief. Leave that." He stares coldly at Clean. "You. Bury it. Again. This time so it stays buried." And his eyes fall on Del. "We'll be back. I'm sure I don't need to tell you. Don't do anything stupid."

The two men climb up past them and onto the tracks. They walk single file into the darkness, pools from the flashlights dancing at their feet. Del stands there, feeling nothing. The darkness is an ocean drowning her. Across the rusted expanse the men are stepping onto solid ground, looking around uncertainly. Bertie bends and picks up something from the ground. He dusts it off and takes a nibbling bite. They move in among the trees and disappear.

The silence takes hold of Del, there on the edge of all that empty air. "Oh, Del," whispers Clean. "I'm so sorry."

But she draws her hand away. "What have you done?" she says.

"I tried. I'm sorry. There was nothing I could do."

"Don't touch me."

"We've got to go."

"Who are you?"

"We can't stay here."

And as if to make the point, the first sounds rise from the darkness beyond. Low coughing grunts, a growl. A long, reverberating howl rises slowly from the distant bank.

"What's that?" she whispers.

"Wolves."

"There aren't any wolves in Connecticut."

"There are always wolves," he says.

And now amid the barking, growling clamor there comes a shout. A cry, rising through the shivering air. A gunshot.

"Jesus."

It freezes them in place. And then a scream. Rising, rising, twisting through the darkness before snapping off like a thread.

BUNNY

31.

The twilight has come, darkening the sky. She wakes to the warmth of the blanket and the red throbbing ache of her shoulder. There is a lightness in her head but no moment's disorientation. Surely that must say something. No bleary wondering where she is, or when or how. The forest seems the natural place, though the approaching night does cause a little worry. How did this happen? How did one thing after another lead her here? Sitting against the rough bark of the oak she tries to conjure up her life. Grocery shopping, Lakeshore Drive, the crowded hubbub of the Water Tower, the bright sunlit echo of lunchtime at Terzo Piano. But none of it is real. The twilight is real. The smell of the earth. She is on a quest. That's what she must remember. She was afraid before; that was the problem all those years ago. She mustn't be afraid again.

The paper bag beside her is cold and slick with grease. She opens the tin canteen and sips the bitter tea. Ten sips, she thinks, and counts them off. The queasiness fades. She touches the watch for courage, for luck. *You are a terrible excuse for a golfer. Maybe it's time to open your eyes. Your last shot has travelled a total of ... zero...yards--.*

--a dogleg halfway up and a water hazard. The trees may prove tricky. It's a hole that rewards pluck and endurance. Remember, if it were easy, a dentist could--.

Smooth and effortless power, isn't that what we all seek--?

Be present in the moment, or the moment will pass you by.

She is a dropped stitch in time. An idea someone else has had. She imagines the padre, distracted by a newer thought, wandering the woods with a nagging sense that something has slipped his mind. But the forest is only trees; and who's afraid of a tree? She is aware of the weight of the gun in her pocket, aware of the sense of order and necessity it provides. Every story has its ending, but it's a rare moment when you hold the beginning and the ending of a story in the same hand. It's sad, she thinks. But some things just are.

From out of sight she hears the crunch of footsteps, the rising murmur of voices strangely matter-of-fact in the creeping otherworldliness of the twilight. The bobbing brightness of their clothes shows through the pale grey and brown of the woods: red, yellow, cheerful and out of place. Bunny climbs to her feet. She lets the blanket drop so that, in her yellow dress, they will think she is one of them. The two hikers emerge, fresh-faced and cheerful, a young man and a woman, stretching their legs in the freshness of the untrammeled air.

They hesitate. The woman's face is clean and unlined, though her expression is concerned. "Hi," she says.

Bunny's throat is dry. She nods.

"Are you all right?"

"I'm fine. Thank you."

"Beautiful day for a walk," offers the man.

"Beautiful," she agrees.

"Do you need any help?"

"I'm fine."

"Are you lost?"

"I'm fine."

"It's going to be dark soon," says the woman. "We could take you back to town."

"I'm really fine. Thank you."

The man is relieved to be convinced, though the woman is uncertain. With a nod they continue past, carrying with them a little bubble of something so ordinary and unthinking that Bunny can no longer recognize it. She waits for the last sounds of their footsteps to fade.

She wonders if they're in love. She wonders if, in twenty years, they will look back on this day. She wonders if love can ever be more than one thin bright thread running through all the warp and weft of things.

She catches a glimpse of something bright, a little beacon of color. When she walks over and stands above it she finds, wrapped in its bright and ordinary yellow, a bag of M&Ms. She opens it and eats them, one by one, marveling at the taste of the chocolate. And now that she knows there is something to be seen, she spots a water bottle, its seal unbroken, dropped by some hiker, perhaps, and waiting for her all this time.

The world is a contest between those who see it for what it is and those who don't. The importance of a quest is not always a matter of the scale of the prize. When there is no pot of gold, the journey, itself, must become the reward. All that she has felt, everything she has held within her heart. It's still out here somewhere, waiting to be found. And the fact that she has so little idea how to find it seems somehow, in her fragile state, merely another aspect of why it must be true.

They tell you if your boat capsizes you're not to leave the wreck. She sits down against her tree again. Drinks the water, watches the night sail in.

She is still waiting for the padre when she hears the screams. She must have been asleep. They drag her from her dreams and into darkness. Solid, thick, the night trembles with the high, piercing cry. It's coming from behind her, the direction of the trestle. And for a moment Bunny thinks she is back in the past: some fantastic transmigration, returning all her most vivid memories to their appointed spots.

But then she is fully awake and hears the growling as well. The yapping of wolves.

She has never heard a wolf, but there is no uncertainty. It's as if the fear is written in her DNA. It is loud, and close. Her legs don't work. The whole idea of rising has been frightened from her mind. She feels the weight of the gun in her pocket, but it is miles away. Her fingers pluck nervously at her wrist; the voice erupts, chirping petulantly. *What is the matter with you? Are you even facing the right way? Your last shot has travelled a total of ...* She scrabbles at it, smothering the voice, snatching at the band. She hurls it away into the darkness, and the voice peters out.

She is a seed in the silence. A tight knot of dread in the darkness. She climbs to her feet. Run, she thinks, Run. While every dragging breath is winding her heart tighter.

And then something. In the distance, no wait, not the distance. In the darkness close among the ancient trees she hears the low, rising tremor of a growl. A rough vibration catching at her ear, catching in her chest. A series of shadows detach themselves from the rising trees and creep into the moonlight. They are low and fierce, tense with energy, smooth in movement. Three of them, four, five. They seem to consider her for a long moment, raising their muzzles to the air, murmuring in a low rustle of hunger and sharpened awareness. "I smell food," murmurs one of them and the others growl approval. "I wonder what the food is doing here. I wonder how it's wandered so far out of its way."

Bunny tries to speak, but her mouth is dry. She is a night-ranger, she tells herself. She is a voyager of Del. She should greet them. She should welcome her fate. She opens dry lips. "I'm Bunny," she says.

"I love bunny. Tender and tasty."

"Not that kind," she whispers.

"What makes you think so?"

Before her eyes the low shadows shift and rise, extending up like smoke in the moonlight, drifting into the shape of men. They close around her, sniffing and growling. "You smell like meat."

"I'm afraid I'm not myself tonight. Someone has taken my medication."

One wolf is bending near, breathing heat on her neck and face. She can feel the rough rasp of fur against her skin. She can see the teeth, long and fearsome, in the faint silver light. "Please don't hurt me," she whispers. "I'm on a pilgrimage."

"Well, why didn't you say so? Where are you going?"

"I'm not quite sure. I've never been this far before."

"Well," says the wolf. "What could go wrong now?"

A claw reaches up and very delicately draws itself down the curve of her cheek and throat. The breath on her face is hot and foul, wreathed in vapors of old meat and blood. Just at that moment the moon emerges from behind the clouds and in the silver light Bunny has to clamp her jaw shut on her scream.

It is a face of fur and long, wicked teeth. A man's face. But the terrible fangs. In the moonlight they gleam, horrid and pale. "It's not so easy to look on your death, is it?" he whispers and grins.

And it is the grin that catches her. It wavers. Shifts. The beard has been shaved back on the upper lip and just below. And she sees that the long and terrible fangs are tattooed on the skin. A set of wilder, more ferocious jaws that frame the human mouth.

He reaches up a hand, a claw—the nails grown long and fiercely sharp, caked with dirt and something darker half-dried under the edge. "Every death has a name," he whispers. "What's yours?"

All she can do is shake her head. The words catch in her throat.

"You don't look good, little Bunny. Have you been sick?"

"I have."

"Nothing catchy, I hope."

"No."

"You're all bones, little Bunny. Hardly worth eating."

"I'm not," she says. "I'm not worth eating."

His voice is close in her ear. "Everything's a trade here in the woods. Everyone understands what's fair. A moment's pain for peace, an empty stomach for a full one. Even a bunny might have something to trade beside its soft and tender self."

Slowly she bends down and picks up the cold paper bag. "I have meatloaf," she whispers. "Hamburgers. With French fries.

And gravy."

The wolf leans in and takes a long deep breath. "And what do you think that's worth?"

"I need to find my way."

The wolf considers for a moment. "Back there is the way you came. Any path you like to the river, then over the trestle. Be careful of the mess."

"I'm looking for a grotto. A magic grotto. And an enchanted cottage. From a long time ago."

"What kind of enchantment?"

"I don't know."

"What's it like?"

"I've never been. But I've heard it described. Golden with candlelight. A whole cave of wonder and delight. A cottage made for love."

His voice is a hoarse whisper in her ear. "That sounds nice." And she feels his tongue, rough and dry, running up the length of her cheek. "And it tastes like the truth. But it doesn't help much. These woods go on for a thousand miles."

"That's not true."

"In the dark, alone, they do. You have to be brave, little Bunny."

"I'm not brave. The only time I had a chance to be, I ran away."

"Then it looks like you've got another chance." Gently but firmly he pries her grip from the paper bag and lifts it from her arms. It leaves her feeling vacant, unanchored, ready to drift. "There's some tea there. I wonder if I could keep it," she says.

"Are you trying to make half a trade? Are you trying to renege?"

"No."

"You need to live off the land, little Bunny. You need to let the woods provide."

"I grew up in Winnetka. I'm not that familiar with the woods."

"I thought you said this was a pilgrimage."

"But which way do I go?"

"You'll know." He holds out something to her, finding her hand in the dark and pressing into it something dry and corky, about the size of a human ear. "Eat this," says the wolf.

"What is it?"

"It's part of our trade."

"I want to know what it is."

"You'll know once you've eaten. Pilgrimage is always an act of faith. You know that."

Reluctantly Bunny brings the corky piece to her nose. It smells of earth, deep and rich and not unpleasant. It smells like long ago, like her first experience of the woods, stepping in among the huge trees, feeling the earth soft and quiet under her feet. She nibbles on one edge. It tastes the way it smells, earthy with a faint, rounded aftertaste of old wine.

"All of it," growls the wolf. "No half-measures here."

Bunny slips it into her mouth and chews. It grows rubbery between her teeth, bringing the saliva welling up. But she finishes chewing and swallows. It sits uneasily in her empty stomach, and she thinks for a moment she might be sick, but the nausea passes. It leaves something in its wake.

It's not so much that she feels more firmly rooted. But the air, and the shadows of the air, seem to draw more closely around her, balancing and steadying. She feels little curlings of sensation at the base of her neck, thin suggestions of color raising gentle fingers to her brain. The brightness lifts itself into her eyes.

"On your way, little Bunny."

"But I can't see."

"Of course you can."

The night is beautiful, the forest is beautiful: everything picked out in moonlight and pearl. The breeze is soft against her skin. The sudden double hoot of an owl arises, loud and close.

"Is that you, Bill? Time to go already? Can't a girl even gather her thoughts?" It hoots again. "Okay, okay. Keep your feathers on."

She feels hollow, ethereal, a creature of mist. She wonders about the tea; she doesn't want anything that will slow her down. But her legs surprise her. One step follows another. The ground is easy, level and soft. The moonlight opens the way; it sharpens her sight. Her ears are tuned. She listens to the rustle of small creatures among the leaves, the noise of her own steps blurring into the general sound of the forest.

She had looked at a map of the Thousand Acre Wood long ago in that first year of her marriage, trying to remember, trying to make sense of it. Trying to feel it again. But the map only showed an irregular pattern of green in an undistinguished stretch of Connecticut. She had been struck by how small it was, how pinched it looked among the cities and towns and roads. How easily it could be missed. But now she is marveling at all that it contains. Memory lives in the heart and the mind, but it lives in the place, as well. It lies deep in the landscape, waiting to be touched again, waiting to be brought to life with its one pure note.

Up ahead in the dark she sees the flicker of a flame. Everything is a trick of the mind; why shouldn't this be, as well? But she finds a candle, wedged between three rocks. On the ground beside it lies a chocolate bar, a bottle of water, and the palely rolled simplicity of a joint. Eat me. Drink me. Smoke me.

She sits and rests. Eats the bar, drinks the water. Leaning back against a tree she lights the joint from the candle flame and draws the smoke in deeply. The queasiness retreats, the ache in her shoulder. The sounds of the forest grow more delicate and complex. She thinks of Del, gathering every one of them, storing them away. The high rusty creak of a frog, the rustle of tiny feet. The owl back again. Who? Who?

She blows out the candle. She tucks it into her pocket. She follows the sound.

There is another candle in the distance. A tiny flicker. And another after that. She moves through the darkness from light to light. There is water, Raisinettes, a granola bar, M&Ms. There is another mushroom, rubbery and dry. She blows out each candle and carries it along, as if she is gathering up the ladder as she climbs.

At some point she's no longer alone. The sounds of low voices come to her. Not wolves, men. The clumsy crunch and rustle of their footsteps. They are not here for the silence. Far out in the darkness she sees the dip and swoop of their flashlights.

"Jesus! It's a fucking big forest."

"She must have come this way. She can't get over the river."

"Well, we're not going to find her like this."

"Do you want to go back and tell him that? What do you think it will be this time? Another fingertip, or your nose?"

"Oh, shut up. Let's go. I hate this place. It gives me the creeps."

Bunny smothers the urge to run. She feels herself grow wily, feels the forest slip its smooth and secret hand into hers. Away in the distance she can make out another familiar flicker of candle-light. Her feet are silent. Her breath is low and quick. With the clamor of voices drawing closer, she hurries.

The candle is lodged in the crack of a low outcropping, a wall of rock rising out of the earth. From the corner of her eye she sees the flashlights weaving through the trees. Quickly she bends down and blows out the flame. Just in that instant she catches the glint of something, thin as a hair. A tiny, single thread of light. It begins at the candle and leads down across the rock face to a deeper shadow, a narrow fissure of darkness that seems to widen under her gaze. It is a narrow opening, a path through the wall of rock. She reaches out.

"What was that!"

"Put it out!" And the flashlights die.

In the widening silence she touches the string. "Thank you, padre."

One hesitant step at a time, she traces her way along the thread, following a narrow path among the rocks. It is almost easier not to look. Inching down the trail she feels the hillside rise on either side. Step by step descending, she hears the voices fade into the past.

What has begun as a hole in the rocks has opened into a wide ledge, and the hillside to her right gives way to nothing but moonlight. It's a canyon cut into the side of the river bank, a quarry hollowed out and abandoned. In the moonlight every cliff is carved and faceted, shaped by the ancient rock drills and dynamite. The sound of water rises to her ears. The ledge goes down and down. Her fingers creep along the string.

She feels water, a fine spray, wetting her cheeks, dampening her dress. She sees a ragged, narrow waterfall, no stronger than a garden hose, tumbling its way down the rocks up ahead. She prepares herself to be drenched, but the trail bends to the left, back into the hillside, and after a little rise and dip she finds herself beneath a wedge of overhanging rocks in a shallow cave above the river.

There is a small flame burning, and the padre sits beside it. "Do you have my candles?"

She gazes out through a gallery of moonlight onto falling water, cliffs, the narrow ribbon of the river. "Thank you," she murmurs. "I never thought I'd feel this way again."

"The lord takes away," he says. "But he doesn't only take away."

He accepts the candles from her and sets them up around the chamber. When they are lit, the rock walls dance and glow. Outside the moonlight is impossibly bright. It catches in the falling water, turns it into strings of pearls. It is all too beautiful to be a dream, and far too beautiful not to.

The padre is sitting on a shelf of rock looking out over the river. He is hunched and rocking a little, as if all this is just too much. Bunny wraps the blanket around her shoulders and settles down beside him. Together they are cloaked in candlelight, sitting on the edge of the world.

"Is this where I was supposed to come, all those years ago?"

"Nothing is lost," he says. "Everything is waiting whether we come for it or not."

She imagines this place waiting for her all these years. She imagines her younger self following the thread along the path, stepping into this bubble of wonder. It is somehow even more vivid to see it through those long ago eyes. To see it transformed by the knowledge of all that it would have meant. It is almost a travail to see it now; what she feels is almost pain. It would have been so beautiful. She could never have gone away from this, never have left after sharing such a sight. And their whole life together would have begun from this moment.

The padre is shaking beside her. She is aware of the dampness, the chill. She is aware of the night air turning cool. She takes the chocolate bar from her pocket and breaks it in half. "This will warm us up."

It is, she knows, so much less than it would have been. She feels it so much less. She has ruined it by coming so late, allowing herself to grow so tired and sick. But still. To know that it has been here all the time. The spill of moonlight on the water, the candlelight. To know that all of it was real. Surely that's something, too.

"Would you put your arm around me, padre? It's all right. It's just a dream."

She draws the gun out, cradles it in her lap.

"What are you doing with that?"

"It was a gift from a friend." The smile feels more wistful than she'd hoped. "Isn't this how it's supposed to work, padre? It's that kind of story, after all. Once you introduce the gun, it has to go off."

"It's already gone off," the padre says gently. "That's why there's a story to begin with. This is a love story, Bunny. It's the opposite of death."

32.

He is standing, caught, suspended between one horror and another. Across the river the screaming dies away, but now, in the silence, the night could hold anything. The images of all that might have happened are there in his mind, but they are nothing compared to the appalling realization that the worst has already happened. The truth is out. And he wonders how he could ever have thought he might keep it at bay.

Book's past caught up with him, that's what the library ladies said. But no one's past is his, alone. And it's always catching up. There is no escape from all that we have done. Clean tries to imagine what he might say to Del, what he might tell her. But words are nothing now.

"You knew," she says. "You knew he was there. How did you know?"

"It's not what you think."

"Did you come back for him, or did you come back for me?"

"For you. Always for you.

"And then you killed him?"

"It wasn't like that. There was nothing I could do."

And standing here now he tries to recall if this is true. The night with Peach, the sudden surprise. After all the years of waiting, his mind frozen into disbelief. He tries to remember the anger of his youth, the fury at Book, the burning rage of betrayal. But all of that is gone. It's just this moment now, and there is nothing to make it right.

"I have to see him," says Del.

"No."

But she isn't asking. And when she leaves the tracks and starts down the hillside to the grave, he follows. His whole life has been leading up to this. He tries to imagine waking up tomorrow without any hope, without any future at all. He tries to imagine what he'll do.

"Do you have a light?"

"A candle," he says.

He takes it out of his bag, and she lights it with her zippo. She steps down into the shallow hole and settles onto the edge, holding up the flame. The patterned glow splashes down over Book. The shadows are a mercy. He might be sitting with his back against a tree, his legs stretched out, a book open on his lap. He might be reading to them both by candlelight. Clean slips into the hole, as well. He sits opposite Del, with the body slumped between them.

"Did you hate him?" she asks.

"I did. I didn't. It wasn't that."

She gathers up her thoughts. "I've been so angry with him. For so long."

"I'm sure he understood."

"I kept thinking there'd be a time when I wasn't. That I'd have a chance not to be. The next time he stopped by. The time after that. I thought we'd talk. Sit down together. Explain ourselves. That's all I wanted. I wanted him to tell me his life. I wanted him to listen while I told him mine. Is that too much? But we never did. He never did. Maybe no one ever does. I wanted him to know me."

"He did. I'm sure he did."

"I wanted him to love me."

"Oh, Del. How could he not?"

She raises the candle toward the face, and gently he stops her, presses the candle back, lets the darkness stay. "Just remember him."

"What I remember is that he was always gone."

"Not always. That's not true."

"What do you remember?" she whispers.

"This," he says. "Sitting together out in the air like this.

Sometimes we'd just be quiet. Quiet for hours. Sometimes he'd read. I loved his voice. You said he never read to you?"

"Sometimes he did. Not often." She manages a smile. "And never the books I wanted. Those are for children, he'd say. So he'd read all this other stuff."

"*Treasure Island*?"

"I liked that one."

"*Huckleberry Finn*?"

She nods and smiles. "But he changed the names. Jane Hawkins. Debbie Copperfield. He told me Huckleberry was a girl's name. He said Sherlock was a just an old-fashioned way of saying Shirley."

"He was a possum, all right. Always two steps ahead."

"It was years later I found out the truth. I still have a hard time believing Sherlock Holmes is a man."

She reaches down, brushing at a sleeve, straightening the jacket. And he can picture her now as a teenage girl, a motherless child with only a father to love. Packing his lunch, washing his clothes, sending him off to work looking spick and span.

"What do we do?" she asks. "Should we call the police?"

"I guess."

"What will they do?"

"I imagine they'll be pretty curious."

"And Bunny? What will Bunny do?"

He shakes his head.

They're straightening him now, smoothing the sleeves, tugging the jacket into place. Clean fixes the glasses, pressing the long hair back. He is careful not to see too much, but in the light he spies a pale margin of white amid the smeared and filthy clothing. Delicately he draws from the pocket an envelope. It is large and almost square, heavy paper and stiff. He peers at it, then brings it to the candle. The address is written in a flowing copperplate hand, laying out with the formality of an engraved invitation the name Barbara Jean Bingham. There is no address.

"Bunny?"

All Del can do is nod. As if it's all just too much, as if, even from beyond the grave, her father is reaching out to somebody else, anyone else but her. She lifts the muddy hand from its grip around the shovel, and she is rubbing it as if the dirt might someday come off.

Clean looks away. He would give her everything, but all he can do is keep taking things away. He looks at Bunny's name, weighs the envelope in his hand. The top has been slit. He draws out a thick sheaf of pages, folded and stiff. They're nothing like the envelope. Four or five sheets of ancient paper, earth-stained and corky, like something forgotten in the earth. He unfolds them.

Since brass, nor stone, nor earth, nor boundless sea,
But sad mortality o'ersways their power,
How with this rage shall beauty hold a plea,
Whose action is no stronger than a flower?

At every secret place he'd buried a little bit of their happiness, and sealed it with a poem. Eighteen years in the earth and here they are: all the cherished moments, stained and water-sodden, dug up and gathered together. All the things they'd buried to preserve. And this is what remains.

Clean holds them gently as you would any figment of the imagination. He lifts them, breathes them in. The smell of earth, paper, the gathered scents of time and rain and the lingering smell of death. What was he expecting? Wood smoke and apples? The dusty smell of a library? Nothing is preserved the way you hope. It's always the least of it that remains.

Del is crying. He hears the soft, broken sounds of her breathing, the low murmur of her voice. He can barely look at her now. Head bent low, she's rocking, whispering. She has the hand in her lap now, holding it as if she will never be able to let it go. Clean's life is over. It's as simple as that. This is all he will have in its place for as long as his memory holds.

He eases across, settles onto the edge beside her. "Del. Del, please." He tries to hold her hands, he tries to comfort her, but her fingers won't be stilled. He leans in close. "I'm so sorry." But it doesn't help. She is holding the hand, the right hand. Long slender fingers caked with dirt. And she is brushing them, stroking them, whispering in a kind of prayer, "Thank you, thank you, thank you." When she looks up her eyes are full of wonder. "Don't you see? It isn't him."

Clean has never known about Book's landscaping jobs, about his accident with the lawnmower, the damaged hand, the missing fingers. To him it is simply a miracle. He doesn't know who it was they had beaten and buried. He doesn't know if he deserved it, or if this is one more weight on his conscience. He only knows that of all the places in the wide world where Book might be, here in the ground is no longer one of them.

BUNNY

33.

She has slept under a blanket on a thin and narrow mattress that magically appeared when the padre lifted his candle above it. He'd held a hand up in hesitant blessing as she sank into sleep, and now she opens her eyes. The cave, which might have been so much less than she imagined, is not. The falling water catches the light, painting the stone with glints of mica and quartz. She can hear the cheerful fluting of birdsong in the unseen trees. Her dreams have filled her with certainty. She is almost unsurprised when she finds, on the rock ledge from the night before, a little cluster of food: bread, cheese, an apple, a bottle of water. The best of dreams always carry their meaning into daylight.

There is a small jeweler's box which, when opened, contains a cardboard ring. It is, she notices, coming undone. She catches at the tape with a nail, and the cardboard unfurls into a curling, narrow strip. A line of elegant engraving.

...request the pleasure of your company at the marriage of
Ruth Anne Bingham and...

It's like the answer to a question she hasn't thought to ask. An invitation cut into strips. And at the bottom, like an afterthought: four numbers printed neatly in ink, 1203. A message without a meaning. A portent wrapped around her finger. It's puzzling, but in dreams even the most uncertain things will eventually come clear.

Bunny re-seals the ring and slips it on beside the other two then steps out onto the riverbank. The walls of the gorge rise above her, the trees high up on the rim. She sits with her back against a rock and lets the sunshine warm her face.

The illness has worn her down; she knows that. It's made

her light-headed and thin. But perhaps it has saved her as well. In the past she has been too afraid, she sees that now. Too afraid and too impatient. But now she understands that her quest, from the very beginning, has been no less than this: to wander through the unknown terrain of her forgotten past, looking for that crucial turning point, that bend in the trail when she could have made everything right. It is a quest without clear guidelines; she can't be sure if she is on the right track. But there is something encouraging in that. It puts the search, if not the goal, within her reach.

She spends the day reading, sunning herself, nibbling on the food. She sits and watches the play of light over the rocks and river. When the sun is at its height and the forest falls silent around her, she slips off her clothes and swims. Her shoulder stings at first, and she worries about infection, but after a moment the water is nothing but a comfort. She lies on the blanket to doze in the sunshine and wakes and swims again. When the twilight begins to gather in the narrow band of sky overhead Bunny slips into her clothes and gathers up her meager possessions. She climbs the narrow path and emerges among the trees, waiting as the sky goes slowly dark.

There's no sign of the padre, but that doesn't worry her. Of course they must wait for the night to travel—every dream requires its own particular darkness.

She begins by following the moonlight: as good a guide as any. Where the trees let in slices and pools of silver, that's where she heads, from one patch of pale light to the next. She doesn't try to move quickly. There is no hurry.

She remembers the screams, of course, and the voices from last night. She remembers the wolves. But even they are part of the quest. The fear is part of the resolve. She concentrates on the silence. Every footfall is its own point of concentration. Sometimes she hears the distant crack of a dry branch, the low complaint of voices. She tries not to let these sounds guide her. She angles her path away until they fade, then she finds her way back to the course she has set.

And then there is the forest itself; it seems to direct her. Standing perfectly still, her breathing shallow, only the sound of her pulse in her ears, she waits for the ache to settle, the complaining voices from her shoulder and joints to die down. Then she reaches out with all her senses for any hint or suggestion. The single crisp trill of a bird's song, the chitter of a squirrel, a low rustle in the forest bed. And she turns in that direction. Finally she sees, among the distant trees, the flicker of light.

It is a candle. But unlike those from the night before, this is burned down to the nub, as if it were somehow left unattended for too long. But there is a chocolate bar. She takes it gratefully. In the distance she can make out another flame. This one, as she approaches it, burns out. Though it's given her a direction. She walks, a note of worry entering in, a thin note of dread.

The next light comes from far off to the side, and it's different. Not a candle. Voices come to her, low and grumbling. The beam of a flashlight. She angles away, silent as mist, until her breathing gradually calms.

Then the rustle of footsteps close behind.

"Padre?" She turns.

"Oh, Bunny! Thank God! It's terrible out here."

"Roger?"

His voice is shaky, though he clings to that last trace of jauntiness. "We've got to stop meeting like this."

She wonders, for a terrible instant, if this means it's all a dream. That such a clear hallucination should find its way in. The thought is a bitter one, that none of it is real. But she sees in the sudden wash of his flashlight that this is not the Roger of her memory. The blonde hair is straggly and damp, the camel coat is stained, his shirt is torn and smeared with blood. He has a thick bandage on one finger, and that's blood-stained as well.

She reaches out and turns off his light. "That's better," she says.

But now that someone has anchored her attention to the things of this world, the nausea returns. She draws the remains of the joint from her pocket. Bless Del for this. Bless Del for all of it. Without her she might never have known she was a night ranger. She might never have known that she needn't be afraid.

Bunny tries to peer ahead, but the shadows are growing deeper. She can sense the light-headedness. She hasn't been eating well, these last few weeks. That will have to change. She needs to make herself stronger if this is to work. The life she is choosing requires strength. She needs to pay attention.

She looks up at the sky where the brightest stars are gleaming through the faint backwash of the city lights. Is that Venus? The bright light there, guiding her way?

She smiles. What a lovely thought. That the sky, itself, might guide you on your way. That love is there to see if you have the eyes. Just to believe it is to make it true.

His hand is on her arm. "This is serious Bunny. You have to tell me. Where's the invitation? Where did you put it?"

"I don't know what you're talking about, Roger."

"This isn't a joke anymore."

The shining lantern of the moon has risen above the tree line and now it coats everything with silver. "You were such a disappointment, Roger. And I was, too. I realize that. But look where we are. And I can remember. Isn't that lovely? Isn't that a gift? I remember walking along one night and we smelled a fire. That little taste of wood smoke on the air. We were hungry and tired, but we felt so—oh, my."

She half-smiles at the little filament of smoke rising from the joint, delicate as a memory. "We had just been making love. And it had been so quiet. And then that first hint of twilight slipped in around us, and the birds started cheeping and fluttering, looking for their places for the night. And suddenly all the trees were alive with birds. It was like applause. That's what Bill said. And it felt like it. That moment deserved applause."

"I don't want to hear about this."

"Oh be quiet. Nobody asked you here."

She stands, balanced on the memory. "We were walking along like this, just like this, and we smelled a fire. That perfect, cozy, fragrant smell. And there was a man sitting there, in a little clearing against a rocky hillside. And you're not going to believe this. It was a priest. Just there. Sitting, cooking his dinner. And he looked so shiny and clean. I don't think he was lost, but he was happy to see us. And we asked him to marry us. And he said, Do you have a ring? And I did. Of course I did. We were laughing, and warm by the fire. Oh, it was beautiful. Like a little chapel. And he married us, and blessed us, and sent us on our way."

Her voice fades into silence, and after a moment even her own imagination shifts uncomfortably. "I couldn't have made it all up, could I?" she whispers. "Not after all this."

"It's just the medication," says Roger.

"There is no medication. That's my problem."

"You'll feel better soon."

"But I won't remember, will I? Isn't that always the trade-off with dreams. They allow you to leave, but not to take them with you."

She hears the other voices. They are drawing close. "Shhh," she whispers.

"This is ridiculous!" Even in the dark Bertie's voice is clear.

"It's a big forest."

"And we've been over most of it."

"Grief!"

It sounds like a curse, but then another voice answers. "It's no good in the nighttime. We'll have to come back in the morning."

Bunny holds her breath. She hears them turning, hears them heading away.

And Roger's flashlight comes on, sudden and bright. "Over here," he shouts. "She's right here!"

Bunny runs.

She presses on, trying to stay silent but aware of every crunch and snap of a twig under her feet, aware of her pounding heart. The beams of light behind her are dancing in the darkness, searching but not finding. The shouts are rising. She doesn't know where to go, so she runs ahead. In the distance the lights go out, the voices die. She is alone once more, but the darkness is not the same. Her breath fills the silence. And then there is another sound, lower than her breathing, underlying every panicky noise she makes. The slow-rising sound of panting roughened into something more. Something edging into the very boundary of a growl.

It's from her left, back among the trees. Growing closer. And she turns, not running now, but fleeing, as if numberless generations of the hunted are shouting at her to fly, hide, climb a tree. But the lowest branches are twenty feet high, and every trunk is less a ladder than a wall. There is growling from the right. She is panting, sobbing. The growls are mixing in her ears with all the sounds of her own panic. She turns again.

She's being herded. She cannot catch her breath. Walking, running, walking. The night is a mass of shadows, and within those shadows, shifting now as if pieces of the night itself are shifting, a pack of low, dark shapes are creeping in. The air, itself, shivers at their growling, at the catch and scrape of claws. Bunny's heart is pounding. Her mouth is dry. She thinks wildly of stories she has heard, hikers in the back country who have saved themselves by lying flat and flinging away their packs and food. But of course she has no pack, no food. She wants to cry out, but her throat is dry. And whatever is left of her voice is caught somewhere deep in her chest and refuses to rise.

She trips, her feet suddenly snagging, and down she tumbles over a log, a bundle of twigs. No. A body. A body wrapped in a familiar old robe with the soft texture of earth. "Padre," she gasps. She feels for him in the darkness: shoulder, chest, head. "Padre, wake up." She shakes him as if he might just be sleeping. As if even now he might leap to his feet and run. And she realizes, even as she touches him, that it's not the Padre. Has never been the Padre. How could she ever have thought it was? And she feels something shift in her heart at the feel of him, that warm familiar touch. Oh, Bill.

Looking up she sees the faint glow of candlelight, but not just a point of flame. It is glowing in a window, a pale golden square of light, mullioned and cozy. There is a building there, dark and low. After all this, a little cottage, with the golden welcoming light within. And she presses herself against Bill's warm body, and even now it is familiar. And when she breathes the scent of him, it is like nothing else she can name or describe, but to breathe it in is to be carried back, to have all her memories returned. "Oh Bill," she whispers. "Bill. We have a daughter, Bill."

The flashlights come on, all of them, it seems. She's in a circle of light so bright she cannot hide.

Roger is panting hard. "Goddammit, Bunny. You've still got some legs on you."

The other figures crowd around, raggedy men, smelling of old alleyways and sweat. The man with the big mustache is there, and he's shaking his head, half-admiring. "This is what we've been chasing? A skinny girl?"

"You don't get paid by the pound." And it's Bertie, bent and panting, hands on his knees, looking ruffled and angry in his stained and wrinkled suit. "Oh, Bunny," he says. "We have so much to talk about."

And as if in answer to that, as if they couldn't disagree, the low growling voices rise from the darkness beyond the blinding circle.

"Goddammit it!"

"Who's there?"

"What the hell is this?"

And the circle of light explodes. It's a cataclysm of noise and bright shards. Bunny feels the weight of the gun in her pocket, but it's nothing to her now. She thought it was all she had, but now she buries her face in the crook of Bill's shoulder, in that loamy, comforting smell of her past, and shuts her eyes tight.

There's a cry, a shriek, a terrible sound ripped out of a throat, and the glare behind her lids darkens. The lights go out. The sound of shouts and running. Then slowly, slowly, just the sound of ragged panting filling the air.

She covers her ears. She huddles low, curled into the smallest seed at the center of the warm, full night. She can feel the presence of the wolves around her. She can smell the wet, mineral scent of blood, thick as the night and filling her nose. She can feel them bending lower, feel the breath on her head, feel the sharp, dry whisper of a single claw against her cheek. And the voice, a low, heavy exhalation of blood and death, whispers, "Wake up, little Bunny. It's time to wake up."

Part Seven

The Cottage

34.

He is free. They are, both of them, free. Free of the past and free of the future. Free of the constant, lifelong, looming threat of Book's death. Free to love.

They call the police from a pay phone at the edge of the train yard. They report the body. Then they ease into the shadow under the catalpa trees.

Bunny. They cannot go through the wolves to get her, so they will have to go around. It feels like a rescue. Love is a rescue. Love is always a rescue.

Two figures watch the slow-panting engine on the middle track. There have been so many trains for one of them and none at all for the other. Part of what Clean wants most, in catching this one, is to mend that distance. He grips her hand tightly. "You're a running machine. You're a running, leaping, catching machine. You leap and you catch and you don't let go."

"Can't we just get on now?" whispers Del.

And maybe that could. The yard is quiet. No guards in sight. They could saunter up and climb aboard. But no moment is simply itself. He wants to find his way back as well as forward. In sharing the leap onto the cattle car—why, oh why a cattle car in Connecticut? Another after all these years?—he is reaching for that single moment that tied him to his life. "It'll be slow, at first. There's nothing to it."

He can feel her, poised like a spring, tuned to that instant. Then the moan of the air horn, the creak of brakes, that long bending instant when the train seems unable to break free. And then it's moving. Slowly at first, but with all the weight and threat, all that terrifying mass in its ineluctable motion. Abruptly they are running.

It catches her on the wrong foot. She stumbles, and he drags her upright with the strength of his grip. She is laughing. Surprised and laughing at her own clumsiness. He glances over. The air is tight in their lungs. He worries about the unevenness of the tracks. His mind flashes back to his blind, childish, stumbling self. He grips hard across the years. They are beside the train. It's a building, creaking along on wheels.

The gate opens more smoothly than it should, showing off for the newbie. He is going to leap in first, but she is eager, and so they find themselves scrabbling on the filthy floor, crawling forward together. He closes the gate and leads them to the front of the car, as if that corner had been reserved and waiting all these years.

For old time's sake he has filled his bag with candy, and he passes a chocolate bar to Del. She breaks off a piece and hands it back, and he can feel this new addition to the fixed shape of his past—the careful solicitousness, the comfort of having someone's particular attention doled out only to him in small, sweet gestures of love.

She inhales the strangeness of it, feels the hard floor beneath her, the judder and sway of the car as it picks up speed. She looks out through the open slats at the nightscape speeding past, the muffled awareness of houses and trees, the occasional smear of a street light hurrying by. It is a new version of the night for her and a marker of all that has been promised and withheld. She snuffs the air as if with one breath she can pick up all she has missed.

The thought comes to him that every life is not just one thread but many, branching and breaking, re-knotting themselves. He wonders what the string of their life together would be if they were to stay like this, if they were to drift past the moment of jumping. Nothing is re-made; that's clear enough. But can you begin again?

Del leans over and whispers, "Read to me?"

He leans into her neck to breathe. Even in the laden air of the cattle car there is the smooth, sweet scent of her. "Is there anyone you want to write a letter to?"

"Not now."

"I have something."

By candlelight he reads the poems, five ancient sonnets made more ancient still by all that they've been through. All of beauty, time, loss and love, each in its moment, preserved forever.

Clean wonders if he will recognize the spot, the long curve of track where they need to jump. The night is rolling past without signpost or mark. Houses give way to forest, and the darkness blurs every clue. But Del is unworried by the prospect; she feels a certain fatedness to things. And so he is grateful both to her and to the shape of the landscape when he feels the train begin to slow. It eases into the long, tight curve. He blows out the candle, folds the poems away. Del gazes up expectantly, her eyes bright even in the dark. "This is our stop," he says.

They brace against the pitch and sway. The door rolls back. They stand like skydivers ready for their leap. The muffled night slips past beyond the hammer of the wheels. Even now he remembers the hand on his shoulder, the voice in his ear. *Tuck your chin, elbows close, springy knees. Straight south. Don't linger in the woods. There's nothing nice that lives in the woods.* He reaches into his bag to touch the compass for good luck, the heavy, hollow copy of *Huckleberry Finn.*

"Aren't we going too fast?"

"Springy knees," he says. "Elbows close. You bounce and roll." He squeezes her hand and lets it go. He counts to three. They leap.

He remembers that long ago journey through the woods as the darkest he's ever known, but now there is moonlight everywhere. It catches in the leaves of the canopy, in the moss and fallen branches. It hangs on the air, lighting their way.

Del hesitates. "It's so dark," she says.

"Give your eyes a moment to adjust."

Clean imagines Bunny now. He wonders where she is. Somewhere up ahead, moving through the forest with her own purpose and goal. He has thought all along that they were all stepping into Bunny's dream, but now he sees that every story is its own. He draws the compass from his bag. The arrow glows in the moonlight. The numbers flicker and shift. The woods are silent; the night is entirely theirs. They head south.

Del's voice is low. "I wish I'd brought my microphone."

"I don't hear anything."

"It's serenity," she whispers.

They move steadily from tree to tree. Her eyes are expanding with the moonlight. She sees that what she has taken for a shadow among some exposed rocks is a small fire pit. And what she has taken for silence is the low whisper of movement at the furthest reach of her senses. She squeezes Clean's hand, bringing them both to a halt.

"Something?"

"I don't know."

The darkness before them seems to grow thinner. A pale figure emerges. Del draws them back behind a tree, and together they strive to make sense of what they can barely see.

It is, Clean realizes, a woman. She hasn't seen them. She appears, at first, to be fleeing from someone, clinging to the trunks of trees, peering back the way she has come. She is, he realizes, naked. A solid smudge of chalk against the darkness of the forest.

"Huh," whispers Del.

"I'm so glad to hear you say that."

She moves from tree to tree, though gradually it becomes clear she is not so much running as hiding; not so much hiding as playing. They can hear her whisper to herself, almost dancing from foot to foot. They hear the laughter under her breath.

Two men come wandering out of the darkness. They are naked, as well, feeling their way as if blindfolded by the night. They are murmuring, calling, not to each other but to the silence at large. Or rather, Clean realizes, to the naked woman, who is now clinging to the back of a wide trunk, spread like a pale butterfly against the dark skin of the tree.

He can make out the voices.

"Marco?"

"Polo." The woman's reply is hissing with laughter.

"Marco?

She slips to another tree before calling back. The voice is so low it seems to have no direction. The men follow as best they can.

Edging around a tree trunk, the woman catches a glimpse of Del, and as she turns it becomes clear she is not entirely naked. She wears, strapped onto her forehead, what looks like a pair of heavy binoculars standing out from her eyes. She turns without haste, moving with the certainty of someone who sees with perfect clarity. She whispers "Polo" into the air behind her, then moves quietly, but without any apparent concern, to get a better look at the intruders.

As the men approach, clumsy in the dark, the woman sidles around, keeping her distance, but peering at Del and Clean, the night-vision goggles making her look like a naked alien with heavy breasts and a dark smudge of pubic hair. She hurries past, murmuring back to the two pursuing men, who follow after, softly calling and feeling their way. They disappear from view.

This is what love does, Del thinks. It turns the world beautiful and strange.

Up ahead is the faintest of glows. A vista of light in the world of darkness. Some time long ago two or three of the big trees have fallen, and they lie now, what remains, in low shoulders of rotting wood, mossed and softened into the earthen floor. Overhead a vast hole has opened in the canopy as if into the sky itself, and the moonlight pours down onto a densely crowded garden of tall and leafy plants. The faint musky smell of the marijuana carries on the thinnest of breezes.

But that is not what takes their first attention. Low sounds of effort rise from the edge of the garden, the sounds of a struggle without conflict. From behind their tree Del and Clean can see, clearer now in the wash of moonlight, the pale shadow of one writhing shape, shifting and remaking itself on a leafy patch of earth while beside them, hunched silently against a tree, the other man, now wearing the night-vision goggles, is the lone, appreciative audience.

Clean's cheeks are burning, but he finds he is holding Del's hand. Neither of them moves. They should back away, they should leave. But something in the strangeness of it, the close and murmuring darkness, keeps them there. Conscious of each other, conscious that the slightest sound would give them both away, they turn. And there behind them is a man and a woman, dressed in jungle camouflage, rifles in their hands.

Clean opens his mouth to speak. "Shhh," murmurs the woman. "Almost done."

A few minutes more, then with a touch on the arm the woman leads them away. The man falls in behind. Clean isn't afraid. That strikes him as odd. Maybe it's the moonlight.

"What are you doing here?" the woman asks.

"We're just passing through."

"We're looking for a friend," says Del.

"Any old friend?"

"A particular one. A woman."

"She's coming from the south," says Clean. "She's in trouble."

"I can't say you're wrong," says the woman. "We haven't heard this much ruckus in weeks."

"Have you seen her?"

"Not many people make it up this far. "

"We've got to find her."

"She been out all night?" the man says doubtfully. "By this time, whatever's going to happen has happened."

"Is there a house?" asks Clean. "A little cottage. South of here?"

"Couple of miles," says the woman. "South-ish. Not that much of a place."

He draws the compass out of has bag. The numbers shift and steady. The woman considers him without expression. "You might be hungry," she says.

"Thanks. But I don't think there's time."

"Maybe you'll stop anyway."

They come to what looks like a large beaver's den, a pile of branches hunched and sagging between two large trees. As they approach the moonlight turns it into a cave, a sheltered hollow: the ground lined with sleeping bags, knapsacks in the corner, a small fire pit out front with a few blackened pots.

"You live here?" says Del. "All of you?"

"Just during the season," the man says. "Though that's nothing you need to remember."

The woman is leaning over the backpacks. She unbuckles one and takes out a zip-lock baggie, rounded and full.

"Really," says Del. "You don't have to." But Clean touches her arm. The lovers have returned. They are dressed now. They also carry rifles.

"Here," says the first woman. She places the baggie gently

in Del's hands. "You'll like this. It's all organic. Sweet as can be."

One of the men is holding out his hand to Clean. "It's a trade." When Clean doesn't move he lifts the compass from his grasp.

"I need that."

"No, you don't."

"It was gift from an old friend."

"You seem nice," the woman says. "You're quiet with each other. I like the way you touch. There's too much death in the world already. Don't come back. Don't talk about this. Don't remember where we are."

35.

They are lost now, without a guide. Yet this, in itself, seems to open their way. Every step is magic. Every glimpse—of a deer, a squirrel, the trundling purposefulness of a possum—is part of the enchantment.

And perhaps this is the blessing of youth: that Clean and Delilah move forward, hearts pounding, ears wide open to every gasp and cry, and they meet nothing. They pass through the forest untouched until, in the darkest moment, when even the moon is afraid to show, they hear a faint and distant cry. A scream. What might have been a shot. It freezes them. And when they move again they are almost on tiptoe, feeling the tilt of their path, the need for a delicate balance. They try to imagine Bunny up ahead. They try to hurry. But every step conveys how fully the night divides us all.

And then there is something new. They hear it, or think they do. The low-pitched sound of breathing, of feet moving almost silently over the forest floor. And then it rises from the crowded darkness, a rumbling growl, like a breath turned fearsome and raw and carrying with it the sweet-acrid smell of blood.

Clean presses his lips almost to her ear. "Don't stop." He grips her hand.

And just for a moment the low surrounding growling seems to part, as if it were a cloud they could pass through by fear alone. And up ahead what else do they see, in a little smudge of moonlight, but a crumbling cottage, ramshackle and dark. They run. The chimney is sagging, the windows are all boarded up. It is an ancient box of stone with a rusted roof, and there are two sprawled bodies in the doorway. No. Just one.

"Bunny?"

"Get the door," says Clean. He is on his knees, feeling for the face, the neck. The throat is torn. There is blood everywhere. It's soaked into the clothing. Men's clothing. A thick camel coat, a suit. Not Bunny! Oh, thank God. A dead man lying on the doorstep.

"It's locked," hisses Del.

"Hurry!"

Because he feels it now. Their fear will only go so far. Their love will not protect them. And hope is just a ragged chance the world holds out to show you all the things that you can lose.

He throws himself against the door—of all the unlikely things to be as solid as the earth. A growl of his own is rising in his throat, part fear, part fury. He dips into his bag and he's clutching the rock—Delilah the rock—so hard and smooth. And Del is sobbing, but there is nothing he can do. He turns. He feels them closing in. And in the corner of his eye there is a tiny gleam. A glint. A little key is hanging on its nail. Nothing more marvelous in all the world.

With a gasp they slip inside and lock the door behind.

The night was dark, but at least there was the moon. Here it is like opening your eyes inside a stone. They stand, listening to the sounds outside, the scuff of footsteps, the murmur and bark of the wolves as they pace and circle.

"Oh god oh god oh god." Del's breathing is a prayer against his neck. But he wants only to be perfectly still, to blend like every defenseless thing into the cover of the dark. "Not a sound," he whispers.

"What is it?"

"I don't know."

Though, of course, he does.

The weight of something solid and furious crashes against the door and a low, hoarse voice shivers the air. "Hey, delicious. You still alive in there? We didn't get much of a look. Are you fat? You get a lot to eat? We're hoping you're plump and sweet and melt-in-the-mouth tender."

He hears the breath catch in Del's throat. He presses his hands against the door.

"What do you want?"

"You're in our forest. What do you think we want?"

"We're just passing through."

"You don't smell like you're passing through."

"We'll leave in the morning."

"I don't think that's true. I think maybe it's too late for leaving. You run like a man with a meaty leg. How do you taste, do you think? Do you taste like chicken?" And there is another horrendous crash, and Clean leaps back. The door shivers and holds. Outside the laughter rises and dies.

They stand together, frozen in the dark.

"I can't hear you," sings the wolf. "You still breathing?"

"Go away."

There's a snuffling sound at the edge of the door, a nose pressed close. "You got a girl in there?"

"No."

"Smells like you do."

"Go away!"

The growling rises again, a ragged tussle of sound, but a few sharp barks quell it, and the wolf returns. "Is that the Book's girl?"

"What?"

"Send a finger out."

"No!"

"Open the door."

"No."

"I can't smell you good through the door."

"You can't taste me, either."

Even the laughter sounds like a growl, as if their teeth were tearing at something amusing. "Just a crack, then, tasty. We're not leaving without a sniff. Just stick her hand out the door. It can still be attached."

"Forget it."

"Then a piece of clothing. Something warm. Something next to the skin. How about her panties? You can spare her panties, can't you?"

She is pressed behind him. Her sweatshirt falls away. In the darkness he hears the rustle as she peals off her t-shirt.

"Uh-uh," he says.

"Be quick."

His shoulder is against the boards, hands on the doorknob and key. Her breath is warm against his ear. "Ready?"

"Hey, tasty. Why don't you—?"

He jerks back the door; Del throws the shirt. In the same motion she has the Zippo out, snaps on the flame. The sudden glare is out of all proportion. It catches the figure full in the face, and for a moment they all stand frozen. There is a dark tangle of matted fur. Terrible, terrible teeth.

He slams shut the door. They stand unmoving. They hear the rustle of footsteps, the grumbling voices, and then slowly it all fades. In the sheltering darkness they cannot let each other go.

After a while he fumbles in his bag. Del has the lighter ready. The candlelight expands the room, painting it with shadows and gold. A narrow table, an iron bed piled high with blankets. The floor is ancient and dark. The walls are stone. There is an oil lamp on the table. The flame catches and climbs the wick.

There is a tablecloth on the small table, and three white chairs drawn against it. There is a bucket on a shelf with fresh water, and a basin for washing, an assortment of plates and bowls, cups, silverware. Three of everything. A little joke, perhaps, or a little prayer. To have just one would be sad. Two might seem presumptuous. But three has such a solid, certain feel. And who knows? You might have guests.

"Do you think we can sit down?" whispers Del.

"I don't think he'd mind."

"Are you hungry?"

"Starving."

He turns to the shelf of food. "There's some sugar. Some powdered milk. There's a big tin of oatmeal. Some jerky. A few cans of sardines. A sack of apples going soft." The stove is a can of sterno and a little rack for the pot. He measures water and oatmeal and sets it on the heat. "It'll take a while to boil."

Del is struck by the loneliness, the residue of years embodied in this tiny place. Her hands feel empty. He gathers them in his own.

It has taken them such a long time to get here, not just to this place but to this candlelit moment. Years of waiting and disappointment, years of wondering at all the ways life offers and takes away. Del feels a little tremor in her knees. Clean's hands are shaking as he lifts them from her grip and lets them settle on her waist.

"Do you want to dance?" she whispers.

"I don't know how."

He kisses her. With all the night around them, this candlelight is theirs alone. They peel away their clothing piece by piece.

"You have so many layers," murmurs Del.

She herself has only two. She reaches down, all elbows, for the hem of her cotton bra and peels it up. Her skin glows in the candlelight: the slope of her stomach, the shallow weight of her breasts, the lush gleam of her shoulders. And for the first time Clean understands all the foolish images of Book's old poetry: lips like coral, breasts like curdled cream. He sees them now for what they are: a true measure of the world.

"You're way behind," she whispers, tugging at his shirt.

He is awkward. Every part revealed is one more clumsy fact, while Del is clearly made for candlelight. He begins to lose his nerve. But her hands are deft and eager. She manages the buttons, the ancient belt. She is smiling in concentration. He is all embarrassment at the stiffness of his flesh, but Del seems merely to grow thoughtful. She grasps him gently, companionably. "So what have you got to say for yourself?"

There is a hiss and a burble from the corner as the oatmeal boils over. It startles them apart. With a gasp he lunges for the pan. Too hot. He sets it down, blowing out the sterno, blowing on his fingers. And when he turns around again, Del is gone. He has half-feared this, of course. That it all might turn out to be a dream.

But then he sees the mounded shadow under the covers of the bed and the dark, shorn head peering mischievously from the pillow. He carries the candle over and sets it on the bedside shelf. The light cascades. She lays a hand teasingly on the blanket under her chin. "What's the password?"

But his mind has shut down with relief. He shakes his head, dry-mouthed and staring, while with a smile she draws the covers down.

"Golly," he murmurs.

"That's correct."

He slips into the bed, whose mattress, he discovers, is neither too hard nor too soft, too narrow nor too wide, but just exactly right.

36.

They awaken to the morning light seeping in through shuttered windows. They are curled beneath the blanket's warmth, but you can imagine the hesitation as they weigh the slow awareness of the moment, images of the night before crowding around them.

"Are you awake?" she asks.

"Don't move."

His breath is warm against her neck. Her hand traps his against the rising swell of her breast. "What time is it?"

He takes note of the weight of birdsong filtering in from the woods. "Morning, I think."

"I have to use the little girl's room."

"Let's make sure the coast is clear."

Naked as a bear he eases out of bed. Del smiles. "There you are."

"I'll check out the window."

"Don't let anybody in."

The shutters look nailed shut but aren't. He slides back heavy bolts, and light pours in.

"How does it look?"

"Nothing but the morning."

Stepping to the door he opens it a crack. It takes a cautious moment to realize the bloody body is gone. The earth has been scuffed clean.

Del gathers the blanket around her, climbs out of bed. She trundles past, pausing to bump against him, once, twice, until he circles his arms around her. "The ladies room is on the other side of that tree," she explains.

"I'll stand guard."

She takes a few steps, folded in her blanket, then seems to notice that, of all the living creatures in her sight, she is the only one wearing clothes. She turns and lets it fall, watching him smile. "How well can you see me?"

"Just about."

She takes a step closer, then another. "Tell me when."

She is less than a foot away when he says, "That's perfect."

"I'll be right back." She slips behind the tree.

The oatmeal is where they left it the night before. There are raisins in a coffee can and coffee in another. They spread the blanket out in front of the hut, but the food is just another form of teasing. She tastes the coffee, eats a raisin, stirs the cold and stiffened oatmeal as he watches. Without clothes he is helpless to pretend. As they make love she watches the moving boughs high over his shoulder, listens to the birds, aware of the breeze, the dusty smell of the earth.

He heats their coffee up again. She laughs, but he won't drink it cold. As they sip from heavy china mugs they balance back to back in the middle of all that flat ground. It is a luxury to turn your back on someone, to feel the pressure of muscle and bone holding you up. They talk in low voices, passing the words back and forth.

They could live here forever without troubles or clothes, without interruption. They would gather nuts and berries and make love over and over.

"But what about coffee?"

"I'll make you forget about coffee," she says, and his laughter warms her, buoys her up.

They have finished the raisins, doling them out. They each hold back the last sip in their mugs until long after it's cold, and in the end, when he gets to his feet, Clean pours his onto the ground, marking the spot with a small damp patch that almost immediately begins to dry.

Del gazes at the shack for a moment, wondering at the sight. It is even more ramshackle in the daylight. The walls are cracked and weather-worn, though now she can see where new stone and concrete have been added, shoring up the sides. A new sheet of tin peeps out from under the ancient roof.

Her heart warms at the thought that her father has, even if unmeaning, prepared this for her. It is his work, his care. And in the light of morning she understands that he and Bunny, no older than themselves, had hoped to stand like this and feel the turn their lives had taken. That they had reached their true beginning.

She glances up. He is peering out among the trees, and now she twines her fingers in his, looking up at the side of his face, willing him to turn, practicing this new power she has over her own happiness.

"Somebody's coming," he says. A sudden chill. "Why don't you go inside."

"Why don't we both?"

He picks up the blanket, wraps it around the two of them.

A man and a woman appear from among the trees. They are still in their camouflage fatigues, but there is nothing of the night's romance. They are grim-faced, hollow-eyed. Their rifles look lean and wicked in the daytime. Del can't look away. The man has Grief's body slumped over one shoulder as if it's just an inconvenience. "Did you do this?" he asks.

Del can't speak, but Clean says, "No."

"You need to cut it out."

"We didn't do it."

"Those fucking wolves," says the woman. "Did you call the cops?"

"Not about this."

"Fucking hell. They're crawling all over the place."

"It's nothing to do with us," says Clean.

The man regards them, empty-eyed, as if whatever he's deciding could go either way. Del feels the glance in the bottom of her stomach.

"This is nothing you want to talk about," he finally says. "You don't even want to remember."

Though of course he couldn't be more wrong.

You begin a story, you think it's going one way, but there is never any certainty.

They wash the mugs and bowls and set them in their place. Del steps to the bed and starts to make it, tugging at the sheets and blankets, smoothing them into place. Beneath the tangled covers at the foot of the mattress she finds a neatly ordered pile, unnoticed until then.

"Oh."

He turns to look. A little collection of candles. A jeweler's box, now empty. A library book, slender and red and improbably clean as if it's only been borrowed once.

"What do you suppose?" he says.

There is a knock on the door. It makes them jump. And then the knob is turning. Before they can do more than stare there is a policeman, mountainous in midnight blue, filling the doorway. His face is pale and tired, his expression stunned. He stares at the naked couple as if they couldn't be less real. "Jesus."

Del snatches up the blanket. Clean grabs his shorts and pulls them on. The policeman is almost too tired to look away. "What the hell is this? Are you all right, miss?"

"I'm her boyfriend," Clean says.

"Miss?"

And Del can't help it. She smiles. "He is."

"I'd ask you what you're doing here...." But then he just lets the sentence drift away. "Have you heard anything? Seen anything unusual?"

They consider for a moment. "It's been pretty quiet," says Clean.

"Do your parents know where you are?" And when neither

speaks, he shakes his head. "Never mind. I got kids of my own. I always tell 'em, if you can't be good, be careful. There's some crazy stuff in the world."

"Thank you, officer," Del says, but he's already closing the door.

She is still smiling as she picks up the book. The pages are clean. The poetry, in neat and nested stanzas, looks hopeful and bright. She turns back to the opening.

The Failure of Love
by
James William Beale

Published by the Fellows and Trustees
of St. Augustine's School,
Philip Hilliard, Chair.

She reads it once and then again. There is a note at the bottom of the page. *James William Beale is the associate librarian of St. Augustine's School.* She shows it to him.

"So?"

"Don't you see?" she says. "Look at the name."

"The Failure of Love," says Clean. "That's got nothing to do with us."

"No," she says. "The other name."

37.

They dress. They close the shutters. They lock the door behind them and hang the key on its nail. They walk south from the cottage. There is no compass to steer by, no need for one now. Just south, that's all they need. The land grows more benign with every step. Their eyes are drawn to the ordinary look of ancient trees, the leaf-muffled ground. Even the shadows seem to glow as if, in the ordinary brightness of the morning, darkness itself is just a kind of muted light.

They rarely speak. Nothing is more fragile than a dream, and with every step the memories of the night before turn more precious. But they have made the world over in its most magical form, and if they can preserve it through the clear and unsurprising daylight, then they can return to it in the darkness—looping one night to the next—and weave it into the rest of their lives.

"Do you know where we're going?"

"Of course," he says. "I just don't know where we are."

And then he does. The silence gives way to the distant sound of water; the endless forest reshapes itself along the edge of the river bank. They can see, perhaps two hundred yards away, the rusted beams of the trestle stretching out across vacant space.

Clean had forgotten—he isn't sure how—that this was waiting for them. That in any voyage like this, the last task is always the hardest. As they approach he cannot shift his eyes away. The rotting steel, the memory of empty air beneath his feet. He cannot still the pounding of his heart. But he moves forward, leading the way, determined to deserve all that he's been granted on this trip.

Easing from the gravel out onto the iron plates, gingerly, gingerly, as if his weight is just an illusion, he takes a first step, then a second. Now he can see the rusted edges, imagine the flaking delicacy of the whole enormous bridge. His palms are slick, his chest is tight. A third step and a fourth. Now he's reaching blindly back for Del.

"Calvin?"

He stops; he hears it in her voice. And when he turns, Peach is standing close beside her, fist bound in the fabric of her sleeve, the open razor floating near her throat. He is grinning. All the blood on his shirt must be somebody else's or he'd never able to stand. "Well, Pisser. If it ain't the devil himself. I wasn't sure we'd ever see you again."

"God damn it, Peach! Put that away! She's got nothing to do with you."

"Is that right?" He glances at Del. "Where's the woman?"

"Cut it out," says Clean.

"No, the other one. The crazy one."

"You didn't find her?"

"Those goddam wolves. They tore us all to pieces. I gotta tell you, I didn't expect to see anyone come walking out of there."

Beside him Bertie Clutter watches with a look of weary resignation. Even he looks bedraggled: his raincoat stained and rumpled, his heavy glasses bent. "I hate the woods," he says. "If I ever see another growing thing it will be too soon." He glances from one to the other. "I don't suppose you came across a truly stupendous amount of cash."

Del just stares.

"I didn't think so. What a calamitous waste of time. It was the goddam invitation. All this while. Clever, clever Roger. Move the money and remember the number: that's all you have to do. So you write it on the bottom of a card and mail it to someone you can trust not to throw it away. And Bunny would never have thrown it away. But what happens? Can you believe it? That fucking Patrick. Why does everyone have to be so goddam mysterious? He never mails it. Gets a sudden fit of the willies and won't let it go. It's sitting in his pocket all the time. And this boob," he nods toward Peach, "throws it away. Buries it with the body. I don't suppose that could possibly be a lie?"

Clean cannot say a word. His eyes are fixed on Del.

"So we're chasing after Roger, after Bunny, we're running all over the goddam country, and the fucking prize is sitting in the ground where we buried it. But then someone finds it, don't they? They dig up our friend Patrick again. Just for the fun of it. But the invitation's gone, isn't it? Who would have done that, do you suppose? Who'd replace a wedding invitation with five moth-eaten poems?"

"Just let her go."

"Yeah. Right. Roger didn't have it. Bunny didn't have it. Who am I supposed to believe?"

"We've got nothing you want."

"I'm sure," says Bertie wearily. "And I'm sure you'd never lie to me. Unbelievable. Can you imagine? This is what I'm reduced to. I used to have standards. I used to have some shred of reputation. Never mind," he says. "Come on. Let's go." He waves him back toward solid ground. Clean has almost forgotten the height. "Take it off."

"What?"

"Everything. The bag, the clothes. Lose it all."

As he hesitates Peach makes a tiny gesture with the razor and a bright bead of scarlet trickles down Del's neck.

"Stop! Okay!"

"This can be easy," Bertie says. "Let's not make it hard. This has already gotten so far out of hand, a few more complications won't even slow me down."

Del is wide-eyed, her face gone pale beside the brightness of her blood. Clean steps off the bridge and sets his bag on the ground. He shrugs off his coat, reaches for the buttons of his shirt.

"You, too, missy," Peach murmurs. He is hovering at her ear. "Let's see what you got."

"Don't you touch her, Peach! I'll kill you!"

"Jeeze, Pisser. When did you turn into such a girl?" But he lets the razor drift a hand's breadth away.

"Okay," Clean calls. "It's okay. Just do what he says."

Stiffly Del unzips, easing her hand beneath the waiting blade. Her face is hot. The embarrassment is good; it crowds against the fear. It's a test, she thinks. She thinks of the blanket at the cottage, the morning sunlight, the magic of the night. She sheds the sweatshirt, the shoes and jeans, and stands in socks, grey cotton bra, and underpants.

Bertie is unmoved. "All of it, if you don't mind. Every little pocket and hiding place."

Almost impatiently she strips off the rest. The voice is hot against her neck. "Now that's what I call nice." He taps her lightly and she flinches.

"God damn it, Peach!"

"Easy, Pisser. Don't get your panties in a bunch."

"Keep an eye on them," says Bertie as he bends to the clothing. Pockets, sleeves, feeling for any secrets. He rips his way through the lining, empties the bag onto the ground.

She doesn't take her eyes off Clean.

He is standing in his skin, every possession scattered before him. He is startled by how little there is. Candles, matches, a water bottle, the round, smiling rock. Bertie gives the bag one final shake, then lets it drop. "Okay," he says. "That's it, then. Off you go."

"What?" Peach turns in disbelief. "What are you talking about?"

"No, no! Leave those there."

Del has stooped to the bag, the clothing, but now she stands again.

"I'll just hold onto all that, why don't I. But you're in luck. It's such a beautiful day. Now, show them out," he says. And when Peach just stares, Bertie shakes his head wearily and makes a little gesture at the trestle. "Do I have to explain everything?"

Peach's grin has returned. He steps to the edge of the bridge, to the narrow lip between the tracks and the fenceless air. He dips the razor in a little bow. "After you."

Clean watches the high branches overhead. He wonders if every life has only a single loop to be played out again and again, as if he was meant to fall all those years ago and the currents have been carrying him back ever since.

Del is aware of the breeze on her skin. She should feel embarrassed, but every corner of her mind is crowded with dread. There is nothing else to do. She sees him there, pale and forlorn, and she takes his hand. She breathes. Her bare feet flinch from the rough gravel and then step onto chilly steel. She has spent the hours of her childhood imagining a life of danger and adventure, but it was nothing like this. She listens for the sounds, the textures of the moment, but there is nothing to hear.

Clean finds himself in motion, drawn by the pressure of her grasp. They are easing out along the narrow edge with nothing beyond. He can't help it; his gaze slips over and down.

"No. Uh-uh," she whispers. "Look at me. Look up at me."

"I can't do this."

"You already are."

Far below the sunlight catches on the rocks and water, glints up through the cracks beneath their feet.

"Now this is what I call a tight fit." Indifferent to the fall, Peach is almost dancing, skipping over wooden ties and steel. The razor is gone now, but his empty hands are out, teasing, touching, crowding them toward the edge. Clean slaps them away, but that alone almost carries him off. He thinks about the fight all those years ago, rolling and struggling over the yawning air. It seems impossible. He thinks about catching himself at the edge: the fear of it all.

He can't lift his eyes from the iron plates. They are pitted and worn, fragile with rust. Peach draws a stone from his pocket and tosses it at their feet. Bouncing, skittering, it finds a hole, falling through in a little shower of flakes. "Oh, man. Will you look at that?"

One step and then another. Clean's hand is slick; the harder he squeezes the more it seems Del will slip from his grasp. He can feel the whole trestle move, catching the harmonics of his fear.

And Peach is in front of them now. He's standing on a patch of sound metal in a little cloverleaf of rust. His voice is cheerful. "Not much to work with here. Boy, would you listen to that?"

The rush and tumble of water thrashing the air.

"You can almost hear the screams, can't you, Pisser? Remember that? A skip and a trip, and over he went."

He has never forgotten the scream, but now it's been replaced by the pounding of his heart.

"Just a little further," Del murmurs. "Almost there."

But Peach is leaning toward them, making little kissing sounds. And Clean can see there is nowhere to go. He is standing on the only good steel. There is the middle of the bridge, but Peach sees his glance. "Oh, no. That would be cheating. There's plenty of room. What are you nervous about? What kind of guy do you think I am? Come on. Here you go. Just enough room to squeeze past."

He can't move. But now somehow, miraculously, Del has slipped ahead. She is drawing him along. Together they start easing around the grinning man. But halfway past, Clean sees it, sees the grin change. A hand comes up. A finger. Just a finger now, taunting him, tapping his shoulder, poking him. And it feels for an instant as if that will be enough.

He lunges for the hand, but Peach snatches it away. "Is that what you want? You want to hold hands?" He is fluttering his fingers now just out of reach, laughing. "Oh, man, will you look at that? It is a long way down." And with a bump, small as a butterfly's, Clean can feel himself go.

He drops Del's hand. It is somehow his first thought, against every reflex. He doesn't want to drag her down. And the knowledge of that will remain a comfort to him for the rest of his life. With flailing arms he struggles for balance, clutching at the air. A foot away, Peach's face is gleeful. "Oh, Pisser. What would your old dad say now?"

And Clean makes a grab, reaching for his arm, his jacket. Anything to hold. There is a fumbling of hands, a slap-fight in the air, and then he fastens onto Peach's sleeve. He's clutching at it, pulling it, dragging himself forward. But Peach is cursing now. He has the razor out, the blade coming open. And Clean's mind is rushing. *Let go or pull; let go or pull.* There is nowhere to duck—the blade so sharp he wonders if he'll feel it. And there is the movement of the wrist, almost graceful. And there is Del, suddenly Del, rising into view. Bright and pale and fierce at Peach's shoulder. And she has hard Delilah in her hand, the smooth and smiling rock, scooped up from his bag, and it's coming down fast, blunt and heavy as fate, hard as the start of the day.

Peach staggers, turns. He is snarling. The blade comes up. But he's slipping now, unanchored. His heavy boots skidding on the rusting steel. And it's his turn to clutch. But there's nothing to grab: no sleeve, no jacket. His nails scrabble on Clean's forearm; there is a bloom of pain almost lost in the moment. And then the world is tipping, tipping.

They turn in the air. They seem to float past each other, falling together and then apart. Peach is suspended like a man in flight. And Clean hears a scream unfurling in his ear, but it isn't his. His knees hit the rotting edge of the trestle and break through. His arms stretch out. Both hands grapple over ancient steel, and he finds it, the rail. He clutches hard, as if everything in the empty air wants to snatch it away.

He will never move. Never move again. He is sprawled, one knee poking through to nothing, cheek flat against the cold deck. *You're a running, jumping, gripping machine.* Del's hand is under his arm. She is breathing hard, as if it's not just him she's holding up but the entire bridge. He feels for her hand, finds it. He drags his knee free.

"Well, fuck me," comes a voice, Bertie's voice, floating from across the way. "What a shitty day this is turning out to be."

Del puts it out of her mind. She turns toward solid ground, leading the way. She is aware of the breeze suddenly, cool against her skin. What it is to be alive. Their nakedness is something distant and strange. A marvel along with everything else. They step onto solid ground. The whining complaint follows after them. "No one's going to be happy with this. You hear me? You tell that to Bunny when you see her. You tell her I'll be talking to her. You let her know-- " The voice breaks off.

"Oh, great," he says. "Another county heard from. Well, who the hell are you?"

Del is still in the lead, easing her way down from the tracks to the river bank below, when the thin, flinty pop of a gunshot comes to them on the air. Clean's heart is pounding so hard he barely hears it, but he lets go of her hand and turns. He strains to see, but to Clean there are only smudges of color. Still, Bertie Clutter is lying dead on the ground. And in that moment two figures emerge from the trees: a blur of forest brown and a bright yellow dress. They stand for a moment at the edge of the trestle as if gathering up all the threads of meaning, present and past together. Then the man steps to the bank and tosses something, small as a stone, into the river below. Clean turns to call, but by the time Del has joined him the figures have vanished.

Naked they walk through the forest, following the curve of the river. In the entrance of his cave the padre is reading to himself, nodding over the words, mumbling his prayers. He is a small, bald man who looks up with an expression of wonder to see the man and woman approaching through the trees with every bird singing their praises and every voice raising itself to the glory of the lord.

Epilogue

James William Beale. Bill Beale.
Billy Beale. Billy Bill. Bill.
Book.

Every name is a life. Every life is a series of names.

JAMES

38.

There is much to be said for a library. A quiet room, a comfortable chair, enough warmth so you can feel your fingers. And, of course, the books.

This one is a cozy place, though not much for research. The donor, a hundred and twenty-five years ago, specified the stone, the architect, the preposterous façade, but thought the books were somebody else's task. The cost of carving his name above the door exceeded the value of the collection for a good many years.

Even now the students don't come for the books. They have their computers for that. They have their phones. But still. It's good to keep some around. The people who end up at the library come for comfort and quiet and a small, cozy space beneath the elegant old roof. They come for the low pool of light in a dark room and a story they can slip into for an hour or two. They come for refuge, though they don't always know it.

There was an evening, years ago. Years ago. He was sitting at his desk in the warm lamplight when the girl came in. He hadn't seen her before, though he'd heard her name. She had about her the thin and prickly self-consciousness of the newly arrived. It was early in the fall semester and her first visit to the library. One of her last, it would turn out. She fit in well at the school. She made friends, man-handled them, shoved her way through a prep-school's tangle of low-grade power politics. She didn't need the library after that.

But this time she was at loose ends, hesitant and blustery. She was slim, dark-haired, with a long face and wide mouth. She stood gazing doubtfully at all the dark shelves as if unconvinced this was anywhere she needed to be.

"Can I help you?"

"No." She gave him a quick once-over. Then perhaps deciding it was better to be safe said, "Thank you. I'm just looking."

"I could give you a little tour."

"That's all right."

She glanced around, as if the thought of a tour had made it clear to her just how small the library was. She straightened up, tucked back her shoulders, gave her hair a quick, impatient flick.

Perhaps that was the moment that got her started at the school, the sudden awareness that, grand as the buildings were, a place with a library as small as this could not, in the end, offer much in the way of intimidation. She took a quick, unnecessary turn around the room.

Afterwards he liked to think she did it for him, did it as a kind of courtesy, offering the room this much attention for his sake. But she only got about halfway around before she decided there was nothing more to see. She turned and headed for the door.

"Thanks for stopping by."

She glanced at him, quick, dismissive, but uncertain. Maybe she was wondering what he meant, if he was somehow making fun of her. Maybe she wasn't sure if there was something she was missing. He'd like to think so. He'd like to think he'd given her that much. When she turned to go he said, "What's your name?" Though he was only doing it to tease her. She seemed in such a hurry to leave.

"Ruth," she said. "Ruth Bingham." As if it were no business of his.

The second time he died he barely noticed; the third time was the charm. But the first time marked the beginning of everything. He was twenty-two. College had ended along with much else. He had lost his mother in his freshman year; his father two years later. The only real thing that happened to him lasted three weeks at the end of his senior year, and when that was over there was nothing.

With Bunny gone he was a ghost haunting someplace he barely remembered. Phil got him a job in the library, found him an apartment in one of his family's buildings with two second-year doctoral students in particle physics. He lived there two weeks.

Then one evening he locked himself out. It was really as simple as that. He was heading to the store. But he had left his keys on the bureau, his phone, his wallet. He stepped outside, heard the door close behind him. The lightness in his pockets only gradually revealed itself as loss. He had been an English major; he knew a metaphor when it bit him.

He thought about breaking in. He thought about climbing the side of the building, though already that was more like a story he was telling than an actual plan. The physics students would be at their lab until midnight. He decided to walk over and borrow a key. He started off.

And came to an intersection: a perfectly ordinary intersection of two ordinary streets.

They had left the art gallery and walked at random. They had stopped for the light and stood right here. They had looked together at the little cluster of shops and the houses and the rusted sculpture of a cow on the front lawn.

He turned.

All that evening he traced their old paths. He had twenty dollars in his pocket. He bought a bottle of wine and drank it on the grass beneath the stone bridge. When he finally returned it was to find the apartment windows lit, the sound of the television. He couldn't bear to let the evening end. He curled up on the ground behind a yew hedge and let his thoughts wander until he slept.

In the morning he washed his face in a birdbath. He bought coffee. He bought a small bottle of bourbon with the last of his cash. The day began to take on its new shape, slack and wide as the horizon. He drank the coffee, then sipped the bourbon. It was as if he could climb right into his memories.

He spent the day walking and reading. The second night, when it came, was warm, and he was more than a little drunk. He couldn't imagine running into anyone, couldn't imagine talking. He had tied himself by the lightest of threads to all that was gone, and he could not risk their breaking.

It wasn't a game exactly. More a test. How long could he hold onto it all?

He couldn't believe she'd been able to leave. He couldn't believe she was gone. He walked through the park down to the tracks. He followed the tracks to woods. There was no path. He wandered. He came to a campfire. A group of men. He had finished the bourbon. He had nothing to offer. But at the bottom of his bookbag there was a copy of *Huckleberry Finn*. He had forgotten it was there.

When the two strangers blundered into the firelight, the blind boy and the thin weasely man, it still seemed merely happenstance—actions that would, at any moment, return him to the life he had known. But one thing led to another led to a another.

When he returned after more than three years there was barely a trace of himself remaining. It was like being at peace. If to be dead is to be outside time, he couldn't imagine anything he wanted more. Until he realized there was no such thing.

He had been walking down an alley, and it was only the sight of the crabapple tree in full bloom once again that told him another year had passed. And he saw the For Sale sign and he wondered if it was a test. To see if he was strong enough now. To see if he could mend. So he'd bought the house. There'd been a little money when his parents had died, and it was a very modest house.

But maybe it was a mistake to see that crabapple blossoming every year. So little that is real could bear up against the pressure of that.

He met Luanne at a retreat for the fragile of spirit. He had decided to stop drinking; she had decided to start. She was pretty and cheerful and determined, and he loved her because of how broken she was. And he loved Del because, with all that she'd been through, she was as strong as he wanted to be. They set out to mend each other. Though of course they couldn't.

A life of love. Who doesn't dream of such a thing? But here's what they don't tell you. Love doesn't make you a better person. It doesn't make you happy. Love feeds on love; love grows from love. But memory devours memory. To say that love is madness is not to say too much.

And happiness?

The nature of happiness is that it has no nature. We think of it as a creature: a bluebird, an angel, a butterfly landing on your wrist. We think we can coax it, welcome it, tame it. We think, if we behave ourselves, if we offer it the appropriate blend of hope and desire and need, it will stay with us. It will make its home in our hearts.

But happiness is not a creature to be tempted or seduced. Not a fickle heart bending its attention upon us. Not a goal or a purpose or a welcome reward. It is nothing you can chase.

But you can turn your back upon it. And then it can surprise you.

There is an old stone building standing in the night. A library, if it matters. You could walk away, but you don't. What if you knock on the door and a wolf answers? What kind of a story do you find yourself in? How can you ever know for sure?

The couple is hesitant, their faces pale in the darkness. The school buildings around them, like an ancient town, are silent and unlit. The young man knocks. This is always the moment when fate is most at risk. When all-that-will-be is still tangled up in all-that-merely-might. The door opens.

"Jesus!"

The wolf says nothing. Wild hair and beard only partially confined beneath a cap, a scarf, a coat. Wild eyes. Bloody fangs tattooed around his lips. "What big eyes you have," he growls. Then he leans forward sniffing deeply, first Delilah and then Clean. "Just so I remember." He steps back out of the way.

They move into the dimness of the room with something like hope. On the table by the door there is a book lying open under the glow of a lamp. It is a brand new copy of *Huckleberry Finn*. Del watches as Clean turns the pages with one delicate finger. They are whole. There is no space cut out, no revolver. The book is untroubled by all that has happened, as if to read it now is to make it all brand new.

They step past, around the corner of the shelves, and there, sheltered in a pool of light, sit a man, a woman, and a girl. They have never before been in a room together. But they have been moving toward this moment all their lives. Bill and Bunny and little Ruth, not so little any more. They are quiet, hesitant. But there is something in their faces, a look, a hint of something shared that binds them all together, like that last warm wash of sunlight at the end of a day. He is reading to them, no, whispering. They are telling each other the stories of their lives.

About the Author

D. K. Smith is a graduate of Yale and the Iowa Writers' Workshop. He is the author of two previous novels, *Nothing Disappears* and *Missing Persons*. He teaches Medieval and Renaissance literature at Kansas State University.

www.ingramcontent.com/pod-product-compliance
Lightning Source LLC
Chambersburg PA
CBHW030420310726
48979CB00009B/1537/J

* 9 7 8 0 9 9 1 4 7 3 7 2 4 *